Born
to
Die

Lee Faulkner

CONTENTS

ACKNOWLEDGMENTS

There are too many contributors involved in getting this from an idea to a manuscript to a novel that to list them all would add tremendously to the page count. Thanks to you all – you know who you are.

PROLOGUE

Around 13.6 billion years ago

There was nothing. There was just space.

Well, there was very nearly nothing. Within that area of nearly nothing there was an incredibly small, dense and hot area measuring only around 1 x 10-33 centimetres across. This area of space contained all the matter and energy that now spans the billions of light years of the universe.

At about 1 x 10-24 seconds later, the incredibly small universe expanded rapidly, doubling in size many times, cooling and allowing matter and energy to separate.

During the next 1 x 10-22 seconds, the universe continued to expand and cool, allowing the formation of subatomic particles that started to bond together to form various elements by the time 1 second had taken place.

After 100 seconds the universe cooled to around 1 billion degrees Celsius and subatomic particles continued to combine creating hydrogen, helium and other elements like lithium.

For the next 100 to 200 million years or so, the universe continued to expand and cool, causing particles of matter to begin clustering together. Gravity was now causing gases to collapse into tight clusters, becoming hotter and denser. These clusters of gas formed stars which eventually clustered together to form galaxies.

Over billions of years, some stars went supernova and, as they exploded, they ejected matter across the universe, including all the elements known on Earth.

Not all of the elements in the universe reached the Earth at the same time. In fact, it is probable that there are many elements that have not yet reached the Earth at all.

Pavia, Italy, 1895

The 15-year-old young man lay in the field at the back of his garden. It was late at night but he had asked his father if he could stay out and look at the stars. The sky was cloudless tonight and with only a faint glow coming from the single gas light in the living room, there was no glare cutting out the vast array of stars in this night's sky.

He had been fascinated by the stars for many years, often sketching their positions in the sky and noting how his drawings varied at different times of the year and, from them, getting some idea of how the Earth moved around in space. He liked watching the moon for the same sort of reasons, sketching the different phases and determining how the moon orbits the Earth and how the Earth, moon and the sun interact.

Tonight, though he had just decided to lay in the field and stare up at the stars. The night sky was so clear that tonight's viewing was already bringing a smile to his face.

He was ticking off the constellation names in his head when he noticed, to one side, low on the horizon, one star appeared to be moving. He watched it for a few moments, soon realising that it was a meteor. He had never seen a meteor before but had read about them and seen drawings of them in books. This was going to be an amazing night.

He sat up so he could see the meteor without stretching his neck. He watched as it hit the Earth's atmosphere and broke into 5 pieces forming a meteor shower. Four of the five meteors flared and then burned out quickly, indicating that they were small enough to be consumed by the atmosphere as they hit it. One, however, continued to glow and developed a small fiery tail, obviously big enough for some of it to survive the journey through the atmosphere.

He continued watching as it appeared to get bigger, then seemed to accelerate and dip due to the curvature and spin of the Earth. It crashed into a rocky outcrop at the far side of the field. Fiery sparks flew up into the air and, a few seconds later the muffled sound of an explosion reached his ears. He looked around back at the house to see if his parents had been woken but there appeared to be no movement or extra lights from the house. He'd always thought his parents capable of sleeping though anything and tonight's events were proving his theory.

There were no other houses in the immediate area so it was possible that no one else had seen this. Without any further thought, he set off towards the glow. The field was full of corn probably half way through its growth so it was going to be hard going and he predicted it would take him a good 30 minutes to reach the rocky outcrop.

He had underestimated the distance and the effort needed to get through the cornfield in the dark so it took around an hour for him to reach the rocks, stopping a few times on route to take a sip from the bottle of water that he had with him.

He looked over the rocks and spotted the small crater the impact had made in one of them. The coolness of the rock had taken much of the residual heat away from whatever had impacted and there was just a small jagged shard, glowing orange, in the centre of the small crater.

He poured some of the water over the glowing shard causing it to sizzle quietly and some steam to rise. The steam quickly cleared and he poured on more water until the glow had subsided. He quickly tapped the shard to see if it was still hot and, once sure that it wasn't, he picked it up.

Though not particularly heavy, it was weighty for its size. He held it up nearer his eyes and realised that it gave off a faint glow. Having studied physics and chemistry at school and also having read many geology books, he didn't recognise the attributes of this meteorite from any of his studies. His keen mind was stimulated by this unknown and he decided that he would do his best to investigate it. Perhaps he had just discovered something new and it could be named after him. He folded it into his handkerchief, placed it in his pocket and headed back towards home, guided by the faint glow of the gas light.

Princetown, USA, April 1955

Sixty years later, the teenager that was had progressed academically, proving to be intellectually gifted and had published multiple papers in various aspects of Physics.

In his earlier days, he had moved with his family to Prague where he had gained an early professorship at the Charles-Ferdinand University and, from there, had spent time travelling to and lecturing and researching in many countries as his fame grew throughout the world. He finally settled in America where he remained for the rest of his life.

During his studies over the years, he had continued to be fascinated by the shard he had found during his teenage years and, a few years ago, had discovered a unique property that could have ground-breaking uses in the future. Despite discoveries in many aspects of Physics he was particularly concerned about the characteristics of the shard and, with possibilities of conflicts in various parts of the world, he was afraid that it could be devastating in the wrong hands. After careful consideration he therefore decided to keep his discovery secret. He authored a couple of private papers on possible future uses for the shard's properties noting that technology and miniaturisation needed to progress before his ideas could come to fruition. For security he tended to keep the shard and associated papers with him on his journeys.

On 17 April 1955 he quickly began to feel very ill and through the day the pains in his abdomen worsened to the point that he could bear it no longer. At the age of 76 he suspected his time may be up and summoned his assistant, Bruria Kaufman, to his side whilst he was awaiting the arrival of an ambulance.

"I fear my time is short," he started, raising his hand in a gesture to stop his assistant from contradicting him, "and I want to pass on something to you that I ask you to keep secure for me until you feel the world is ready for it."

Bruria had spent the past 4 or so years assisting the professor and she had grown a close working relationship with him. She could see he was serious and was obviously in pain so allowed him to continue without interruption.

The professor handed over a wooden box about the size of a cereal packet and Bruria placed it to one side as she listened. "In the box is an item and some papers explaining what it is and ideas of what could be done with it. I ask that you keep it secure and do not open it until I have gone. Then I ask that you read the contents and decide if the world is ready for it to be introduced. If you decide it should be kept secret for longer, I urge you to keep it secure until you feel the time is right." He winced as the pain in his abdomen became worse.

"Are you sure you want to continue with this now, Professor?" asked Bruria concerned.

"We must make time for me to finish the hand over to you," he said through gritted teeth. "If you feel the time is not right in your lifetime then please pass it on to someone you trust."

"I ask again, Sir," said the assistant, "are you sure you want to do this?"

The professor grasped his abdomen as the pain increased. In the distance the siren of an approaching ambulance could be heard. "We must finish this before the ambulance takes me away," he said now struggling to speak clearly through the pain. "I seriously believe that the item in this box could be world-changing in the correct hands at the correct time but could also be world destroying if the wrong people have access to it.

"You must promise me ..." he paused mid-sentence as the pain took his breath away, "... you will do this for me ..." he paused again before adding, ".... Please." The pain got the better of him at that point and he passed out, his breathing still steady but faint.

The ambulance arrived and Bruria let in the crew. They examined him briefly and quickly determined he needed to get to a hospital. The crew got him onto a wheeled stretcher and began to move him towards the ambulance. He came to and cried for them to stop as he beckoned Bruria to move close to his face. "You must promise me that you will look after it for me," he said faintly between sharp breaths due to the pain.

"But, Professor..." she started.

"Please," he said struggling to speak clearly. "I must know it will be kept safe. Just tell me now."

She considered her options briefly and decided that she had none and that it was obviously important to the professor. "Of course, I will do as you ask," she said trying to sound reassuring, "but you can have it back when you come back home. Until then I will do as you say." Nothing more was said but her pledge was received by a weak smile. "Now let the crew take you to the hospital and get you treated. I shall see you tomorrow, Professor Einstein."

Albert Einstein died the next morning caused by the rupture of an abdominal aortic aneurysm. Bruria Kaufman never saw the professor again but she would never forget Einstein's last words to her as long as she guarded that wooden box and its contents.

One year ago

Professor Norman Smythe knew he was going to die.

Or, rather he knew he was going to have to die rather than give up his secret.

He'd had a decent turn in life now that he had reached 90 years old. Or, that was what he was telling himself. Now, strapped to a metal chair, the only item in the middle of a sterile room, he wondered how it had come to this.

Having graduated from, and progressing to lecturing at Oxford he had always wanted to work in the sciences, to make that discovery that would improve all of mankind – the sort of dream that every scientist aspires to so he thought. Well, it had eventually happened to him and, like many discoveries, it had happened by accident. He had been experimenting with fundamental electronics, trying to find an element of resistance that could dissipate the most power without burning up which, in turn, could lead to smaller circuitry and further miniaturisation and greater efficiency. During one experimental setup, he had used a small shard of silicon that had been shared with him by one of his professors at Oxford.

In an effort to distract his mind from the pain of the plastic ties biting into his wrists and ankles, his thoughts wandered back to the day when he was first given the shard. His professor was a Jewish national who was related to a research scientist from during the war but the scientist had held back on the discoveries, knowing they would have been used for wide spread human destruction. Though it was soon after the end of the war, his reputation had allowed him to return to his life he had in England before the hostilities and he had taken up professorship back at Oxford. He had formed a close professional relationship with Norman, seeing early Norman's potential for scholarly greatness.

At the end of a particular in-depth lecture, he had signalled to Norman to stay behind as all the students were leaving, giving him the shard once he was sure they were alone. "This was given to me by a very esteemed colleague, in my early academic years, in much the same way I am giving it to you. And I pass on the same warning that was given to me. Guard it carefully my boy. One day I am sure you will discover what is unique about it, as did I after many years of possession. Then perhaps it will be at a time when it can be used for the good rather than be abused by the bad. There are people out there who will do anything to gain possession of this so remain silent about it until you are in a position to utilise its properties."

"But what is it and what are these unique properties?" Norman has asked.

"It is better that you find out for yourself, as I did when the time was right," came the reply.

That had been the last time he had seen his professor as a short while after, he had been killed in what was reported as a car accident though, following investigation, a reason for the accident was never discovered. As a result of his suspicions, Norman had kept the shard hidden and never mentioned it throughout and beyond his university years, only ever performing any work on it when he was in complete isolation.

After many years of on and off experimentation with it, Norman had finally discovered the unique attribute of the piece of silicon and, in doing so, had also discovered why his former lecturer was reluctant to disclose it to the world. In fact, even at the time of his discovery, with all the conflicts going on throughout the world, Norman was unsure whether it was the time for general disclosure.

Due to the potential of the shard's properties, as a precaution, he had mailed it and a copy of his notes to a long-trusted friend that he had known for many years, originally as one of his students and later becoming a sounding board and fellow researcher. However, he now knew there was a leak somewhere in his contact chain. Either in his political connections or perhaps his phone calls had been intercepted. Maybe both. He certainly couldn't believe his friend had betrayed his confidence either deliberately or accidentally. However, a leak was definitely present as, this morning, as he had left home, he had been bundled into a car by a couple of unspeaking suited giants, blindfolded and transported to this room where he'd been strapped to this metal chair.

His mind was brought back to the present by a metallic voice echoing around the room, coming from some hidden speakers mounted into the ceiling. "We are tiring of asking. Give us the substance or its formula, Professor."

Truth be known, Norman had no idea of the formula. Having analysed the shard, there were elements within it that were unknown to any sciences he was aware of. He knew how to get it to exhibit its incredible properties but had yet to discover why they were triggered and how to make copies – certainly not until he had discovered what these 'yet unknown' elements were. In the meantime, he certainly wasn't going to give up the shard or any of its details to these thugs.

"Never!" he shouted defiantly. "Go to Hell!"

"I'm sure if there is an afterlife, that is where I will be heading, Professor," said the metallic voice. "Now, don't make it any more painful than it needs to be. You will tell us in the end."

Norman wasn't a fan of bad language but, he decided there was a time and place for everything in life. "Fuck off!" he shouted at the top of his voice.

The speaker to the sterile room was shut off and the metallic voice was then directed at the technicians monitoring the proceedings. "Do we have any further information since picking him up?"

One of the technicians spoke up. "We've searched his house and found nothing pointing to the shard."

"Nothing!" said the metallic voice, its frequency rising.

"Er, nothing. But he was picked up coming away from a post office, having deposited a parcel."

"And you have the parcel?" asked the metallic voice with menace.

"Er, no," said the technician with a shaky voice. "The post office van was there and picked it up before we could get to it."

"And do you know to whom it was posted?"

"Er, no. We didn't get a chance to see the parcel up close to see an address and a van was there so the parcel was transferred straight to it before we could get sight of the label."

The metallic voice now sounded perfectly calm, something that always worried the technicians more than when it was raised. "Are you telling me you failed?"

"Er no," said the technician now sounding more nervous. "We picked up a contacts file from his smartphone and we're analysing the data to find out who is most likely to be the addressee."

"We can ask him to tell us," said the metallic voice. The speaker to the sterile room was switched back on. "Okay professor, I will ask you one more time, what is the formula and where was the parcel going?"

Norman looked directly at one of the small cameras suspended from the ceiling. "And I will tell you one more time," he said, "fuck off and fuck you!"

"You will tell us," the voice shouted menacingly. "Release the first phase."

There was a faint click from within the ducting of an air vent on the wall that Norman was facing and, a few seconds later, a small, wispy, smoke-like cloud came into the room through the slats. Unlike a smoke cloud from something like a cigarette that tends to disperse quickly, this cloud kept its form and moved across the room towards the stricken Norman. As it approached him, the cloud split into seven smaller wisps resembling tendrils. Each tendril settled over Norman's eyes, nostrils, ears and mouth and then, in synchronous formation, seemed to flow into each orifice. Immediately Norman's eyes, inner ears, sinuses and throat erupted in intense pain. It was so sudden, unexpected and wide spread that Norman screamed out uncontrollably, writhing and fighting against his bindings.

"The pain is excruciating is it not?" said the metallic voice, now increased in volume so as to be heard over the screams. "You know how this can be stopped. Just tell us what we want to know. No one can resist this pain for long."

The pain continued to the point where Norman just wanted to die. At that point, it seemed to reduce slightly then increase again moments later, keeping Norman from passing out and keeping the suffering at its maximum. It was so intense that Norman couldn't take it any longer. "Okay, I'll tell you," he panted through the pain. "I've given the details to the government. So, you can't get hold of any of it you fuckers!"

"Can I be sure you're telling the truth?" asked the metallic voice.

"Yes, yes, yes!" he shouted, gasping in pain between each word.

"Okay," said the voice and immediately the pain stopped.

Norman slumped in the chair, drawing deep breaths into his lungs, the sweat pouring off his forehead. The pain had stopped in an instant as if it had never happened and he was just about to shout more abuse when he heard the metallic voice again. "Thank you, Professor. We believe you."

Norman relaxed a little. Was the pain finally over for him?

Then the metallic voice spoke again. "And the parcel, professor?" it asked.

"No, you're not getting that from me," said Norman between gasps of breath, blinking repeatedly at the camera as the sweat pouring down his forehead was going into his eyes.

"Come now professor, you know how much pain I can

inflict to you. And I can make it last much longer if necessary."

"You can smother me in your fucking clouds as much as you want you bastard," said Norman defiantly. "I'd rather die than give you any more details."

"I think I believe you when you say you will not tell me anything more," said the voice. Norman relaxed a little when he heard that. Was the pain really over? "So now," continued the metallic voice, "I shall take you at your final words."

There was total silence for about 10 seconds then the metallic voice spoke again. "Phase two," was all it said.

Norman tensed as he heard those words. Another click sounded from the air vent and then a larger cloud came through. Norman watched it wide-eyed in fear as it approached him, straining again against his bindings so hard this time they cut deep into his wrists and ankles. The cloud split just like the previous one and entered Norman's body in the same way.

Immediately the pain started again but this time it spread inwards throughout his body. He screamed in absolute agony for some seconds, unrelenting, then abruptly went silent, slumped down in the chair, his lifeless eyes staring ahead, no longer in any pain.

The person with the metallic voice showed no concerns for the dead scientist in the room. "Report on phase two," he instructed.

"Power drained 5 seconds after death," came a reply.

"Shit!" shouted the metallic voice. "We need greater capacity, more power. Find me more power."

"With respect, Sir," came a voice from the technician area, "we have a solution. We just needed the details from the professor."

The sound of the metallic voice increased to an insane screech. "Are you telling me that I shouldn't have used him for Phase 2 experiments?"

The technician was silent for a few moments of

contemplation, deciding whether he should say any more. He took a look at the lifeless body of the professor on his monitor screen. "Er, no Sir," he said thoughtfully, "we're ready to continue when you are."

"Good," came the metallic voice sounding a little calmer. "As the next person to question my planning will be in the chair for Phase 3."

A couple of months later

The sea was calm for as far as the eye could see and reflected the clear blue sky making it difficult to distinguish the water from the sky. The air temperature was in the mid-twenties centigrade and the breeze was blowing gently making it feel very hot in the sunshine.

The 30-foot sea-going yacht was cruising at around 20 knots, travelling from the Canary Islands in a south-westerly direction and had been doing so for the last couple of hours or so.

Karen Egan, a twenty-five-year-old, blonde-haired woman with a figure that could easily be mistaken for a fashion model, sat up from the prone position she had been in for the past hour and called across to her new husband of 3 weeks, Marc. "Are you sure we should be this far out? We lost sight of Gran Canaria ages ago."

Marc Egan, was twenty-seven, six foot tall with relaxing blue eyes and a toned body rather than over-muscled. He was a successful internet start-up entrepreneur but had refused to let the success go to his head. Yes, he liked the 'good life' but he was hard working and never asked a member of staff to do something he wouldn't do himself. He kept his staff on good salaries and also gave them a share of the profits and, as a result, was considered by most to be an all-round good bloke.

He had met Karen two years ago whilst on holiday and knew she was the right girl for him to spend the rest of his life with from very early into their relationship – something she had confessed to having the same thoughts at the same time. She was also successful in business having designed web sites for many of the top global companies and still had a waiting list of clients wanting to tap into her talents. Though they could afford to holiday in the majority of locations throughout the world, they both had spent many seasons when younger in the Canary Islands and had continued to visit the islands, even choosing to get married on Lanzarote 3 weeks ago. Now, they were chilling out for the final week before travelling home to Hampshire in England and back to work. They had hired a sea-going yacht so they could cruise around the islands, choosing to anchor off some secluded coves for the nights so they could be alone and totally relaxed.

Today, however, the sea was so calm, the breeze slight and the sun not too hot, Marc had decided to venture out away from the Canaries and the African coast so they could really spend the day in the middle of nowhere. He was determined to get to a point where the GPS display would only show the sea, even at a zoomed-out scale. He had reached that point, where the nearest of the Canary Islands had cleared the right-hand side of his GPS display about ten minutes previously and was contemplating stopping the engines and drifting for a while when Karen had sat up and spoken to him.

"It's okay, Kaz," he said looking towards her but having to shade his eyes with his hand to cut out the glare of the sun. "We're well within the range of this boat and I wanted to feel the relaxation of true isolation. I was about to stop and cut the engines for a while but just spotted something ahead as you spoke."

"What can you see?" asked Karen turning to look straight ahead, also shielding her eyes.

"It looks like a little island on the horizon but it's not showing up on the GPS."

"Do the GPS units show all the islands around?"

"They should do," he said still looking ahead at the small

land mass. "It's a proper maritime GPS system so the mapping should be pretty accurate."

"I see it now," said Karen adjusting her hand shade to cut out the glare. "Looks big enough to be classified as a proper island surely."

"Well, it's definitely not on the GPS even if I zoom right in. There should be nothing here. Perhaps we could claim it," he laughed.

"Yeah," agreed Karen playfully, "but I'm not sure if 'Egan Island' sounds good.

"Then perhaps we should call it 'Kazegan Island'" said Marc. "Let's have a closer look," he added, "I can't see anyone about. Maybe it's uninhabited."

"I wouldn't be surprised," said Karen giggling. "It must be a long commute to get the shopping."

Marc continued to steer the yacht towards the mystery island keeping a keen eye on the coastline as it continued to become clearer as they neared it, so far seeing no signs of life.

Ten minutes later, having still seen no signs of habitation, Marc dropped the anchor with the yacht in the shallows, placed a temporary ladder at the beach side of the yacht and followed Karen down into an inflatable and paddled the few metres to the white sandy beach.

The beach was like a postcard scene. White, untrodden sand that stretched for the entire visible side of the island, palm trees dotted every few metres providing the only shade and rocks every ten metres or so dividing the beach into smaller sections and also beyond the trees creating a small barrier between the beach and the inner island. On first visual inspection, there appeared to be no life, human or otherwise, that was going to spoil a lazy time for two on the sand.

"This is perfection, Mrs. Egan. Our own private island, at least for the next few hours."

"Mm, I could get used to this," said Karen smiling. "Now what shall we do?" she asked moving closer to Marc.

"Well, I can think of at least one thing that it would be rude not to do in this secluded environment," replied Marc as they sat down next to each other on the pure white sand. "And I think it's a good thing you're only wearing a bikini. Saves a lot of time undressing and dressing.

They twisted to face each other and kissed deeply. Marc reached around Karen's back and pulled open the bow holding her bikini top in place allowing it to fall down on to the sand. Karen took off his polo shirt leaving him wearing only swim shorts. They embraced again feeling the warmth of their near-naked bodies pressing tight into one another and kissed passionately, their mouths now able to explore other parts of their bodies. They parted briefly so that they could remove their bikini bottoms and swim shorts then rolled back into an embrace with Marc on top. Their passion was interrupted as Karen froze suddenly.

Marc stopped his kissing. "What's the matter?" he asked concerned.

"That noise," said Karen sounding concerned. "I can hear a clicking sound from behind the trees inland. I think there's someone here."

Marc sat up and peered beyond the trees. "There's nothing th —"

He was cut off by more clicking sounds. He pulled on his swim shorts and, keeping his gaze towards the direction of the sounds, said to Karen, "Put your bikini back on, Kaz," and towards the trees shouted, "Who's there? Show yourself."

For a moment there was silence then the clicking sounds started again. Marc stood up and headed towards the trees.

"Marc, no! Stay here," said Karen as she covered herself with her bikini.

"You stay there, Kaz. It's okay." Marc picked up a fist sized stone from the beach and headed into the trees looking around for the source of the noise.

Beyond the tree line he saw a large number of metallic cannisters standing in what appeared to be a random formation, each the size of an average soup tin. The clicking sound was being caused by the lids of some of the cannisters springing open.

"What the hell," Marc quietly said to himself as he walked slowly towards one of the open cannisters trying to see inside.

As he got to within a body length of an open cannister, a wispy smoke-like cloud emerged from four of the open ones. Marc covered his mouth and nose with his hand and turned to head back to Karen on the beach. The clouds from each cannister moved together and combined then quickly headed in Marc's direction, catching him and surrounding his head. He jerked from side to side to try to free his head from the cloud but, as fast as he moved, it moved with him. He held his breath in an effort to avoid breathing it in but the cloud separated into a number of tendrils and flowed into his ears, eyes, nostrils and mouth through the gaps in his fingers. Immediately immense burning pain erupted throughout his head. He let out an involuntary scream and fell to his knees, clutching his temples to try to stop the agony.

Karen heard the screaming and ran through the tree line towards the source of the cries. "Marc!" she shouted, "Marc! What is it?"

Through the intense pain Marc heard Karen's shouts. "Karen," he screamed still clutching his head, "Kaz, stay away. Get away from here. Run!"

Suddenly he felt another level of pain and appeared to see a blinding white light though his eyes were tightly shut. He roared a long, terrified scream at the top of his voice, then his lifeless body fell to the ground, eyes wide open in terror, mouth open in a silent scream.

Karen ran beyond the tree line and stopped, frozen in horror as she saw Marc's lifeless body lying on the ground.

"Marc!" she screamed in terror. "Marc! Oh my god, no!"

She stared at his eyes as they peered blindly towards the area of cannisters. Tears flowed down her cheeks as she tried to comprehend what was taking place. Then she heard the clicking sound again and, looking beyond Marc's body, saw the cannisters as four more of them sprang open allowing wispy clouds to rise from each one.

Karen turned and ran back towards the beach in blind panic. She didn't know what these cannisters or their misty contents were but instinctively knew to be afraid of them.

She made it back to the beach and started to push the dingy back towards the water. Suddenly, in one continuous movement, the wispy cloud surrounded her head and flowed into her eyes, ears, nostrils and mouth. She screamed hysterically as the intense pain erupted all over her head and tried to claw at her temples in an effort to stop it. She spun on the spot and jerked and spasmed to try to stop the searing sensation that felt it was all over her body but there was no way to stop it.

She screamed an almost inhuman noise as the pain intensified and a blinding white light seemed to appear in her tightly closed eyes then she collapsed, first on to her knees and then forwards, half in and half out of the boat, mercifully now lifeless, no longer having to endure the constant agony.

From beyond the small field of cannisters came three people, one with a tablet and radio in each hand. She was studying the data on the tablet as she talked into the radio. "We had around one minute of operation from each cannister set. A marked improvement over the previous trials."

"Better," said a metallic voice from the radio, "but still not good enough. We need longer operation times."

"Without the formula we are struggling to achieve more power with the existing size limitations. However, we have progressed much in the last few weeks."

"But it is still not good enough!" stressed the metallic voice. "You need to make further improvements quicker. I hope you are not suggesting you are content with what you have achieved now."

Without betraying the worry in her voice, the woman replied. "No, of course not. It just would have been more straight forward if we had the formula."

The owner of the metallic voice appeared to mellow slightly. "Keep working on it and report your progress back to me daily. Get your men to dispose of the bodies and then take the boat out to sea and sink it. We want no traces of them left on the island."

"That's all being taken care of," said the woman, waving the two men into action as they picked up Marc's body and carried it back to where Karen's was lying in the dingy.

The metallic voice continued without acknowledging the woman's competence. "I suppose with the unscheduled trial caused by our uninvited guests being a success, we can declare that Phase 3 is effectively underway."

Within the hour, the two bodies and the dingy were returned to the sea-going yacht which was sailed a mile or so out to sea from the island and then scuppered. At that point there was no trace of Marc and Karen Egan or of what happened to them or their boat. As far as any investigations went, they had just vanished without trace, leaving no signs and no distress calls.

CHAPTER 1

He should've been a dead man.

He'd been lucky.

If the road hadn't recently been mortar-bombed. If he hadn't stumbled on that loose piece of tarmac. If that hadn't thrown him off balance, jerking him quickly to his right, the sniper's bullet would've hit his neck, most likely destroying his throat and windpipe and causing him to drown in his own blood.

As it was, the high calibre round had hit his shoulder, missing the joint, but penetrating close enough to take a chink out of his collar bone. It had entered at his front, expanding slightly as it continued through, the exit wound creating a cavity larger than the entry.

As a result, he'd fallen to his knees, was losing a fair amount of blood, and was fighting not to pass out due to the pain.

But he was still alive.

So, he'd been lucky.

He should've been a dead man.

He was confused for the moment. His mind was wandering as it was trying to deal with the pain. It must have been only moments ago but he had a vague memory of leaving the three other members of his covert team back under the cover of some dense bushes whilst he went ahead to do ….

What was it?

The pain was filling his mind. He'd been trained to deal with bullet wounds, maybe into fleshy areas of the body but when it came to shattered bones the pain interrupted the thought process.

Concentrate!

Now, what was he there for?

Yes, to scout the target house. But for what?

It came to the top of his mind again – the intense burning, throbbing sensation in his shoulder, tempting him to think of nothing else.

Concentrate, concentrate!

They'd known he was coming; they were waiting for him. How could they have known? The mission was code red, secret.

The burning was taking over now. All he could think of.

Concentrate, concentrate!

Yes, think, dammit! Yes, clearer.

Few people knew about the mission, very few, top secret.

Pain!

There must be a leak within the squad. Jeez! That can be the only explanation, we have a spy –

The second shot hit him.

Again, he was lucky, if you can call that luck.

The second bullet hit him on the temple – this time grazing him, passing through skin and etching a groove into his skull.

A few millimetres, maybe a centimetre, to the side and it would have pierced his skull, literally blowing his brains out.

But it hadn't and he was still alive.

So, he'd been lucky…. again.

He fell to the ground, now in a state of semiconsciousness where his vision appeared a spinning haze and his hearing was muffled – as if he was listening to everything around him from a long distance – the only sound in the foreground a loud high-pitched whistling.

He was aware of someone shouting, "Covering fire!" and could hear muted sounds of rapid gunfire. It all sounded faint. Was it a long distance away? He wasn't sure due to the intense, overwhelming ringing in his ears. He couldn't see clearly what was going on around him as his hazy sight seemed to be darkening at the edges. He felt like he was spinning fast though he knew he was lying still on the ground.

Then the order of events became confused. He was having trouble concentrating, the pain in his shoulder, the pounding in his head and the piercing ringing in his ears were becoming unbearable. His senses were quickly surrendering the pain they were currently experiencing to a far more peaceful unconsciousness. He heard voices and was aware of contact and movement but the order they happened wasn't clear anymore.

He had the vague sensation of being grabbed and pulled back through the bushes. Then he thought he heard a voice shouting, "I'll get us a clear way out."

Then more muffed sounds of gunfire and another faint voice shouting, "Noooo!"

Then another faint shout of "Leave him!"

Then a closer voice saying, "This is gonna hurt like shit!"

Then the faintest smell of antiseptic and the momentary feeling of something being placed on his wounded shoulder and his temple.

Then penetrating, searing pain. His shoulder felt on fire, his head pounded like thunder.

Then a fleeting sensation of intense white light in his vison, bright at last.

Then darkness.

He awoke.

It was dark but he knew he was in a hospital; he could tell by the smell. No matter where in the world, all hospitals have a 'hospital' smell: a mixture of bleach, lemon, pine, ionised clean air, antiseptic, the scent of 'get well soon' flowers and questionable food smells. The 'hospital' smell.

There was some light in the room coming from a small window in the door and filtering through the edges of the curtain pulled across the window. He could see he was in a single-bedded room, sitting up, though slightly angled, in the bed. There were various small machines and displays on wheeled stands around the bed and, from these, various leads and tubes attached to various parts of his body.

He felt numb; that sort of feeling you get if you haven't moved in a long while. Why was he there? Everything seemed blurred. He tried to move to sit himself a little more upright and a breath-taking pain shot through his shoulder and a lightning bolt blazed through his head. He then remembered being shot, falling down and being dragged backwards. He wasn't aware of anything after that, until now.

The door opened and a nurse quietly entered the room obviously unaware that he was awake. She checked some of the instruments, made some brief notes on a chart at the end of the bed and went over to the door ready to exit and go on to her next routine stop. Before she could open the door, she was halted by his voice, faint and croaky as though it hadn't been used for a while. His throat felt dry and raw and, when he tried to speak, it felt like he was swallowing a bag of nails.

Through the discomfort he managed to mumble, "Where am I?"

The nurse turned away from the door and walked to his bedside. She smiled and poured some water from a plastic jug into a small cup.

"Have a drink. It will make your throat feel better. Just sip it for the moment."

She held the cup up to his lips and he took a sip. Though

he could see from the condensation on the jug that the water was cold, it felt like it was burning. He grimaced and she tilted the cup away from his lips.

"You haven't drunk for a long time so it's going to feel sore. Take a few more sips and it will feel easier."

She tilted the cup back to his lips and he took more sips. As she had said, as his throat became less parched, the water went down feeling less and less painful with each sip. It wasn't long before he could swallow a larger quantity without much discomfort so he tried speaking again.

This time his voice sounded louder and clearer and was formed without the previous accompanying pain. "Thanks," he said now with a small smile of his own. "Where am I?"

"It's okay," said the nurse placing the cup down on the bedside cabinet, "No need to worry. You're in hospital and safe now."

He matched her smile and took a glance out of the window. Through the net curtains he could only see what looked like an inner courtyard so it gave him no clues to where the hospital was situated. "The hospital bit I'd guessed," he said with as little sarcasm as possible, "but where is the hospital? How long have I been here? What happened?"

"Woah!" she cried putting up her hands in front of her defensively. "One question at a time." The smile returned to her face as she counted off her answers on her fingers. "The hospital is in London. You've been here for 48 hours. And I don't know what happened to you. You arrived with gunshot wounds to your head and shoulder. Your collar bone had splintered where one of the bullets had hit and you'd lost a lot of blood. You had to be patched up in theatre."

He paused briefly, taking it all in. He was still groggy from long-term sleep. "London!" he cried in a surprised manner. "How did I get here? I didn't get injured in London……did I?"

The smile still remained as she said, "I'm afraid I don't know how you got here. I don't know any more than I've already told you but there are a couple of friends outside waiting to see you when you're up to it. Perhaps they could help with the details. Let's get you smartened up a bit and then, if you feel okay, we'll let them in."

The nurse went out into the waiting area and approached a man and a woman sitting down alone in the room. She smiled and said, "Your long wait is over. He's awake and would like to see you."

The woman returned the smile, "Excellent, thanks. That's great news. How is he?"

The nurse's smile continued. "He's okay, considering what he's been through. He's only been awake for a few minutes after being unconscious for a couple of days so he's still quite groggy. That and the fact that he's on strong painkillers means that he's a bit confused. He was asking where he is, how long he's been here and what happened to him so his memory is lacking at the moment. He took a blow to the head so that could account for some short-term memory loss. If you've known him for a long time, it may be worth talking about a few things from his past history to help the memories return."

The woman continued with her smile and the man now joined in. He said, "Many thanks," as they both stood up from their chairs, "Please lead the way."

The nurse led them to the private room and showed them in, leading with, "Here are your friends. They've been waiting a long time to see you." She looked around as she was speaking and added, "I'll get an extra chair so you can both sit down." Thanks were said and she left the room.

The woman spoke first but they both said, "Hello Sir."

The patient stared at them; his face creased trying to reach into his memory. He kept looking at them for some time visibly struggling with his thoughts. Finally, looking towards the woman, he said slowly, "it's……. erm…… Lisa?"

"That's correct, Sir," she said cheerfully.

He then looked at the man pensively and said, "And...... erm...... erm..... Paul?"

"Erm, it's Phil, Sir," said the man.

"Ah, Phil. Sorry, my mind's not working at a hundred percent at the moment. More like ten percent I think!"

"That's no problem, Sir," he said, "You've been through a lot. It's no surprise your mind needs to warm up a bit."

"Talking of having been through a lot, what have I been through? Are you able to fill me in?"

Lisa spoke up. "We can fill you in, Sir. Give you a full briefing. Is there anything you can remember regarding what brought you here?"

The patient was about to speak when there was a knock on the door. Without waiting for a reply, the door opened and the nurse walked in with an extra chair. She was still smiling and said, "I've brought you a chair so you can both sit down."

Phil took the chair and said, "Thanks," and placed it next to the one already beside the bed and he and Lisa sat down side by side. The nurse maintained her smile and backed out of the room closing the door behind her.

The patient waited for the door to shut and then said, "I can remember –"

There was another knock on the door. The patient said, "Come in," but was already too late as the door was already opening.

The nurse walked in carrying a tray. "I thought I'd make you two a nice cup of coffee and a nice jug of cool water for our patient."

All three said, "Thanks," and then remained silent; their eyes aimlessly glancing around the room as they waited for the nurse to leave.

She soon got the hint. "I'll leave the tray here," she said, placing it on the bedside cabinet, "and I'll leave you to it."

All three said, "Thanks," again and the nurse again backed out and shut the door.

The patient took his cue to speak again. "As I was saying, I can remember nothing at the moment. I've been shot, twice, so I've been told. I have a sore head and a sore shoulder. I have a vague memory of being somewhere hot, staking out a house. Then it's all blank at the moment. I don't even remember being hit."

Lisa turned to Phil and said, "I'll lead on this if you like," to which he responded with a nod. She turned back towards the patient and began. "You, Phil and I are part of a team. We were –"

She was interrupted by the patient. He said, "Hang on, erm, Lisa, you're gonna have to go further back than that. For instance, perhaps you could start with my name."

"You don't know your name," exclaimed Lisa, eyes wide open in surprise.

"Nope," he replied, "I've been awake for a short while now and don't remember anything. I know I've been shot only because I've been told, and because it bloody well hurts but, for the moment, I can't remember why, when, where or by who!"

"Then we'll start from the beginning and see when it starts to jog the memory," she said in a serious tone but with an understanding smile. Perhaps we'll see if this kick starts your recollection. Your name is Saten. Nick Saten."

CHAPTER 2

"Satan!" he said sitting himself a little more upright in the bed, startling himself and wincing due to the pain it caused.

"Not Say-Tan with an 'a'", said Lisa smirking, "It's Say-Ten with an 'e'. Saten." This caused Phil to chuckle too.

Nick looked a little puzzled but shared the smiling too. "What's so funny?"

Phil spoke up this time. "It's what you always say to people you are newly introduced to. They always think of Satan and you always correct them describing it to be with the 'e' rather than an 'a'."

That sparked a memory in Nick. Various flashes went through his mind of him saying that phrase. Many faces flashed through accompanied by his voice uttering those words. His memory stopped at a past instance where he was saying the speech to Lisa, Phil and another man. He grimaced as he tried to recall the name of this third person. It was coming back to him in small parts – they were his team. The four of them often worked together, he was pretty sure of that. In fact, they were pretty inseparable. More flashes appeared in his head, briefly and far from complete. The four of them in combat, raiding locations, freeing people, covert operations, behind enemy lines. He couldn't focus clearly on any of his mind's depictions but he was sure they were all relevant to him and the team. But that third person was eluding him. Whenever he thought about the 'team' there he was, a face with no name. Maybe he now remembered Lisa and Phil's names only because they were here with him and, after all, they had to jog his mind first of all. He closed his eyes and pictured the man's face, trying to dig out the missing name. He saw more flashes of the four of them together then some of just the two of them but still no name was coming.

"We're a team, yes, it's coming back – a little at a time. But there's another member who's not here. I can picture him but cannot put a name to the face."

Lisa and Phil glanced at each other briefly and then looked back to Nick. The effort of trying to re-awaken his mind was placing a strain on him. A few beads of perspiration were appearing on his brow but he kept digging deep, knowing this was what was needed to quickly get his mind up and running. He tried to roam deeper into his memory. The flashes were clearing a little but it was still like he was trying to focus through fog.

Then the fog started to clear. "His name is, erm, erm, Carl. Yes…. No, not Carl. Starts with a 'C'. I'm sure it does. Erm…. Chris. Yes, that's it, Chris! Chris, erm, Wynter that's it." He gave a big smile at this point as he'd managed to overcome one memory hurdle at least.

So, he asked the next, obvious question, "Where's Chris?"

Lisa and Phil glanced at each other briefly again before she said sadly, "Chris didn't make it back from our latest mission. He broke cover to get to you after you went down. He dragged you back but was hit just as he got you safe." She swallowed deeply to stop her voice from choking up, then continued, "Unlike you, he showed no signs of life and his position had become compromised for a no life sign retrieval as it was under constant sniper threat. So, we had to leave him and get you back to the extraction point."

It came back to him now like someone had magically flicked a switch in his head. It was no longer separate small flashes; the whole picture had appeared in a flash. They were a small Special Ops team attached to the UK Special Forces comprising of personnel from the Army and Navy. Formed to go in behind 'enemy' lines in order to sabotage, rescue, disrupt or distract prior to Special Forces team's engagement. They had gone in to perform a hostage rescue prior to a full air-to-ground missile attack on the location. The rescue mission was a Code Red Top Secret task but it seemed that the 'enemy' was prepared for their arrival, hence the ambush and the sniper.

Nick looked from Lisa then to Phil and said quietly, "They knew we were coming."

Lisa and Phil glanced at each other again and they both lowered their heads to face the floor before she sheepishly said, "Yes, it would appear they did."

Nick felt pained to think a top-secret mission had possibly been leaked. "How?" he said turning himself gingerly to look at each of them. "How can they have found out we were coming?"

"We don't yet know, Sir," said Phil tiredly. "Mission knowledge was restricted to the usual few as far as we know. We're still looking into where a leak could have originated."

Lisa then took over. "Meanwhile we've been stood down on home leave. With one member down, you out of action for the moment and possible compromise of security we are currently out of action."

"Jeez!" said Nick, "What a mess! Has anybody else been to see me?"

"No," said Lisa, "As a minimum, one of us has been either outside the door or in here since we brought you in here a few days ago. Very few people know where you, in fact, we are. We've no intelligence to suggest we are still being targeted but have taken precautions anyway. After all, there was no intelligence to suggest the mission had been compromised either."

Phil now spoke up. "The Home Secretary knows we're here, and has been briefed of the mission issues, but nothing has been mentioned in Parliament and, for obvious reasons, the Prime Minister has been made aware of the situation."

Nick looked puzzled, his mind not fully up-to-speed. "Obvious reasons?" he said without looking up, "What obvious reasons?"

Lisa's face showed itself to be troubled again. "Oh, Nick, I thought your memory had returned. You don't remember?" Nick gently shook his head, that detail was yet to return though it was clearing as Lisa was speaking. She continued. "The Prime Minister's daughter, Charlotte, was the hostage. We'd got intel on her location. We'd gone in to get her out."

That was the jolt his mind needed. His memory flashes were becoming longer and clearer now. He now recalled studying the picture of Charlotte, a briefing by a distraught Prime Minister, a further briefing by the Home Secretary, ops planning with the team, a rush to board a plane, a HALO jump in order to get near to the target house without being seen, the approach and then the ambush.

"What happened to Charlotte?" he asked wondering whether he really wanted to hear the answer he was expecting.

"We suspect they had already moved her, that's if, due to the leak and possible misinformation, she was ever there at all." She lifted her smart phone from her pocket, performed a few swipes and taps, then turned it to face Saten and continued, "The day after we were there, this picture was posted online; the newspaper was current on the day."

The picture showed a full-length view of the Prime Minister's daughter with a newspaper next to her.

"Unlike the previous picture that led to clues as to her whereabouts and us going in to retrieve her, our digital forensic team confirmed this one showed no detailed background, no clues at all. There were no signs of injury but no signs of life either." She walked over to the window and looked out as if trying to see the missing daughter but really looking at nothing. She turned around facing the two men and said through gritted teeth, "So, so far they have made no demands for a ransom for her return. We don't know for sure if she's alive and, if she is, we currently have no idea of where they're keeping her."

At that moment there was a crash from somewhere outside the room; the sound of metal trays and various plastic items falling to the floor. Then there was silence.

Lisa said, "If that was the nurse dropping things, shouldn't we now hear the sound of her picking them up?" She and Phil drew their pistols from their shoulder holsters and went over to the door.

Phil held up his hand with three fingers in the air. "We go on zero. You left, me right. Three, two, one, ze –"

The door burst open, hitting Lisa's outstretched arm, knocking her over and her pistol out of her hand. She crashed to the floor over by Nick's bed. At the same time two men in white surgical coats, and carrying some sort of suppressed hand guns, entered the room. Phil took one shot at the nearest, hitting him in the chest area causing him to stagger back slightly but apparently having no stopping effect. The man then took a shot at Phil whilst the other took a shot at Lisa, both shots sounding like a muffled thud. Phil fell to the floor by the door and Lisa lay by the bed where she had fallen.

The intruders ran into the room, one kicking the pistol out of Phil's grip and the other kicking Lisa's pistol further away from where she had fallen. In the time taken to relieve them of their weapons, Lisa and Phil had become motionless.

The two assailants advanced over to the hospital bed where Nick was laying, one on each side. "What the fuck is going on!?" shouted Nick. Neither of the white clothed people spoke. One raised his unusual hand gun, aiming it at

Nick. "Woah, hang on," shouted Nick, "can't we talk about this?"

Another muffled thud came from the weapon pointing at Nick and he immediately felt a burning, stinging sensation in his chest He tried to call out but could make no sound. He tried to swing around out of the bed but was unable to do so; he seemed to have lost feeling from his legs downwards. The two assailants just stood beside the bed watching Nick, pointing their weapons at him but not firing any further shots. He tried to swing his good arm at one of the two but it felt too heavy to move. He tried to move and shout once more but could do neither.

His vision started to spin and waver, the spinning getting faster and faster.

Then everything went black.

CHAPTER 3

Saten came to.

He started to become aware of his surroundings again. He had no idea of how long he'd been unconscious, his head was pounding and he felt like he could puke at any moment. His limbs felt leaden and his vision was like he was looking through murky water. He tried to move and the sharp pain in his shoulder brought him abruptly out of his groggy state.

"Jeez!" he mumbled, his lips feeling slightly numb making the word slur.

"Nick, you ok?" he heard in a soft, female voice.

His vision was clearing as was his spatial awareness. He could see that he was still in his hospital room but the room looked like a tornado had swept through it; contents of cupboards and drawers were strewn across the floor, medical monitoring machines were on their side where they had been pushed over and various boxes of gloves, masks and aprons had been torn up and emptied over the carpet tiles.

The question had come from Lisa who had been picking things up over by the window but, having heard Saten speak, now made her way over to the bedside. "You ok?"

she repeated.

"Er, yeah," said Nick looking around the room. "What the Hell happened?"

Lisa looked very serious. "You remember those two men who ran into the room? They shot the three of us, and the nurse outside, with tranquiliser darts. God knows what was in them 'cos they worked damn quickly. And they came prepared. Phil got off one torso shot at one of them with no effect so they must have been wearing body armour."

Saten still had a puzzled look on his face. "So, they were pros. What were they doing here? Why rip the place apart? And why use tranquilisers?" He looked around the room once more. "And where's Phil? Is he ok?"

"Phil's ok. He's outside making sure the nurse is alright."

Just then the door opened and Phil walked back in. "Thought I heard you two talking. You alright boss?"

"Yeah, okay," said Saten, "You? And the nurse?"

Phil nodded, "Yeah, I'm okay and the nurse is shaken but she seems strong so should get over it. Has a bit of a headache and feeling a bit nauseous, much like the rest of us, but apart from that she seems fine."

"Good," said Nick smiling. "Now you're both here, I was asking if we knew what they were doing here and why they should choose to use tranquilisers."

Lisa spoke again. "We think they, or someone controlling them, weren't sure whether we had got into the house during our last mission before we had to get you out. We think they must be concerned we may have brought something back with us. Hence why they've ripped up the room, searching for something. We've had reports that our homes have been turned over too. How they got to know where we all live God only knows. No-one injured at the homes, they chose times when all occupants had gone out."

The puzzled look returned on Nick. "But what the Hell were they looking for? We didn't get to the house and didn't get the PM's daughter." He pondered for a few moments then said, "And they couldn't be the same people that were holding her as they would have known whether we'd been inside the house."

"Er, no boss," said Phil, "They must be another group looking for the same thing we were and, not being sure whether we had it, is why we assume they kept us alive whilst they searched rather than taking us out."

"Looking for the same thing as us?" asked Nick, the puzzled look gaining strength. "We went in to rescue the PM's daughter, didn't we? That's what you told me earlier, wasn't it?"

They both said "Yes" at the same time and then Lisa continued, "Our mission was to go in and find the PM's daughter but it seems your memory obviously hasn't fully returned."

"I assume not," said Nick, "What am I missing?"

"We were briefed that the PM's daughter had something with her that must be retrieved. Whatever it was, was so secret that we weren't told what it was until we were over there ready to move in. Even then we were only told it was a small silicone orthotope that had been embedded in her stomach area and we were never told what was in the orthotope."

"An ortho-what?" Nick asked with a quizzical look on his face. "What the hell's an ortho … thing?"

Lisa smiled. "I asked that," she said lifting her hand and spreading her thumb and finger about 5 centimetres apart, "and was told that it's about this big and it's a posh, technical term for a rectangle."

"Why don't they just call it a bleedin' 'rectangle' then," said Nick.

"I think, 'cos it's something special, whatever it is, they thought they'd give it a techie name to make it sound more important."

"So, we were to go in, rescue the daughter and bring her and the 'rectangular' implant back with us," said Nick trying to sum up the mission. "What would they have been looking for if they knew we didn't have the daughter with us?"

Lisa added to her explanation, "We were told that the silicone orthotope was so important to retrieve that our orders were to bring it back at all costs."

"Yeah, I got that part," said Nick, "But I –"

"No, Nick. You haven't got the full story. We were ordered to cut the fucking thing out of her, bring it back and leave her there if necessary."

"Jeez!" said Nick again. "Who the fuck gave that directive? If I remember right, the PM absolutely adores that kid. He'd surely have the person who ordered us to do that shot!"

"That's what concerns us," said Lisa. "We were briefed personally for this mission. The orders didn't come through the usual channels, from the Home Office, Army Command or the secret services." A look of grave concern appeared on Lisa's face. "The exact order was to bring her back if we could but, in order to get the orthotope, we were to cut it out of her if we had to. I quote, and I think I've got this bit word for word, 'The orthotope must be retrieved with or without its carrier. If the carrier has to be eliminated in order to retrieve the orthotope, then so be it.' He was willing to sacrifice his daughter's life for this thing so I don't suppose he had much value in ours. Makes you wonder who sent those goons in earlier! He's not sure if we got it. We haven't told him one way or the other yet so he sends in the heavies to find out."

Nick took a few moments to contemplate what had been said then spoke up. "We need to keep the lid on this for the moment, until we find some evidence to back this up. For the time being our stance is that we have no idea who the two 'visitors' are or who sent them. Meanwhile let's look into this and see if we can find anything further. If, and I mean if at the moment, the PM is behind this in any personal way, we have a loose cannon here and there's no telling how deep this goes. And, once the whereabouts of this thing is known, or at least it becomes known that we don't have it, we suddenly become surplus to requirements!"

CHAPTER 4

Kenneth Grantham, 85, loved walking his dog, Laddie, in these woods close to home. Laddie had been a companion for Kenneth for the past eight years following his wife succumbing to the ravages of melanoma. He glanced up at the sun shining through the trees and thought back to how she had loved to soak up the sun at every opportunity and always going a gorgeous golden-brown following exposure. Then the mole on the side of her neck was spotted which neither of them could remember seeing in the past. After a little persuasion she went to her GP who sent her for tests. He could still remember the specialist, word for word, explaining that it had already spread and was the reason for the various pains she was feeling. He remembered the haunting words 'incurable' and 'six months' hitting them like a hammer blow.

Neither of them was particularly religious but they prayed following the prognosis and, towards the end, they talked about meeting up again one day in the heavens. He had his doubts that that would happen but it seemed to keep her happy.

He sat down for a moment on the trunk of a fallen tree and patted and stroked the Old English Sheep Dog. Laddie responded by snuggling up to Ken, licking his hand as it swept past his muzzle.

Ken looked around the wood and, without looking down, spoke to Laddie.

"She loved coming here you know, Laddie. This was one of the main reasons we moved local to this wood, she loved the peace and quiet, just being able to hear the birdsong and the leaves rustling in the wind."

Laddie had heard these words almost daily. He didn't understand them but recognised that they seemed to make Kenneth sad so he always snuggled up to him when he said these things and showed his affection by licking his hand or face when they could be reached.

It was during the words being said that Laddie detected an unusual smell. It was faint but his keen senses could tell it was coming from further into the trees. It was a smell that was not usually present in the woods and he instinctively knew it was not good. Laddie sounded a mild, friendly growl and gave a slight pull on his lead.

"What is it, Laddie?" said Ken. He was used to Laddie being so well trained that, even these slight differences in his behaviour could be significant.

The dog mumbled a growl again and gave another little tug on his lead.

"What's wrong, Lad?" said Ken becoming curious. Laddie didn't usually behave like this – especially at his age. In dog years Laddie was around the same age as Ken.

Kenneth gingerly stood up from his makeshift seat and allowed Laddie to lead him into the woods. They hadn't gone far before Ken could now smell an odour, slightly metallic, almost tinny. Another few steps and Ken could now see the cause of the smell. In amongst a pile of old leaves, laying face upwards, was the body of a girl. She was clothed but her blouse had been ripped open at the front leaving her naked from the waist up except for her arms which were still through the sleeves of her blouse. Her skin looked pale, a grey-white shade which was probably due to her blood loss. Her tummy area had been sliced open deep enough for some of her intestines to be visible and her belly, stomach and chest area was covered in a dried layer of her blood. Parts of her ripped blouse had become stained with her blood where it had flowed down her side from the huge open wound.

Ken kept the lead short so Laddie wouldn't venture over to the body and walked a little closer. He considered himself quite easy going when it came to gruesome sights — he'd watched enough documentaries on the television showing death, destruction, operations, etc. after all — but this turned his stomach. This was no accident nor was it an animal gorge of any type. Someone had inflicted this upon her. It was murder.

Ken looked around quickly. Was the person that did this still around? He couldn't see anyone and Laddie didn't seem to be acting as if there was anyone else nearby. He took a deep breath and looked again at the body. There was no point in checking for vital signs, there was no way anyone could live with that much damage to their torso.

He took a longer look at her face and thought he recognised her. Now, where from? Yes, he'd seen her, or someone that looks like her, on TV. Yes, he thought he knew who she was.

He pulled his mobile phone from his pocket and checked if it had a signal out here in the woods. One bar, that would have to do, so he dialled 999 and was put through to the Police.

"Yes, you can help me," he said rapidly, "I've found a body in the woods, dead, and I think it may be the Prime Minister's daughter."

He was asked to describe exactly where he was and then asked to remain close by. "Someone will be with you as soon as they can," said the emergency operator.

It took thirty minutes for the sound of a car arriving somewhere in the distance and a further five minutes for two men to walk to where Ken was standing. During that time Ken had walked with Laddie back and forth within sight of the body glancing at it each time they passed and each time thinking more and more that it was the face of the PM's daughter.

One of the men went over to the body, the other stood close to Ken and Laddie and introduced himself.

"Hello, Sir. My name is Detective Inspector Smith and over there is Detective Sergeant Jones."

Ken thought to himself 'Smith and Jones, I suppose it's possible. You couldn't make up a more common set of surnames' but said out loud, "I'm Kenneth Grantham and this here is Laddie."

"Pleased to meet you, Sir. Thank you for calling this in. It must have been quite a shock for you."

Ken took a huge gulp. "Yes, it was. I'm not easily shocked but that sight shook me up a bit. Is it the Prime Minister's daughter? It certainly looks like her."

"We'll be waiting for confirmation of identity and hope to have it as soon as possible. Meanwhile is there someone at home who can be with you for a while? We want to make sure there is no shock after effects."

"Er, no, not really," said Ken, "I live alone, and I've no family apart from Laddie."

The Inspector took a step closer to Ken. "And have you told anyone else about this?"

Ken thought that a bit of an odd question to ask. Did it really matter if he had called and told anyone else? But Police no doubt have their procedures.

"No, I haven't told anyone," he said nervously, "I've been too shaken to phone anyone else and have to explain what I've found."

"Okay, that's good," said the detective cheerfully, "we don't want word spreading around too soon and getting loads of people descending on the crime scene."

"Oh, no, I suppose not," said Ken looking over his shoulder as Laddie had become restless due to the sergeant approaching the trio.

"Can we confirm identity?" asked the detective looking beyond Ken at the approaching policeman. The sergeant gave a slight nod and the detective gave a pre-arranged nod and hand signal reply. The sergeant pulled out a hand gun with a large suppressor fitted. There was a slight hiss and a muffled thump as the sergeant shot Laddie in his head. Laddie collapsed instantly.

Everything then happened very quickly.

Ken glanced down at his dog and then turned back in a rage to face the inspector.

He just had time see a suppressed gun barrel pointing at his forehead.

He just had a moment more to exclaim "Wha …!"

He just had a moment longer to think that he may finally find out if he will see his wife again.

But he didn't have time to register the second slight hiss and muffled thump.

CHAPTER 5

4 months following the bullet wound

Nick woke with a start. He'd rolled over in bed onto his wounded shoulder and, catching it in certain positions, still meant it produced a bloody sharp pain; bad enough to wake him up. Physio was on-going and the shoulder, in fact his whole arm, was probably about ninety percent fully operational but, as he often told the trainer, that didn't stop it fucking hurting when it felt like it.

He glanced at the bedside clock. Seven in the morning, time he was up anyway. Not that he had much to do while he was off with this shitty shoulder. Rest, physio, rest, eat, sleep. That was his daily routine and had been for the last three months.

He gingerly sat himself up, stood and went into the bathroom to shower and freshen up for the day ahead. Ten minutes later he emerged, dressed in the first things he could reach from the wardrobe – jeans, tee shirt and trainers, went downstairs and made himself a light breakfast.

Having finished that, he carefully stacked the dishwasher and then started to pace around the house waiting for the time to go to his daily physio workout.

"I'm going stir crazy," he said out loud but to himself. "If I'm not careful I'll start talking to myself and that really would be a sign I'm going round the twist."

He paced around the room, stopping by the window during each circuit to nose though the slats in the window blinds – though there was virtually nothing going on outside.

He mumbled to himself, "There's old Joe opposite washing his car as usual, trying to wash it back to the bare metal at the rate he's going and there's Mrs. Whatshername chatting to Mrs. Thingamy two doors down. What they find to chat about I'll never know. And there's the standard set of cars parked along the road, as always. Hang on, someone's got a new car, we have a new black saloon outside Mrs. Thingamy's. Not seen that one before. Makes a change."

He had the usual three hours to get through before he could head out to his physio appointment and the usual three hours of nothing lined up to keep him occupied. He couldn't spend another three hours looking out the window seeing as he could already picture the scene he would see day in and day out – well, apart from the new car. He made a mental note to find out who's car it was so he could thank them for giving him something different to look at. In the meantime, he was quickly going stir crazy.

"Arfur!" he shouted, again to his audience of one, him. "Arfur Fucksake, this is getting so boring it's driving me mad. What am I gonna do for the next three hours? Same as I did for the morning hours of the last three months – absolutely bugger all. There must be something I can do to keep me from going 'kin mad. Can't go anywhere, except for bleedin' physio. No one ever comes here, except when the bleedin' physio does home visits. It's not as if I even get a bleedin' phone call anymore. I reckon the phone's seized up and that it's never gonna ring again!"

The phone rang!

"Jeez!" he exclaimed staring daggers at the handset, "I

swear that sort of thing only happens in movies and books!" He tapped the speaker button so that he could talk hands free and answered in his best telephone manner. "Yeah. It's Nick speaking. Who is it?"

The voice at the other end of the line sounded anxious, hurried. "Nick, it's Linda."

Nick heard the unusual tone in her voice, sounding frightened. This wasn't like her at all.

Nick had known Linda since they were in the army together and they had become good friends, growing closer since leaving. Linda Andrews was one of the few women to join the special forces having passed all the courses fair and square scoring higher than many of the men. She came with strength, agility and a high IQ and was very well respected by her peers. She wasn't the type to be afraid of a battle and had won awards for bravery during many fiercely battled conflicts. At one point in their relationship Nick had wondered if it would become serious enough for marriage but it never came to that and they drifted apart though remaining very good friends. That's why Nick was concerned hearing the frightened and anxious way her voice sounded on the phone, she was always strong and was never one to display her emotions easily.

He decided not to show his concern until he knew what could be bothering her. "Hi Lin. How's things?"

She continued on without acknowledging his question. "I need your help, Nick. I've stumbled into something I can't handle on my own. I don't think they're gonna stop until they get me. I'm managing to keep a step ahead at the moment but they're closing in. They're gonna kill me if I don't give it back to them."

Nick tried to calm the situation. "Woah there," he said in a commanding manner, "you're not making any sense. Who's gonna kill you? And what have you got that they want back from you? Try to calm down and tell me what's going on."

His commanding manner had no effect on her. "I can't

tell you now Nick. I don't have time. Can't stay on the phone for too long. Have to keep moving or they'll find me."

"Who are you talking about Lin? This isn't like you at all. Tell me what's happening."

"I told you I can't now. They can't be too far behind me. Jesus, Nick, I'm scared."

"Where are you, Lin? I'll come to you. Just tell me where to go. I'm sure this can be sorted calmly."

Her voice raised at this stage. "Have you been listening to anything I've said? I'm not making this up Nick, not exaggerating. Fuck me, I really think they'll kill me!"

Nick tried to keep the conversation calm. "You still haven't told me who they are and what they are after. Tell me what's going on."

She sounded bordering on sobbing at this stage and her speech started racing. "I really can't tell you on the phone Nick. I don't know who might be listening. And I can't stay here for too long as they must be close behind." She paused briefly and then sounded a little more in control. "Do you remember our favourite place? Our favourite place we used to often visit. If you do, don't say where it is"

"Er, yes. I think I know where you are talking about."

"Can you meet me there tonight?"

Nick involuntary checked his watch. "I can do it in 90 minutes if you like."

"No!" she said hurriedly then slowed herself down. "No, thanks, Nick. Safer if we're there later. Can you make it end of the day? Eleven or eleven thirty?"

Yes, I can do eleven thirty. I'll be there."

Now the gratitude could be heard in her voice. "Thanks Nick. You don't know what this means."

"You're right, I don't," he said in a confused tone, "but I'm hopeful you will explain when I see you."

"Oh yes, yes I will," she said in a relieved tone. "But, in case I'm, er, not around when you get there, I'll put it in our favourite spot – our secret favourite place."

Nick had a fair idea that she wouldn't tell him anything further until they met, including any further explanation as to what 'it' may be so he just said, "Okay."

Before he could say anymore, Linda said tearfully, "Thanks mate, bye," and then she ended the call.

"Arfur...!" Nick shouted again. Then he spoke out loud to himself, "What the hell's going on? She's not one to go looking for trouble. What the hell does she have that people want?" He made a little involuntary shrug of his shoulders and said, "Only one way to find out I suppose."

Years ago, more years than Nick cared to remember accurately, their favourite place had become a permanently fixed open-air funfair situated just on the western outskirts of London on converted farmland. They'd often visit it during their 'going out' stage whenever they could get leave and their favourite ride was the Love Boat, a leisurely water ride where two to a boat could meander slowly along a winding mini river – much of it secluded – forgetting the world around them and allowing them a few minutes of 'private time' together. One stage of the ride was the imaginably titled 'Tunnel of Love' in which the boats entered a man-made enclosure that was dark enough for privacy, according to the sign 'allowing our customers a few minutes to get to know each other in a more intimate way'. Within the tunnel was an area at a turn in the river where a large love heart had been strategically placed and back lit in a soft golden glow to create a particularly romantic area. At times Nick and Linda would board separate boats and leave each other romantic notes hidden behind the heart, invisible to all in the dim light but known so well to them that they could reach behind as the boat drifted past and retrieve the message for reading when they came out of the tunnel into the light. This they had joked had become their favourite spot, naming it their secret favourite place, keeping it secret as they didn't want their friends to know and label them as 'lovey-dovey'.

This is where he was now about to visit. He hadn't been

there for years but knew it was still there as he'd seen adverts for it in the newspapers recently. He remembered remarking to himself how much the area had developed since the days of going there with Linda. There were more rides, some leisurely, others white knuckle, a kids' area where smaller rides kept children and parents occupied, an adult go-kart track and an open-air pool with a wave machine and a few water chutes curling around each other at one end. He thought to himself that it must look so different from the old days but time moves on and, from what he had gathered from the newspaper ads, the Love Boat ride had been kept pretty much as it had always been.

Nick went about his daily routines as normal. A trip to the physio, the local shop to get lunch, a workout then a meal rescued from the freezer. Then came the evening and he decided it was time to get ready for the trip. Better to be a little early than late.

Nick went to his bedroom, reached into his clothes wardrobe and released a hidden catch that allowed a false back to slide aside revealing a large safe with a keypad and fingerprint reader. He keyed in an eight-digit code and then placed his right-hand index finger to the print reader. His print was recognised and with an audible click the safe door opened.

Inside was a small collection of pistols, assault rifles, explosive devices and associated accessories. He picked up a shoulder holster, a Glock 17 pistol and two spare clips full of 9mm ammunition. He also chose a covert body armour top that could be worn under shirts and tee shirts without being seen. He put on the body armour, shoulder holster, checked the Glock was full with one chambered round and then placed it in the holster. He closed and locked the safe, slid the rear wardrobe panel back into its closed position, grabbed a leather jacket placing the spare clips into the inside pockets and headed downstairs. He then grabbed his wallet and car keys, set the intruder alarm, went out locking the front door behind him and approached his car.

This year Nick had bought himself an Audi R8. He'd loved the look of the car as soon as he'd entered the showroom but had fallen for it on hearing the sound of the V10 5.2 litre engine the moment it had been started. It was fast and classy looking as far as he was concerned – a real head turner.

The R8 detected the keys in his pocket as he approached and automatically unlocked the doors and adjusted the seat, steering wheel, mirrors, air conditioning and digital dashboard to his pre-set favoured settings. He got in, started the engine savouring that V10 growl and drove out of the driveway heading for the fair.

Moments after the R8 was out of sight, the black saloon pulled away, heading in the same direction. Inside the saloon three of the passengers loaded and readied their weapons, SIG Sauer 516 assault rifles with laser red dot sights.

Earlier, one of the occupants had placed a micro tracker – self-adhesive and magnetic nowadays as more vehicles no longer had steel bodywork – on the underside of the car so that the tracked vehicle could remain out of sight but still be followed. A GPS map was showing on the centre console display and, on this, was Nick's R8 showing as a moving dot a few hundred yards ahead of the saloon.

They followed the R8 at a safe distance so they couldn't be spotted, heading west out of town, weapons ready for use.

CHAPTER 6

The fair had certainly expanded since Nick had last been there. He remembered it as being an area in the middle of a muddy field, now it looked like it took up the entire farmland. Tall, brightly lit towers with all sorts of fast-moving revolving seats whizzed around causing occupants to scream with delight whilst roller coaster tracks coiled like giant snakes in between the towers daring passengers to loop the loop and twist and turn with nothing but a metal bar between them and disaster. A large arena stood at one end of the fairground where knights in their bumper cars did battle whilst loud mood music played and sirens blasted to increase the tense atmosphere. In the middle of the main stretch of rides was a huge archway with hundreds of multi-coloured lights spelling out the fair's name, enticing thrill seekers in and giving an advance notice of what sensory stimulation a visitor would be met with upon entering.

At the other end of the fair, looking like a poor relation to the modern rides, was the Love Boat. Apparently kept going partly due to an agreement of sale during the early expansion as the farm owner was an avid user of that ride in the 'good old days' and partly due to many people still using it reliving their youth.

Next to the Love Boat ride, making it look so small in comparison, well-lit but only in white lighting, was a car park large enough to take around 1000 cars. This had been a small muddy area of the field during Nick's original visits where cars would often get stuck in the winter times when the ground was soft, requiring good natured fair goers to assist in the pushing of vehicles to allow their occupants to head home. Nowadays, in contrast to its original self, it's a level, tarmac covered area marked out in numbered parking spaces. Sharing the tarmac with the car park is a go kart track situated at the far side from the fairground and now chargeable rather than provided for free for uses of the original fair.

"What is free nowadays," said Nick to himself. "Won't be long and they'll charge us for parking even when we turn up on foot!"

Currently, it was a quiet night for the fairground and at this late time the car park was around a third full. Nick drove his R8 up to the gate, paid the entrance fee and drove in to the designated numbered parking space. He got out and locked the R8, looked around for anyone or anything suspicious, saw nothing, checked his watch and found it was 23:20 so headed slowly towards the Love Boat ride.

He looked around for any sign of Linda. The place was fairly quiet with a few people heading between their favourite rides but he couldn't see her and saw no obvious signs that she may have left for him. Remembering what Linda had said during her message Nick walked up to the Love Boat ride, getting immediately to the ticket booth as there was no queue and said, "One please."

The ticket seller grinned slightly and questioned, "Just the one?"

"Yes!" said Nick, raising his voice a little and putting the correct money on the counter.

The grin broadened a little more. "Oh, it's just that we usually get asked for tickets for two for this ride," sniggered the seller sliding the ticket across.

Nick gently but firmly snatched the ticket from the seller's fingers, looked him in the eye, winked and said, "Can I help it if the person I'm most in love with is me!"

He walked to the decking area where the small boats were waiting for boarding and sat down in the front one waiting for the ride to start.

As Nick was making himself comfortable in the boat, a dark saloon had entered the car park and had driven in to a parking space. As the car was parking, the occupants had watched Nick as he approached the Love Boat ride and got in to one of the boats whilst they were checking their weapons again. They got out from the saloon, concealing the weapons under their coats, and headed towards the ride entrance.

Nick sat back in the chair steadying himself as the boat gently rocked from side to side as it set off into the ride through the silk curtains as they automatically parted with an aging hum and with an added grind as they were brought back together. It brought back old memories for him of the days when he and Linda used to sit side by side as the boat meandered along the water watching the tranquil scenes from various romantic films and books depicted on the shoreline lighting up as the boat passed by.

He then realised why it was bringing back such vivid memories and remarked to himself, "It hasn't changed a bit. In all these years they haven't added a thing. There must've been some newer romantic films and books since I was last here. No wonder it was quiet at the entrance."

He decided to relax and check out the remainder of the ride – if it was exactly the same as before then chances are the Tunnel of Love and the Love Heart would still be present.

The boat rounded another bend and the Tunnel of Love came into sight. Nick sat up a little more so that he would be able to reach out from the boat if the Love Heart was still present. He heard the hum and grind of the curtains and thought to himself that someone else must actually be using the ride as well. As the boat entered the tunnel, he saw the old sharp bend was still there and he prepared himself for reaching around the love heart. The boat turned at the bend and the heart came into sight, the same as it always had been, maybe looking at bit more faded in the spot light that came on as the boat neared it.

He was struck by another thought. What if Linda hadn't got here yet and therefore hadn't had a chance to place anything behind the heart. What if that was her in the boat he heard entering a while ago. He may have to go around again. That'd give the ticket seller something extra to grin about.

The boat approached the heart and Nick leaned over to reach behind it. He moved his hand around but couldn't feel anything.

"Shit…!" he said, "will have to go round again."

Then he felt something. It felt cube shaped, cold, metallic and small enough to easily fit into his gripped hand. He grabbed it, brought his arm back round from behind the heart and sat back in the boat to stop it from rocking again. He was now past the heart so the spot light had switched off. He waited to get to the next scene so its spot light would give him some illumination but it wasn't working so all he could do is feel it and try to peer through the semi-darkness. It was roughly cube shaped and felt like it was made from metal of some kind. It felt very cold, as if it had been out in the open for a long time and, in this light, he couldn't see a lid or an obvious way that it might come apart. It looked smooth and, in the dim lighting, he could just make out some markings on the sides he could see but was unable to make out what they were. As he moved the cube in his hand to get a feel for it, he felt the corners of the cube weren't pointed, as if it had had the corners smoothly filed flat. He wondered why it should be that shape and, from initial quick looks at it, he had no idea what it was or what it might do. He placed it in his pocket for safe keeping. If Linda had put it in the special place, she must have had a good reason and she sounded so scared on the phone. So, it must surely be important –

Suddenly the boat stopped moving and the spot lights and subdued lighting went out leaving only the faint glows coming from the emergency lighting.

"This could be dodgy," he thought to himself. "Just in case, this is no time to be sitting here."

Whilst his eyes were getting used to the dim lighting, Nick couldn't see anyone but could hear faint footsteps on the bank side approaching the area where he was. "Definitely getting dodgy. Too quick for a breakdown rescue party."

As quietly as he could, he got out the boat and into the water on the far side from the direction of the footsteps. The water was only deep enough to reach his thighs so he crouched down to use the boat as cover. The footsteps became louder and, as Nick peered around the side of the boat, his improving sight could make out four figures coming out of the shadows. As they drew nearer, he could see there were three people forcing the fourth to walk with them, obviously reluctantly as the figure was trying to get free from the grip of the two figures either side and the one behind. They approached the heart and it became clear that the reluctant figure was Linda, hands bound in front of her and tape across her mouth.

One of the captors switched on a powerful torch angling the beam directly at the boat, causing Nick to quickly dart back under cover. The torch beam swept back and forth around the boat and surrounding part of the river in a search pattern telling Nick that they didn't know for sure where he was. He kept low and could hear there was movement happening sounding like Linda was being dragged around. The torch beam settled back on to the boat and an accented voice, possibly oriental, loudly called out, "We know you are out there Mr. Saten. Please show yourself or we will be forced to permanently disfigure your friend."

Nick kept perfectly still not revealing his position whilst

trying to gauge if the oriental voice was bluffing. He heard what sounded like muffled cries and deep, fast breaths.

The oriental voice spoke again, "My colleague is now holding a razor-sharp knife against your friend's cheek with the point only millimetres away from her eye. You have ten seconds to come out of hiding or he will be pleased to press the point home and draw the blade down to her jaw. Ten…, nine…"

Nick peered around the boat again and his eyes had now adjusted to the dim lighting to allow him to see that the voice was being truthful – though Linda was trying to move away, she was being held tightly while a knife blade was being held against her face.

"Eight…, Seven…"

Nick had to think fast. There were three of them, spaced apart. So, unlikely that he could take all three out before Linda was injured or worse.

"Six…, Five…"

The muffled cries and deep breathing were getting louder and faster. There could be more of them. He could see three but there could be more somewhere watching. Even if he managed to take out the three, if there are more, they could still harm Linda.

"Four…, Three…"

The breaths were getting more fraught, loud sounds as heavy breath was drawn in through the nose and a rasping as breath was blown against the tape covering Linda's mouth.

He needed to stall for time. Give himself a bit longer to discover if they're alone and hope that he gets a chance to make a rescue attempt.

"Two…, One…"

"Okay, okay," shouted Nick, "I'm coming out. Take the knife away. Leave her alone." He checked the small cube was deep in his pocket then stood upright with his hands raised loosely at the elbows and slowly made his way over to the river bank.

The countdown stopped and the oriental voice calmly said, "Please get out of the water Mr. Saten then stand on the bank keeping you distance."

Nick climbed out of the water up on to the grass. As he stood up, two of the trio trained high powered assault rifles on him whilst the third had swapped his knife for a pistol that he was now pointing to Linda's side. "Please give me the item you have retrieved" said the oriental with a menacing tone.

"I don't have anything," said Nick using his best Poker playing, non-committal voice.

"Please do not play games with us Mr Saten. My colleague would take great pleasure in killing your friend. He likes to improvise and has pleaded with me to give him the opportunity to experiment with how many shots or cuts he can make before death occurs. We saw you reach behind the heart so just hand me what you found behind there."

"There was nothing there," Nick shouted. "I reached behind but couldn't find anything there." He gauged the situation, one holding a gun to Linda and the other two pointing rifles at him. The odds weren't good. However, if he gave them the little cube then they would have no reason to keep Linda or him alive.

"Ok Mr. Saten. To demonstrate we are not bluffing, Mr. Li please prepare to take the first non-lethal shot on my command."

The one being referred to as Mr Li smiled and moved the pistol so it was pointing at Linda's elbow. She struggled more but was still being held firm by two of the captors. The oriental shouted again, "Ok Mr. Li. On my command. Three…, Two…" –

"Okay! Okay! Stop!" shouted Nick. The countdown stopped again. "I'll give you what you want, just don't harm her." He could see that Linda's eyes had become fully opened as she faintly shook her head indicating that Nick shouldn't hand over anything. He met her eyes with a hopeless expression silently saying what else could he do.

"How can I be sure that you will not harm us if I give you what you want?" he asked trying to stall for more time.

"You cannot," came the reply, "but I can guarantee you will both die very slowly if you do not. You are in no position to bargain Mr. Saten. Just hand it over or I will instruct Mr. Li to proceed with no further countdown this time. Mr Li......."

"Okay, okay," said Nick, "don't shoot. I have it right here for you. I'll hand it over n........."

He stopped in mid-speech and a puzzled look came over his face. At that moment three red dots had appeared on the side of the heads of each of the captors.

"Erm...," was all he could think of to say.

Three shots were fired and all three captors' heads exploded as hollow point bullets burst out of their exit points taking an eruption of blood, bone and brain matter with them. The three captors were dead before they had registered the sound of the shots and their lifeless bodied slumped to the ground, weapons falling around them.

Nick reacted quickly, old forces training still in memory. He leapt at Linda catching her in a rugby tackle to the ground and then rolling with her down the bank back into the water. Once there he quickly untied her hands, took off the tape covering her mouth and removed the handkerchief that had been stuffed in her mouth.

"What the fuck happened?" she said, clearly shocked to still be alive.

"No idea," he said quickly, "whoever did that aren't with me. Let's get the hell out of here."

Nick grabbed her hand and made to run away along the river but she stood firm and stalled his momentum.

"Wait!" she shouted. Did you pick it up? We can't go without it."

"Yes, I've got it. Now let's g........."

He stopped in mid speech for the second time as two red dots appeared on Linda's and his chests, hovering over their hearts.

"Erm …," he said again.

CHAPTER 7

MI6 Headquarters, Vauxhall

MI6 or the Secret Intelligence Service giving it its correct title has always been a secretive organisation working behind the scenes helping to keep the UK safe from threats from other parts of the world. Since its early beginnings in 1909 as the Secret Service Bureau Foreign Section it has always worked gathering intelligence that can be used to thwart potential attacks on the UK and its nationals both in country and abroad. In times of various wars over the years, its brief has expanded and further sub-sections have been introduced. Since the introduction of Section D in 1938 it and subsequent sections have been performing clandestine operations some so secret that they will probably remain undisclosed, known only to a very few high-ranking UK officials.

David Wilmott was one such official. Having been monitored in his university years and then through his five years in military intelligence where he speedily rose up through the ranks by merit rather than due to connections, he was recruited into MI6 to head up one of the Section D ultra-secret sub divisions where he had remained achieving many successes that, by their nature, can never be applauded. Now fifty-five but looking ten or so years younger due to his disciplined fitness regime, he was just over six-foot-tall and toned rather than rippling with muscle. A few stray grey hairs were present around his temples but these were kept from being prominent by a short hair style that he regularly cut himself, often enough for it to appear that his hair never grows. Unmarried, having never found a female that he thought would be able to put up with him on a permanent basis, he had had a few short-term relationships in the past but, due to the nature of the business, work tended to come first, so long hours were spent in the office rather than at his out of London home by the river. He was friendly, well liked and well known for being persuasive and getting the best out of people. This side of his nature would likely be put to the test in the near future with the next task he was planning but, before he could plead success, there were a few more things he needed to get straight, a few more local agents he needed to get 'on board'.

He leaned back into his recliner chair mulling over his plans for the near future, gazing out of his large office window across the Thames watching the water buses go by and the many cars and pedestrians traversing Vauxhall Bridge.

There was a double knock on the office door. David swivelled around on his chair so that he was sitting neatly at his desk facing the door. "Come in," he said cheerily.

The door opened and in walked Andrew Fleming, current Chief of MI6 and David's direct manager. Like Wilmott, Fleming was toned, choosing regular gym visits over sporting activities. Five years older than Wilmott and a little greyer but also looking younger than his age. Having worked his way up through the ranks following joining the service from university, he professed to understand the needs of his agents and, as a result, he was well liked throughout the organisation and by his political governors.

As well as having a good working relationship, Fleming and Wilmott were friends outside of the work environment and therefore kept their private conversations informal, leaving the 'Yes sir, no sir' sayings for the benefit of the media.

David had been expecting a visit for a while. The boss was getting worried and trying his best to pass his concerns down the line. He decided to do his best to look calm.

"Andy," he smiled, "what can I do for you?"

"Dave," he said making sure the door was closed behind him, "have you found him yet?"

So, that was definitely why he had called in person; this wasn't a discussion that could be written down or recorded over a phone line.

"No, not yet," said Wilmott, "but I've got some of our best out there searching for him. We'll find him soon."

"But, what if we don't?" said Fleming in a worried tone.

"Andy, relax," said Wilmott still sounding calm. "They're the best at hunting people down. They have all the known places covered. They will find him."

"And, when they do, I don't see him likely to just give in to them without putting up a fight. Can you really guarantee this will be concluded favourably, and quietly?"

David smiled in a genuine way.

"Andy, we've already discussed this, at length, and were both going with it, or so I thought. This needs to be done for the good of the country. And, as previously agreed, I still feel it's vital that we carry this out without the knowledge of our leaders including the Prime Minister and the Cabinet. My searchers are the best at what they do. They will find him and they will carry out their instructions and they will not cause a scene. That's what they do."

Fleming hesitated for a moment. He was used to having the weight of life-or-death decisions on his shoulders but that was usually with the approval of Whitehall or the Palace.

"Yes, but we're talking about taking the law into our own

hands. It's the sort of thing '6' has only done in the past during times of war."

David leaned forward resting his elbows on his desk. He wasn't going to take the responsibility for this on his own; they had debated this at length and agreed the action.

"Effectively we are at war this day and age. War on terror – from various directions, a digital war – hackers from various countries trying to destabilise economies and the occasional mad ruler trying to take over the world starting with his own country or province. It's got to the stage over here where we have to make decisions on behalf of the politicians. They're often powerless in these matters nowadays. Stopped from taking action by political ties, threats of legal action, media coverage and, dare I say it, influence from the enemy countries involved."

Fleming looked pensive. "I know we've discussed it and, yes, I'm for it in principal but whatever you say, however you put it, we are not at a declared war with anyone. So, the buck stops with us if this goes ape shit. We could be hanged for this!"

Wilmott swallowed hard. It's a lot to be asking of his friend but there's a lot to be gained from it too if it goes well. He'd thought about it for a long time and still considered it to be the right thing to do.

He spoke slowly and cautiously, "That's why we must be very careful that there are no records of this. That nothing can be traced back to us or to '6' itself. That the people involved have no direct connections to the service nor to us."

Fleming allowed a faint smile to materialise. "Okay, okay Dave. So, we go ahead with it. Then what?"

A large smile appeared on Wilmott's face.

"Once he's been found and dealt with, we'll be free to control any actions or hits considered necessary. We'll then be in a position to regain some control for the country, get some status back for the UK without involvement of politicians."

Fleming sounded surer of himself now.

"And this all has to start with this one action on this one man?"

Wilmott sounded very confident.

"Yes," he said now with a tone of authority, "once we have him it will be the catalyst for many other actions." Wilmott stood up, turned and gazed out of the window. "There'll be no going back once we have dealt with Nick Saten."

CHAPTER 8

The Fairground

The red dots continued to hover over the hearts of Nick and Linda. They both stood still, barely daring to breathe. Nick glanced around moving only his eyes, looking to see if there was any way he and Linda could get away but they were in the open and there was no way they could escape the time it took to pull a trigger. He glanced at Linda and their eyes met. He could see the look of realisation on her face that they couldn't get out of this. Nick was expecting a shot to happen next but, instead he heard a voice.

"Mr. Saten and Ms. Andrews, please remain still whilst we approach."

Nick then heard faint footsteps approaching where he and Linda were standing, then spotted four silhouettes coming out of the low light, two of them keeping their weapons steadily aimed at Linda and him. They drew near enough for Nick to be able to see them in the low lighting; they appeared to be wearing Special Ops combat outfits but had no insignias on their uniforms. Their assault rifles looked like Sig MCX variants, also what Nick would've expected Spec Ops to be using. They were all wearing balaclavas, with cut-outs for their eyes and noses, under what Nick also recognised as Ops-Core FAST ballistic helmets. This all pointed to them being a Spec Ops team but with no identifying marks.

The one that appeared to be the leader spoke out again.

"Mr. Saten, Ms. Andrews, please come with us if you wish to get out of here safely."

"Who the fuck are you people!?" exclaimed Nick.

"Right now," answered the same person, "we're the people keeping you alive … Now, please come with us!" he said with urgency, "the Prime Minister would like to see you both."

Nick and Linda took another look at each other with both signalling surprise at who their apparent appointment was to be with. Nick raised his eyebrows and Linda made a slight shrug of her shoulders, signalling to each other that they thought they didn't have much choice at the moment.

"Then, lead the way," said Nick.

"I think you'll understand if you two go first but, please bear in mind, that we will be a couple of steps behind you and you will still be red-dotted even though you won't be able to see them. We'll tell you where we want you to go."

They guided Linda and Nick out of the Love Boat ride, into the car park beside it and over towards a dark saloon that had two equally dark people carriers parked nearby. Nick suspected this was the same saloon that had been the additional car along his street though he didn't remember the people carriers.

Nick realised now that the small amount of people that were currently attending the fairground had been kept away from the ride and this area of the car park by some men and women dressed in standard police uniforms. Whether they were genuine police he didn't know but, now that Linda and he were approaching one of the people carriers, the police were heading towards the other.

Linda and Nick were guided into a people carrier along with the two armed-guards, the apparent leader getting into the passenger seat of the saloon. Not a word was spoken but, once they were all in and the doors were shut, the vehicle pulled away and, once out of the car park, picked up speed with the saloon following close behind. The vehicle now containing the police had pulled away in the opposite direction, following hand signals from the leader.

The side windows of the people carrier had been blacked out and the view through the front windscreen was obscured by one of the armed guards so Nick had no idea where they were heading and could only see the two people in the front seats of the saloon through the rear window. He kept his head angled towards the floor on the vehicle but the angle was such that he could still see out the rear window. The internal light had been left on in the saloon so the faces of the driver and the leader were both lit up fairly clearly even in the dark of the night.

Nick had picked up some lip-reading skills during his covert ops training some years ago, so was keen to read what the leader was saying. He couldn't make out every word and would only 'hear' one side of the conversation but often that was enough to be able to get the gist of what was being said in many conversations.

As the vehicles had pulled away, the apparent leader had produced a mobile telephone and tapped at the screen. Now, the call had connected and he was speaking quite fast down the phone. Nick couldn't make out every word but was getting used to the leader's pronunciation and, hence, picking up more and more words as the discussion continued, he put the conversation together.

It appeared that the leader was reporting in to someone. "Yes, we have them … No, we don't have it but he told the … he has it." Then there was a long pause as he listened to the person at the other end. Then, "Are you sure you want them brought in? They may be seen." Then another long pause. Then, "Okay, if you really need it, we can get it from him now … Okay, okay, if you must speak to them, we'll bring them in." Then another pause. Then, "Yes, after that we can take them there. As long as you keep them on side and they trust us, then we can get them there without trouble … Yes, yes, I understand there must be no trouble when they're near to you … Yes, yes, of course we'll ensure they're seen by few people." Then there was another long pause. Then, "Yes, that can be done. Both? … No, they'll never be found, that's our guarantee."

Nick then saw him tap to end the call, put down the phone, turn to the driver and say a few words that had couldn't make out whilst side on. The driver then spoke into a radio handset and the people carrier then increased speed which was matched by the saloon.

"Oh shit!" Nick said to himself, then continued the thought, "we've got to get away but Linda won't know any of this. She thinks these are the calvary and that we're off to see the PM. I need to get the message to her so we can get away. How?"

He sat silent for a while, thinking. He needed to act fast, he didn't know how long before they reached their destination. If the two of them weren't ready then or before, they were up shit creek. He thought for a bit longer….

"Oh shit!" he exclaimed loudly. The armed guards sat impassively but Linda reacted to the first words spoken for a long time.

"What is it, Nick?" she asked quietly.

"Oh, erm, I just remembered I left the gas on!" he said keeping close eye contact with her.

"The gas?" she said sounding confused.

"Yeah, at home. I left the gas on. I need to get home as quickly as possible."

"Well, there's not much hope of that at the moment," she said glancing around the vehicle, "I don't think we'll be heading your way for a while. I think –."

"Shut the fuck up!" said one of the impassive guards robotically, emphasising he wanted quiet by raising his MCX to point directly at Linda's head.

"Okay, okay. Just saying," said Nick raising his hands, palms outwards, as a sign of surrender. He stared forwards again whilst thinking to himself, "Did she understand? It was some time ago. Did she remember?"

When they were 'an item' a good few years ago, if he needed to get away quickly or urgently, to get back to camp or to get them away quickly from somewhere they shouldn't be, he used to say he'd left the gas on and had to get home quickly to sort it. The saying had come from her, back from a time when she had left the gas on and did need to get home quickly. He just hoped she remembered it was a bit of an unofficial coded phrase. "Oh well," he thought, "let's hope she understood and will be ready if and when we get a chance to get away."

The journey lasted another 40 minutes and Linda and Nick were both covered by the MCXs all the time, there was no chance to make an escape. The final 10 minutes of the journey had been stop-start and slow when moving so, Nick assumed they had driven into a built-up area – which meant they may be able to lose themselves behind buildings or around corners if they got the chance to get away. He just hoped Linda had got the message. He looked across at her and she gave an almost imperceptible nod of her head which he took to mean that she was ready to make a break for it whenever he was.

As the people carrier was slowing down at the end of its journey, the guard that had been obscuring the view out the front windscreen, shifted to one side allowing Nick a view outside. He knew London very well, his Special Ops advance driving and abduction avoidance courses had required him to do 'the knowledge' in a similar fashion as taxi drivers, and, even though it was now some time in the middle of the night and the only lighting was the glow of the street lights, he immediately recognised they were in Thorney Street at the rear entrance to Thames House.

When the vehicle came to a complete stop, the guards made their first mistake. As the car pulled up and, before the saloon had come to a halt behind them, they started to get their captives out via the side sliding door. The guards remained inside and indicated that Linda and Nick should disembark together. They both stepped through the side door, Linda slightly ahead of Nick, with one of the guards close behind him, weapon raised. As Nick stood on the pavement he stumbled slightly and grabbed hold of the door for balance. The guard still slowly walked forward preparing to step down from the vehicle floor—

Nick slid the side door as fast as he could, pushing the gunman's arm sideways and then crushing his wrist between the door and the car's frame with a scream and a crunch of breaking bones. At the same time Nick had deflected the MCX upwards in case the guy had pulled the trigger. The gunman got one suppressed shot off harmlessly into the air before his wrist and tendons were crushed and then his now useless hand could no longer grip the weapon allowing Nick to take it from him.

Nick flipped the MCX so it was facing into the gap being created by the guy's arm, took a shot at the guy then angled the weapon at the other gunman whose vision had been blocked by his comrade until then and double-tapped two rounds into his neck sending him sprawling to the floor. As he was firing, Nick slid the door open, jumped back inside the people carrier and crashed the butt of the rifle into the side of the driver's head.

At the same moment, Linda had reached into the open doorway, picked up the second MCX and fired a burst of rounds at the now stationary saloon, peppering its windscreen with holes, hitting the driver and blowing out its front tyre.

Nick's actions had happened so quickly that the occupants of the saloon had not had the chance to leave the car. Now the leader was opening the car door and starting to draw his Glock. Nick opened the driver's door and pushed the unconscious driver out onto the road. He jumped into the driver's seat, checked that Linda was still in the vehicle, shouted, "Hold on to something," and floored the accelerator. The turbocharged engine roared in response and pushed Nick back into his seat and Linda off her feet onto the side chair where she had been seated for the previous journey.

The leader of the gunmen had exited the car and shot at the disappearing people carrier but, due to the distance already achieved by Nick's floored accelerator and the limitations of a suppressed Glock over distance, the shots went wide.

"Shit! Shit! Shit!" he shouted watching the rear lights of the people carrier disappearing around the corner at the end of the road.

"Shit! Shit! Shit!"

Then he came to his senses. "Unit 2, read? Alpha vehicle has gone rogue. Track and attack. They must not get away"

CHAPTER 9

The people carrier sped around the corner of Thorney Street, now out of sight of the saloon and its occupants.

"Are they following?" yelled Nick concentrating on keeping the vehicle's four wheels on the ground as he guided the people carrier fast around the bend in the road, tyres squealing.

Even though she was confident, Linda took a cautionary look out the rear window. "No, they're not," she shouted above the engine noise, "I shot out their tyres. That saloon won't be going anywhere for a while."

"Excellent," Nick smiled through his concentration, "then we're home and dry."

"Don't say that," Linda scolded, "they've probably got other patrols out in London."

"Nah!" said Nick confidently, "they had a two-vehicle armed escort for us. I doubt they would've thought they needed backup."

By now they were on Millbank speeding south. As they hurried past The Tate Britain Gallery a black car with darkened windows pulled out behind them.

"I wouldn't be so confident about your last statement," shouted Linda, tension now sounding in her voice. "We've got company!"

Nick glanced in the rear-view mirror and saw the black car increasing speed behind them.

"Aww, faff! Hold on!" he shouted hitting the brake pedal with his full force and, at the same time, spinning the steering wheel causing the people carrier to skid into a turn with a squeal of rubber on tarmac. Nick steered into the skid and floored the accelerator again once traction had returned and the vehicle sped across Vauxhall Bridge leaving a trail of burnt rubber in its wake. The black car also took the turn onto the bridge, the superior road holding compared to the people carrier, allowing it to perform the manoeuvre at a greater speed and to reduce the gap between the two vehicles to around 30 metres. The passenger side window wound down and a man dressed all in black produced a suppressed assault rifle and aimed it at the people carrier.

Even in the dim light provided by the street lamps, Linda could see rifle being prepared. "Jeez, Nick!" she shouted, "they're gonna start shooting."

"Faff again!" exclaimed Nick hurriedly. "Hang on to something!"

He spun the wheel to the right and moved the car over to the opposite side of the road. Being the early hours of the morning there were only two cars heading across the bridge in the other direction to the people carrier so Nick could easily steer around them, though close enough to be able to see the look of surprise on the occupants' faces. As there was little traffic, the black car was also able to follow across the carriageway. The man in the passenger seat fired at the people carrier causing distinctive 'ting' sounds as the bullets punctured the vehicle's metal panelling.

"Nick, they're shooting back here!"

"I know," he shouted back, "I can hear it from here. You're not hit, are you?"

"No, not so far," she said in a voice sounding relieved.

"Good," he shouted, "in that case, shoot back!"

There were no other cars on the road at this time and

Nick was able to steer the people carrier the wrong way along the one-way road in front of Phoenix House and perform another screeching turn onto Nine Elms Lane. The black car followed keeping the distance between them constant, the passenger firing further shots, one of which shattered one pane of the people carrier's rear window, another hitting the rear top corner of Nick's seat, not stopping and taking out a wadding of stuffing close enough to Nick's arm for him to feel it go by.

"Faff!" he shouted again, "they're getting too close. Shoot the bastards!"

Linda picked up the MCX which had fallen to the floor when the people carrier had first accelerated off, poked it out of the shattered window and fired a couple of rounds at the black car. One round skimmed off the front wing of the car making the driver lift off the accelerator to allow a greater gap between vehicles.

Nick took advantage of a lull in shooting and spun the car sharply right onto Prince of Wales Drive, heading towards Chelsea Bridge. The people carrier couldn't handle the fast turn and skidded again causing Nick to have to compensate, slowing him down and causing Linda to lose her footing again.

"F'kit!" she shouted, "I think I need to be strapped in back here!"

"Sorry," he said loudly, "needs must…"

"If you want me to shoot the bastards then you need to drive steady or at least tell me if there are sharp turns coming up."

"What can I say," he shouted back, almost apologetically, "this ain't no pleasure ride!" Then he thought for a moment, "but I'll see what I can do."

He took a look in the rear-view mirror and saw the black car had regained the 30 metres distance and the passenger was starting to make ready to fire again. Up ahead Nick saw the entrance to Battersea Park on the left before Chelsea Bridge. He glanced in the mirror again and saw the black car getting still closer and the passenger taking aim again.

He had an idea. "Hang on, Lin," he shouted, "sharp turn left coming up. Once I've turned, I'll level up and try to hold it steady. As the car turns to follow us, take another shot. Aim at the driver."

"Okay," she shouted grabbing hold of the inner door handle with one hand and bringing the MCX up near to the broken window with the other.

As the next burst of bullets were fired from the black car, Nick took the sharp left turn into Battersea Park, a couple of rounds passing harmlessly past the rear lights and one hitting one side of the rear bumper. Linda managed to stay in position this time as the forces tried to throw her across the back of the vehicle. When the people carrier had straightened out Nick took his foot off the accelerator and held a steady straight line. As the black car made the left turn to follow, the passenger was unsighted and would remain so until the car had straightened up but he readied himself to shoot in preparation for the car to finish the turn.

Linda however, had a full view of the driver as the black car was turning. She let go of her hand hold and gripped the MCX tightly whilst resting it on the bottom of the broken window and took aim. As the black car turned, she fired three shots at the driver position. The first shot hit the driver in the upper chest area, lodging harmlessly into his body armour and winding him slightly. The second shot hit him in the neck, passed through destroying his windpipe and exited spraying blood over the headrest and over the passenger's face. The driver only had a fraction of a second to register the neck shot as the third bullet hit him in the forehead, killing him instantly. His dead body slumped uncontrolled and his foot pressed full down on the accelerator whilst his body weight turned the steering wheel sharply to the right.

The black car veered right away from the park road, sped across some grass, through a couple of small trees and launched off the small embankment plunging into the River

Thames. The passenger had been preparing to fire his weapon and was leaning out of the window when the driver was hit. The events then happened so quickly that he didn't have time to fully lean back in to the car. The sudden deceleration caused by hitting the water caused him to crack his head on the door frame, knocking him unconscious. The car was carried by the strong Thames current and also sank quickly due to the open windows, dragging the unconscious passenger down under the water from where he would never return.

Nick had stopped the people carrier after seeing the black car veer off the road and he and Linda had watched to see the car sink into the murky water. After waiting a few moments to see that there were no further cars chasing them, Linda got into the passenger seat and they set off at a sedate pace so as not to attract any further attention.

Though London is teeming with people and vehicles during the day, at night parts of it can be virtually empty and, apart from the few cars on Vauxhall Bridge, they hadn't passed any further cars or pedestrians during the chase. However, they knew that they would have been picked up on numerous cameras that are all over the London streets so priority was to ditch the people carrier for another vehicle as soon as possible, preferably out of view of the cameras.

They drove around until, in a small backstreet near to the Saatchi Gallery, they spotted an older car that looked as if it was in good condition. They needed an older car so that it didn't have an immobiliser radio linked to the keys and could therefore be easily hotwired. They parked up near to it and managed to force the window down far enough for Linda to get her smaller arm in so she could operate the door release. Nick then got in to the driver's seat, removed the steering column cowling, found the correct wires stripping them back with his finger nails, joined a couple of them together and then momentarily touched another to them effectively bypassing the ignition key. The car started and the engine sounded smooth. Nick was satisfied that it was unlikely to let them down so Linda got into the passenger seat and they set off at a sedate speed. They should now be safe at least until the owner awakes in the morning and finds the car is missing. They were finally able to relax a little.

They drove in silence for a few hundred yards then…

Linda smiled. "Faff?" she said.

"What?" said Nick.

"During the chase you said 'Faff' back there.

"Did I?"

"Yes, you did."

A moment's hesitation then, "Are you sure?"

"Yes, I am sure," she said, the smile growing. "You actually said 'Faff'. At least a couple of times."

"Well, if you're sure," he said, "erm, this car drives well for an old banger, don't you think?"

Now she laughed. "Don't try to change the subject."

"There's no subject to change."

"Yes, there is. Nobody says 'Faff' anymore."

"I do," he said, keeping his eyes on the road with occasional glances in the rear-view mirror.

She scoffed. "Apart from you. You had the choice of 'fuck', 'shit', amongst numerous other great words and you chose 'Faff'?"

"Yeah, well, it's an old saying of mine."

"I've never heard you say it before."

"Well, maybe not that old then. Or maybe really old, before your time"

"So, what made you choose 'Faff'?"

"Well, it seemed appropriate for the time. It stands for 'Fart and Follow Frough'."

Linda stared at the side of his face aghast. After a few seconds Nick glanced at her staring at him then back at the road. He glanced again and she hadn't changed her stance.

"What!?" he said incredulously, "what's the matter with that?"

"Fart and follow through?" she said now laughing.

"Not 'through' with a 'tee, aitch' he said also smiling now. "it's got to be 'Frough' with an 'F' otherwise it doesn't work."

Linda laughed some more, at least the silly banter had eased the tension for a while.

"You were right," she said through her laughter, "maybe we should have changed the subject. You know what's gonna happen from now on, don't you? If I ever hear someone say 'faff' or 'faffing about' I'm gonna think of farting and following through!"

They both laughed then went quiet again, still smiling to themselves. The night's events put to the back of their minds for at least a while.

They headed out of London driving carefully, ensuring they committed no traffic offences that may attract unwanted attention. After driving for about a half hour they found a motel that had a room available for the rest of the night, paid for a twin room in cash then drove the car a few streets away, parked it up wiping it for prints as best they could and walked back. Linda showered first and, once Nick had freshened up and came back into the bedroom, she was asleep on her bed.

Nick smiled, she looked as beautiful as ever just lying there breathing quietly.

"So, what is all this about?" he spoke softly to himself so as not to wake her. "Perhaps we'll get a chance to find out in the morning."

He laid down on his bed, turned out the bedside light and was also asleep as his head touched the pillow.

CHAPTER 10

Nick woke slowly from a deep sleep. The sun was shining through the sides of the curtained window bathing the room in a semi-bright light which his eyes were quickly adjusting to. He looked across to the other bed and found it empty. The door to the shower room was open and he could see that Linda wasn't there. On his bedside cabinet was a notepad and pencil set featuring the motel logo. On the notepad in Linda's handwriting were the words '11.30 Gone for grub. See you soon'. He smiled at the thought then looked at his watch. It was midday. He had slept through from who knows what time until now. Unusual for him but he must have needed it. He got out of bed and went into the shower room.

By the time he had freshened up and stepped back into the bedroom, the door opened and Linda walked in carrying a full supermarket bag. She smiled. "I thought we could do with a bite to eat. There's a convenience store a couple of streets past where we left the car. I paid cash."

Nick smiled too. "Good thinking. It's only now I've seen a bag of food that I realise how hungry I am."

Linda emptied the bag on a bed and they each tucked into a pre-packed breakfast sandwich and a couple of precooked chicken drumsticks washed down with a small bottle of fresh orange juice. Linda had also bought a twin pack of toothbrushes and a small tube of toothpaste so that they could freshen up their mouths as well as showering.

It was only after they had finished that Nick decided it was time to get some answers. "So, Linda, what the hell is going on?"

She looked guiltily at him. "Yeah, I owe you an explanation."

"Yeah, I think you do. It'd be nice to know what I've got mixed up in."

"Mm, okay," she said, "I'll tell you the whole story but first, you did pick it up, didn't you?"

"Yes, I did," he said walking over to where he had hung up his clothes. "So, where are you going to start?" he asked as he reached in to his jacket pocket, pulled out the small cube and placed it on the bed.

Linda had followed Nick's hand as he was talking and was now staring quizzically at the small cube.

"What's that?" she asked.

"What do you mean, 'what's that'? he countered, having the first chance to take more notice of what he had picked up.

"I mean what's that? Why have you put a poker dice on the bed?"

Nick looked properly at the cube. On the sides facing him were King, Jack and Ace symbols.

"Well, technically it's a die as there's only one of it!" he said smiling.

Linda looked quizzically between Nick and the poker die. "It's not funny, Nick. I don't care if it's a die or a dice, why have you put it on the bed?"

"Cos that's what I picked up from behind the heart."

Linda's eyes went wide open and her face quickly became a pale white. "Oh, no, no, no," she mumbled softly, "no, no, no. That's not it. That's not it" She looked deeply into Nick's eyes. "You picked up a ... die?"

Nick returned the deep gaze. "That's the only out of place thing I could feel behind there so I picked it up."

"Oh my god!" said Linda quietly, "that's not it. No, no, no. That's not it. You didn't feel anything else?"

"I picked up the only thing I could feel when I reached behind the heart. You didn't tell me what I should be looking for so, once I'd felt that, I picked it up. I couldn't see what it was in the dim light so I put it in my pocket for safety and then you turned up with your oriental pals in tow and all hell let loose."

Linda had stopped smiling now. She knew Nick wasn't joking about this. "Well, that's not it."

"Not what?"

"Not what I fucking put there. Not what I wanted you to pick up for me."

"So, what did you put there for me to pick up?"

"It's a thing called a silicon orthotope. It's –"

"Arfur!" he interrupted loudly.

"Arthur?" questioned Linda in a daze. "Who's Arthur?"

"Not Arthur with a tee-aitch, Arfur with an eff. As in Arfur Fucksake!" clarified Nick.

"Not that 'kin thing again!"

"You've heard of it?" asked Linda, "it's supposed to be top secret. Need to know only"

"Top secret," laughed Nick, "you're kidding. The amount of people that seem to be after it, it's far from 'kin secret."

"But why have you heard of it?" asked Linda.

"It was my team that was sent in to retrieve it when the PM's daughter had been kidnapped whilst it was in her possession."

"Jeez!" exclaimed Linda, "I was never told. Word was that it was a rescue attempt for the PM's daughter. It was never mentioned that she had it with her."

"It was kept very quiet," said Nick. "This damn orthotope seems to be valued over life. We were instructed to retrieve it even if we had to cut it out of her and leave her there – dead or alive."

"It was in her!?"

"Yep. The PM had it surgically implanted in her tummy region. He'd figured it was the best hiding place for it. Though it obviously became known 'cos, when her body was found it had been cut out of her."

"Jeez!" she said again. "It's still fucking important. I was instructed to infiltrate our oriental friends' setup, get it from them and return it directly to the PM. I'd spent some time getting their trust but somehow, they were on to me, hence my call to you, Nick. They followed me to the fair, saw me leaving the Love Boat Ride but presumably didn't see where I'd hidden it. They must've tapped phones somehow as they knew about our conversation but didn't know where it was hidden due to our codes. They were taking me back into the ride to find it when we came across you."

Nick was silent for a few seconds whilst he took this in. "Well, that explains the Orientals but doesn't explain who 'disposed' of them for us." They both remained silent for a few seconds trying to understand who may have saved them. Nick then continued, "They were kitted out in forces garb and were taking us to Thames House. I can only assume that the PM didn't trust you to get it back for him on your own." Then he looked at Linda and then made an involuntary glance around the area. "Or he didn't want any loose ends once you had got it back," he said suspiciously.

"You think he could be behind our rescuers?"

"I think he may be behind them but I'm not so sure if they were rescuers. Not for the long term anyway." Nick looked around the area again, more by habit than thinking anybody else was there. "I have my suspicions that he may have sent them to retrieve us and then dispose of us once we had handed over the orthotope."

"What, the PM!?" said Linda.

"I have my suspicions," Nick repeated.

Linda was silent again, thinking through the events from the PM giving her the mission through to the chase through

London. Much of it was clear and seemed possible in her mind except for the point when they fled central London.

She adopted a needy look on her face as she spoke again. "Look, I trust you completely, Nick. You came out to save my life without question but what prompted you to flee when we got to Thames House?"

"I was lip reading the lead guy in the car behind ours. He was talking to someone and confirmed that, once we had handed over the 'item' we were to be made to 'disappear'. They, of course, thought I had the orthotope at that time. From what we know of how few people should know about this, they could well have been talking to the PM."

"You think he was 'approving' our disposal?"

"It certainly seems like it."

"So, what the hell is this thing that it's worth the lives of so many people?"

"I have no idea, Lin. We were never told what it was. It was just described to us and we were told to get it."

"Same here. I was told to get it but the rest was 'need to know' and, apparently, I didn't."

"It seems our lives have become redundant since we got involved with this 'kin thing."

"Jeez!" she said again. "So, what are we going to do now?"

"Well, I don't think we have much of a choice. The first thing we need to do is go and get it."

"What!" said Linda, "Go back to the fair. They'll be watching for us."

"Not necessarily," said Nick thoughtfully, "they think we have it. They think I picked it up so they wouldn't think we'd have a reason to go back to the fair."

"It's still risky, Nick. They could be staking it out in case we return."

"I really don't think we have a choice, Lin. Without the damn thing we don't have anything to trade for our lives. I think it's our only hope. We're going to have to risk it. We've got to go back."

"So, do you have a plan?"

"Erm no, not yet. I'm sort of thinking this through on the run at the moment – no pun intended."

"We should go back soon in case somebody finds it. I know it's unlikely that anyone will clean behind that heart but the sooner we get it the better."

Nick thought silently for a few moments then said, "We should go back today. As you say, the sooner we get it the better and they'll probably be concentrating their searches for us elsewhere. If they've stationed any lookouts at the fairground, it will probably be minimal amounts. Plus, my car should still be there in the car park – it shouldn't've been clamped or towed yet – so we could leave in that."

Linda nodded in agreement, "So, when do we go?"

Nick picked up the telephone on the bedside table. "We should go now, during the day, when it's likely to be quieter." Then he spoke into the telephone receiver, "Erm, hi. Could you organise a taxi for two people in about half an hour? Erm, yes you can, it's a London address. Erm, no thanks, it's a one-way journey. Okay, thank you." He then turned back to Linda, "Okay, let's be ready to go in 30 minutes. Taxi to meet us outside Reception."

"Okay, ready in 30" said Linda drawing out the words, failing to hide her concerns, "but I've got a bad feeling about this."

"Yeah," said Nick displaying his concerns too, "so have I. We're an expendable commodity in this. And, if our suspicions are correct, there's no-one at the top who can help us."

CHAPTER 11

Linda and Nick were outside the hotel reception in twenty-eight minutes and then had to wait for another eight minutes before the arrival of the taxi. Nick told the driver the destination and they headed off, Nick appearing relaxed but, though he was sure nobody knew where they were staying, he regularly glanced out the back window to see if they were being followed.

When they arrived at the fairground, Nick instructed the driver to park up opposite his R8 so that Linda knew which car they would be heading to when they were leaving. He paid the fare with a reasonable tip and they got out and stood chatting until the cab drove away.

"So far, so good," said Linda slowly looking around, "I've not seen anyone obviously looking for us."

"Me neither," Nick said whilst also looking around casually, "and I didn't see anyone tailing the cab during our journey. Maybe they really didn't think we'd be returning."

"Yeah, maybe," muttered Linda, "but let's go on the assumption that they're watching out for us somewhere."

They headed across the car park to the Love Boat ride and approached the ticket booth where, Nick noticed, the same ticket seller was present. Nick placed the correct money on the counter.

"Two tickets this time," he said quickly. "I've found someone as equally adorable as I am this time."

The seller gave him the two tickets without saying anything this time and they sat down in the front boat. This was not a busy time of the day for the fair and, for the less popular ride like the Love Boat, the two of them were the only ones preparing to go in.

As their boat started moving, Nick again glanced around warily but saw no one looking suspicious.

"Oh well, let's sit back and enjoy the ride," he said putting his arm around Linda's shoulder.

"It sure brings back old memories," said Linda leaning in to his embrace.

The boat entered the main ride and slowly continued until they were approaching the heart. Nick turned his head to face Linda.

"If for any reason we get separated, as planned, meet back at the motel."

"Okay," said Linda as she prepared herself to lean around the heart.

As the boat aligned with the heart, Linda reached behind its base and felt for the orthotope, picturing in her mind where she had placed it – and felt nothing.

"It's not there!" she said, "It's not there!"

Nick stood up in the boat and reached across, grabbing the heart, holding the weight of the boat against the current. "Feel again," he said straining to hold the heart in his grasp whilst keeping the boat from moving with his feet, "we don't want to have to go around again."

With the boat relatively still, Linda was able to reach a little further around the back of the heart and moved her hand back and forth still feeling only grass.

"It's gone," she said hurriedly.

"Keep feeling for it," said Nick as the boat began to slip away from his hold.

Linda could feel the boat gradually moving with the

current and knew that Nick would have to let go soon or he'd be out of the boat which may attract unwanted attention. She reached further around the heart and felt the edge of something thin and smooth. She snatched for it as the boat moved her a few more centimetres away and managed to grip it by the corner. She brought it around from the back of the heart and placed it properly in her hand, checking her recognition of the shape by touch in the dim light.

"I've got it!" she shouted eagerly, "got it!"

Nick let go of the heart causing him to fall onto his side in the boat due to its continued movement under him. He quickly righted himself and sat back down beside Linda.

"Okay, play it cool when the ride finishes," he said, "we don't want to give the staff here any out of the ordinary stories to relate to anyone who comes by to investigate."

Linda placed the orthotope deep in her pocket and they sat in the boat, arms back around each other as the ride ended and they exited back into the daylight. Nick looked around quickly, anticipating possible trouble. He couldn't see anything out of place, then his eye caught sight of the ticket seller standing by the ticket booth. Even from the distance between them, Nick could see the seller looked wide-eyed and agitated whilst talking on his mobile phone and looking their way.

"I don't like the look of that," he said gesturing towards the ticket seller, "I was wondering why the ticket seller wasn't touched last time we were here with our friends. He's looking too nervous. I think he might be their eyes and ears."

Nick looked around again and this time some people stood out from the others around. They were dressed casually to blend in with the other fair goers but, from the directions of the main entrances of the fairground and the car park these people were walking at pace towards the exit of the Love Boat ride where he and Linda were standing.

Nick reached into his pocket, took out his car key and

handed it to Linda. "You take my car and get the orthotope out of here. Meet back at the motel as soon as possible."

"What about you?" she asked worriedly.

"I'll try and lead them off. There's a few more people walking towards the fair entrance now, let's head towards them. You mingle with them. I'll make myself seen and try to draw them away. You get the thing back to the motel and I'll meet you there."

"How are you gonna get there?" she asked.

"I'll think of something," he said leading her towards the small crowd of people heading towards the fair entrance.

The people heading from that direction slowed upon seeing Nick and Linda coming towards them whilst the ones from the direction of the car park increased their speed. Nick and Linda moved into the small crowd and then slowed to remain central. Linda ducked down slightly, lessening her height so she was a little below the heads of the crowd but continued walking with them. Nick turned and started to walk back towards the car park glancing first back and then forward at the approaching possible bad guys. He spotted a coach parking up in the car park and started running towards it. A number of the pursuers from the fair entrance gave chase and the ones from the car park changed course to head in his direction. Thinking on his feet, Nick arrived at the coach and continued running beyond it heading towards the go kart track.

His pursuers had anticipated him heading towards a car so had stayed around the parked cars whilst running in his direction. Now they changed direction and headed towards the go karts to try to head him off.

Nick's distraction was creating a clear area within the car park so Linda took the opportunity and sprinted away from the small crowd in the direction of the R8. This took her pursuers by surprise giving her a head start and they then had to make their way through the small crowd giving Linda a few more seconds' lead.

Linda was extremely fit and a fast runner so was nearing

the R8 very quickly. Once she was within twenty metres or so she touched the remote unlocking button on the key fob allowing the doors to be unlocked as she reached the car. The modern car had keyless start so there was no need to fiddle with the key in the ignition, so Linda just fell into seat, closing the door, pressed the start button causing the car to roar into life, put the selector into 'drive' and floored the accelerator.

The car sped off and raced through the car park exit causing her pursuers to veer off towards a car of theirs parked close to the exit. They clambered in, started the engine and moved off to follow the R8.

Meanwhile, Nick had reached the kart track just as one racer was about to get into his idling go kart. Nick pushed in front of the startled driver, jumping down into the go kart, putting it into gear and speeding away out of the track and onto the road. One of his pursuers jumped into another go kart but had to start it up giving Nick a precious few seconds' gap. The rest of his pursuers turned and headed back towards their car within the car park in order to give chase once they reached it.

Go karts vary in performance depending on whether they are fairground, hobbyist or professional types. Fairground models may only reach around 20 mph whilst hobbyist versions may be capable of around 60 mph. The karts being used on the track adjacent to the fairground were professional types, fully geared and capable of top speeds of around 150mph. Nick had driven such karts in the past so was able to control the sensitive steering – the slightest turn of the small steering wheel amplified through to the front wheels creating sharp, sudden turns – and master the small movement involved in the gear changes. His pursuer in the second kart had not driven such vehicles before and, having floored the accelerator, had caused the kart to shoot off at an unexpected speed. He managed to hold the steering towards the exit gates but, as he turned the wheel to drive on to the road to follow Nick's kart, he over steered the front wheels effectively causing them to be near to ninety degrees to the direction of travel, creating a pivot to the momentum of the speeding kart, tipping the kart over, crashing it and him against the gate post, knocking him at least unconscious.

In the distance Nick saw his R8 exit the car park pursued by a black saloon and he increased his speed in an effort to catch up with them. As he chased after the two cars, he sped past the car park exit and just had time to register another similar black saloon turning on to the road. He chanced a quick glance behind him and confirmed that the second saloon was also part of the chase.

"Shit!" he shouted loudly, his voice getting lost in the air rushing past his face.

Linda glanced to her rear-view mirror and saw the black saloon closing on her. She was also surprised to see a small vehicle on the road catching the saloon and realised that it was Nick on a kart of some kind. She saw up ahead a slip lane that joined a dual carriageway both of which appeared to be virtually empty of traffic and steered the car onto it whilst increasing speed.

Part of the specification of the R8 was cornering at high speed so Linda was able to easily drive the car onto the dual carriageway and accelerate along the long straight she had joined with barely a squeal from the tyres. The saloon following her wasn't built for such manoeuvres and skidded as it took the corner leaving a trail of black rubber on the road in its wake. The driver of the saloon was skilled and steered into the skid bringing the car onto the carriageway following the R8.

Nick saw where the two cars ahead of him were going so turned after them without lifting his foot off the accelerator. The go kart took the turn with ease, Nick shifting his weight to counter balance it as the outside wheels lifted slightly off the ground. The saloon chasing him struggled with the speed causing the driver to lift off the accelerator increasing the distance between the two vehicles as it came into the straight. The saloon had a fast-straight-line speed so the driver was able to start to lessen the gap at the current speed the kart was travelling.

The passenger of the fourth vehicle in the chase lowered the window and leaned out aiming a suppressed pistol at the go kart ahead. He fired a couple of shots but was too far back to guarantee a hit and the bullets went wide of the kart pinging off the tarmac beside Nick as they ricocheted into a parked car at the roadside.

"Faff!" shouted Nick as he turned the steering wheel left and right slightly so that the kart snaked along the road presenting a lateral moving target to the shooter. This manoeuvre presented a lesser target but also allowed the saloon and R8 in front to get farther away.

"Shit!" he shouted as he saw the gap widening in front of him. He had a pistol in his jacket pocket but there was no way he could shoot behind him at the speed he was driving – he couldn't risk twisting around to aim with the kart steering as sensitive as it is – so he eyed an approaching exit lane and decided to take it thinking that he can at least take one of the pursuers away from Linda.

Nick left it to the last second then turned the wheel as sharply as he dared causing the kart to skid slightly on its rear wheels as it took the turn. He turned and leaned into the skid as before and the grip soon returned so he could accelerate again. The saloon tried to match the cornering speed of the kart and lost grip on the rear wheels. It slid across the road out of control, the driver battling with the steering wheel to regain traction. The rear wing made a glancing hit to a crash barrier on the angle of the exit lane, effectively slowing the slide, allowing the driver to gain control of the saloon, enabling him to straighten up and speed after the kart again.

Nick saw this unfold in the kart's small wing mirrors, first thinking the saloon was going to crash out of the chase, then seeing it fortuitously hitting the barrier and righting itself.

"Faff! Faff! Faff!" he shouted. "Are we gonna have any 'kin luck today?"

At the end of the exit lane was a roundabout and, just about to enter the roundabout, was an articulated lorry moving slowly due to having a full trailer. Nick had a plan. He floored the accelerator again, the roundabout seemingly approaching at a startling pace, the saloon keeping up as it too increased speed.

The kart arrived at the roundabout as the cab of the lorry had passed by the first exit to the left, the trailer now across that exit. The lorry, now in motion, was beginning to speed up.

Nick steered left and ducked at the same time. The kart continued under the trailer bed between the trailer's wheels. As he entered under the trailer bed Nick thought he had misjudged the vertical gap and that he was now going to literally lose his head as he felt his hair brushing against the underside of the trailer.

In the few moments it took to enter the gap beneath the trailer, the lorry had picked up more speed which meant that its rear wheels were getting perilously close to Nick's kart; if they touched, he'd be crushed.

As the nose of the kart exited from under the trailer, the inner rear trailer wheel made contact with part of the kart's body panelling creating a horrible squeaking noise. Nick held his breath….

….and the kart emerged on the far side of the truck to the saloon.

Nick let out the breath and concentrated on steering the kart straight and fast to get maximum distance between him and the saloon before the lorry cleared the exit and allowed the saloon to proceed again.

The saloon had to slow and wait for the lorry to clear the exit as there was no way it could fit under the trailer like the go kart. As soon as the exit was clear, the saloon accelerated again after the kart. It wouldn't take too long before they would catch it again.

Nick scanned the road ahead for an area he could out manoeuvre the saloon but it appeared to be fairly straight with no slip lanes or junctions nearby and very few other cars to hide amongst. He glanced in the wing mirror again to see the passenger lining up the pistol in readiness to shoot again.

"Shit! Shit! Shit!" he exclaimed as he started to weave the kart from side to side again.

The passenger fired another three shots, one going wide of his elbow but close enough for him to feel the hairs move on his arm and the other two hitting and smashing one wing mirror.

"For fuck's sake!" shouted Nick, now effectively half blinded to the happenings behind him. "I repeat, are we gonna have any fuckin' luck today!?"

He stopped weaving the kart, dropped a gear and floored the accelerator but was soon catching up with the small amount of traffic that was taking up the road width ahead. He was going to be an effective sitting target at this rate. He looked at the approaching cars and determined that there was no way past them if they remained in the current formation and, if he got too close to them, they could get caught by any stray shots.

"What the hell do you do when you're right out of luck," he mumbled to himself.

At that time the cars that were ahead had created a small space between them as one overtook another. This gap would only last for a few seconds until the overtaking car would move out again performing its next passing manoeuvre. Nick steered for the gap with his foot to the floor, the kart still increasing its speed.

"C'mon, luck, luck, luck!" he shouted at the approaching cars.

The saloon also accelerated in an effort to catch the kart or, at least keep up with it and the passenger steadied himself for his next shots. He had Nick in his aim this time. Nick could just about make out the passenger's movements in the one unbroken mirror and swerved the kart slightly to line up with the varying gap between the cars ahead –

Just as the passenger fired his next two shots.

Had Nick not swerved at that moment, both shots would have hit him, one in the back of his neck and the other around the base of his spine. But his swerving had repositioned him as a target far enough for the higher shot to pass within millimetres of his shoulder, continuing harmlessly through the gap in the cars ahead, and the lower shot to hit the kart's engine cowling. This was a professional racing go kart with the engine cowling being made from carbon fibre. Carbon fibre is extremely light weight but extremely strong making it ideal for racing where strength is required but weight is always an issue. Along with those two useful characteristics is one not so good: carbon fibre is brittle.

The second shot hit the carbon fibre engine cowling, causing the brittle substance to explode into hundreds of sharp shards. These shards landed and spread out across the road behind the kart. The following saloon tried to steer around them but was too close and only managed to veer across the lane, approaching the shards at an angle.

All four tyres hit the broken carbon fibre causing them to violently blow out as they were instantly shredded. As the saloon was travelling at an angle at the time, momentum effectively turned it into a sideways motion. The tyres blowing out so quickly caused the wheel rims to drop quickly, digging themselves a little way into the tarmac. The built-up energy of the sideways momentum caused the car to flip up and spin in mid-air before crashing back down on to the road rolling side on before coming to rest on its crushed roof. The saloon's occupants were not wearing seatbelts so were thrown around the inside of the car like rag dolls in a tumble dryer. They were dead before the car had come to rest.

Nick had seen some of what had happened in his mirror and could guess the rest. "Shit!" he said to himself, quietly this time. "I take back what I said about luck!"

He was pretty sure that no one would have survived the crash but he didn't have time to stop and find out, he needed to try to catch up with Linda and help her if he could. The cars he was preparing to overtake before seeing the saloon crash were now out of sight giving him a view of the road into the distance. He could see that some distance ahead the road re-joined the dual carriageway that he had exited earlier. If he got back on that road then perhaps, he could catch up with Linda and the car that was chasing her.

He floored the accelerator again, changing through the gears as fast as possible and was soon back on the main carriageway where he allowed full acceleration to continue in the hope of catching the R8 and the other saloon – providing they hadn't turned off the road.

CHAPTER 12

Linda had remained on the dual carriageway and, in the minute or so since Nick and the other saloon had turned off, she had travelled a couple of miles farther on, dodging in and out of the few other cars that were on this quiet road. The saloon had been keeping a steady distance behind her throughout the chase proving that, despite its looks, it was a high-performance version.

On two occasions during the chase the R8's speed limiter had cut in with a warning on the dashboard announcing that 155mph had been reached. The first time the electronic speed limit had been reached Linda had cursed the car's UK legislative background – in many other parts of the world there was no electronic speed limiter set allowing the R8 to reach speeds in excess of 200mph – and the second time it was reached she cursed Nick.

"Saten, you dipshit!" she had shouted to anyone who may be listening. "Saten, I can't believe you haven't had the limiter programmed out. Jeez!"

The electronic speed limitation of the R8 meant that the chasing saloon was able to keep up in straight lines as it too was capable of similar speed. It was at corners that the R8 showed its superior engineering, edging away whenever there was a bend in the road. Unfortunately for Linda, this part of the road had been relatively straight for a number of miles and looked similar up ahead for as far as she could see.

She wondered if Nick was okay. She'd seen him turn off a few miles back and saw the other saloon follow him and he had very little protection in that small kart.

A small, dull thud brought her back to concentrate on what was happening around her at the moment. The noise had been caused by a bullet hitting somewhere on the R8's bodywork. She glanced at the rear-view mirror and saw the passenger of the chasing saloon leaning out aiming an assault rifle her way. She saw a small flash from the rifle's suppressor and another dull thud could be heard from the back of the R8.

"Nick's not gonna like this," she said out loud, moving the steering wheel a little, hopefully putting off the shooter's aim.

The driver of the saloon matched the motion of the R8 allowing the shooter to line up ready for another shot. He fired two shots in quick succession. Both blew two small round holes in the R8's rear window. One buried itself in the back of the passenger seat. The other grazed Linda's upper arm, carving a slight groove in her deltoid muscle. She screamed at the shock of being hit and immediately felt the warmth of her blood running down her arm. The graze caused her nerves around the wound to react making her arm feel temporarily numb and her to lose control of its movement as it lost its grip of the wheel and fell uselessly to her side.

She resisted the natural urge to hold and squeeze the wound, instead holding on to the steering wheel with her other hand. The distraction had caused her to slow the car slightly allowing the saloon to gain ground and she was unable to operate the manual or paddle gear changers at the moment so was relying on the auto mode which, though still fast, was not as quick.

The saloon was gaining, matching the R8's movements

as Linda steered from side to side as best as she could one handed. The shooter steadied his weapon and took aim. He was close enough to be sure of a good hit now and, even with the target car weaving a little, he was able to keep the target's head in his sights.

Linda was now able to see the shooter clearly in the mirror and could see the suppressed barrel pointing at her. She tried to move her wounded arm but there was still no feeling there, it just stayed lifeless by her side. Everything was happening so fast and she was unable to swerve to avoid being targeted. She looked in the mirror again and could only focus on the suppressed barrel.

The shooter began to put pressure on the trigger, the target's head still in his sights.

Linda did the only thing left for her to try. She stamped down on the brake pedal.

Being a powerful supercar the R8 had powerful brakes and, being in 'auto' rather than 'sport' mode, the anti-lock braking system was operating. This caused the car to slow down considerably quicker than the saloon throwing the shooter's aim off completely and his shot went harmlessly over the top of the R8 as he tried to compensate for the fast-decreasing gap.

The saloon didn't have brakes as efficient as the R8 and the driver swerved to avoid the possibility of crashing. Linda however didn't wait for the R8 to stop, she stamped back on the accelerator and raced off again. The saloon's driver reacted quickly too, starting to accelerate after Linda again, whilst the passenger readied himself again for another shot.

She had only postponed the inevitable.

The road was still pretty straight and still surprisingly low in traffic so Linda was stuck with the saloon gaining a little each time she had to slow slightly to steer around the few vehicles she came across. Déjà vu was setting in as she glanced in the mirror and saw the passenger readying his weapon again. However, this time the driver wasn't going to be caught out so easily again and was holding back a little further to give him a little extra manoeuvring time.

This time Linda had run out of ideas. The saloon was matching her speed and direction, was too far back to be caught out by braking and there were still no exit lanes to drive off the road. She looked in the rear-view mirror and saw the shooter preparing to fire again. She carried on swerving and varying her speed, she wasn't going to let them have an easy time with this.

The shooter had his target in his sights again; a clear head shot.

Linda could see the shooter was steady and ready to fire. She held her breath.

The shooter relaxed and started to apply pressure to the trigger –

A loud, unsuppressed shot rang out and blood erupted from the back of the shooter's hand as a 9mm bullet passed through it ripping bone and tendons. The shooter's hand released all pressure from the rifle's trigger, cancelling the shot, as he screamed in agony looking at his smashed hand.

Linda had heard the shot too and, realising quickly that it wasn't a shot from the rifle, she struggled looking in her mirror to see what had happened.

Nick lined up the go kart beside the saloon, matching its speed – both vehicles now reaching around 120mph at this point. He had re-joined the dual carriageway and floored the throttle and changed up through the gears as quick as he could. Being so small and manoeuvrable the go kart didn't have to slow down to pass the few other cars on the road and so caught up with the R8 – saloon chase relatively quickly.

As he'd approached the two cars, he could see the passenger preparing to fire at the R8 so he had adjusted his speed and positioning, got out his pistol, aimed at the shooter's hand and fired. Luckily has aim had been good and he had disabled the shooter, stopping him from firing.

However, he had not disabled the driver who swerved the saloon towards the kart trying to force Nick off the road.

Nick's reactions were fast and he jerked the steering wheel and braked moving the kart farther aside and behind the saloon. He steadied the kart, matching the speed again but now behind the saloon, and he took aim and fired another shot. He could see blood splatter the windscreen followed by the passenger's lifeless body slumping over towards the driver. The driver was trying to push the passenger's body away from him whilst steering the saloon chasing Linda in the R8 so Nick took advantage of the distraction and took aim at the driver's head. He fired and the bullet penetrated the saloon's rear window and continued through the car missing the driver's ear by millimetres and exited through the windscreen. He aimed and pulled the trigger again but nothing happened – the gun had jammed. He realised now that the previous case had not ejected and there was no way he could clear the weapon one handed whilst speeding in a kart. He put the pistol back in his jacket pocket and concentrated on keeping up with the saloon while trying to work out his next move.

The driver of the saloon noted that the gunshots had stopped and now pulled out his own pistol and fired at Linda in the R8 whilst keeping Nick in sight in the rear-view mirror. The two cars were far enough apart for the aim to be ineffective and the shots fell harmlessly short of the R8 causing lines in the road as they scraped along the tarmac. The driver accelerated in an effort to make up the distance so that he could get a clearer shot.

Linda could see in her mirrors that the saloon was gaining again and she could also see that Nick was behind it in the kart. Should she stop and help him? No, he wouldn't want her to do that. He'd want her to keep going and stick to the original plan of meeting back at the motel. She pressed down on the accelerator and maintained the gap.

Nick knew this part of the road and, in about two miles, there was a large roundabout which would cause Linda to slow down allowing the saloon driver to be within accurate firing range. He had to do something before then, she'd be an easy target if the saloon got up close.

But what could he do?

It's not as if he could run the saloon off the road with a go kart, is it?

Or could he?

He had a plan. Crazy, but the best he could think of given the short time.

With the saloon driver concentrating more on the R8 ahead of him, Nick floored the throttle and sped around the back of the saloon on the blind side to where the driver was seated. He matched the speed of the saloon so that he stayed in the blind spot of its wing mirror. If the driver lost his concentration on the R8 he'd be unable to see the go kart without turning his head to look behind him.

Looking at the back of the driver's head from his low position, Nick was pleased that all his attention was on catching the R8. Nick just had to keep his position until Linda started to slow down in preparation for the roundabout.

Linda glanced in her rear-view mirror and saw she was keeping the saloon at a safe distance – safe in that the driver didn't seem to want to shoot at that range. She couldn't see Nick so ventured a glance in her wing mirrors. There he was, just behind and to the side of the saloon. What was he doing? Why was he staying there? She had no more time to think about that as, she saw she was approaching a 'roundabout ahead' sign.

"Shit!" she said out loud and then softly to herself, "he's gonna be in firing range when I slow down!"

She weighed up the situation as quick as she could. She couldn't take the roundabout at the speed she was travelling – the R8 was still speeding at around 120mph – if she clipped a kerb the car would flip over. She would have to slow down and take her chances.

At 120mph the point had already been reached to slow down so Linda took her foot off the accelerator. Though the car's momentum carried it forward, there was some engine braking that caused it to start to reduce in speed. Linda glanced nervously in her mirrors and saw the saloon closing. She looked ahead and saw that she would very soon have to start braking which would give the saloon driver the opportunity for a clear shot. She glanced back in her mirrors and saw the saloon getting nearer. She also saw the go kart start to move up alongside the saloon.

"What is he doing?" she said to herself.

The saloon driver was no longer aware of the go kart; he was more concerned with the R8 that was fast getting into a range where he wouldn't miss. He prepared his pistol ready to fire the fatal shot.

Nick saw his chance. The saloon was slowing down as well as the R8 but at a slower rate. Rather than slow down with the other two vehicles, he sped up. The go kart overtook the saloon very quickly as it was the only one of the three now accelerating. It caught up with the R8 in a matter of seconds and Nick now matched the speed of the supercar. The gunman saw the go kart as it hurtled past and, with a confused look on his face, prepared to aim at Nick instead of Linda.

Linda saw the go kart was now right behind her but had to concentrate more on the fast-approaching roundabout.

Nick lined up with the R8 only inches behind it, matching its speed, and also checked his mirrors to ensure the saloon was still in line behind him.

It was.

In one continuous movement he stood up in the kart, stepped onto its front bonnet and leaped forwards towards the R8. As he jumped, his trailing foot trod down hard on the kart's steering wheel causing the front wheels to turn too far for the speed it was travelling. The forward momentum of the kart onto the front wheels that were virtually side on to the direction of travel, caused the kart to jump up pivoting on its front axle. The kart spun 180 degrees so it was now upside down but the jumping action had taken it about a metre or so off the ground.

Still travelling at around 80mph the saloon driver had no time to react and the upturned kart ploughed into the car, through the windscreen, crushing the driver's head and upper torso and producing a gory mess of twisted metal, broken carbon fibre, blood, flesh and bone. The saloon veered out of control over to the side of the road and crashed into a large tree causing the front of the car to crumple up like a concertina.

At the same time, Nick was sailing through the air, hoping his momentum was enough to reach the R8. As he'd leapt, he had cleared the roof and his outstretched arms were in line with the R8's bonnet. However, he was fast losing any forward movement and, as gravity started to take him downwards, he could see the still-speeding car – now beginning to travel forwards faster than him – inching ahead below him. He reached his arms downwards rather than forwards, his fingers now sliding against the smooth paintwork of the roof. He stretched his fingers as straight as he could –

And his fingertips found a hold in the bodywork to the rear of the side window. He held his grip and pulled himself further down and landed with a thump across the rear window and spoiler.

"Stop the car!" he screamed not knowing if he could be heard.

Linda had seen the leap which had taken her by surprise as much as the saloon driver and she reacted instinctively when she felt the thump on the bodywork by stamping on the brakes. The car stopped very quickly and would have thrown Nick forwards had he not have trapped his boot around the spoiler. Instead, it jolted him down onto the roof and rear window, cushioning his contact. He then let go of his gripping hand and boot and rolled off the car to the side and fell onto the road.

"Fuck! Fuck! Fuck!" he shouted to try to dull the pain, "To quote a well-known phrase, I'm getting too old for this shit!"

Linda got out of the car and ran round to Nick. "Are you okay?" she asked looking concerned at him still laying on the ground.

"Hmm. Next time I say 'you take the car' and I throw you the keys, remember to throw them straight back. Next time you can take the go kart!"

"Oh, so you are okay," she said helping him up.

"Well, it's not every day you get to be an R8's roof rack," he said dusting himself down. "Let's get back to the motel. I'll drive. We'd better get out of here before any of their friends turn up."

Nick walked around, stiffly, to the driver's side and got in, Linda taking the passenger seat. He took the pistol from his pocket and cleared the stoppage – taking only a couple of seconds now he had both hands free.

"They don't make guns like they used to," he said smiling. "That would never have happened in the good old days!" He then saw the blood on Linda's sleeve. "You're arm?" he said. "You've been hit. Are you okay?"

Linda glanced down at her sleeve. "Oh that. Just a scratch luckily. Looks worse than it is."

"Okay," he said as he put the pistol back in his jacket pocket and pressed the button to turn off the engine, then pressed the button again without his foot on the brake, turning the ignition on without starting the car. He then pulled on both steering wheel paddle gear changers at the same time, released them, hit the stop/start button again and then hit it once more with his foot on the brake pedal. The engine roared into life and, at the same time, the digital dashboard speedometer changed from showing a maximum speed of 180mph to a new display of 240mph.

Linda stared at the changing speedometer then turned her gaze to Nick.

"What?" he asked as she looked back down at the speedo. "Oh that. I had the ECU reprogrammed so that the speed limiter could be switched off."

"Well, when you said to take the car and threw the keys

at me, you could have told me that little trick. I could've outrun them easily."

"We were a bit hard pressed for time for a driving lesson. Besides, I wouldn't have had the chance of catching up with you and would've missed the opportunity to leap from go kart to R8. It would've been dull if I'd told you."

He smiled but didn't get it returned as they drove off heading for the motel.

CHAPTER 13

As they drove into the motel's car park, Nick parked the R8 in a space away from the other cars and they remained seated, looking around, scanning the car park and surrounding area for anything out of place. Happy that all seemed well, they got out, locked the car and walked into the building and along towards their room.

As they arrived at their room, they saw the door was slightly ajar. Nick took his pistol out from his jacket and motioned for Linda to stay where she was. He opened the door slowly, gun at the ready to fire. The blackout curtains were closed so the room was dark except for the light from the corridor slowly spreading across the floor as the door was opening.

Nick carefully glanced either side of the door opening and couldn't see anyone so he stepped into the room casting a shadow across the floor. One hand still readied to shoot, he reached to the wall, found the light switch and clicked it on. The main ceiling lamp came on, lighting up the room and illuminating a man sitting in a chair next to the bed. He had his empty hands raised, elbows resting on the chair's arms and was squinting, showing that he'd been sitting in the dark for some time.

He said calmly, "Hello, Mr. Saten. It's nice to meet you."

Nick quickly regained his steady two-handed grasp on the pistol and changed its direction to be pointing at the head of the man.

The man remained calm. "I am unarmed Mr Saten and can assure you I mean you no harm."

Nick kept his gun trained on the man. "Who the fuck are you!?" he said aggressively. "What the hell are you doing here!?"

"I'm here to speak to you, Nick. Is it alright if I call you Nick? I just want to talk but I could talk more easily if that gun wasn't pointing at me."

Nick held his ground. "You can call me what the fuck you like but this gun stays where it is until you tell me who you are and what you're doing here."

"Okay Nick, okay. My name is David Wilmott. I am the head of Section D, a department of the Secret Service. My ID is in my pocket, if you'll allow me to get it out."

"Don't move!" said Nick staring menacingly at Wilmott. "You move and I will fire."

"Okay, okay," said Wilmott remaining in the chair.

Nick kept the gun pointing at Wilmott's head but quickly looked around the room and assessed there was no obvious other danger. He then called out to Linda, his gaze never shifting from the man. "Lin, come in slowly. I'm gonna ask you to frisk a guy in here and find his ID in his pocket."

"Okay," she said as she edged into the room looking around Nick at the man sitting in the chair. "Oh," she said softly as she shut the door behind her, "Nick, it's okay. This man is David Wilmott, he works for MI6."

Nick held his position. "You're sure?" he checked. "You know this guy?"

"Yeah, Nick," she said, "I know this guy. In fact, for the past few months I've been working for him."

"You've been working for him?" said Nick still keeping his eyes on Wilmott.

"Yeah, Nick. It was David that asked me to retrieve the

orthotope. I've known him for years. I'm pretty sure he can be trusted."

Nick lowered his weapon, though kept it primed and in his hand, ready for use. "Okay," he said warily, "forgive me if I'm not as trustful as Linda but, after what we've been through in the last few hours, I'm a bit nervy around surprises."

Wilmott motioned with his eyes indicating that he'd like to lower his hands and, with a nod from Nick, he slowly rested them on the arms of the chair.

"I don't blame you, Nick," he said calmly, "and, if you'll allow, I'd like to explain why I'm here."

"It's not just why you're here. We were pretty careful renting this room so, I'd like to know how you got to be here too."

"I'll explain all but, first I can assure you that your location is still secure. It is known only to me and one other member of my team whom Linda has also known for some considerable time." He glanced over at Linda to see a look of curiosity on her face. "It's Larry Stevens, Linda."

Linda's curious look changed to a smile. "Oh, Larry. Yes, I can vouch for him too, Nick. I trust him as much as I trust David."

Nick relaxed a little and sat on the bed facing Wilmott. Linda walked over and sat next to Nick and she said, "Anyone want a drink? I can boil the kettle and make a cup of tea or coffee."

"There's some bottles of beer in the mini bar, still sealed and in their box. I brought them in with me in case you could do with one when you got back," Wilmott said in a friendly manner.

"Well, in that case, can I get anyone a beer?" said Linda. "As my mum always used to say, everything'll look better over a nice bottle of beer."

"Shouldn't that be tea?" asked Wilmott visually relaxing.

"I'm paraphrasing a little," she said playfully. "Though mum was ahead of her time with her sayings."

Linda went over and opened the mini bar, broke open the box, took out three bottles, lifted the caps with a bottle opener that was in the fridge and handed one each to Wilmott and Nick, keeping one for herself. "Cheers," she said, raising her bottle a little into the air. The others joined in too, raising theirs though Nick still kept one hand on the pistol.

"Okay David," said Nick, "I'm ready to hear what you have to say."

"Right," said Wilmott taking a swig from his bottle, "I'll start from the beginning. I head up a highly secretive department within the Secret Service, Section D. A small team of specially selected people, originally started during the war to gather data and disrupt the Nazi war effort. Since the end of the war, Section D now has a similar role but the 'enemy' so to speak is terrorism in any of its many forms. I effectively hired Linda to get the orthotope – of which I'll try to explain more in a while – from the Orientals that we were pretty sure had it due to them leaving their signature marks when they took it from the Prime Minister's daughter. Linda managed to infiltrate the group that had it and get away from them with it in her possession. However, somehow, they knew she had it and pursued her at which point you became involved and you know the story from there."

Nick still looked confused at this point. "But, if it was your lot that took out the Orientals at the fair, why did they give chase in an aggressive manner? That is, do their utmost to kill the two of us!"

"Ah, I'm coming to that," said Wilmott hastily not wanting Nick to lose his calmness towards him. "Whoever intervened at the fair were not Section D."

"Who the hell were they then?" Linda and Nick said together, glancing at each other and then back to Wilmott, who appeared strangely thoughtful.

Out of a nervous habit, Wilmott performed an involuntary glance from side to side as if looking to ensure the room has no other occupiers. "I strongly suspect they were working directly for the PM," he said.

"What!?" they both said together, briefly glancing at each other again.

After a moment for thought, Nick then said, "So, you are trying to tell us that the PM is trying to get hold of this orthotope but not through legal channels. He's running autonomously from the rest of the government."

"Yes, that's what I strongly suspected for some time and, the events tonight have strengthened my suspicions," said Wilmott taking another swig from his bottle.

Nick continued. "Are you saying that the PM is on some personal vendetta to avenge the death of his daughter?"

"No, I'm not saying that," said Wilmott. "My suspicion is that it's not a personal vendetta at all. I think he's beyond personal care about his daughter. I think he proved that by placing the damn thing inside her in the first place. He could have just kept it then but I'm assuming there were too many witnesses to see him take it away. I think he's gone rogue and is working with someone – as yet unknown – to take control of this orthotope for his and, or their personal gain."

"Jeez!" exclaimed Linda, "you didn't tell me that before."

"I wasn't sure before and it was, for obvious reasons, highly classified. Even now, it is only known to me, the Chief and you two. Hence why I'm telling you here in this room. Larry swept it for bugs before you arrived. It's clean."

"So, why tell us now?" said Nick glancing at Linda momentarily, suspecting she may say the same thing at the same time again. She didn't. She was sitting on the bed trying to make sense of the information.

"That does sort of make sense," she said before Wilmott spoke again. "I never heard the Orientals mentioning the PM nor found any evidence he was connected to them. And the team that took them out then took after us were wearing UK Special Forces or Police SFO outfits but with no insignias."

Nick spoke out again. "So, if what you're saying is correct, that still doesn't explain what you're doing here, how you got to be here, what you want from us and what this damn thing is."

"I'll continue," said Wilmott. "The first part is simple. Since Linda has been working for Section D, she has had an encrypted tracker inserted under her skin allowing me to trace her here. As to what I want from you, that will become apparent but, first I'll try to explain a bit about the orthotope and then it may become a little clearer why it's wanted."

"Okay, go ahead," they again both said together glancing at each other suspiciously.

If Wilmott had noticed that they kept speaking as a team, he said nothing about it. He looked from one to the other and said, "Do you know the fundamentals of superconductivity?"

They both nodded and Nick spoke up. "It's where a substance gets to be in a state where it has no electrical resistance, allowing extremely high current flow without any build-up of heat."

Linda added, "And it means that a city could be supplied with electricity through small diameter cables. Power would be ultra-efficient as there would be little if no loss."

Nick continued. "Problem with it is that, in order for substances to become superconductive they need to be cooled to extremely low temperatures – around minus 250 degrees centigrade – and the power it takes to get the temperatures down out ways the advantages of superconductivity in all but very specialist equipment."

Wilmott spoke again. "That's right up till now. Until now superconductivity has been used in magnetic body scanners and particle accelerators, high end expensive products. The power needed to cool the superconductive lines is extreme and expensive therefore usage has been very restricted."

Nick and Linda did their 'trademark' curious glance at each other then said together, "What do you mean 'until now'?

Wilmott continued. "Back in 1911 superconductivity was first observed in Holland by accident when mercury was cooled to minus 269 degrees centigrade, the temperature of liquid helium. At that temperature the electrical resistance was observed to have just disappeared. From that time onwards, scientists all over the world have been searching for the substance that will allow superconductivity at room temperature or above, that is, without the need for cooling. Various different substances have been tried with some past success at minus 20 odd degrees but it still meant that, in order to achieve, the conductive material had to be kept cold and remain cold in order to work.

"What we now have is a material, silicon that's impregnated with some other substance or substances, that is superconductive at plus 5 degrees centigrade and above. A proper room temperature superconductor."

"Well, that's a good thing, isn't it?" asked Linda.

"It's good and it's bad, depending on your point of view. It could be the breakthrough that's been looked for allowing enormous amounts of power to be generated cheaply. As you said, Linda, it would allow comparatively huge currents to be carried in small conductive cables as no resistance means no heat build-up. It would no longer be necessary to transform electricity up to high voltages in order to transfer them around countries. In fact, it may be possible for power stations to transmit at useable, safe voltages – it could be that future mains sockets in homes would be replaced by 12 volt or 5-volt outlets eliminating the need for inefficient transformers in electronic equipment. The computer chips of the future could work at unthinkable speeds as they wouldn't overheat and, due to another superconductivity characteristic, there would be no electromagnetic interference between tracks within the silicon chips."

Linda spoke again. "As I said, that all sounds good."

"Yes, all good so far," Wilmott said carefully, "but not everyone would want the good points. Energy companies would make far less as very little power would be needed.

In fact, many devices could be run by battery in the future. Vehicles will be able to be powered efficiently by batteries that will seldom age and fail to keep their charge. Such vehicles will be able to have extensive mileage ranges without the need for topping up. So, energy and oil companies may pay big money to keep such superconductors from being manufactured."

"That's not so good," Linda added.

"And that's not all," said a very serious looking Wilmott. "Various government departments have previously discussed the possibility of immensely powerful weapons – hand held and bigger – that could be produced using super conductive components. It's the old adage 'whoever gets the super weapons gets control'. When they find out about this substance, whoever gets hold of and can reproduce it would be able to impose control on the rest of us if they decided to do so."

Nick had been silently listening but now cut in. "Are you trying to tell us that the world's super powers don't know about this stuff yet?"

"Sort of," said Wilmott. "We at Six were pretty sure, up to about 8 months ago, that no-one but us and the PM knew the whereabouts of the superconductor or if it really existed. Then, around that time, there started to be whispers in corridors around Westminster – nothing formally spoken or written. The foreign agents of my department also started reporting of rumours that such a thing existed. These rumours were coming from various parts of the world so the 'whispers' were spreading. However, it appeared that it was just rumours being reported. No one appeared to be sure of the physical existence.

"Then the PM, in his infinite wisdom, hid the substance inside his daughter as you know and it became obvious that others not only knew about it but had an idea where it was when she was kidnapped. Your team was sent in to retrieve her and the orthotope but operational security was compromised and your team was ambushed and unable to complete the mission. Then, after that, her dead body was found and the orthotope had been removed. That meant it had become known how the orthotope was being hidden.

"GCHQ got wind of a group that was behind all this and had the orthotope so, whilst you were recovering from your injury, Nick, I sent in Linda to infiltrate them and get the orthotope. She managed to obtain it and make her escape but not before her mission had also been compromised and she was being pursued when she contacted you. You know the rest from there."

Nick's face formed into a puzzled look. "That's not all," he said, "there are still pieces missing. My mission and Linda's were compromised and you're telling me that only your team and the PM knew about the plans.

"Then there's the people in the anonymous SFO outfits. They saved us from the Orientals but then wanted the orthotope from us and would have killed us for it if they had the chance during the chase from London. Where did they come from? And who authorised them to do what they did? And … why do they need to go to so much trouble for this damn orthotope? Why not just make another one?

"And …, why are you here to meet us when you could have instructed Linda to a drop off point somewhere."

"Firstly, I can tell you that they're all out to get this bloody orthotope 'cos, as far as we know, this is the only piece in existence and no-one seems to know what it consists of. Everyone needs it to be able to reverse engineer more of it."

"How can it be so rare and be worthwhile?"

"We'll only know that when we analyse it and see if it can be replicated," continued Wilmott.

"What about the bloke who invented it, or claims to have done so?" said Linda.

Wilmott looked serious again, "He was involved in an accident and died soon after the announcement. Can't be proven but the accident was suspicious."

"Fucking politics!" exclaimed Nick. "One day perhaps

all countries will work together for the 'greater good'."

"Yeah, Earth to Nick!" said Linda. "What colour's the sky in your perfect world?"

"Yeah, exactly," Nick laughed.

"And, talking of politics," said Wilmott with a faint smile on his face, "I'm here because, as already mooted, I'm afraid to say that I have grave suspicions that the PM is behind this. I suspect that he has plans to weaponize the superconductor and exert control over other nations. I have reason to believe he is not in this alone but has been corrupted by a third party or parties. I suspect he has gone rogue. And I'm here to give you a proposal which I hope you will accept.

"I would like to ask you, Nick, to head up a new small team that would be based within my Section D and would report only to me or to Andrew Fleming, The Chief. The nature and mission instruction of this team would not be known to anybody else. This team would perform those functions that, politically or maybe even legally at times, the government would deny any involvement. If your team was compromised, you would be on your own as far as the country is concerned. We at Six would do what we can to help but, officially, we would deny your existence. It would be high risk but you would be rewarded well and, being 'unofficially' linked to Six, you would have access to all the latest equipment, including those currently at beta testing stage.

"Before you consider my proposal, there are two other things. One, you are free to choose your team members for each mission and, I suspect she would be in your list anyway but I would like you to include Linda as it's the two of you that I have complete trust in. Two, if you choose to accept, your first mission will be to investigate the PM, his possible involvement in the superconductivity issue and to discover who is in it with him, who is financing his operations.

"You don't have to answer straight away and, if you have reservations about this, I'd like to discuss them here in this clean room. However, I'll be straight with you. I came here personally in the hope of a swift answer and I shall admit that I came in the hope of a positive swift answer."

Nick looked across at Linda, thoughtful for a few moments, then smiled. Linda returned his smile in a knowing way. "There's not much for me to consider, David. You've described what I do best. No doubt you're already aware of my previous team's role, one similar to your description but perhaps known to more people. The answer is yes, you have me with a new team and, if Linda wants to be part of it, I'll gladly have her on side too."

Linda continued her smile and gave a slight nod of acceptance. "First job for me as part of our new team is to hand over this for safe keeping," she said taking the orthotope and putting it in Wilmott's top pocket.

Wilmott continued to look very serious. "Thanks," he said tapping his pocket, "I'll not acknowledge your acceptance with a joyous reply. Truth is, I'd prefer not to have to set up such a team but nowadays I consider it a necessity. I'm glad you've said yes and I think the country would be indebted to your successes if they were to know about them.

"You'll be known by the code name 'DAHRT', the Deniable Actions High Risk Team. If we can sit down here for a while, over another beer perhaps. I fully stocked the fridge when I got here. Just in case of a positive answer," he added when he saw the look of realisation on their faces. "We can go over the 'admin' parts: renumeration, budget, reporting, pre-authorisation for mission decisions, etc."

Nick went over to the fridge, opened the door and got out three bottles. He offered them up to Linda and Wilmott, got a nodded thanks from both and popped the tops from all three bottles. He passed one to each of them and they clinked them together as a toast, all three saying "Cheers".

They then settled down to make themselves comfortable ready to discuss business.

CHAPTER 14

10 Downing Street, London.

10 Downing Street, in the heart of Central London, has been the official residence of British Prime Ministers since 1735 and has been host to some of the most famous political figures of modern history. The house is larger than it appears from the front, having been joined to a building behind it in the 18th century and spilled over into much of 12 Downing Street in more recent times. In addition to being the home of the current British Prime Minister, it doubles as their office outside of Parliament and has been the location of some of the most important decisions affecting Britain for the last 275 years.

It was in the office of 10 Downing Street that the current British Prime Minister, Chayton Jameson, was sitting, behind his ornate desk, in conversation with his Private Secretary, Sir Kit Jenkins.

"And tomorrow morning you have a visit from the Overseas Trade Minister," continued Jenkins, "then lunch with the Governor of the Bank of England and then Prime Minister's Questions in the House in the afternoon."

"Do I need advance briefing for any of these, Kit?"

asked Jameson.

"No, Prime Minister," replied Jenkins in his usual confident manner. "We have had no advance list presented to us so tomorrow's meetings are just routine and for Question Time, no one has submitted any for consideration."

In his usual efficient style Jenkins had researched any current issues that may arise and was happy to be able to report that there were no major issues that should crop up unannounced. There were still some issues simmering in the background that may be worth committing to memory and, as always, he had prepared a short briefing for the Prime Minister.

For some time now Jenkins had been the right-hand man to Jameson, spanning his years of being an MP through to his current time of Prime Minister. He had helped him through the struggles in the bad times and been there to support during the good times. Some tabloids had joked in the past that it was actually Jenkins that was controlling the country – the headlines sometimes referring to Jameson as the Prime Minister and Jenkins as the President.

Jenkins cleared his throat and continued speaking. "However, there are some possible issues that may be worth considering so you are prepped for an answer. Firstly –"

He was interrupted by a ringing coming from the direct line telephone on the desk.

Most calls coming into Downing Street were routed through the main reception so that callers could be assessed and only relevant calls put through to the PM. However, the Prime Minister had a private line that could be dialled to directly call the telephone on the desk in the PM's office. This number was known only to a few world leaders and close kin of the PM. Therefore, if the telephone rang, it usually would be for an important reason.

It was this telephone that was ringing now.

Jameson said, "Excuse me," to Jenkins and picked up the phone. "Jameson," he said in an authoritative voice.

On the other end of the line a muffled voice spoke. "The target was missed. The captors were lost."

Jameson stared at Jenkins with a shocked and puzzled look on his face and spoke into the phone. "What did you say!? Who is this!? How did you get this number!?" he exclaimed. He was met by silence on the other end of the line followed by the click of the call being ended. "What the hell was that?" said Jameson placing the handset down onto its cradle.

Jenkins looked concerned as his eyes tracked the lowering handset. "Who was that, Prime Minister?" he asked also with a puzzled expression.

"I have no idea," said Jameson. "A muffled voice saying something about targets being missed and captors being lost. No idea who it was, they didn't say. How did they get this number?"

Jenkins looked concerned. "I'll look into it right away, Sir," he said getting his mobile phone out of his pocket and tapping a speed dial number. A few seconds later he was connected. "Reception?" he asked and after receiving a reply, continued, "This is Private Secretary Jenkins, can you trace a call that just came in on the PM's private line? Yes, just now. Lasted only a few seconds before the caller hung up."

Jenkins waited for a couple of minutes with the mobile phone at his ear, occasionally giving a 'yes' and 'no' to some questions at his ear piece, then said, "Okay, thanks. Keep on it," as he ended his call. Jenkins looked across at the Prime Minister and said, "Reception have got no details of the call. In fact, they've got no record of a call coming in to your line."

The PM looked even more puzzled. "Nothing!?" he exclaimed. "How can there be nothing? The call only came in a couple of minutes ago!"

"I don't know, Sir," continued Jenkins, "they're looking into it now. In fact, if that will be all I'll go over there now and see if they're coming up with any info."

"Yes, please do that Kit," said the Prime Minister. "It would be nice to know who has obtained access to the private line."

"On it right away," said Jenkins as he opened the door and stepped through, closing it behind him.

"Yes, keep on it," Jameson shouted at the door and then looked down at the private phone with a shocked expression on his face again. He shook his head a couple of times then picked up the private line handset and dialled a number from memory. After two rings the call was answered.

"It's happened," said Jameson and, without waiting for a reply, ended the call by placing the handset back down on the receiver.

CHAPTER 15

Cheltenham.

Harry Wilkinson was content in his job. No, not just content, he was happy. He was doing a job he was good at and he was making a difference. At school he'd always been referred to as 'the geek' as he seemed to have a natural understanding of electronics and computer programming. In the days before voice recognition, they used to say that Harry could talk to the computers and understand their replies.

This 'geeky' way of life continued all the way through his education and used to carry over into his non-scholarly life too. It was therefore no real surprise that he ended up working for the Government Communications Headquarters, more commonly known as GCHQ.

He'd been working at GCHQ for 16 years now, having been recruited directly from university. He'd passed the interview, impressing the bosses so much that he had bypassed the bottom rung of the ladder and been thrust straight into the world of data decryption. He had excelled in that field, often writing his own software coding to allow codebreaking of text and decryption of scrambled voice lines, and had worked his way up to heading the Data and Audio Decryption Department.

Though in charge of 30 or so staff members, Harry still liked to get his hands dirty when he could and was the person of choice for any high profile or extra sensitive monitoring work that came to the department.

A few weeks ago, he had decided to get his hands dirty again. His department was busy so it was the perfect excuse for him to knuckle down just like in the old days. He was pleased he had taken it on as it soon developed into what was likely to become a very high-profile operation if the information he was acquiring was correct. He had concentrated on this task full time since starting it and had decided to keep it close to his chest until he was sure about it. In the meantime, he would continue monitoring this particular phone line and any data transmitted along it too.

Today had been no different from any other day from the past weeks. There had been some calls and some possible text messages, some of them of interest and others certainly not. Sat in one of a large number of cubicles, in front of a bank of monitors, a pair of headphones covering his ears, he tapped an icon on the tablet in front of him and completed typing in the latest text of the speech that had recently taken place on the line he had been monitoring. He ensured the file was time stamped and then tapped another button to save it on to his secure area of the network drive.

He was particularly pleased with his recent work as, for this type of secure line, it wasn't always easy to find the correct decryption algorithm as it changed following each call. But he had suspected this line was following an offset-step pattern similar to one he had seen once before and he had successfully developed the decryption code that had enabled him to monitor all calls over the last three weeks, building up a large portfolio featuring some interesting dialogue.

He was pleased this latest conversation had been short as it was the end of his official shift time and he was looking forward to getting home and unwinding in front of the tv with a decent takeaway and a beer. He signed off from his terminal and, after checking that his remaining staff were all set for their evening's work, he put on his jacket, picked up his bag and headed to the exit. As a matter of routine, he went through the standard body and bag searches with his mind on whether to treat himself to a pizza, fried chicken or a burger.

He was brought back to real time by the sound of being 'buzzed' out of the building and now concentrated in putting his pin number into the secure locker so that he could retrieve his smart phone that always had to be surrendered for the duration of each shift. He powered it on and checked for messages that he may have missed during the shift. The usual spam messages were present but nothing else of interest. He thought of phoning ahead for his takeaway order but decided against it as he still wasn't sure what he really wanted. He'd decide during the journey home.

It had been a successful day so he felt good. He took a deep breath to take in the fresh air that he hadn't experienced for the past eight hours of his shift before getting into his car for the anticipated hour's journey that would get him home.

He loved his Audi RS5 and the growl of the engine even at tick over. He had treated himself to the car about a year ago; the first brand new car he had ever bought. It had been a big expense but, being single, he'd decided that it was about time he had a little fun in his life. Though capable of travelling very fast, the car was a delight to drive even at slow speeds so he hadn't regretted the outlay. As he started the car now, he still couldn't help but form a small smile as the engine came to life and he felt the restrained power as he pulled away from the parking space.

He gave a slight nod to the security guards on the gate as they opened it allowing him to drive out into the wooded area surrounding the workplace. He drove on for a few hundred yards reaching a crossroads in the woods. As he pulled up at a stop sign in the road the car engine stalled and all the electrics in the car stopped working.

"What the hell," he said to himself, sitting momentarily stunned at the complete car electrical failure, staring down at the dashboard in the hope of finding some indication of what had happened.

This had never happened before; the car had been completely reliable up until now. He couldn't believe it. It just had to be the day when he was really looking forward to a relaxing evening at home. He pressed the start button a few more times but got no response from the engine. He looked up, out of the windscreen to see if there was anyone around that may be able to help but there were no other cars in sight. He took out his phone to call the breakdown services and touched the fingerprint sensor to wake it from standby but the screen remained blank. He tried switching it on again and nothing was happening.

"This is weird," he said out loud to himself. "What the hell's going on?"

Those were the last words he ever said.

He didn't have time to register the sound of the 7.62mm bullet breaking a hole in the side door window as it continued on, hitting him, entering the side of his head just above his ear, destroying his brain stem, killing him instantly.

CHAPTER 16

Nick Saten felt relaxed, something he hadn't felt for a long time. It was a week since the 'business' discussion with David Wilmott – which he had to admit had gone very well – and he had only seen him once since then, when he and Linda had gone into the SIS Building to be 'kitted out'. Since then, they had been told to have some time off whilst the boffins at HQ do a bit more digging into the orthotope and they weren't going to disobey those orders.

At the moment, following an early drive into the countryside, they were having a leisurely stroll along the bank of a very quiet stretch of the Thames. The sun was shining brightly but the temperature was pleasant rather than hot and the air was fresh rather than humid. There were no people around and no boats and the only sounds were of the gentle flow of the water, birds singing to one another and the buzz of insects in the fields.

They had spent most of the week in places similar to this, wanting to have some time in contrast to the turbulent life style they had been through lately and it had given them a chance to catch up.

"I want to thank you again for answering my distress call, Nick," said Linda smiling at him.

"You know there's no need," said Nick returning the smile. "We've already been through this and I'm sure you would've done the same for me."

"You're sure about that are you?" she said playfully.

"Or maybe you would've seen my number on your phone and not taken the call."

"Yeah, that's more like it," she said putting her arm around his waist and they walked along.

"Ohh!" he winced causing Linda to take her arm away from him. "Still a bit sore from leaping onto speeding R8s."

"There you go exaggerating again. As far as I remember it was only one R8."

"Oh, okay Miss Pedantic! If it wasn't for the fact that you know my current sore spots, I'd challenge you to a fight."

"Oh yeah? I'd win sore spots or not."

"Oh yeah?"

"Yeah!"

They both broke into laughter at that point, moving close and turning to face each other. They looked into each other's eyes for a few seconds then Nick said, "It's been really good to be with you again."

"Yes, it has," agreed Linda.

They continued the eye contact as they moved their heads slowly towards each other, lips parting, preparing for contact. They closed their eyes and, as their lips touched –

Nick's mobile rang!

They both froze in frustration, then parted.

"Unbelievable!" exclaimed Nick as he picked out the mobile from his pocket. "I thought they were supposed to be smart phones. If that phone was smart, it would have known not to bloody ring just then!"

They both laughed but knew it could be an important call. This was Nick's new encrypted mobile that he had been issued with as part of his new role. Very few people knew the number.

He swiped the 'answer' icon and just said one word,

"Yeah?"

A voice at the other end of the line said, "On for a darts match tonight?"

Nick looked at his watch and said, "Yeah. I can be there in an hour or so."

The call ended and the two of them headed back across the field to the car in preparation for the drive back to London.

The journey back was uneventful and traffic was surprisingly light so they arrived at the outskirts of Central London in just under an hour. Nick parked in a street that was populated by three-storey townhouses, they got out from the car and walked to the door of one of the central townhouses that looked in need of a little paint and let themselves in.

Inside it was a complete contrast to the outside look, modern wooden panelled flooring throughout with an entrance hall lit by recessed LED spotlighting. Nick touched a small tablet computer mounted on the inside wall beside the front door, his fingerprint was immediately recognised and the graphics of a red keypad appeared on the display along with the digits '10' in the same colour that started to countdown in seconds. Nick tapped in a six-digit code on the keypad and the remaining digits turned green indicating that the house alarm had been deactivated.

They walked into the living room, similarly floored and lit to the hallway with a modern lounger on one side of the room across from a 72-inch flat screen tv mounted on the wall, sat down and Nick picked up a wireless keyboard that had been resting on the seat. He placed his thumb on the fingerprint reader and the tv screen became a monitor for a computer that was hidden in the room somewhere. He tapped in another six-digit code and the pc desktop appeared and he used the touchpad on the wireless keyboard to place the cursor over and double click an icon in the shape of a dart. The desktop on the screen was replaced with a window showing a box with the message 'input password' and Nick tapped in sixteen characters from memory for another window to appear with the message 'input code'.

"Now let's see," he said out loud glancing back at the screen of his mobile.

Once he had touched the finger print reader again, a further six-digit code appeared on the phone's display. He tapped in the code followed by the phone's code and the image of David Wilmott appeared on the screen. Somewhere above the monitor was a concealed webcam as Wilmott obviously had a view of the room. "Good afternoon, Linda, Nick," he said smiling.

They both said 'good afternoon' in reply and then Nick said," I take it there's been some developments."

Wilmott looked stern. "Developments, yes. We have a mission for DAHRT."

Linda and Nick looked at each other and then back to the screen. "We're all ears," said Nick.

"Yesterday evening," continued Wilmott with a serious look on his face, "a GCHQ operative was killed in his car about a mile or so from the base."

"These things happen," said Nick, raising his hands and shrugging his shoulders to indicate his puzzlement of their involvement. He assumed there must be more to the story so he as encouraging Wilmott to elaborate.

"Yes, these things do happen, but not usually due to a sniper's bullet."

"A sniper!? exclaimed Nick, "close to GCHQ. Isn't the area policed and covered by CCTV?"

"Normally, yes," said Wilmott, "but this happened in the wooded area near to the base. No extra patrols around there but plenty of CCTV cameras, all of which were taken out of action by EMP. As was his car to leave him stranded in the woods."

"We're talking pros here, "said Linda. "Electromagnetic Pulse generators, especially mobile ones, aren't easy to get hold of. And a sniper you say?"

"Yes," said Wilmott, "we're talking a precision shot through a car window hitting the target around the ear. Probable brain stem destruction, instant take out."

"This all sounds pretty bad," said Nick, "but why us?"

"I was coming to that," said Wilmott. "Henry Wilkinson was head of DaAD, the Data and Audio Decryption Department, within GCHQ and was usually desk bound nowadays. However, he was one of the best engineers, writing many of his own sneak algorithms for intercepting video and audio. And for the past few weeks he had gone back to basics and had been call monitoring."

"So, he'd trodden badly on someone's toes," said Linda. "Do we know who he'd upset?"

Willmott turned his head from side to side, evidently checking that he was alone where ever he was currently based. Happy that was the case, he continued. "For the past few weeks, he had been doing sensitive work for me, known only to me. He had been monitoring the PM's private phone line."

"And what had he found?" Linda and Nick asked together.

"He'd been in contact saying that he had something to report and we had agreed to meet up later today to discuss."

"Had he sent you the data covering his findings?"

"No, he was due to update me today when we met up."

"Okay, so what do you want us to do?" asked Nick.

"I'd like you to go up there and take over the investigation. A few days ago, Wilkinson made contact with me and said he had some information that would, I quote, 'blow the investigation open'. A bit cliché granted but I think he thought he had something substantial. He wouldn't tell me remotely so we were setting up a meet. Then he was taken out.

"Find a link between the assassination and the PM. I think he may have slipped up this time. Sanctioning a hit on a UK citizen on UK soil seems a bit of a panic situation so it's likely that he's not covered his tracks fully. We need to get evidence to bring him down but also find out who's financing him and who else he has under his control.

"I need your team to go in as, currently, we have no evidence against him so, if our efforts are discovered before finding anything, it would be very embarrassing for Six.

"The crime scene, in fact the whole wooded area, has been cordoned off by local police. Well, that's the power of Six," he said with a slight smile. "I'm using the excuse of a possible terrorism incident. It only happened yesterday evening so we're still preserving the scene ready for you two to arrive as SIOs to investigate. You can go to the scene and enter GCHQ having full access to all areas – your security clearances are higher than those at the base. Report directly back to me with any updates. Look for any connections and gather any evidence."

"We're on our way," they both said together.

"Good," said Wilmott then paused briefly. "Beware though when you get there. Wilkinson was reporting directly back to me. As far as I know, no-one else there knew about his eavesdropping work for me but his murder, and the way it was carried out, tends to suggest that somebody knew what he was doing and reported it to Downing Street. We may well have another traitor or traitors at one of our most secure and heavily-vetted buildings in the UK."

Wilmott then showed a concerned face and said, "Of course, until we have evidence to use against the PM, we can't be seen to be investigating him. Therefore, if you're exposed, you're on your own. We will deny any involvement with you or your team's activities. As it will always be, due to this lack of support, you are free to decline the mission and no less will be thought of you."

Nick looked at Linda and got the slight nod he was expecting. "We understand and we'll be there," he said causing Wilmott's face to show relief. "We'll be there in a couple of hours at most," he added as he and Wilmott ended the secure connection.

Linda looked at Nick. "You sure you want to be doing this?" she asked. "We'll be going against the British Prime Minister. Not only will he have the backing of the majority of the population, he's going to have most of the security services at his disposal – those that are loyal to him are likely to do whatever is necessary to stop us and those impartial members will just need to have a story made up for them to be equally dangerous to us."

Nick pondered her words for a few moments then said," Yes, I'm sure. If David is correct, I want to expose this corruption through to its roots. Are you okay with this?"

"Yes, I am," she said quickly. "He's already sent people out to kill us, he's sanctioned the death of others and must be stopped. So, I'm in."

Nick smiled and led Linda from the TV room up the stairs to one of the spare bedrooms. He slid open the doors of the fitted wardrobe to reveal a compartment with only a few shirts hanging up. He pressed a concealed button and a small panel slid away to expose a pin pad and a finger print reader. He touched his index finger to the reader and the numbers on the pin pad changed colour form red to green. He then keyed in a six-digit pin number and a quiet click could be heard. At the sound of the click, Nick gripped the rear wall of the wardrobe and slid it sideward revealing a further wardrobe space which was full of an assortment of weapons, body armour and various other gadgets that the department's techie team had put at their disposal.

Nick and Linda both put on concealable body armour, chose suppressed Glock 19s in shoulder holsters along with a few other items that they thought may be useful. From a wardrobe in the main bedroom, they dressed in casual clothes in an effort to blend in with local CID, both checking in mirrors that the covert body armour nor the Glocks couldn't be detected easily.

From Nick's collection of vehicles, they decided to choose the RS5 as the R8 would've come across as too flash for an investigating officer. The RS5 was no slouch so would not really impair a fast getaway or a chase if needed.

They got in the car, Nick driving, heading out towards Cheltenham, starting the first mission for DAHRT.

CHAPTER 17

Traffic was minimal and they reached the woodland area on the outskirts of Cheltenham in just over an hour. They showed their passes to the officer guarding the cordon's entrance and were directed to where the Audi RS5 was located. They parked up at a distance they considered to be 'forensically safe', walked over to the sports car where two forensics officers were working."

"Jeez! Said Linda, "David wasn't wrong when he said they were keeping the area cordoned off. The body's still in the car."

"Yeah," said Nick, "he obviously knows some influential people."

They introduced themselves to the forensics officers as the SIOs. The older of the two officers replied. "Good to meet you. I'm William and this is Edward."

"Hi," said Edward, smiling as he continued with his work.

"Where is everyone else?" Nick asked.

"We're here on our own," William said. "we're the only ones to have been allowed within the woods until you two."

"Oh, fair enough," said Nick. "Have you found anything of interest?"

"Not regarding the shot as yet," said William, "but we have found something of interest regarding the car. Well, the electronics of the car."

"Not just the car," added Edward. "There's his watch and his mobile too."

"What about them?" asked Linda.

"The circuits in all the electronic parts around here, car ECUs, the guy's watch and mobile, they've all been fried.

"Fried?" said Linda. "What do you mean, fried?"

"They've all been overloaded and burnt out, probably by some sort of EMF pulse. Probably aimed at the car in order to immobilise it. His watch and mobile were probably just in the firing line."

"EMF pulse," said Nick. "We're talking some expensive, high-tech stuff here aren't we?"

"Yes, we are," William and Edward said together.

Nick and Linda gave themselves a knowing look at each other before Nick said, "Do you know where the shot was fired from?"

"Way over there," said Edward pointing to a large fallen tree trunk a few hundred yards in the distance. "We found some disturbances in the earth the other side of the trunk and some new scratch marks on the trunk where the rifle may have been steadied. No spent cartridge cases so far though."

"Ok, thanks," Nick smiled. "We'll go over and look around the firing position. You two carry on here and let us know if you find anything else."

The forensics officers both said, "Will do," and turned back to examining the car.

Linda and Nick then started towards the fallen trunk, leaving the officers to continue searching the car.

"Seriously," said Nick as they walked.

"Seriously what?" asked Linda.

"Our two forensics guys back there."

"What about them?"

"How did they manage to team up together?"

"Why do you say that? They seem okay and know what they're doing."

"Yeah, they're probably fine," said Nick with a cheeky smile forming. "But we've got Bill and Ted back there. I bet they've had some excellent adventures!"

"I reckon you're the only person who would've thought of that," said Linda with a stern look on her face. Her lips then curled into a smile too. "Though, at least they're not dumb and dumber!" she added sniggering. "As far as I can tell anyway."

They reached the overturned tree trunk and looked around it taking notes of what Bill and Ted had said about the ground and the scratches on the bark. Nick stood and looked towards the car where the forensics officers were working.

"It's a fair distance to the car. Whoever made the shot was pretty accurate."

"Yeah, probably a pro," added Linda still looking around. "Nothing's been left. No shell casings and the ground's too dry for any decent shoe prints."

"Yeah, I think you're probably right," agreed Nick. "We're not gonna find much around here. As you say, we're likely dealing with a pro here so unlikely to find any evidence. Let's head back to the car, more likely to find something there … I hope."

They started to head back towards the car. As they got about half way back, Edward looked up from examining the body and shouted towards Nick and Linda. "We've got something here that you need to see." They quickened their pace in the hope that they may finally have a lead.

As they got within about 50 yards, Edward smiled, pointed towards the body and called out, "I think you'll want to investigate this. This should not –"

His speech was stopped as his chest exploded in a huge splash of blood and he slumped to the ground, dead before he landed.

William saw his colleague fall to the ground and started

to head over to him.

"Get down!" shouted Nick as he and Linda dived to the ground and rolled behind a wide tree withdrawing their Glocks from their holsters as they went. "Get down!" he shouted again but William was intent on going to his fallen partner.

It all happened so quickly. William took only a couple of seconds to reach the fallen Edward but, as he looked down at the body, his neck exploded in the mass of blood and gore. He fell next to his colleague, dead within seconds of falling.

Nick lay next to Linda behind the tree, both had their Glocks at the ready. "You ok?" he asked.

"Yeah," she replied. "No sounds, he's using a good suppressor. Any idea where the shots came from?"

"Somewhere beyond the fallen tree to the right judging by where the shots hit. Question is, is he still there?"

Nick raised his gun and slowly started to edge his sight around the tree. There was a thump as part of the bark beside his head splintered, again with no sound of a gunshot. He instinctively jerked his head back behind the tree.

"He's still there!" he said alarmed.

"The shot came from about 2 o'clock judging by where the tree was hit," Linda added.

"Okay," said Nick, "I'll draw another shot from him, then you shoot in that direction. With a bit of luck, it might give me a bit of cover to get nearer to him. Then I'll put up some covering shots for you to move in."

"Okay," she said, "ready when you are."

Nick edged over to the other side of the tree trunk and darted his head out from behind it and quickly back again. There was no gunshot sound again but there was another thump and a spray of bark from a tree ten yards back in line where Nick's head had been.

"Go!" shouted Linda as she spun out the other side of the tree and fired a short spread of three rounds at the 2 o'clock position and either side of it.

As soon as Linda has shouted, Nick took off and sprinted for another large tree ahead of him. As far as he could tell from his moving vision there had been no further shots from the sniper which presumably meant that Linda had spotted the correct location. He reached the tree he was aiming for in a couple of seconds, crashing hard into the trunk to stop his momentum. He immediately leaned around the trunk and fired a couple of rounds in the direction Linda had indicated. It was his turn to shout "Go!" and, as soon as he did, Linda was running to another large tree ahead of her. Nick watched as she reached the trunk that was over to one side and slightly ahead of his position. As she leaned around the trunk to give him covering fire, there was a loud clang this time and Linda slumped to the ground.

"No!" screamed Nick, eyes wide with anger. He ran out from behind the trunk and sprinted towards the 2 o'clock area, gun held out in from of him. Now he was near enough to see movement in the bushes as the large suppressor was swinging round in his direction. He fired a couple of shots above the suppressor and it jerked upwards slightly but continued moving to line up with him. Nick altered his sprint direction a little to be farther away from the swinging rifle and ran as fast as he could towards the side of it. The suppressor continued its swing, now only a few degrees from being in line with him.

He was now only about 8 metres from the barrel end as it was finishing its line up to have him in its sights. He took one more stride and then leaped up and towards the rifle as he felt a bullet whiz by underneath him. He flew through the bush's leaves and landed on the rifle butt and tumbled into the sniper, grabbing hold of him and rolling him away from the weapon. As they stopped rolling, Nick hit out and landed a punch to the side of the sniper's head. Though the punch landed as aimed, the sniper was strong and, though slightly stunned, didn't let go of his grip on Nick, now trapping his arms down by his side.

Nick tried a head butt catching the sniper on the bridge of his nose. He landed it perfectly and heard a crack as the cartilage broke. Now with blood running out of his nostrils, the sniper taunted him by smiling and landed a punch into Nick's stomach. The punch was hard and the air was forced out of his lungs as he doubled over in pain. The sniper threw Nick to the ground and fell on top of him, landing with his knees on Nick's chest making it hard for him to catch his breath. Nick tried to push the sniper off him by placing one hand on a shoulder and the other on his chin but he was too heavy and Nick was still weak from being winded.

The sniper grasped his hands around Nick's neck and began to squeeze hard. Nick tried to kick out but the way the sniper was kneeling over him, it was stopping his legs from any useful movement. Nick tried a punch to the sniper's face but he had no room to get a good swing. He couldn't breathe and he felt the grip tighten on his throat. His vison started to darken around the edges as his body fought to stay conscious. He tried again to push out to stop the sniper but his strength had gone as his body was fighting the encroaching darkness.

He looked up defiantly at his assailant's face in an effort to show he would never give up. As his vision was blacking out in all but a small centre circle of sight, he saw the sniper's head jerk sideways as blood and bone sprayed out from one of his temples. The sniper slumped to one side of Nick, releasing the grip on his neck.

Nick gasped for breath as his vision started to return to normal and strength began to return to his muscles. He looked around to try to take in what had just happened and saw Linda standing to one side, a recently fired gun in her hand.

"I thought you were dead," he said hoarsely, "but I'm glad you're not," he added quickly.

"You can't get me that easily," said Linda smiling. "That sniper's bullet hit my bloody pistol and ricocheted up catching me on the temple. I was lucky, it only grazed me but dazed me for a while. Knackered my Glock too. Lucky we both brought a spare."

"Well, I'm sure glad it only dazed you," said Nick, his voice now sounding less gravelly. "And I must thank you for suggesting we bring an extra pistol each. Not that I had a chance to use mine."

Linda smiled again and helped Nick stand. He wobbled a bit but soon got his balance back.

"Let's see if we can find out if this bastard has any ID," he said.

They searched the dead sniper but he had nothing to identify him and the rifle had had its serial number removed too. They headed back to the forensic officers and confirmed they were unfortunately dead too.

Their training overcame their emotions – it would be time to sort out the officers later – and they headed back to the car.

"So, what was it they had found that they wanted us to see?" wondered Nick.

"There's obviously something here for the sniper to still be around trying to keep people away from the scene," added Linda.

They approached the car, looking around the area surrounding it and could see nothing of interest. So, they moved on to the car, Nick taking the front and the body with Linda taking the rear seating area and the boot. It appeared that the body had not been moved and the driver's area of the car had not been cleaned up. It was slumped over towards the front of the car, the seatbelt stopping it from being draped over the steering wheel. The passenger side seat and side window were covered in blood due to the bullet's exit wound. Nick searched the body then scanned the seat and there appeared to be nothing else of interest amongst the blood.

The centre console between the front seats had missed most of the blood spray and, looking it over, Nick noted that the gear selector was still in 'D' where the occupant had been driving, approaching the junction. The tray next to the gear lever had a couple of small post-It notes, both with initials and what looked to be phone numbers handwritten on them and some loose change: two One Euro coins, an American Dime, two UK Pound coins and two UK Two Pounds coins. As Nick picked up the coins to check what they were, one of the Two Pounds coins felt different to the other – lighter and not evenly balanced across its surface. Upon closer examination, Nick could just make out a join line going across the diameter of the coin. He gripped the coin between the thumb and first finger of each hand either side of the join line and he pulled. The Two Pounds coin separated into two halves, one half having a hollowed out rectangular hole in it and the other having a USB connector protruding from it.

"I've found something here," Nick called over to Linda holding up the USB storage device. "I wonder if this is what the guys had found. It was hidden in plain sight amongst a selection of proper coins."

"It could be," said Linda holding out a small re-sealable bag for Nick to drop the device into. "So far I've found nothing of interest here at the back. I'll pass judgement until I've checked the boot."

"And I'll check in the glove box and under the bonnet," said Nick. He opened the glove box and found it to be empty. He then pulled the bonnet release lever to find it offered no resistance. He went around to the bonnet to find that it was already open but resting down on its latch. "It looks like the guys had already looked under the bonnet," he called out to Linda. "Or they were just about to start."

He lifted the bonnet which stayed open, resting on two hydraulic struts either side of the engine compartment. He scanned over the engine components and everything looked correct.

Or did it?

Something looked a little odd but what was it?

He scanned the area again slowly then spotted what didn't look quite right. The leads connected to the car battery terminals seemed stretched so that they only just reached the terminals and were tight against the side of the battery. Usually, he noted to himself, car battery leads had a bit of give in them to enable them to be disconnected easily if the battery needed to be removed or replaced. He glanced down the side of the battery and could just make out that the bottom of the battery seemed to be slightly off the bottom of the battery tray. There could be something underneath it. He looked a little closer but couldn't see anything so he squeezed his hand down between the side of the battery and the engine compartment wall and could detect what felt like the edge of a plastic bag with his fingertips but he didn't have enough room to move his hand to grip it.

"Is there any sort of tool kit in the boot?" he called out to Linda as he twisted his hand out from the small gap.

"There's a small bag of screwdrivers and spanners," Linda replied bringing the bag around to the front of the car and handing it over to Nick. "I've finished at the back. There doesn't seem to be anything. You found something here then?" she asked.

"I think there's something under the battery," said Nick as he opened the bag and found a spanner to fit the battery terminals. He loosened the nut on the negative terminal and had to use a screwdriver to prise the connector from it as it was so tight. He then did the same for the positive terminal and lifted the battery up from its housing revealing, as he'd suspected, a plastic bag. Linda reached in and grabbed the bag, unwrapped it and pulled out the contents.

"It's a notebook," she said flicking through the pages. "All hand written."

"We need to get these back to get them looked at," Nick said. "There's nothing else under the bonnet. I think we've probably found the things of interest."

Linda agreed as she placed the notebook into another

resealable bag.

Nick pulled out his mobile as they were heading back towards their car and phoned David Wilmott and gave a brief explanation of what had been happening.

"You're on speaker now by the way," said Nick, "so Linda can contribute. And we need an express clean up team to be deployed to deal with the car and the four bodies, one in the car, two near the car and one further out in the woods."

"It's on its way," said Wilmott, "and we'll get liaison officers involved if there are any friends and family involved with the forensics guys. You get yourselves back with your findings. I'll have a lab tech on standby to investigate the USB stick."

"You might need two lab techs," said Linda with a little smile forming.

"Why two?" asked Wilmott and Nick together.

"Because the notebook appears to be written entirely in shorthand," she said. "I've learned shorthand in the past and it's not a version I recognise."

"I'll see what I can do," said Wilmott.

"We certainly need to find an expert," Linda added. "Unless you can find someone who knows this particular form of shorthand, we may as well have a book of blank pages."

CHAPTER 18

Houses of Parliament, Westminster

The Palace of Westminster, more commonly known as the Houses of Parliament, is situated beside the River Thames in the centre of London. A constant attraction to tourists from around the world, it is easily recognised by its bell tower that houses the famous great bell nicknamed 'Big Ben'. Originally built in 1016, it was formally the monarch's principal residence in the late Medieval period and has been the meeting place for the English Parliament since 1295. Demolished in 1834 due to fire, rebuilding commenced in 1840 forming the building that can be seen today.

In an isolated corner of the building, in an unused office, a figure was sitting in the shadows at the desk at one end of the room, telephone in hand, a conversation in progress.

"No, it will not be traced. No one knows this phone line is connected. Even if someone sees the line has been used, it cannot be traced back to me – I have no direct connection with this area of the building."

The distorted voice on the other end of the line made no comment on the safety of the communication. "What is the situation at Cheltenham?"

The shadowed figure continued. "The two forensics officers were eliminated at the scene... before they had the chance to report their findings so I believe."

"And Ms. Andrews and Mr. Saten. What became of them?"

"They survived a shoot-out against the sniper – the sniper did not. And, no, there was nothing on the sniper to trace him back to me ... or us."

"And did they find the USB stick?"

"Yes, they did. They are taking it back to their lab for evaluation. It will not take long before their crypto-analysts gain access to its contents."

"And did they find anything else?"

"Nothing else has been reported. As far as we know, they have only the data on the USB once it has been decoded."

"And have you discovered the location of the orthotope?"

The shadowed figure swallowed hard before answering. "No, I –"

"No!" the distorted voice rose in volume as the shadowed figure was interrupted. "Your task was to retrieve the orthotope. Without it the formula is useless."

The shadowed figure's nerves started to show through into the speech.

"I, I, I am working on it. There are a number of locations it could be being kept. If I make the wrong move for it and show my hand, it will be guarded so closely I will never be able to get to it. It is difficult to second guess Wilmott and Saten. They are very experienced agents."

The distorted voice lowered in volume again which brought a shudder of terror through the shadowed figure – it was more frightening somehow when everything stayed calm.

"You are being paid well to retrieve it and you were chosen for your experience. Are you telling me that I chose wrongly!?"

"N, No. I can get it. Our problem is getting it without arousing suspicion. It may take time."

"You have until this time tomorrow. Otherwise, I will have to find someone with better experience!"

The line clicked and went dead as the call was abruptly ended. The shadowed figure wiped away sweat from his forehead and the palms of his hands. He took out a cheap 'pay as you go' mobile from his jacket pocket and dialed a number from memory. The call was answered at the first ring.

"Sir?" came the response from the other end.

"We need that orthotope now," the shadowed figure said with emphasis on the 'now'. "Put people on all known locations of Wilmott and Saten. Enter and search and find that orthotope."

"And if there are people present, in the way, Sir?"

"No one must be allowed to stay in the way. Take all necessary action to ensure no witnesses remain. Do you understand what I am saying?"

"Yes Sir! Does that instruction include Wilmott and Saten, Sir?"

"I repeat, no-one must be allowed to stay in the way. No-one."

"Understood, Sir."

The shadowed figure ended the call. There was nothing more that need to be said. He placed the mobile back in his jacket pocket, stood, wiped the desk phone with a handkerchief to obscure any fingerprints, opened the door slightly and, once sure no-one was in the corridor, exited the room and headed back towards the busier, more populated area of Parliament.

CHAPTER 19

At the end of their call to David Wilmott, Linda and Nick were told to take the USB stick and the notebook to a Self-Store-It warehouse on the outskirts of Southampton and to ask for him at Reception. They waited for the clean-up team to arrive which took only 20 minutes to get there – where Wilmott got hold of these teams so quickly was anyone's guess – and, having briefed them on the situation, they drove off in Nick's RS5, Nick driving. They drove around Cheltenham for a while until they were sure they weren't being followed and then headed down towards Southampton.

After some time in silence, Linda turned to Nick.

"So, what the hell's going on with all this, Nick? There's an awful lot of people getting killed for what amounts to be a lump of silicon."

Nick glanced at Linda then back to the road ahead.

"Gawd knows what the mentality is of the people involved in chasing after it. And it's not the silicon they're after, it's whatever's been embedded into it that apparently makes it so special."

"And can you really see the PM being implicated in this?"

"Nowadays nothing surprises me, Lin," said Nick glancing in the rear-view mirror, satisfying himself that there were no tails. "Though I would've thought even this PM wasn't quite so stupid as to get involved in such things. But one never knows. Perhaps if we can get the notebook deciphered it will give us some clues."

"And why are we meeting David at a storage warehouse?"

"I dunno, Lin. Maybe Six has a secret storage box or two within the place. Or perhaps it's just a neutral location to meet away from prying eyes. I s'pose well only find out when we get there. Which won't be for a while yet. He could've chosen a meeting place a bit nearer to Cheltenham."

They travelled for much of the journey in silence until they drove into an industrial estate, turned a corner and saw the Self-Store-It warehouse in the distance in front of them. Nick drove the RS5 into a space marked with the Self-Store-It logo and he and Linda climbed out of the car and, after a scan of the surrounding area to check for anything suspicious looking, they went into the reception area.

Unusually for a self-storage facility, there was a proper desk in the reception area with a proper person sitting typing on a computer keyboard. The receptionist, a pretty brunette who looked to be in her early twenties, wearing a badge with the Self-Store-It logo at the top and the name 'Carol' printed in the middle, looked up and smiled upon seeing the two visitors. A camera mounted near to the entrance door had taken a head and shoulders picture of Nick and of Linda and fed them through to the central server. In a fraction of a second, the server system had matched the facial features to those on file, identified the visitors and displayed their details on the computer screen at the reception desk.

With the identities confirmed, Carol was able to relax her grip on the Glock G26 she had holstered to her thigh.

"Hello Ms. Andrews, Mr. Saten. Mr. Wilmott is

expecting you. If you go through the doors to my left and head down the corridor, Mr. Wilmott will meet you at the lifts."

They said their thanks and headed as directed. As they entered the corridor, they could see Wilmott already at the lifts waiting for them. As they drew near, he smiled and swiped a card across a reader that was mounted on the wall in place of any 'lift call' buttons. The doors slid open and Wilmott ushered them inside and followed, the doors sliding closed behind them.

"Welcome to Self-Store-It, Southampton," he said with a smile on his face.

They said their hellos and Nick added, "What is this place, David?"

Wilmott continued smiling and said, "All will be revealed in a few moments. Bear with me until we reach my office."

An LCD touch screen was mounted on the lift wall and, rather than buttons, it displayed icons showing ground, two floors up and minus one down. Wilmott touched his thumb on a hidden reader at the bottom left of the screen and his name appeared on the display at the top of the buttons. He then touched his card momentarily against the screen and two extra floors appeared on the display, minus 2 and minus three. He tapped the icon for minus three and, though smooth, the lift started heading down fast. It quickly passed minus one and two then continued down for a few seconds extending its travel before reaching the third basement level. The doors slid open and they exited, Wilmott allowing them out first.

They were greeted by another receptionist, also badged Carol, at a similar looking desk to the one on the ground floor. She checked her monitor for confirmation of the facial recognition from the camera in the lift and relaxed her grip on the holstered weapon on her thigh, hidden by the desk. She said hello to all three of them by name and they returned the gesture as they headed down the corridor where Willmott showed them into his office. The office was large but all space had been used. A desk was at one end with a chair one side and two on the other. On the desk was a keyboard, three flat screen monitors in a line, a desk phone, a charger mount for a mobile phone and a pile of papers in a tray. On the two walls not occupied by the door and the desk, there were four large flat screen monitors, two on each wall and on one side of the room there was a meeting table with eight chairs. Wilmott gestured Linda and Nick to sit in the chairs at the desk as he sat on the chair across the desk facing them.

Nick smiled. "So, this is how you finance your operations is it? By having a storage facility as a second job."

Wilmott accepted the jibe though he had heard similar before.

"We figured it would be a good disguise for our offices. In fact, it's a fully operative storage facility, open to the public. They don't know about the extra floors and we charge them the going rate so it all looks fairly innocent.

"We've set up a number of Self-Store-It warehouses around the country, all with virtually identical basement and subbasement floors that can be accessed as we did here, by card swipe and fingerprint. We'll be giving you a special version of your driving licences that double up as swipe cards for the lifts – for use in all the warehouse locations. Every Self-Store-It warehouse around the country is ours, all kitted out the same. Entry by face recognition, card swipe and finger print – we'll program yours in later – so you can access any of them at any time.

"Each warehouse has a floor encompassing office space, meeting rooms and armouries and another floor where the computer and lab geeks work their magic. I'll give you a tour in a moment then you'll know the layout of each warehouse – they're all the same. We can then drop off the orthotope and the USB stick with the lab guys and give the notebook to the geeks."

Linda spoke up at his point. "This is all very impressive, Dave. How long have you been building these places? How many are there?"

"Andrew Fleming and I have been planning these for some time. The building on the Thames is sometimes a bit too public for certain people to be seen too often – much like yourselves, so we've had three of these built so far dotted around the UK with another three at the planning stage. It's taking a while to get them all sorted as they are ultra-secret. Neither the PM nor the Cabinet Office know about this."

"How have you done it then?" asked Nick.

"Originally using CT funds for the first build, we then found that storage is so popular that they'll end up paying for themselves in a couple of years. That's the beauty of basing ourselves in these working self-store buildings – loads of people are paying to use them plus we can store stuff here tucked away that we would have trouble getting in and out of London."

"It's all pretty impressive," said Linda and Nick together.

"You'll see how impressive as we have a walk around. In fact, rather than delay the lab guys any further, we'll have the items delivered there so we can see if they have any joy with them when we get there."

Wilmott pressed a button on his mobile charger and within a second a voice was heard on the intercom.

"Yes Sir?"

"Ah, Carol," said Wilmott sounding official, "could you come into my office please. I have some things for you to take into the labs for me."

Within seconds there was a gentle tap on the door and Carol from the lower reception walked in. Wilmott got Linda and Nick to hand over the orthotope, USB stick and notebook and Carol took them away heading straight to the labs.

"Are all the receptionists named Carol?" asked Nick, smiling.

"Yes, they are," said Wilmott noticing Nick's smile vanishing. "All receptionists at all the warehouses are or will be named Carol as they are placed. That way, if you arrive and find a receptionist with a different name badge or calling themselves something different, you'll know to be suspicious. On the other hand, if you arrive at a reception desk and ask a Carol where the 'usual' receptionist is quoting another name, she'll know you're having problems and can summon security."

"Sounds like a good plan," said Nick, "but won't regular public visitors find it strange that all receptionists they meet are all called Carol?"

Wilmott was hoping that question would be asked and smiled. "We'll be rotating the receptionists between the various locations and varying their shifts and from time to time we'll change the name being used – notifying our agents of course."

Linda and Nick nodded their approval and Wilmott gestured for them to stand and exit his office. He led them along the corridor to a door that looked like it belonged at the entrance to a bank vault. He swiped his card against a reader, keyed in a passcode on the LCD screen beside the door which triggered a scan of his face. Within a second, the LCD screen background colour turned from red to green and a series of substantial clunks could be heard as the locks were released. He pushed open the door and ushered Linda and Nick inside, following them and shutting the door behind them.

Now inside, Nick and Linda were surprised to find a large, well-stocked armoury. The room was about 10 metres square with shelves along the side walls and in rows across the floor. On the visible shelves Linda and Nick noticed an assortment of weapons and ammunition; rows of Glock 19 and 26 pistols, SIG MCX assault rifles, AI sniper rifles and their associated ammunition. It was anyone's guess what else was on the shelves they couldn't see.

"This is an impressive collection," said Nick. "Are you expecting a war?"

Wilmott looked serious for a moment. "You never know

what might occur. These stores are accessible back up to the special forces and police SFOs in the event of trouble. And they're available to us whenever we want to use them. Each location has an identical armoury so you're never too far from backup weapons if you need them. Out the back of each armoury there's a 20-metre range for testing the weapons if needed."

Wilmott took them back out into the corridor and headed for the lifts.

"The rest of this floor is made up of offices and meeting rooms," he said as they reached the lifts and he went through the motions of swiping, and finger print reading to get them to the next floor. "And this floor is where the labs and techies are," he said as the lift doors opened to reveal a small corridor with a couple of doors on either side.

As they walked along the corridor Nick and Linda could see that, on one side was a large lab area with many rows of work benches, everything looking white and sterile and on the other side, where they were heading, was a smaller area full of work desks with computers, monitors and all sorts of other boxes and gadgets on each. They entered the computer area and Wilmott took them over to the only two desks currently occupied, stopping nearer to one of them occupied by a man who was busily tapping at his keyboard.

"This is Keith Turner, head of the section and that guy over there is Tony Chapman, Keith's deputy head. Guys, this is Linda Andrews and Nick Saten."

Keith stopped typing and turned to greet his visitors. For the first time Nick and Linda could now see him properly. He appeared to be in his mid to late twenties, having shoulder length hair and wearing jeans with designer rips in them and a tee shirt with 'Beware of geeks baring GIFs' written on it. He looked the stereotypical computer programmer/hacker.

"Hi," he said smiling. "Pleased to meet you."

"Don't let this guy's appearance fool you," said Wilmott, "there's nothing he doesn't know about computers. I think, if they cut open his head, they'd find a chip rather than a brain."

Keith didn't blush but added, "It's a perception that I like to keep up. I just blind Dave here with science most of the time. Luckily there's only Tony here who can tell him whether I'm right or wrong."

Tony Chapman stood briefly to say hello then sat back down in his chair facing the visitors. Tony was of a similar age but more conservative in appearance compared to Keith. Still looking casual, he wore a plain shirt and jeans and had his hair cut short.

"Pleased to meet you too," he echoed.

Wilmott smiled and added, "Well, we've not had cause to think either of these guys wrong so far." He then looked more serious and said, "Early yet I know but have you got anything for us?"

It was Keith's turn to smile this time.

"Yes and no. Yes, we have broken into the majority of the USB stick and are retrieving data from it as we speak. There's one fairly small area on it that seems to be protected with a much stronger code that we haven't been able to break into as yet. It's only a matter of time. And yes, we are analysing the orthotope but no, we haven't sussed its constitution yet. And no, we haven't found a matching short hand coding to match that in the notebook as yet. We wonder if it's a version that the author has made up himself. If so, it will take longer to crack as our decrypting software will have to take it line by line until it breaks the code."

"Excellent start," said Wilmott genuinely impressed with how far they had got in the short time they'd had the items to analyse. "So, what have you got from the USB stick?"

"This should interest you," Keith said as he turned to face the second of the terminals lined up across his desk. "We've found a load of info on the drive. It was encrypted but our decryption algorithms soon broke through its defences." He tapped a few keys and pages of data started to appear on the monitor. "What we've got here," he said pointing to an area of data on the screen, "is a list of dates of calls to and from this phone number here, which is the Prime Minister's private line at his desk at Number 10. There's obviously no interest in many of them but you'll notice that a few have been highlighted. The transcriptions from the highlighted calls are then displayed to the side of the number list."

"So, is there anything interesting about the highlighted ones?" asked Nick.

"I'll send you the full transcriptions but many of them are quick calls with one- or two-word conversations that may or may not have any hidden meaning. However, there's a couple here dated a few months back and another here dated a few weeks back that may be significant. They mention shipments and deliveries but never state what is being sent – it's only referred to in cliché as 'the merchandise'."

"No!" sniggered Nick. "The 'merchandise'. Sounds like we're in some 'B' movie."

"However," continued Keith, "the timings of these 'merchandise' movements coincide with what we know of the PM's daughter's movements and the reference to 'merchandise' stopped just before her body was found."

"Jeez!" said Linda staring at the monitor. "Are you saying that the PM coordinated his daughter's kidnapping and her death?"

"Well," said Keith sounding very serious, "the final 'merchandise' call sates that the 'item' should be retrieved and the 'merchandise' should be disposed of."

"Jeez!" exclaimed Linda again. "He orchestrated her death in order to get the orthotope. We've got him."

"Well," said Keith again, "we've only got this Harry Wilkinson's word on this. The dates of the calls are from a printout so we can be fairly sure those calls were made when it says. However, we've not yet found any recordings of the phone calls, only this transcript that Wilkinson has typed up. We can be pretty sure that Wilkinson wouldn't be lying but we have no proof as yet."

"This is ridiculous," said Linda crossly. "He can't be allowed to get away with this."

"Well," repeated Keith, "we may not have lost out here. The transcript of a call made the day before Wilkinson died mentions a meeting that will be taking place between the PM and his contact."

"When and where?" said Wilmott. "And I take it there's no way of knowing who this contact is?"

"They never state any names during any of the transcripts we've seen so far, so I'm betting they don't at all. We only know it's the PM because it's his phone and Wilkinson refers to the voice as being 'CJ'."

"Ok," said Wilmott. "So, they're not stupid whoever they are. So, do we know when and where?" According to the transcript it's going to take place," said Keith made making an involuntary glance at his watch, "at 12 midnight tomorrow."

"And does it say where?" Wilmott asked again.

"Er, yes it does," came the reply a little hesitantly. "It says Bournemouth."

"Bournemouth!" Wilmott, Linda and Nick all cried together.

"That's what it says," Keith said pointing to the screen where the transcript showed the seaside town. "It says, and I quote, midnight, under the pier, Bournemouth."

"Why the hell would the PM choose Bournemouth for a midnight meeting?" asked Nick.

"He's not chained to Number 10 you know," Wilmott answered. "He can get out and about at times and I suppose he knows the town from the old Tory conferences. I assume at around midnight he expects to be able to sneak out past security."

"That's if his security team aren't in on this as well," Linda added.

"You're sure it says Bournemouth?" asked Nick staring at the screen then at Keith.

"That's what it says," he said placing his finger over the word on the screen. "And I don't know of any other Bournemouths he could reach for a quick rendezvous from Number 10."

"Well. It looks like we might get a day out to the seaside tomorrow," smiled Nick. "Or a night out anyway."

"We really need to know who he meets," said Wilmott. "Find out who's controlling him so we can plan how to shut this down."

Linda added, "Well, if he meets with someone tomorrow, we'll be there and find out who it is. Meanwhile we need to find somewhere to put our heads down for the night."

"There's no need," said Wilmott. "We have apartments here on this floor. They're for our teams that need to work late or through the night. You two can stay in a couple of them. They're well equipped so you shouldn't have too much to complain about."

"Okay. Lead the way," said Nick.

They said their goodbyes and were led off towards the apartments by Wilmott, leaving Keith already returning his attention to the USB stick. He didn't like being beaten by computers or electronics. He muttered to himself or maybe to the flash drive.

"C'mon you bastard," he said tapping additional lines to the code he was using to break into the device. "I'm not giving up this easily." He executed this latest piece of code and was surprised at the way it appeared to be rejected by the USB stick. "Mm, it's as though it is actively blocking any code from accessing it."

"Maybe it's a hard-wired firewall type of area within the device," said Tony walking over to Keith's desk.

"We'll it's not gonna beat me," he said staring at the stick with a look of hatred, "even if it takes all night or more." He continued to type lines of code, executing them and cursing under his breath when the area of the device remained inaccessible.

"You should call it a night," said Tony, stifling a yawn. "You're tired and, if you're not careful, you'll find yourself going around in circles."

"I'm gonna keep at it for a while longer," Keith said through gritted teeth. "You go off home and get some sleep. We can start again in the morning."

"I'll take you up on that as I feel knacked. I'll go as long as you're not far behind me," Tony said showing concern for his boss.

"No, I won't be far behind you, Tone. See you tomorrow."

Tony shut his system down, grabbed his jacket and headed off giving Keith a gentle tap on the shoulder as he went. Keith continued running code and cursing when it failed to produce desired results.

Nick awoke and looked at the digital alarm clock on the bedside table. Three thirty in the morning. He'd slept for a long time having retired early, not realising how tired he must have been and the bed and pillows were very comfortable. There were no windows in these apartments as they were below ground but what would have been total darkness was gently lit by some faint mood lighting within the recessed ceiling so he could make out the layout of the room.

His mouth felt very dry so he got up out of the bed, went over to the mini bar and picked out a bottle of flavoured water, downing half of it in a few gulps. He felt more awake than tired now as many thoughts were whizzing around in his head: is this bit of silicon really worth lives, who are the different factions that seem to be after it, can the PM really be involved in this and who's in it with him?

He could see that there was a faint glow of light from under the apartment's door so he opened it a little and determined it was coming from the computer rooms. He put on one of two gowns that were hanging on the back of the door and strolled towards the lighted room. There, hunched over his keyboard, busily typing was Keith. There was a small convex mirror clipped to the corner of one of Keith's monitors so he only had to glance from the monitor to see who was approaching from behind.

"Hi Nick," he said appearing to be just as dynamic as he had much earlier.

"Don't you ever sleep?" asked Nick smiling.

"Not when there's a challenge like this," said Keith still tapping away at his keyboard. "It's not letting me into one area. The rest of it is accessible but this one area is blocking every attempt to read it."

"Do you think this Wilkinson guy was clever enough to program such a thing?"

"He may have been. He was bright enough to create his own version of short hand, that we haven't yet deciphered either I may add. So, it's possible but, if he has coded this, he should have been working here, not at GCHQ."

"And you've still got no idea of what that area of the USB stick contains?"

"No, that's right. I have no idea. Though I'm thinking that it's been hard wired into the device rather than being a coded bit of memory. Which means that, without the trigger entry code, the only way into it may be to take the thing apart and wire in directly to the isolated memory area. However, it could be tamper proof and set up to wipe the memory if the case is opened."

"Where would this guy have got hold of such a specialist device? I take it, it's not standard GCHQ issue or you'd know how to get into it."

"No, it's not standard issue, Nick. I don't think a USB device disguised as a coin has ever been issued to any of our guys. It's possible that he has modified this device himself or had it modified especially for him but we don't know what for and won't know until we can talk to it."

"Maybe we won't need to get into this secret bit. If we find who the PM is meeting tonight maybe that information will lead us to what we need to know."

"Maybe, Nick. But I still don't like to be beaten by these sorts of things. There's got to be a way in. It's just a matter of finding it."

"What I'm trying to say, Keith, is that we have our next lead in the meeting tonight so, getting into this device is not mega urgent so you could get some sleep."

"Thanks, Nick but I'll keep on for the moment. I get a bit of shut-eye at my desk when I need it. I'll be fine. I'm used to it. And Tony can take over in the morning when he's back in"

"Okay, fair enough," said Nick stifling a yawn. "It's making me feel tired again just watching you so I'm going back to bed."

"Okay then, bye for now," said Keith still typing at great speed.

Nick shrugged his shoulders and headed back to his apartment.

"Computer geeks," he said to himself with a slight smile. "They have an extra power pack hard wired in somewhere."

He got back to his room, disrobed, had another small swig from the bottle of water, got back into bed and though his unanswered thoughts were still going through his head, they soon started fading as he drifted back into a comfortable sleep.

Nick slept through the night, getting up late morning. Once he'd showered and shaved, he discovered that his clothes had been cleaned, dried and pressed – another service that Wilmott had attached to the unit to allow 24/7 working when necessary. He wandered to the canteen area to find Linda had also slept late and was now eating a large brunch.

After eating they headed back towards their rooms, passing the lab areas and seeing that Keith was still sat at his desk, head down, typing.

"I was up during the night," said Nick looking Keith's way, "and he was in there then. Does he ever stop?"

"I think he's a robot," Linda said through a large smile. "It's another technology marvel that David is gonna reveal to us soon. He'll slip up soon and introduce him as 'Keith Version 3.4' or something."

"As long as he doesn't point out where his on/off switch is, I'll not mind."

Keith spotted them in his rear-view mirror and looked up, turning around from his keyboard and gave them a small wave. Nick gave a thumbs up with one hand, an 'ok' symbol with the other and silently asked the question whether he had cracked the USB stick with a silent but inquisitive look on his face. Keith gave a thumbs down, shook his head and turned back to his computer.

"I think they could've programmed his human side to be a bit more realistic, "said Linda.

"Yeah," agreed Nick. "He doesn't resemble a typical human at all. He's friendly and hardworking and spot on with the correct level of support for us. He'll be out on his ear, or powered down as soon as they know he's on our side."

They got back to their rooms, rested for a while and then met up at the armoury to get kitted then headed out for their night out.

CHAPTER 20

Bournemouth

Bournemouth, on the central south coast of England, was heathland until the mid-nineteenth century when the small village with a population of around 700 people started to grow into a popular seaside resort. In 1870, when the railway system arrived, the number of visitors increased dramatically and, by the 1890s the population had expanded to around 37000 people and Bournemouth began extending its boundaries absorbing surrounding villages.

By 1901 electric trams were introduced across the town and the population reached 59000 and then continued to grow throughout the twentieth century, with a Pavilion theatre built around 1930 to provide further entertainment for the visiting populace.

In 1979 the now corroded pier from the late nineteenth century was rebuilt into the form it is today and the town continued growing from then onwards with the population now standing at around 200000. During the mid-1980s, Bournemouth International Centre was constructed as a concert and conference centre in order to attract more tourists from competing resorts along the south coast, hosting many famous performers and large businesses and political parties.

It was in a hotel directly across from the International Centre where Nick and Linda had checked-in in the early evening and were now sitting in the hotel's restaurant at a table overlooking the pier.

After loading the car with their weaponry and protective equipment, they had set off, driving along the coastal roads until they had reached the seaside resort. They'd pre-booked the hotel and a space in its underground car park so they were able to drive straight in, the automatic barrier system recognising the car registration from the booking. They'd signed themselves in as Mr. and Mrs. Dobbs, unpacked their small amount of luggage and were now enjoying a meal in the hotel's restaurant before their trip to the pier.

"What is this we're eating?" whispered Linda with a cringing look on her face. "It said potted crab on the menu. It tastes more like potted crap! I think they used the wrong final letter."

Nick smiled. "I didn't book the place for its cuisine. More for its guaranteed parking and its location," he said looking out the window at the entrance to the pier. "I ordered the beef skewers but, looking at the ones that bloke has over there, I wonder if they meant to write beef spewers!"

They both laughed as the lone waitress came over to their table.

"Are you ready for your main courses now, Sir?" she asked pleasantly.

"As we'll ever be," said Nick cheerily adding "gawd help us!" under his breath as the waitress headed towards the kitchen.

After a few minutes the waitress returned with two plates in her hands.

"The chicken skewers for you madam and the beef skewers for you sir," she said placing the plates down on the table. "Is there anything else I can get you?"

They both said there was nothing else they required and the waitress left. They studied their skewers and looked up at each other, both with surprised looks on their faces.

"They look okay," said Nick cutting off a piece of his skewered beef and eating it. "Mm, and it tastes really good."

"Mine too," said Linda with a suspicious look on her face.

Nick added, "I don't think they like that bloke over there. He got some real shitty looking ones. And I think you must've got his crab!"

They both laughed again and tucked into their meals.

Back at the Self-Store-It warehouse in Southampton Wilmott was preparing himself for another night in the place. This time he'd be monitoring the progress of the mission in Bournemouth. He was on his way to the control room where he could stay in contact with Linda and Nick, when he stopped in on Keith and Tony who were still tapping out lines of code.

"Still no joy, Keith?"

"Oh, hi David. No success yet. It's a real challenge."

"Have you slept, Keith?" asked Wilmott genuinely concerned.

"Oh yes I've had a few hours here and there. But I find it difficult to get any deep sleep when I have a challenge like this. Tony's been keeping things going when I've had a few hours away"

"Do you still think this is something this GCHQ guy could have made himself?"

"Well, I have been wondering, Dave. It's got to be very sophisticated hardware to withstand all we're throwing at it. Unless it's something he's acquired somehow and then put into his own case. I've never come across a USB stick this advanced that's been constructed in the form of a coin."

Keith continued typing on his keyboard, hitting the enter key and looking fed up when the pc pinged and 'No entry' was displayed.

Nick and Linda had finished their meal and, feeling pleasantly surprised at the quality of the food, had gone back to their rooms to change one at a time so that the other could stay at the table watching for any movement at the pier. They had both changed into jeans, polo shirt and jacket with covert body armour under the tops and covert shoulder holsters containing their Glocks.

They left the restaurant and started down the hill towards the pier entrance. It was now 11.30 p.m. and there was no show on at the pier theatre tonight so the pier appeared to be dark and deserted. According to Keith's findings, the meet was supposedly going to be taking place under the pier so, rather than head for the pier entrance, they veered off, on to the beach where they could see the underside of the pier without being spotted by anyone who may turn up there.

Wilmott smiled at Keith.

"I'm sure you'll crack it soon. I doubt there's been many bits of computer coding that have beaten you."

"No," said Keith glumly, "it's usually just a matter of time. The right code here at the right time and we'll be in. With the two of us working at it, it shouldn't be too long"

"Have you got anywhere with any of the things found at his house?" asked Wilmott trying to give Keith the chance to tell him some good news.

"We've been through all the IT from his place with nothing to report. This is the last piece from his place and the only one proving to be trouble."

Wilmott frowned a little, puzzled at what had just been said.

"No, Keith, this USB stick was found in the car. So, you've processed all the bits from the house."

Now it was Keith's turn to look puzzled.

"No, David. This wasn't from the car. It must have come from the guy's house."

He looked over towards Tony.

"Tone, didn't you tell me this had come from the guy's house, not from his car?"

Tony looked up from monitor.

"Er, the USB stick, Keith. Er, yes, I thought it was from the guy's house."

"I'm pretty sure it was from the car," said Wilmott tapping at his smart phone.

He accessed the inventory from the secure link to the server and scrolled down until he came to the entry he was looking for.

"Yes, it says here in the car contents listing, 'one USB stick shaped as coin'. And this inventory was published before we had got to the guy's house so, it must have been in the car."

"No, no. It couldn't've been," said Keith glazing over, looking from the USB stick to his display.

"Why are you so sure?" asked Wilmott following Keith's gaze at the screen.

"Because the car was fried by an EMP. We've since tested everything and everything electronic was fried – all the chips in the car's ECU, the infotainment centre, the guy's watch and his phone are all completely dead. Destroyed by a huge electro-magnetic pulse that was presumably used to stop the car. Nothing electronic inside that vehicle would have survived."

"But we've got information from it," said Wilmott pointing at the USB stick. "It's working."

Keith stared eye-to-eye at Wilmott. "That can only mean the stick was placed in the car after the pulse. After the car had been stopped."

"Shit, shit, shit!" exclaimed Wilmott. "We've been set up."

He tapped his smart phone into phone mode and speed dialled Nick's number. After a second or so the message came through, 'The number you have dialled has been switch off. Please try again'. He hung up before the message had finished, his thoughts racing to Linda and Nick at the pier in Bournemouth.

"Shit, shit, shit!" he shouted again.

CHAPTER 21

The first shot burnt its way through the air, close enough to Nick's head for him to feel his hair moved by the passing bullet.

He was lucky to be alive.

Had Linda not stumbled on a large stone in the sand a split second before the shot, she wouldn't have fallen against Nick causing him to sidestep a little – enough for it to miss his head by a few millimetres.

The bullet continued on its way, past Nick's head and hit a concrete pillar supporting the pier, producing a loud crack and a spray of small rocky shards.

Nick grabbed Linda and dived to the ground, pulling her down with him. Holding her tight to him, he rolled them in the sand towards the pillar as the second shot hit the ground where they had fallen causing an eruption of sand into the air. Nick and Linda used the sand cloud that had been produced to stand up at a crouch and run behind the pillar whist the gunman was temporarily unsighted. They both grabbed for their Glocks but stayed sheltered behind the pillar.

"Any idea where the shot came from?" asked Linda.

"No idea. Suppressed, didn't hear a thing. And where's

the PM?"

Nick stole a quick glance around the pillar to see if he could get an idea of where the shooter was located only to have the concrete at head height erupt with the impact of another bullet.

"Can't see anything but he must be along the seafront to get a shot at us. Keep low and in line with the pillar. Maybe we can stay unsighted."

They crouched again and backed away from the underside of the pier, keeping the same line with the pillar and the shot direction. No further shots were fired so they turned, still crouched, and started to run, all be it slowly as the sand was soft.

In the dim light of the crescent moon, the beach was very dark but, at the same time, they both spotted the silhouettes of three or four armed figures advancing towards them from farther along the coastline. They stopped and looked towards the land only to see another three figures advancing out of the gloom towards the beach.

"Jeez, we're surrounded," cursed Linda.

"Not quite," said Nick quickly. "Fancy a swim?"

"What about the sniper?" asked Linda worriedly.

"I'm banking he won't fire if his colleagues are moving in."

Nick grabbed Linda's arm and ran with her towards the sea. A suppressed bullet hit Nick's Glock with a loud bang. Sparks flew from the impact as the shock wave forced Nick to drop the weapon.

"Dive and head for the end of the pier," he cried.

They reached the water's edge and dived in, pushing themselves forward and down. From under the water, Nick could see some faint lights glowing through the gloom at the end of the pier so he swam towards them guiding Linda. They were both good swimmers and had no trouble reaching a little mooring area at the head of the pier. In contrast to the blackness of the sea stretching to the horizon, the dim lamps on the pier gave faint illumination to a bank of jet skis for hire that were tied up for the night, bobbing up and down gently on the gentle waves. They surfaced on the far side of the jet skis and took in some deep breaths of air.

"Don't suppose they've left the keys in for safe keeping," whispered Nick.

Though the sea was lapping at the base of the pier and against the jet skis, it was relatively quiet so Nick didn't want to be heard from the shore.

Linda glanced around the side of the jet ski she was sheltering behind and quickly darted back behind it.

"Keep your fingers crossed," she added, "our friends have reached the shoreline and I doubt they're gonna worry about getting their feet wet."

Nick gently swam around the nearest of the jet skis, reaching up, feeling for the ignition switches and finding them keyless.

"No luck," he said, shaking his head.

Linda stole another glance towards the shore. "We need to think of something, Nick. Some are wading in and the rest are making their way along the pier."

"And we have no keys for the getaway cars and one Glock between us," said Nick looking around for inspiration.

They both glanced from the side of the jet skis to the pier and back. The gunmen in the water were now up to their waists and preparing to swim and the gunmen on the pier had advanced about half way along. Linda aimed her Glock from one set of gunmen to the other then lowered her weapon.

"It's no good," she whispered to Nick. "I'll only be able to get a couple of good shots off at one of the groups and that will then pinpoint our location for the others."

"We'll just have to take out as many as we can and then swim for it," said Nick still trying to gauge which would be the better target.

The gunmen in the sea were now standing still and

keeping their heads above the water as they raised their weapons, pointing them towards the area of the jet skis. The ones on the pier had now reached the end section and were also taking aim at the moored craft. Linda and Nick looked around the jet ski where they were sheltered and two of the gunmen on the pier drew their weapons to point at their heads.

Linda started to bring her Glock up to aim at the gunmen as they started to tighten their pull on their triggers. Linda was in despair. They were hopelessly out numbered and had walked right into this ambush but she was determined to take as many of them with her as she could. She picked a target that was also targeting her and took aim. The gunmen and Linda all started to apply the necessary pressure to their triggers and –

Sirens.

The noise of loud sirens, many sirens, cut through the quiet seafront.

The gunmen on the pier and in the water withdrew their weapons and all started to retreat to the entrance of the pier. Linda kept her Glock aimed at her target but didn't shoot.

As the sirens increased in volume, the gunmen all met at the pier's entrance, mumbled something to each other and then ran off at pace heading away from the noise. Linda and Nick stayed where they were, Linda covering the area as best she could with her single weapon. They assumed the sniper had moved off with the other gunmen but they couldn't be sure.

The sirens were getting louder but their sound was drowned out by the screech of tyres on tarmac as a fast car was making a quick getaway.

"They've probably all gone now, Lin," said Nick as he edged out from the shelter of the pier supports. "Now all we have to do is explain ourselves to the cavalry."

The 'cavalry' cars gave off further screeches as they skidded to a halt at the entrance to the pier. A number of officers disembarked, shouting "Armed police!" all brandishing assault rifles, half running on to the pier and the other half running down under it, rifles pointing in the direction of Linda and Nick with the attached torches illuminating their faces.

Squinting in the torch light, Linda held the Glock by barrel with her finger tips and slowly placed it on the ground in front of her then raised her hands.

Nick also raised his hands, one shading his eyes, and said, "Guys, I can explain…"

He was stopped in mid-speech by one of the armed officers.

"Mr. Saten and Miss Andrews, if you could please remain where you are whilst we secure the area."

"You know who we are… er… obviously," said Nick with a puzzled look of his face.

"Yes, we do," came the reply. "We're here courtesy of David Wilmott. He sends his regards."

Various shouts of "Clear!" came from the officers searching on and under the pier.

"Okay," said the officer facing Linda and Nick, obviously the guy in charge. "Cease search, form protective cover." Then to Linda and Nick, "Okay Miss Andrews, Mr. Saten. Area now appears safe."

"Well, thanks," said Nick, still puzzled. "You say David Wilmott sent you?"

The officer smiled. "I don't know who you guys are, in fact you were never here so I've been told, but we received an emergency call from Mr. Wilmott to scramble to the pier – possible armed hostiles. Unfortunately, it seems the intel was inaccurate and we found no-one here. That's what's going in my report anyway."

"Glad you came out," said Nick smiling, "we were in a bit of a tight situation until you arrived."

"Say no more," said the officer. "We're just local plod. I suspect, as 'they' say, you're operating above my pay grade. Glad to be of service."

"Well, thanks anyway," Linda and Nick said together.

"Pleasure was ours. Okay, stand down. Back to base."

The armed officers grouped up from their protective locations and headed back to their cars. Linda and Nick walked with them back to the road, gestured their goodbyes and headed back to the hotel.

Linda followed Nick back to his room where he retrieved his mobile, switched it on and phoned Wilmott. The call was answered on the first ring.

"Nick? You both okay?" asked a concerned Wilmott.

"Yes, both okay, thanks to you. What the hell happened? There was no sign of the PM."

Wilmott explained about the discovery that the USB stick must have been planted and that, once discovered, Keith had determined the area of memory he couldn't access was in fact a hard-wired processing unit that was trying to transmit burst code information back to an unknown source.

"So, we were set up completely," said Nick. "Those bastards knew we'd break the coding and set up an ambush for us here. And we didn't get any of them so we're still no closer to any proof of who's behind all this."

"We may be a bit closer," said Wilmott. "In the last hour or so, Keith's latest algorithm has broken the short hand code in the notebook. It's deciphering it as we speak."

"Some good news at last," said Nick hopefully.

"Yeah, we hope so," said Wilmott. "Get your ass back here. Hopefully by the time you're back, it will have finished decoding."

"We're on our way."

Linda returned to her room to pack her bag whilst Nick gathered up his belongings, ensuring his room was clear. They met at reception ten minutes later where they handed their keys to the desk clerk.

"I trust there was nothing wrong to make you check out early, Sir, Madam?" asked the clerk tentatively.

"Not yours or the hotel's fault," said Nick. "It's just that we found Bournemouth a bit uneventful."

They walked back to the car, stowed their bags and sped off out of Bournemouth anxious to get back to discover the contents of the notebook.

CHAPTER 22

Houses of Parliament, Westminster

Back in the shadows of the unused office in the isolated corner of the Parliament building, the figure was sitting at the desk with the telephone receiver in hand. On the other end of the line was the distorted voice, calm but menacing.

"Saten and Andrews are still alive. Explain!"

The shadowed figure gulped down some bile that had risen into his throat.

"I... I don't know how b... but armed police arrived before our men had a chance to take them out."

The distorted voice continued, seemingly unconcerned with the excuses.

"Your men, not ours failed in their task. You are responsible for your men. Their failure is your failure and failure is unacceptable."

"It w... won't happen again. W... with the police on th... the scene, I didn't want any of our ... my men captured. They h... had to get away. S... Saten and Ms. Andrews were very fortunate that the police were in the area."

The distorted voice remained calm but rose in volume.

"You think fortunate? The police were summoned by Wilmott!"

"N… no. Th… that cannot be possible. H… he couldn't have known what we were planning. The USB stick was still transmitting during the Bournemouth exchange."

"They realised the USB stick had been planted in the car, so then determined that information on it was probably false. You made a grave error placing the USB stick inside the car rather than on the ground nearby."

"B… but we didn't have much time before someone else was likely to spot the disabled car."

The distorted voice still remained calm but slowed down the speech to instil dread into the shadowed figure.

"You have failed me on two occasions. This cannot be tolerated."

The shadowed figure sobbed.

"N… n… no. I can put this right. Just give me a chance."

"You have had chances. Failure is no acceptable."

The owner of the distorted voice tapped an icon on his smart phone. In another shadowed corner of the unused office a small container clicked open and a small, wispy, smoke-like cloud emerged, headed over to the shadowed figure, split into smaller tendrils and entered the figure's eyes, nostrils, ears and mouth. The shadowed figure's eyes, inner ears, sinuses and throat suddenly flared up in intense pain. He dropped the telephone and screamed in agony pressing his hands against his temples in a vain attempt to stop the suffering. The pain continued for what seemed like minutes but was actually only seconds and then abruptly stopped. The shadowed figure slumped in the chair, sweat soaking his body from the exertion involved in fighting the pain. The tendrils left his body from where they had entered, reformed into the smoke-like cloud and returned to the container. Other than his panting, there was complete silence in the room.

The silence was broken by the distorted voice, loud

enough to be heard in the silence.

"You will not fail me again. If you do, next time the pain will not stop until it stops you. Now go and make contact again at the next scheduled time. At that time, I want to hear that Saten and Andrews are dead."

The call ended leaving the room in silence again except for the heavy breathing still coming from the shadowed figure. After a few minutes he composed himself, tidied and wiped the telephone and left the office, creeping along the corridors back towards the populated area of Parliament House.

CHAPTER 23

Southampton

Back at the sub-basement level of the Self-Store-It warehouse in Southampton, Linda, Nick and Wilmott were in the main meeting room awaiting the arrival of Keith. Wilmott was using the waiting time to explain what had happened whilst Linda and Nick were in Bournemouth.

"Once Keith had fully understood the USB stick had been found in the car, he realised that it must have been placed there after the incident as the pulse that stopped the car took out all the electronics within it. Having realised it had been planted, chances are all the data on it was false and, we quickly sussed that we had all been set up and you had been lured to the pier at Bournemouth. I called in a few favours and got the local armed response team to attend, having mailed them pictures of you two first."

"Well, they arrived without a moment to spare," said Linda looking relieved. "We were hemmed in and only saved by the sirens. Well done, Dave."

"It wasn't just me," said Wilmott graciously. "It was Keith who sussed the set up, and talking of 'the devil' here he is."

Keith walked fast into the meeting room carrying the notebook and the orthotope and wearing a large smile. Tony followed him in a few steps behind.

"We've broken the code," Keith said excitedly. "We can now tell you the contents of the notebook and also go a lot further in telling you what the orthotope is."

"It's a superconductor," started Wilmott, then trailing off he added, "Isn't it?"

"I'll explain," said Keith, "but first I'll cover the notebook then lead into the orthotope."

He moved around to the front of the large meeting table and handed a remote pointer for the large, wall-mounted flat screen monitor to Tony.

"Can you work the graphics please, Tone?"

Tony pressed a few buttons and two pictures appeared on the monitor, the notebook on the top left and the orthotope on the top right.

"The bespoke shorthand was a challenge," started Keith. "In some places he had split the words making it more difficult to find patterns but once the software had focussed on some repetitions it then was just a matter of time until it had decoded it all. We were going around in circles for sometime weren't we Tone?" Tony acknowledged with a slight nod and Keith continued, "That is until I tried my beta AI coding, that effectively learns from its mistakes and that made the code make sense after a bit of trial and error. I think Tony would still be struggling with it now, as he had been for a good while before hand, if the AI hadn't found the patterns. I have print outs for you of the entire book but I'll sum up a few interesting pointers. It talks about the monitoring of a phone line in Parliament House. It mentions conversations regarding the orthotope. There is a piece in there that talks about arrangements for meetings. When we correlate the timings, it becomes clear that one of the so-called meetings is the arranging for you two to be 'met' at the fairground."

"Does it state who was making these calls on this phone

line?" asked Wilmott.

"It mentions no names," clarified Keith, "referring to the side giving many of the orders as 'unknown' and the side based at the Parliament House phone line being 'CJ'. In fact, it refers to the initials 'CJ' many times."

"Shit!" exclaimed Linda. "So, we're definitely talking 'CJ', Chayton Jameson, The PM."

"It's certainly the right initials and, from the information written, it appears to pinpoint the phone to the PM's private office."

"Jeez!" exclaimed Linda again. "What else does it say?"

"The person referred to as 'CJ' has many conversations with another person who remains unknown. By the way the conversations go, I'm not sure if CJ knows the identity of this other person. It's certainly never mentioned in the text. Early conversations talk about general government business but they progress to the unknown person heavily influencing decisions being made by CJ."

"So, someone is manipulating the government," said Wilmott.

"If all the info in the book can be believed," continued Keith, "then there's someone controlling most of the major decisions that CJ is making and worse."

"That's if the decoding of the text is correct," said Tony, "and the original text in the notebook is correct too. We have one man's hand-written info that we can't talk to him about and we have an AI program that is still in beta coding. It's possible that the AI is making the documentation into something we want to see."

"Is that possible?" asked Wilmott in a concerned tone.

"It's possible in theory," replied Keith, talking to the group but looking sternly at Tony, "but, in testing, the AI coding has been successful so we have no evidence to dispute what it's decoding. At the moment it's safer to assume the decoding is accurate than not. However, as Tony pointed out, there's no way of telling if the contents of the notebook are a figment of the guy's imagination."

"That's what I'm concerned about," said Tony, "we could be relying on bad info if –"

Keith cut into Tony's speech stopping him from saying any more.

"However," he said, his voice slightly raised for emphasis, "the cross reference of timings to calls being logged and personnel being at the right place at the right time all seem to fit with what has been logged."

"So," said Nick trying to steer the conversation back to the contents of the notebook, "we're going on the most likely assumption that most, if not all, of the decoding is accurate."

"Yes," said Keith whilst Tony remained silent.

"So, getting back to what you were saying about the contents, what do you mean by 'worse'?" asked Nick.

"More recently the conversations have included instructions to 'dispose' of people though no methods were mentioned."

"You're saying that the Government or, at least, someone in it, 'CJ', is involved in assassination plans?" asked Linda.

"That's exactly what I'm saying," replied Keith.

"Well, that's certainly worse," said Nick.

"In fact," continued Keith, "yours was one of the names mentioned in the 'disposal' instructions Linda. Your 'disposal' was suggested as a possible way of obtaining the orthotope."

"It's getting even worse," added Nick.

"And recently your name was in there too, Nick."

"Even worserer," said Nick grinning at his grammatical error.

Wilmott cut in at this point.

"Seriously folks, we'd better be careful with our communications from now. Lin's and Nick's involvement with me and with the orthotope is known to very few in government circles. Andrew Fleming and I have kept this secret for obvious reasons – or we thought we had. We have to assume that our phone lines are being tapped somewhere so use only our encrypted smart phones from now on."

He received nods in agreement so looked at Keith giving him the hint to continue.

"So why do they need the orthotope so badly?" asked Linda.

Keith continued, "To answer that I first need to tell you about the picobots."

"Picobots?" Wilmott, Linda and Nick said together.

"Yes, they've been working on picobots according to the notebook."

"Surely we've reached the realms of sci fi," said Linda.

"A few years ago, that may have been the case," said Keith. "Picobots have been in development for many years now. We've been experimenting with them ourselves for a while. It appears that these guys have taken things a step further and, according to the notebook, they've created working bots that can be remotely programmed, can communicate with each other and can fly."

"Fly!?" all three said together again.

"Yes, they've apparently created picobot versions of drones that are 'smart' in that they can virtually team up and work together in an organised fashion. However, where medical type picobots that may be injected into the bloodstream can obtain their power from the electrolytes in the blood, these bots have been designed to fly in the air and, therefore need a proper power source. According to the notebook blurb, they've been testing their bots in air and they have a very limited battery life, even minute propellers presumably taking up a lot of the juice. Therefore, with the announcement that this room temperature superconductive orthotope has arrived, they want it to power the bots to give them a much-extended operating time."

"So, why didn't they use the orthotope and analyse and create more of it when they had it?" asked Linda continuing her questioning.

"I think they tried. Reading 'between the lines' of the

sometimes-cryptic conversations noted in the book, I think they analysed the make-up of the orthotope and, maybe even created more, but they couldn't get it to superconduct. According to the latest conversation instalments, they're still trying to get it to work, but they're not going to have much luck."

"What makes you say that?" asked Linda again.

"Because," continued Keith, "we've cracked its code and now know its secret."

They all looked at Keith with wide eyes, willing him to continue.

"And?" said Wilmott eventually when he realised Keith was slow to reveal.

"And," he finally continued, "we originally went down the same route they did and tried to determine what was so special about this piece of silicon that made it different to other pieces. Then, when one of the techies was looking at it under the electron microscope, she noticed that a possible circuit had been etched on to part of the silicon surface and, being very techie, she then noticed that it was arranged similar to other memory chips she had seen in the past."

"She recognised the layout of a silicon chip?" asked a bemused Nick. "That could be a good party trick!"

"She worked with them a lot in the past, so had her suspicions when she saw it. She then bonded electrodes to it, powered it up and confirmed it was a memory chip."

"And, what…" Wilmott's question was stopped by Keith holding up his hand.

He continued. "It's not straight forward to determine the contents. Unless the program used to store the information is known, it's a bit of a guessing game to make any sense of the binary coding."

"So, we know it's a memory chip but we don't know what info is stored on it," stated Wilmott with a touch of defeat showing in his voice.

"No. We were lucky again," said Keith, smiling. "She noticed a number of repetitions in the coding and therefore suspected it to be a picture file or files. After trying a few different picture file formats, she determined there to be a jpeg file in the coding and, maybe, another one too but that one is corrupted, probably due to being deleted in the past. She's still working on the possible second one but successfully decoded the first file and came up with a picture of an A4 sheet taken from a notepad with the whole page full of formulae. It was then passed to our chemist techies and they analysed the data and determined it was the formula for doping silicon to make it superconduct. They're trying it out now but it takes a while for the doping to take place so we don't yet know if it actually works."

"But," said Linda thoughtfully, "what we're implying by all this is that they, whoever 'they' are, don't have this formula."

"That's what the text implies," Keith stated. "However, at the bottom of the formula page there is a reference to a shard of the superconductive material. On one occasion of the telephone conversations, they mention that they are trying to locate a shard – believing it to be another superconductive piece of silicon. They hoped it may prove easier to analyse than the orthotope was proving to be. Of course, we now know that they were unable to 'crack' the orthotope because the silicon was just that – silicon. If they realise this, they are likely to increase their efforts in searching for this shard. Whether they have any clues to its whereabouts is never mentioned and whether the second page gives any further information about it or its present location, we'll have to wait and see. It's not easy to determine the missing bits of information when the result is unknown."

"But, if anyone can do it, I'm sure it'll be the person who is capable of reading silicon chips," said Nick with a friendly chuckle in his voice.

"Exactly," added Keith. "She's determined not to give up. She'll sort it but how long it will take is an unknown."

"Well, keep us informed of any developments," said

Wilmott preparing to leave the meeting.

"Hang on," said Keith. "I haven't finished yet. There's a further important revelation in the notebook."

Wilmott got himself comfortable again. "Please carry on," he said also displaying a surrendering gesture with his hands.

"During the last few entries in the notebook, they talk about a project where they intend to launch the picobots and, I quote, 'destroy' a large number of people, the identities of which they don't disclose. Without the superconductive material they are limited by operating time and, in order to do what they are talking about, they need to manufacture more of the bots so one set can be launched when the previous ones exhausted their power packs."

"Jeez!" said Linda. "Do you think they're capable of all this?"

"I think they are," said Keith. "They mention a successful 'Phase 3' test and then talk cryptically about it. Apparently, various recent so called 'natural disasters' that have taken place around the world were part of 'Phase 3' of their so called 'Project'.

"Jeez!" Linda exclaimed again. "Then they're already responsible for a great number of indiscriminate deaths and planning more. You say they're manufacturing more of these things, Keith. Any indication of where this is going on and how they're getting them to the destination?"

"They mention an island, they refer to it as Diabolus Island, where design and manufacturing are taking place and the transportation by boat. Of course, these things are so small that millions of them don't take up much space so huge container ships aren't needed. They could be transported on larger ocean-going yachts.

"And, before you ask," Keith added, anticipating what question was about to come his way, "there were some references to possible locations of this island and possible points of reference on it. This info has been passed to our geography boffins and I'm expecting an update from them any minute."

"And there's no clue as to the other conversationalist is who seems to be controlling 'CJ'? asked a hopeful Wilmott.

"Nothing further we've come across so far," said Keith glancing down at his smart phone as it beeped. He read a short message and then tapped the screen a few times then added, "Right on time, the boffins think they've discovered the location of the island."

"Anywhere nice?" asked Nick cheekily.

"They're saying it appears to be located approximately 50 miles south-west of the Canary Islands."

"Yeah, that's nice enough," said Nick.

"However," continued Keith, "looking at maritime charts of that area, there are no islands mapped within a hundred-mile radius. Nothing until you get to the Canaries." Keith read further into the email and performed a couple of taps to the screen. "They've forwarded a link to a satellite picture of the area taken a month or so ago. It's not high res at all as there are no known land masses around there and it's not on a main shipping lane so there's not usually much interest in the area." Keith clicked another link and a photograph appeared on his monitor. On the right-hand side of the screen the islands making up the Canaries were shown and on the far left a small pixelated blurred area was present.

Keith continued, pointing at the pixelated blur. "That blob is in the area that is being mentioned according to the boffins. They've double-checked official charts and there should be no land masses in that area. That appears to be the Diabolus Island being referred to in the text."

"But, how can they magic an island out of nowhere?" asked Linda. "Is it a shallow area around there where they could've built upon?"

"Don't know and no are the answers," said Keith. "I don't how they could build one and, no, the water isn't shallow in that area. According to the charts the sea is about 4000 metres, over 12000 feet in that area and there's no known recent volcanic activity around that region that could have created a land mass. So, we don't know. There it is on the photograph and there it isn't on the charts."

"Maybe it's time we had a look at this Diabolus Island," said Nick looking towards Wilmott. "What do we have in the way of water crafts?"

"Walk this way," said Wilmott strolling off, thanking Keith and Tony as he went.

"If I walked that way… Ow!" Nick was cut off from saying anymore by a sharp elbow to the ribs by Linda. They then followed Wilmott in silence, Nick smiling to himself.

Wilmott led them back to his office where they all sat down and he gestured towards one of the monitor screens on the wall whilst tapping a few times at a tablet on his desk. A picture of a mid-sized ocean-going yacht appeared.

"We have access to this," Wilmott said, tapping at the tablet causing more pictures to scroll through on the screen.

"Now we know where you spend your holidays," said Nick.

"It belongs to a friend…. of the organisation," continued Wilmott laughing, "but, when not operational, can be used as we wish, for vacations, cruises, etc. Though the waiting list is rather long."

He tapped at the tablet again and a small submarine appeared on the screen.

"And this three-man sub is available to us too which may be ideal for getting near to the island unseen."

"Where are they now?" asked Nick. "How long before we can get them into location?"

"The sub is already on board the yacht and the yacht is currently being serviced in Cyprus. It can be in the area of the Canaries in 48 hours."

"Ideal," said Nick looking thoughtful. "That gives us enough time to get a couple of things done before then."

"What do you need to get done?" asked Wilmott.

"Well, for one thing, this can't be done by Linda and me alone. We need to get another recruit into the team to man the sub while two of us go on to the island." Nick turned to Linda. "Phil will be ideal; he's manned small subs loads of times in a past life." With Linda nodding her agreement, he turned back to Wilmott. "David, can you arrange for Phil Webbe to meet us on the yacht by the time it's in the Canaries?"

"Okay, no problem. Leave it with me," Wilmott agreed. "You said 'a couple of things'. Anything else you need?"

"Yeah, that gives us a day or so for a more in-depth investigation into this 'CJ'. So, we need to be able to get into the PM's private office for a look round."

"Is that a wise thing to do before we look into the island?" questioned Linda.

"Probably not but, as far as we know, this 'CJ' knows nothing about the notebook so is probably under the impression that any information regarding bots and islands was lost along with the GCHQ guy. Maybe we can find some info on the subject if we have a rummage through his office. We may be able to get a clue as to who the person is that's controlling him."

"Okay," said Wilmott. "Your passes can get you into Parliament House. From there you'll have to find your own way into the private offices. If we arrange for any appointments, the element of surprise will be gone. I'll organise the yacht, Phil Webbe and a small crew for it and get it to the Canaries in a couple of days. Then you can fly in and rendezvous at the Canaries and we can then head off to Diabolus Island from there."

"We?" questioned Linda and Nick together.

"Yes," said Wilmott. "I'm still a field agent at heart and am ideally qualified to pilot the yacht." He thought for a moment. "And the sub," he continued, "so there's no need to involve Phil on this occasion."

"Yeah! And?" they both said together again, suspecting an ulterior motive to surface.

"And," continued Wilmott with a smile on his face, "once we're finished, if there's enough time, I can slowly sail it back to Cyprus, possibly enjoying a few stops along the way. So there's no need to have another person in competition for its use on the way back."

"A, ha!" said Linda, smiling. "It's all coming out now."

"I'll have you know," grumbled Wilmott, "I had it ear marked for me for last week and next until all this crap started."

"Okay, we'll let you off the hook," laughed Linda. "In fact, once this is all over, perhaps we'll join you on board for a while."

"Okay," said Nick, grinning, "that's enough of the date arrangements. Let's focus back on the job. David, you get the ball rolling regarding the yacht and Linda and I will concentrate on getting more information on this 'CJ'."

"We'll all get in touch to discuss plans before we go separate ways," said Wilmott as Linda and Nick headed out of his office, back towards their rooms.

After Wilmott, Linda and Nick had left the meeting room, Tony walked over to Keith. "I only wanted to point out that we can't rely one hundred percent on the data, Keith."

"Yeah, I gathered that, mate," said Keith in a friendly tone, "but, at this stage, I think they wanted some assurances that we are on the right track. Yes, we need to inform them that there could be errors but we don't want to be too negative."

"Okay, boss. Just doing what I thought was best."

"No probs, Tone," Keith smiled.

Tony smiled too and then headed out of the meeting room leaving Keith alone. Keith turned back to the monitor, tapping a few more times on his tablet and concentrated on the satellite picture of Diabolus Island. The picture he had showed the trio was from a month or so ago so he had logged into the satellite system over that area and had requested a download of an up-to-date photograph hoping it would be of a better resolution.

It had taken a little while to download and, after looking at it on his monitor, he had requested another download from the satellite system. He was now looking at the second download. It was the same resolution as the one he had shown the trio so didn't give any further detail. However, he was studying the pixelated picture of the island. He brought up the original picture onto another monitor so that the two pictures were now side by side and moved his head from one to the other with a puzzled look on his face. He picked up his phone and called the department of the geography boffins. After a couple of rings, the call was answered.

"I'm looking at the satellite picture of Diabolus Island you sent to me a while ago," said Keith whilst still staring at the two displays. "Are you sure there was no distance distortion on the picture file?"

"Yes, we're sure," the boffin replied. "We checked it when we were trying to clean up the file to try to enhance the resolution. The distance is uniform throughout the file. What you see is a true representation. Why do you ask?"

Keith was still staring from one screen to the other as he continued speaking.

"I know the resolution isn't great and I've downloaded an up-to-date picture from the satellite that's exactly the same resolution and I know the actual picture of the island is very low res due it's size compared with the size of the area shown but both pictures show the island to be the same size; the same number of pixels contained in each."

"So, what's the problem?" asked the boffin.

"The problem," said Keith, still staring at the screens, "is that, on the new picture, the island appears to the two pixels closer to Lanzarote."

"It could be an error in the file download," said the boffin.

"Yeah, I thought of that," said Keith, "so I downloaded another copy and it's exactly the same."

"In that case both pictures should be the same. If you

can send us the new picture we'll investigate and get back to you."

"I intended to do that," said Keith as he clicked at his mouse. "It's on its way to you now. I was going to ask you to look into it as I believe that, if both pictures are accurate, then two pixels difference means the island has moved approximately two to three hundred yards. I'd be grateful if you could confirm that as soon as possible cos, if it's right, we have an island that, until a month or so ago, had not been seen before and now also seems to be able to move around in the sea!"

CHAPTER 24

Houses of Parliament, Westminster

Parliament Square was never quiet, even at night. Lorries crossed the Thames from the south at Westminster Bridge, delivering their goods into London taking advantage of the hours without the congestion charge. Private vehicles threaded their way through Central London, their occupants heading to bars, night clubs and restaurants or to their homes if they had had an early session. Many of the vehicles were the traditional London Black Cab, the taxi, an iconic sight on London streets at any time of the day and night.

The sun had set around 30 minutes ago and the dense clouds blotted out any moonlight creating a dark evening, lit only by the minimal illumination from the street lights around the Square and by the faint glow coming from some of the windows in the Houses of Parliament.

A London Black Cab came from Westminster Bridge, turned into parliament Square and pulled over to the side of the road just along from the entrance to the Houses of Parliament, attracting interest from the police officers guarding the entrance. The rear passenger door opened and Linda stepped onto the pavement. A few seconds later,

Nick had paid the driver and got out allowing the taxi to drive off before any of the officers felt the need to approach.

"Do you know how much that cost?" exclaimed Nick, still staring at his wallet. "London is 'Rip-off City'. I told him we weren't tourists but the price didn't change."

"Oh, stop moaning," said Linda playfully. "You'll get it back on expenses. Just keep the receipt."

Nick looked at her sheepishly. "I didn't get a proper receipt; the driver just jotted the price down on a scrap of paper he had lying about and gave it to me. Ridiculous. No wonder I usually drive everywhere."

"If what you have doesn't equate to being a receipt, I have a solution for you," said Linda looking serious.

"What's that then?" Nick enquired.

"Easy, just keep moaning."

"Oh, thanks a lot!" said Nick. "That's really helpful."

"Well… shut up anyway! It's your own fault. Parking on the outskirts then getting a cab when we could have got the Underground. You've only got yourself to blame."

"Yeah," said Nick showing the scrap of paper to Linda, "but I could've bought the damn taxi for this."

"Bloody hell!" exclaimed Linda. "That's ridiculous. You've been conned. Jeez!"

"See, I told you."

"Anyway, we're here now," said Linda as she walked towards the entrance. "Let's worry about it later. Has David got our emergency extraction set up for us?"

"Yes, I could see it as we drove over the bridge but I'm hoping we can walk in and walk out without being noticed."

"That would be nice," Linda smiled at him, "but this is us we're talking about. Since when has anything gone correct and to plan?"

"You never know, our luck must change one of these days," said Nick also smiling. "Anyway, this is it. We're being looked at by the gate keepers. Time to get to work."

They walked side by side up to the Houses of Parliament

entrance and were stopped by the officer at the gate.

"Hello Sir, Madam. Can I help you?" he said.

They both said their 'hellos' and 'thanks', showed their security services ID cards and, on the strength of them, were waved straight through, bypassing the x-ray and metal detection area. They casually walked across the courtyard idly chatting and entered the Parliament building.

They'd timed their entrance carefully to coincide with a debate taking place in the Commons Chamber which many MPs, including the Prime Minister, were attending. This meant the foyer and surrounding corridors appeared to be relatively empty. They calmly made their way to the Prime Minister's private office, without attracting the attention of the few people they passed. They had dressed smartly and were displaying their passes, as were all others, and so blended in with the populace.

Nick had prepared their excuses for being there in case they met anyone as they arrived but the corridor was deserted and the office was empty and locked up; any staff either attending the debate or already left for the evening.

Nick looked at the lock, "Standard Yale-type, no problem," he mumbled to himself.

He took out a small soft case from his jacket pocket and extracted the necessary lock-pick tools he required and, fifteen seconds later, the door was unlocked and open. They went inside the office, gently shutting the door behind them in case anyone wandered past. There were blackout blinds on the windows and the glass of the door so Linda made sure they were fully extended then pushed a small rug that was by the doorway against the bottom of the door and then switched on the main light.

"Ok," whispered Nick, "I'll get the filing cabinet open and check in there, you have a look in the desk drawers."

The filing cabinet was locked but it took Nick only a few moments to pick the lock and he was soon searching through the files. Linda found the desk drawers locked too but was just as adept with her set of lock picks as Nick was with his and she was soon flicking through the paperwork within them.

After a few minutes of searching neither had found anything incriminating. Nick still had a couple of filing cabinet drawers to go through but Linda had finished the PM's desk so she locked the drawers again and moved on to a bookcase that was between the two windows and started to pull out the books to see if there was anything of interest in them. She finished looking through the top row and moved down to start on the next. About six books in there was a set of four that didn't sit flush with the rest; protruding by a couple of millimetres or so. She was drawn towards these as all the others on that row seemed to be flush with one another. The row was tall enough for the books to be tilted outwards without pulling them fully from the shelf. Linda tilted all four at once and peered in behind them and saw some folded paper flat against the back of the shelf. She supported the tilted books and reached in and pulled out the paper, pushing the four books back upright. She unfolded the paper to discover it consisted of two sheets of A4, both more or less full of text. She tilted them towards the light and scanned through the contents. After reading through she stopped for a moment, starting at the sheets then re-read them.

"Jeez!" she said in a low voice. "We've been idiots."

Nick stopped going through the cabinet drawers and looked over to Linda.

"Have you got something?"

"Jeez, Nick! Yeah, I think I have. Do you want the good news or the bad first?"

"You know me," he said smiling. "Always the good news first."

Linda still kept scanning through the two sheets.

"The good news is that I've found a document that has some references to the island and manufacturing."

"Excellent," said Nick. Then a little warily, "And the bad news?"

"The bad news is that the document has been signed off by a 'CJ' and –"

"That's not bad news," interrupted Nick, then looking at Linda's facial expression, added, "…is it?"

"That's not the bad news," Linda continued. "The bad news is that the 'CJ' initialling has been expanded to a full signature – Sir Kit Jenkins." Nick looked at Linda with a puzzled expression so she continued. "I thought that strange at first too then I thought again and it's been staring us in the face since the notebook had first been translated."

"What?" said Nick still looking puzzled.

"What's Kit short for?" Linda asked but didn't wait for an answer. "It's short for Christopher of course. Bloody Christopher! Christopher Jenkins. CJ. They're both CJ. The notebook could have been referring to Sir Kit rather than the PM and, now this paperwork has surfaced, it appears it was referring to Sir Kit all the time."

"So, we've been researching the wrong man," said Nick angry with himself for not even considering the name shortening. "For fuck's sake. We need to get in touch with David and Keith to get them to investigate Sir Kit's background. And we need to get out of here otherwise we'll have a lot of PM questions to ans…."

Nick broke off his conversation and held up a hand to stop Linda from saying anything. He could hear the footsteps of someone walking along the corridor outside the office.

"Lights," he said quickly as he positioned himself beside the hinge side of the door.

Linda hit the light switch and darted to the other side of the doorway. They both waited, holding their breaths, willing the walker to continue on. That wasn't to be though. The footsteps stopped outside the main door and a key was put into the lock. The key turned, unlocking the door, and it started to slowly open as the person outside pushed against it. Nick and Linda braced themselves, ready to pounce once the person had entered the room.

The door opened and a figure reached an arm into the room to switch on the lights. Before the switch could be reached, Nick grabbed the arm and pulled the person inside the room, spinning him around, twisting his arm behind his back, forcing his other arm against the wall and placing a hand across his mouth to stifle any cries. The figure tried to struggle out of Nick's grip but was held firm. At the same time, Linda had quickly shut the door, placed the rug back against the gap at the bottom and switched on the light.

In Nick's full body lock, struggling but unable to escape and murmuring behind Nick's hand, was the Prime Minister, Mr. Chayton Jameson. All three stood silent for a moment. Nick's mind raced to decide what he was going to say to and do to the PM. He decided to go with the truth and see what reaction there was from Jameson.

"Sir," he said calmly but quickly, deciding to keep things formal even though he had the man in a painful armlock, "we don't have much time to talk to you alone. We are here under the authority of David Wilmott and can prove our identity once I can safely release my hold on you. We are investigating the death of the GCHQ operative and have uncovered evidence that steers us towards wanting to seek the cooperation of Sir Kit Jenkins. We are here without his knowledge and would prefer to keep it that way."

Nick released some of the pressure of his hold on the PM but still kept it strong enough to hold him in place.

"If I release my hold, Sir," he continued, "will you give us enough time to show our credentials without crying out?"

Jameson gave a slight nod of his head, signalling his agreement, and Nick slowly released his hold but kept his arms poised ready to restore it again. He showed the positive mindset that a Prime Minister requires to hold office and, outwardly at least, revealed no signs of panic.

Nick reached into his jacket and produced his photo ID pass, holding it so Jameson could see it. Linda did the same with hers.

"Thank you, Sir," he said continuing in the calm manner.

"My name is Nick Saten and this is Linda Andrews. We are part of a small undercover team working for David Wilmott. We are on your side, Sir."

"You're the new team David and Andrew Fleming were talking about forming," said Jameson confidently, seemingly a little more relaxed now he had an idea of who they were.

"Yes, we are, Sir," assured Nick, showing no surprise but making a mental note to ask Wilmott how many people had been told about the supposedly 'top secret' DAHRT team.

Jameson continued. "And what's this nonsense you were saying about Kit?"

"I'm afraid I don't think it is nonsense, Sir," Nick countered. "And I'll prove it to you shortly. First though, can you tell me where Kit is? And your security officers? I'm surprised to find you alone."

"I sneaked out from the Chamber a few minutes early. The debate had concluded but idle chatter was continuing. So, I headed back to my office for what I thought was going to be a few minutes' peace."

"I see," said Nick. "So, we only have a few minutes until Sir Kit and your security contingent will be back in the office."

"That should be the case, yes," said the PM.

"Then Linda and I need to get out of here quickly," stated Nick. "We really don't want him to know we've been here talking to you at this stage. But first you need to see this, Sir."

Linda handed the sheets of paper to Jameson who started to read through them. After a short time, he finished reading and looked up from Nick to Linda and back again.

"I don't understand," he said with a questioning look on his face. "All these papers refer to are an island and some sort of manufacturing. I take it I'm supposed to read more into this than it seems."

Linda spoke up at this point. "The murdered GCHQ operative was monitoring communications from this office."

"This office?" said Jameson looking surprised. "You mean the phones in here were tapped?"

"Yes, they are," continued Linda. "We thought you were made aware of this following the murder."

"Not to my knowledge," said Jameson cautiously. "I've not seen any memos or reports on this."

"Well, that's what he was doing; listening in to any comms from here. However, he didn't just listen in, he kept records of the calls in the form of an encrypted notebook. This was hidden in his vehicle when he was assassinated and wasn't found by his assassins when they searched it. Our techie guys deciphered the contents and found it contained references to picobots, the manufacturing of them, plans to use them and an island base somewhere near the Canaries. The decoded text mentioned the person involved from this office having the initials 'CJ' so we suspected he was referring to you until we found these pieces of paper with the initials and the name 'Christopher, Kit, Jenkins' on them along with references to the island and manufacturing."

"This is absurd," exclaimed Jameson. "Are you sure about all of this. I've known Kit for over twenty years. I can't believe he is involved in any of thi –"

Jameson was interrupted mid-sentence by his office door bursting open. In the open doorway stood Sir Kit Jenkins with a smart phone held out in front of him. Either side of Sir Kit stood a couple of security officers with their Glocks drawn, pointing towards Jameson, Linda and Nick.

"You should start believing it Chayton," said Jenkins with menace gesturing with his smart phone. "I've been monitoring all you've been doing and saying and can confirm it's all true."

"But, why?" asked Jameson looking genuinely aggrieved.

Jenkins ignored the question and continued speaking, waving his security officers into the room. Following them in, he shut the door and gestured towards Linda and Nick.

"Cover them and check them for weapons."

The officers moved over to Linda and Nick and one

covered them with his Glock whilst the other frisked them, removing a small Glock 26 from each one's shoulder holster.

"All clear," he said once he had finished, placing the Glocks into his jacket pockets. The officers then returned to positions out of reach of Jameson, Linda and Nick and resumed covering them with their Glocks.

The Prime Minister stared at the pistols being pointed in his direction.

"Chris, stop. Why are you doing this?" he asked, almost pleading.

Jenkins acted as if there had been no question and continued speaking.

"So, there is a notebook detailing my conversations."

Linda glanced in the direction of Nick who gave a slight shake of his head.

"You've been listening in to our conversations," he said glaring at Jenkins.

Jenkins formed his face into a smug grin.

"Yes, of course I have," he said in a mocking tone. "I have been monitoring all audio from this room straight to my mobile here. I know what all of you have been saying."

"But that's impossible," said Jameson. "The whole building is swept for bugs every few days. Any bug you planted would be detected."

Jenkins walked over to the Prime Minister thrusting his smart phone up towards his face.

"You are so stupid, Chayton. In fact, you're all so stupid, all your security teams. They look for radio transmissions from bugs that they suspect need to reach to the outside world. I use a blue tooth transmission, something going on all over the House and therefore allowed, that transmits locally to a smart phone in my desk in the next room. That in turn uses another allowable source of transmission, Wi-Fi, on to the secure Government network which I then pick up on this phone here. Security are briefed to look for transmissions from external, hostile devices and ignore all transmissions from internal sources."

"But you still haven't answered why you are doing this," said Jameson ignoring the phone being waved at his face.

"I'm doing this for the good of mankind. For the good of the world. Once Jonathon Caymes has control of the world's super powers, they can be controlled to all work together. No more conflicts. No more wars. Just a world at peace."

"Who the hell is Jonathon Caymes" asked Nick.

"He is a person of great vision," replied Jenkins. "The head of The Syndicate, a group who want nothing more than peace throughout the world."

"And to get this peace," continued Nick, "Caymes resorts to violence, murder even."

"He says the world will not listen. All the super powers have their own agendas and will stop at nothing to come out on top."

"But it seems to me," Nick didn't feel like stopping at this point, "like this Caymes will also stop at nothing to come out on top. He is as bad as the ones he says he wants to stop."

Jenkins would not be defeated. "Jonathon realises how his actions will be interpreted but says this is necessary in order to stop all the disagreements and conflicts."

Nick laughed. "Can't you see, Jenkins, he is doing exactly what he says he wants to stop. And how will he keep the world at peace? By violence or, at least, the threat of it."

"That is enough!" said Jenkins in a raised voice, gesturing to his guards in Nick's direction.

One of the guards walked over to Nick and swung the Glock, hitting Nick hard on his temple with the butt. Nick fell to the floor, dazed but still conscious.

Linda went to move towards Nick to help him but was stopped but the guard pointing his Glock at her. She stopped moving.

"Nick, are you ok?" she said concerned, looking from him and then glaring at Jenkins.

Again, Jenkins chose to ignore the hatred looks and continued with his speech.

"You do not understand, any of you. You're all fools. Someone has to be in the position of peace keeper."

"So, he will be peace keeper by dictatorship," said Nick as he slowly got to his feet, dabbing at the point of impact on his temple and checking his fingers for blood. "And exactly how does he intend to keep this peace?"

"He will be explaining all tomorrow when I finally get to meet him. I have been graciously invited to his island, the island that appears to be known to you, where he will explain my part in the new world order."

"You've never met him?" said Nick in a surprised tone.

"No, I have never had the privilege until now."

"You've never met him yet you are prepared to carry out his 'dirty work' for his goal of world domination."

"Without his what you refer to as 'domination', the world is destined for mutual destruction. He will prevent this from happening and allow all to live in peace."

"It will never happen," continued Nick. "There will always be someone in this 'ideal world' that wants more from it. In this case, it's him. He's no better than those he supposedly wants to control. He's mad and so are you for listening to him."

Jenkins was looking angry at this stage.

"I said that is enough!" he shouted, nodding at one of the guards again.

Obediently, the guard advanced and pistol-whipped Nick around the head again. This time was harder than the first and Nick could do nothing to stop the blackness closing in to his eyesight as he collapsed to the floor again, knocked out cold.

CHAPTER 25

The darkness receded as Nick started to slowly open his eyes. The light caused a shooting pain at the back of his eyes and an area at the side of his head felt like it had been cracked open. His sight started to come back into focus and he could see a blurred version of Linda's face as she concentrated in dabbing a tissue onto an open wound at his temple.

As Nick's vision became clear he could see Jameson standing behind Linda watching her wipe some blood away from his temple. He gingerly looked around the room and could see no one else. He was laying on his back on the floor and, when he tried to sit up, became giddy and nauseous.

"Lay still for a little longer," said Linda still dabbing a tissue to Nick's temple. "You received quite a blow and have been out cold."

"How long have I been out?" he asked, wincing as the movement of his talking caused further pains behind his ears. He slowly moved his head from side to side and saw only Jameson and Linda. His mind was clearing and the memories of before he was knocked out were returning. "And where is Jenkins?" he added.

"You've been out for about twenty minutes," Linda

answered, speaking softly, "and Jenkins has left the room, leaving his guards outside the door."

Nick went to get up again and, this time, the giddiness was much less. He was helped into a chair by the desk by Linda on one side and the PM on the other.

"While you were out," Linda continued, "Jenkins gave us some more info. Seems it's difficult to stop him talking if it's about him."

"Yeah, I get the impression he likes the sound of his own voice," said Nick grimacing as he gently touched a lump forming on his temple. "What did he say?"

"It would appear that he's been brainwashed by this Caymes bloke. How it's been done is anyone's guess as I'm pretty sure he wasn't kidding when he said he hadn't met him. Despite all his chattering, he didn't seem able to describe this bloke at all. In fact, he seemed really proud of the fact that he's finally been invited to the island where he will meet him in person. He's got the two guards outside the door on his side obviously but he also appeared to refer to others around the building so we're unsure as to how many hostiles we have to deal with here. He got called away, telling the guards that he'll be back as soon as possible, then left them outside whilst he rushed off. They've got suppressors for their weapons so may well be unafraid to use them."

"Well then, it's time we got out of here by the sounds of it," said Nick as the situation was quickly clearing any grogginess that was left. "I take it the desk phone's not working."

"No, the line's dead and he's enabled some sort of signal blocker to stop our mobiles. I heard him telling the guards that one of them would have to move away from this area if they needed to call him. So, it can only be local interference."

Nick's mind was racing. "So, we need to cause a distraction," he thought out loud, looking around the office. "We could set off the fire alarm. Anyone got a match or lighter?"

Linda and Jameson both shook their heads. "Oh well," continued Nick, "that probably only works in the movies anyway." He turned to Jameson with a thoughtful expression appearing. "Sir, with all that's happened today, do you know of any security officers that would definitely be loyal to you?"

Jameson shook his head. "I can't be sure anymore," he said apologetically. "Until today, I wouldn't have suspected Jenkins or his protection officers of being anything but on my side."

"That's a point," said Nick, still looking pensive. "Where are your protection officers? I take it that's not them outside."

"No, that's definitely not them outside. They're the ones assigned to Jenkins. Mine should be here by now. Once they would have become aware that I'd slipped away early from the debate they should have come here as the first place during their search for me. I can only assume that Jenkins may have told them to have a break."

"Or maybe they're loyal to him too."

"That's possible as they are new to me. They have only been assigned to me for a few days so I can't vouch for them as such. My regular two officers are on a week's break at the moment."

"Okay," said Nick, a possible plan forming in his mind. "We'll have to take that chance that they'll be with us. We'll soon know when they get here, I suppose. So, when they're not by your side how would you summon them in an emergency?"

"I have a panic button installed on my phone for when I'm out and about, said Jameson.

"And we know the phones aren't working in here," added Nick.

"Yes," said Jameson with a slight smile, "but from this office I have a panic button that's hard-wired into the alarm system. If I press that they should come running."

"And is it silent?" asked Nick. "I'm assuming it's

designed so as not to alert whatever or whoever is causing the panic situation."

"Yes, the alarm system sends a signal to their mobiles so, as long as they are not in this locality, they should receive the signal."

"Okay," said Nick glancing over towards the door, "can we see anything through the keyhole as to what's going on outside?" There was an old, unused deadlock in the door and the keyhole had never been sealed up.

"Yes," said Linda, "that's how we can be sure the guards are still out there."

She quietly stepped over to the door, crouched down and peered through the keyhole, then moved away, back towards Jameson and Nick.

"They're both out there, standing a couple of metres away from the door, one on each side of the corridor."

"And is the door locked?" asked Nick.

"No," Linda replied, "there's no deadbolt visible. I don't think it's been used for years and I don't suppose they're too worried as they're waiting outside."

"Right, so we need to be ready by the door to distract the guards if and when the other guards come running." Nick turned to face Jameson. "Okay, sir, time to press the button."

Jameson walked over to his desk, sat down and reached under the desktop. "Button pressed," he whispered.

"Okay," said Nick, "you stay behind Linda and me but be prepared to run when we say so."

Linda and Nick walked over to the door and Linda went back to looking through the keyhole whilst Nick gripped the door handle ready to throw it open as soon as the officers arrived. Nick gestured for the PM to move behind him and then moved his hand near to his mouth to indicate silence.

They waited.

After a few minutes waiting, Linda was still crouched, peering through the keyhole with Nick standing by the door and the PM behind him.

"There's still just the two guards," she whispered, maintaining her view of the corridor outside the office. "No one else has appeared."

"They're not coming," said Jameson. "The panic switch has been disabled."

"Seems overly thorough to me," Nick thought out loud. "As far as we know, they had no idea we were going to be here today so why take the potentially unnecessary precaution of disabling the alarm. From past knowledge I believe the whole alarm system is checked once per week so they couldn't disable it too far in advance without it being noticed."

"That's correct," added Jameson. "It's still tested weekly so, maybe my security guards are on Jenkin's side too."

"It's possible," said Nick, "but I wonder if, even if they were part of the Jenkins goons, they would have turned up to alert the guards outside that we had tried to summon them."

"Still nothing," Linda whispered again.

"Perhaps we should try it again," Nick suggested.

"Okay, I'll give it another go," said Jameson making to move back to his desk.

"No, you stay by the door," said Nick guiding Jameson to a stop. "I'll do it. You stand behind Linda ready to move out if we have to. Whether we can get your guards here or not, we'll have to make a move soon otherwise we'll be in their hands."

Nick walked over to the desk and sat in the chair. He reached under, located the panic button and pressed it noting to himself that it was a bit stiff to engage.

"Okay, done," he said as he walked back to the door. "Let's give it another few minutes to see if we get any results."

They waited again.

This time, after around 90 seconds, Linda tensed.

"The guards have moved," she said softly. "They've looked at each other and then towards the end of the corridor. I think they may be able to hear someone coming."

"Right," said Nick, "if it is the PM's security then we need to be ready to move as soon as they appear. Lin, tell us as soon as you see anyone come into the corridor, whoever it is. Sir, you be ready to move out with me as soon as I open the door. We need your security to see it's you here with us."

After a few more seconds, Linda spoke again.

"It must be them and they must be on alert. They've just glanced around the corner, guns raised, and darted back again. Standard defence action."

Linda moved her face away from the keyhole and Nick opened the door. At that point, events happened quickly. The security officers, having glanced into the corridor and seen two other Parliament guards present outside the Prime Minister's office, had assumed the situation to be safe and under control. They had therefore stepped around the corner into the corridor, still on alert with their guns drawn but pointing upwards. The leading security officer was asking the two guards if they knew what had triggered the alert as Nick opened the door. At the same moment the two guards were raising their weapons, pointing them towards the officers.

"No!" Nick shouted but it was too late. The guards fired, double tapping their pistols, at the unsuspecting officers. Before they could respond, the officers were hit by hollow-point 9mm bullets, one in the head killing him before his body had fallen to the ground and the other twice in the lower centre of his neck, falling immediately with death to follow in a matter of seconds.

Nick reacted instantly. With both guards facing away from the door having engaged the officers, he had a vital couple of seconds before the guards would react to his shout. He sprinted at the nearest guard that still had his arms extended, pointing his pistol at the fallen officer. The guard started to turn towards the sound of running approaching him but Nick was too fast. He leapt at the guard, grabbing one arm with his left hand and the pistol with his right. The momentum of Nick's leap started the two of them falling towards the floor. On their downward journey Nick pulled at the guard's arm and gripped the hand that was holding the pistol. Nick positioned the guard's weapon to point at the second guard and pushed his finger against the trigger. The pistol fired, sending another bullet into the second guard's neck causing an explosion of soft tissue and bone fragments onto the wall behind. The second guard was dead instantly.

The first guard hit the floor with Nick on top of him. Nick angled his grip on the guard's arm and hand, using the momentum to smash the back of the guard's hand that was holding the pistol onto the floor. There was a loud crack as the guard's wrist snapped and his grip was immediately loosened on the pistol. Nick took advantage, grabbed the pistol and took out the guard with two taps to his chest. Nick sprang quickly to his feet and ran over to the two security officers to check them but could see they were both dead before he reached them. He ran back to the office where Linda and Jameson were now exiting after Linda had read the situation to be safe.

"Okay, we've got to get moving. Sir, you need to come with us. Even suppressed, the pistol shots may echo around here. No one's turned up so far but we don't know who may have heard anything. And we have no idea at the moment who Jenkins has on his side. The only way we can guarantee your safety is for you to stay with us for the time being."

If the Prime Minister didn't like the idea, he didn't say. He just nodded and said, "Lead the way."

Nick considered the PM's request for a moment then said, "In fact it may be better for you to lead the way, Sir. We need to get across the House, through the libraries and onto the terrace. There's a boat waiting for us there. It'll probably look less conspicuous if you lead the way and we play your security for the journey."

The Prime Minister still didn't appear to object to the

idea. "Okay," he said, "let's go."

Linda and Nick collected the suppressed pistols from the fallen officers and guards, each putting one in their back waistband and taking the loaded magazines from the other and putting them in the front, covering them with their tops. All three then strolled along the corridor heading in the direction of the libraries.

Nick took his smart phone out from his pocket and tapped a speed dial key. The call was answered on the first ring.

"Nick," said Wilmott. "Progress report?"

"Long story, Dave," said Nick as he continued walking, glancing from side to side, looking out for anything suspicious. "I'll fill you in later. Need to know now, we have the PM in tow and we're heading for the boat. I hope you got the correct permissions for it to be there. I don't want it to be towed away. And I hope you left the keys in the ignition."

"Permissions granted, it's still there and not only are the keys in the ignition, I'll switch it on now so it's ready for your arrival."

"Eh, you're there with it?" asked Nick surprised.

"As I've said before, I was a field agent and still have it in me. You just get here and I'll be ready to get us on our way."

"Okay, we'll be there soon."

"By the way Nick, there are three boats moored along the terrace now. Ours is the one in the middle. Don't want you getting on the wrong one."

"Understood, Dave. Be there as soon as we can."

Nick ended the call and focussed his full concentration back on the surroundings. Jameson was leading the way, strolling at a seemingly casual pace. Linda and Nick were just behind him, one on each side. Amazingly they had not met anyone so far.

"Where is everyone?" asked Linda. "I thought this place was usually full of people."

"They were all in the Chamber," said Jameson. "It was an important debate so they had all come in especially for it. However, many of them would have left the building at the end of it or returned to their offices to brief their local councils. The House may be surprisingly empty at the moment."

"Let's hope so," said Linda. "It's certainly making our journey easier, so far."

They turned the next corner to see two suited men heading towards them.

"Shit!" said Linda quietly. "Me and my big mouth. If they speak to us, it's down to you Sir. Don't forget, we're just your security officers."

As they continued walking towards the suited men, Linda and Nick slowly moved one of their hands behind their backs ready to pull out their pistols if necessary. Looking calm and professional as the PM's security, they kept their gazes on the suited men, looking out for any movements out of character. The suited men smiled, looked at each other briefly and one of them glanced behind as they walked. As the distance between the five people continued to lessen, one of the men whispered to the other and they started to reach inside their jackets. Linda and Nick gripped their weapons and began to draw them from their waistbands –

All four stopped grabbing for their pistols as chatter and footsteps could be heard from behind the suited men. The suited men stopped walking, moved to one side of the corridor and leaned against the wall appearing as if they had been there talking for a while. A small crowd of people walked around the corner from beyond the suited men and continued towards Jameson, Linda and Nick.

"Keep walking," said Nick quietly. "Get through the crowd as quickly as possible and don't stop."

Jameson, Linda and Nick continued along the corridor and met up with the small crowd of people as they were in line with the suited men. Jameson replied to a few of them who had said, "Hello Prime Minister" but kept walking. Linda and Nick stayed by his side gently forcing the small crowd to part for them. As they passed the suited men, Nick stared at them and smiled receiving two sneers in reply.

Once they were in clear space again, Jameson led Linda and Nick around the corner and, a few metres in front of them, was the entrance to the Commons Library. They could see that there were people within the library so, after glancing at Nick and receiving a slight nod, Jameson led them in.

Inside the library there were a number of people seated at desks reading, many of them making notes. On the far side of the room, beside the door that leads to the terrace was Jenkins and a number of his security guards. Jameson stopped, unsure of what to do and Linda and Nick stopped beside him. Nick glanced back towards the door and saw the two suited men enter, each gripping their pistols under their jackets.

"Keep going," whispered Nick. "Looks like we have a mixture of goodies and baddies in here. So, we might be okay whilst the goodies remain."

Jameson led the trio over to the terrace door where they were approached by Jenkins before they could get outside.

"Ah, Prime Minister," said Jenkins loudly but innocently so the room could hear. "We need an urgent word with you back in your office."

"Er, it will have to wait," said Jameson looking to Linda and Nick for reassurance. "I have some urgent business here."

"I'm afraid this is a very urgent situation," said Jenkins as his guards motioned towards their shoulder-holstered pistols. "With respect I must insist that we go and deal with it now, Sir."

Jameson glanced from Linda to Nick again with a pleading look that was asking what he should do now. Nick spoke to Jameson so that all interested parties could hear.

"Perhaps, Sir, we should go and attend to this urgent

business."

"Okay," said Jameson.

"I'll lead the way, Sir," said Nick turning around and heading back towards the door.

The two suited men were standing side by side to one side of the door and, as Nick became in line with them, he darted out a hand, not at the men but aiming for the glass-protected fire alarm switch. His fingers met the alarm's glass panel, breaking it and setting off the fire alarm. Immediately, loud, high-pitched sirens could be heard echoing around the House along with a recorded looped message saying 'The fire alarm has triggered. This is not a drill. Please proceed to thew nearest fire exit'.

The occupants of the library all rose from their chairs and headed for the nearest fire exit which, in the case of this particular room, was the terrace. They began to exit through the door onto the terrace beyond. Nick turned around facing away from the door into the corridor and made sure all the people were facing away from him as they headed outside. The two suited men were looking over towards Jenkins for guidance on what he wanted them to do so they didn't see Nick as he leant over to them and thrust his outstretched hands into each man's throat, crushing their Adam's apples into their windpipes. They collapsed to the floor unable to breathe. Nick walked back with the occupants and re-joined Linda and Jameson as they headed for the terrace.

Jenkins walked over to Jameson with his security guards beside him.

"You're only putting off the inevitable, he said. "Once the all clear is sounded, then everybody will be going their own ways. Then we can finish our urgent business."

"Maybe. Maybe not," said Nick mocking Jenkins. "We'll see."

They all headed outside onto the terrace which had filled up with people from other offices and libraries. Nick led Linda and Jameson slowly over towards the middle boat of the three moored at the terrace. Jenkins and his guards were caught in the crowd so had not yet extracted themselves over to be beside Jameson.

Nick quickly assessed the situation and took advantage.

"Oh my god!" he shouted towards the crowd. "The fire's outside here. Quick, back inside. Fire!"

This had the desired effect on the crowd. They performed an about turn and started to go back inside from the terrace into one of the libraries. Jenkins and his guards were caught in the middle of the crowd and were being taken with the flow, backwards, off the terrace.

"Okay, we have a few seconds before they get back through the crowd," Nick shouted. "Quickly, all on to the middle boat."

Jameson and Linda climbed on to the boat. Nick untied the mooring rope and jumped on board too. As he jumped, the pistol became dislodged from his waistband and fell into the river.

"Oh shit! I don't believe it!" he exclaimed. "After the trouble I went through to get that."

Wilmott stood up from the chair by the steering wheel on the upper deck. "We okay to go, Nick?" he asked.

"Yes. Go, go, go!" shouted Nick as he coiled up the mooring rope whilst looking back at the terrace.

"David?" questioned Linda. "What are you doing here?"

"Story for another time, Lin, if you don't mind. Are we ready to go?"

"Yes, go!" shouted Linda.

Wilmott pushed the throttle a little forward so he could slowly steer the boat out from in between the two other boats. Once clear he pushed the throttle all the way and the boat took on a surprising burst of speed for its innocent look, leaving a vee shape of waves in its trail. Wilmott gazed behind at the terrace to ensure they were currently clear of danger. His concentration was interrupted by the blast of a ship's horn. He turned his gaze forward to face the direction of the sound to find his boat heading straight for the side of a tourist ferry about 50 metres away. He spun the wheel forcefully and the modified engines, propellers and rudders quickly responded, causing the boat to lean into a tight turn and change its course now taking it speedily along the side of the tourist ferry almost at touching distance. As he passed by the ferry's windows he shouted "Sorry" to the many occupants who were taking photographs of the events taking place. He checked there were no other floating obstacles in the near vicinity and steered the boat on course away from the terrace. Knowing it was now safe to glance behind him again, he looked to find the other occupants laying where they had tumbled due to the momentum of the tight turn.

"Sorry," he shouted again.

Jameson, Linda and Nick righted themselves into seated positions on the deck and smiled back at Wilmott, grateful that the turbulence had subsided at least for now.

Back at The Houses of Parliament, Jenkins and his guards ran out onto the terrace, they could see Wilmott's boat speeding off, already. The people that were left on the terrace following the commotion caused by Linda, Nick and Jameson rushing onto the boat, scattered when they saw the guards openly carrying pistols.

"Shoot them," shouted Jenkins. "Now!"

The two guards drew their pistols, stood on the edge of the terrace and fired at the speeding boat. The boat was already too far away for anything but a lucky shot to reach its target.

"Quickly into the boats," shouted Jenkins to his guards. "Get after them!"

The two guards stopped firing at the fleeing boat, untied the mooring ropes of the two remaining boats and jumped onboard, one with Jenkins and the other on his own. They selected full throttle and sped off in pursuit.

CHAPTER 26

On the leading boat, Wilmott was at the helm pushing the vessel to its top speed, heading up river, away from the Houses of Parliament. Nick had shielded the Prime Minister from the initial shots as best he could but, now they had subsided, he motioned for him to remain sitting on the deck, told him to keep low and joined Wilmott. Linda was at the transom, keeping a look out at what was occurring back at the terrace.

They had passed through an archway of Lambeth Bridge and were quickly approaching the slight bend in the river before Vauxhall Bridge when Linda spotted the two boats leaving the terrace in pursuit.

"They're after us!" she shouted loud enough to be heard at the helm. "Two boats on our tail."

Wilmott glanced around. "I see them," he shouted in reply. "Let me know if they get close or they do anything else of interest."

Linda formed the 'ok' sign with her hand and turned back to watch the pursuers as they continued under Vauxhall Bridge, keeping to the shorter route around the inside of the bend in the river.

Keeping the boat speeding along whilst avoiding any

others either moving or moored in the water, Wilmott turned his head slightly so he could see Nick and still see the river ahead.

"What's the story about the PM?" he asked.

"It wasn't Jameson behind all this," said Nick. "It turns out that the 'CJ' being referred to in the notebook is Sir Kit Jenkins, Kit being short for Christopher of course."

"Shit! Of course," exclaimed Wilmott grimacing. "So, there were two 'CJs' in the Private Office. Easy to assume that Wilkinson was referring to the PM. Why the hell didn't he write 'Kit' in his notebook? It would have stopped any possible confusion."

"I suppose, being a decryption operative, he was used to putting everything as he heard it plus, I assume he was always of the thought that his notebook was exactly that; notes that he would refer to when reporting to others. Still, it caused us a bit of grief in the House. Jenkins has security officers on side but we don't know which ones or how many so, the only way to keep Jameson safe was to bring him with us."

"If you can call being in a boat chase along the Thames safe," added Wilmott.

"Quite…," agreed Nick. "Well, we certainly couldn't guarantee his safety if we had left him there. Until we know for sure which of the security officers are on side, he'll be better off with us."

Their conversation was interrupted by a shout from Linda.

"They're gaining on us. At least, one of them is."

Wilmott and Nick looked behind the boat and saw the leading pursuit boat was now only a few hundred metres behind them whilst the second one was about a hundred metres behind that one.

"Take the wheel Nick," said Wilmott as he reached into his pocket for his smart phone. "I need to make a call to clear our way and to hopefully arrange an interception for our friends behind us."

Nick took over the controls while Wilmott stood to one side to make the call. He kept the boat to the inside of the bend, avoiding the various barges moored beside what was left of Battersea Power Station swerving slightly inwards to steer clear of some barges that were anchored in line with the right-hand arch of the Chelsea railway bridge. The noise of the motor and the waves created by the boat cutting through the water echoed as they passed under the bridge. He now had to steer towards the centre of the river as he could see a number of stationary barges moored to the right of Albert and Battersea Bridges.

His concentration was interrupted by a shout from Linda.

"Now only about a hundred metres behind us," she reported loudly. Then increased her urgency. "He's drawing a gun!" she shouted. "Get down!"

Nick and Wilmott crouched down slightly as they heard a couple of rounds whistle past the boat but the gunman was still too far away to get an accurate shot.

Linda steadied her arms on the transom and took aim to return fire. Before she had a chance to shoot, a lucky shot from the gunman hit her pistol, ricocheting off it, deeply grazing her hand causing her to release the Glock which fell into the river. The bullet imbedded itself into the deck causing no further harm. Linda fell to the deck clutching her hand which was bleeding along the graze across her palm.

"Not again!" she shouted through the pain. "Unbelievable!"

Wilmott had seen what had happened. "Linda!" he shouted, not knowing the extent of her injury.

"I'm okay," she shouted back. "It's not bad. Lost my weapon though." She looked up at the pursuing boat. "And he's still on our tail."

"You sure you're okay?" shouted Wilmott.

"Yes, yes," replied Linda looking back at the gunman as he fired off a few more rounds then suddenly stopped. "I think he may have emptied his weapon," she shouted. "And he either hasn't got any spare mags or can't reload whilst steering 'cos his boat is being kept unsteady by the waves in our wake. It's not stopping him from closing in on us though."

"I see him," shouted Nick, glancing backwards again. "Going as fast as I can."

Linda continued watching as the gunman's boat slowly approached still clutching her bleeding hand tightly. Jameson crawled across the deck, keeping low, and handed Linda a handkerchief. Linda gestured her thanks and wrapped the handkerchief tight around her hand and tucked in the ends. A red stain quickly started to appear through the cotton layers but she still used the hand to motion the PM back to where he had been.

"He's less than fifty metres away now," she shouted. "Nick, I think he's trying to come along side."

Nick chanced a glance behind and saw the pursuing boat was only a few metres behind. They were fast approaching the Albert Bridge and Nick steered right to take his boat under the far arch. The pursuer took his boat under the bridge through the next arch on the left. He had now gained enough for both boats to go through the arches at the same time causing a roar as the noise from two engines echoed around the underside of the bridge. As soon as they were both out the other side, the guard turned his wheel sharply to the right and his boat shot across the water towards Nick's. Before crashing headlong into Nick's boat, the guard lined his boat up so that it butted into the side of Nick's. He then turned the wheel sharply right again trying to force Nick's boat into the shallows or into some boats that were moored at the side of the river. Nick countered the force with a swift turn of his wheel to the left. All this was happening as both boats were hurtling along at top speed side by side, quickly getting nearer and nearer to Battersea Bridge. The guard tapped a few times keeping Nick's boat and his on a straight course through the water. Nick was concentrating on the guard's boat, trying to counter each nudge from the other boat so that his stayed on an even line.

His concentration was interrupted by Linda shouting. "Nick! The bridge. Watch out!"

He looked up to see they were headed directly for one of the bridge columns, realising that the guard had been deliberately trying to make them crash into it. He spun the wheel to the right and felt the boat responding relatively slowly to the response he was used to from a car. In the next second or so he watched the column close in on his vison, close enough now for him to make out the individual bricks that went into constructing it. Keeping his hands firmly gripping the wheel, he willed the boat to respond.

Within a few metres of the column, the boat turned far enough for it to scrape along its side as it sped under the bridge. The guard had steered his boat the other side of the column so they both came out from under the bridge side by side again, separated by a few metres.

"I've had enough of this," he said angrily to Wilmott. "Take over the steering."

As Wilmott came back to take that wheel, Nick turned it so that the two boats were close to touching each other again. Wilmott took the wheel as Nick jumped down to the deck and ran the few steps towards the guard's boat.

"What are you doing, Nick? Don't…" shouted Wilmott but it was too late to stop him.

Keeping to his stride, Nick jumped on to the gunwale, pushed off and leapt across to the other boat, crashing into the surprised guard and knocking him to the deck with Nick landing on top of him. Nick's impact on the guard, caused him to spin the wheel sharply before he fell. The boat veered away from Wilmott's boat cutting diagonally across the river, heading for the far left-hand column of Battersea Rail Bridge at full speed. Nick used the element of surprise to punch the unprepared guard hard on the temple. The guard was strong and, though a little dazed, kept his concentration and gripped Nick's arms whilst bringing his knee up into Nick's torso, throwing him off and to the side. They both got to their feet, Nick now beside the wheel and the guard a few metres behind him.

Nick prepared to run at the guard but detected the sound of a train close by. He looked ahead and saw the boat was now only a few seconds away from hitting the bridge column. He grabbed at the wheel and turned it causing the boat to lean to the right and now head under the first arch. The guard took advantage of Nick's distraction and ran over, putting Nick into a powerful arm lock around his neck. Nick let go of the wheel instinctively grabbing for the guard's arm as he could already feel its grip tightening on his larynx, cutting off his air supply. He tried to pull the guard's arm away from his neck but the guard was strong and he had no way of getting any extra leverage. Nick could no longer breathe and thought his vision was already dimming through lack of oxygen but it was the shadow caused by the boat speeding through the bridge arch. As the boat came back out into the light, the guard's grip tightened further and Nick could now feel the cartilage around his trachea starting to give way. He had to do something now or his windpipe would be crushed.

Back onboard Wilmott's boat the fight was being watched as Wilmott concentrated on lining up to steer through the middle arch. His concentration was broken by Linda.

"Dave, the other boat's catching us now. Fifty metres," she shouted. Then her tone changed. "Keep down!" she yelled as a few more rounds whistled past the hull.

The shooting stopped so Linda risked another look. "Jeez!" she shouted. "How the fuck?"

"What is it now?" shouted Wilmott.

"Shit, Dave! Four jet skis have just come out of Chelsea Harbour. Lining up with the other boat. What else are they gonna throw at us?"

Wilmott decided to concentrate on trying to get back beside the guard's boat. Priority was to help Nick unless the shots from behind started again. He steered a diagonal course as he came out the other side of the rail bridge to hopefully intercept.

With his vision now beginning to fade at the edges, Nick was still able to see that they were fast approaching Wandsworth Bridge.

It was now or never.

He increased his grip on the guard's arm and, in a set of smooth moves, he lifted himself off the deck, balancing on the guard's taught arm, quickly used his feet to turn the wheel so the boat was heading for the main central arch, then pushed away from the wheel with his legs as hard as he could, forcing the guard to fall backwards onto the deck. As they were falling, Nick forced himself further out straight so that most of his bodyweight was concentrated on the guard's chest. At the moment of landing on the deck, the force of impact concentrated Nick's weight onto the guard's ribcage. There were some loud cracks as a number of the guard's ribs broke.

The guard screamed out in pain and involuntarily released his grip on Nick's neck. Nick took a great gulp of breath, clearing his vision almost instantly. He quickly spun around so he was now straddling the guard who was still dazed from the pain of multiple broken ribs. Nick punched the guard hard on his Adam's Apple causing another loud cracking noise. The guard clutched at his throat and could only make a slight hissing sound as his windpipe had been crushed by the blow. He wasn't going anywhere.

Nick now looked forward again and saw that the boat had luckily steered itself between a number of moored barges and was now heading for the central arch of Fulham Railway Bridge. He tweaked the wheel slightly so that the boat was heading safely under Putney Bridge and then took a look behind. He could see Wilmott's boat on an angled course, heading for him with another boat and some jet skis close behind.

"Shit!" he said to himself. "It never rains…"

Keeping his boat inline for the middle arch of Putney Bridge, Nick adjusted the course so that he would meet up with Wilmott's boat quickly. As the two boats neared each other, Nick steered an about turn so that they would pass side by side with Nick's going in the opposite direction, heading towards the pursuing vessels. For the brief moment that the two boats were next to each other, Nick spun the wheel hard to the left forcing his boat against the side of Wilmott's. As soon as he had done that, he leapt again from one boat to the other, landing hard on the deck and rolling into the Prime Minister who put out his hands to grab him and slow him down.

As Nick's boat cleared the back of Wilmott's, the wheel being hard over made the boat turn behind the other into the path Jenkins's pursuing vessel. There was no time to steer clear and Jenkins's boat crashed into the side of the one vacated by Nick. Unlike in the movies, there was no massive explosion as the impact had been nowhere near the fuel tanks of either boat. However, there was major damage to the bow of Jenkins's and the hull of the other and both boats began to quickly take on water.

The jet skis, being more agile than the boats, managed to steer around the collision. Jenkins angrily shouted across at the jet ski riders to be rescued then he watched, grimacing, at the boat with Linda, Wilmott, Nick and Jameson getting away. He then ordered two of the jet skis to continue the chase whilst the other two circled back to pick him and the other guard from the sinking boat.

Wilmott's boat had recently passed by Bishop's Park and Fulham Football Ground and was now coming out of a bend in the river to be in sight of Hammersmith Bridge. He steered to the left of the river as near to the bank as possible, knowing they were approaching a long left-hand bend. Taking the shortest route was gaining him a few valuable seconds as the pursuing jet skis were still regrouping. Every second allowed more time to plan their next move. The jet skis were faster than the boat and would soon catch up with them.

Nick stood up, glanced behind and saw two leading jet skis starting to close the gap and another two behind them going a little slower as there were two people on each of them. Nick moved over to Wilmott, steadying himself using anything secured on the boat.

"Four jet skis approaching fast. Two of them will reach us within a minute or so."

Wilmott glanced briefly at Nick then looked back to concentrate on lining up for the far left-hand side of Hammersmith Bridge.

"What was all that about, Nick?" he asked. "Jumping from one boat to another. A bit risky to say the least."

"I've been without any weapons since before I got on your boat. So, I had to jump the guy before he had a chance to fire at us."

"I gathered that bit," said Wilmott smiling, "but I wondered why you didn't ask me for one first." He jerked his head down and to his left. "Under the chair."

Nick bent down and looked under the chair. He reached under and pulled out a SIG MCX Rattler assault rifle along with a box of 5 full magazines.

"You could've told me you had this, Dave," said Nick as he checked the magazine and clicked off the safety catch.

"We've hardly had the time," said Wilmott apologetically, "and I didn't know you were about to leap between boats."

"Well, it may just come in useful now, mate," said Nick as he looked back along the river. "We've got company… again."

By now Wilmott's boat had reached Hammersmith Bridge and was speeding under the farthest left arch, still close to the bank. The two jet skis with one rider on each were now only about 50 metres behind with the other two about 100 metres farther back. Nick hurried to the transom and crouched down next to Linda eying the blood-soaked handkerchief wrapped around her hand.

"You okay?" he asked.

"Yeah," said Linda looking around to face Nick. She followed his eyes to her hand. "Oh, this," she said holding up her hand. "It's just a big graze. Looks worse than it is. I'm fine."

Any further conversation was halted by a number of rounds hitting the rear hull. The jet skis had reached within 30 metres of the boat and both riders had opened fire.

"Get down!" shouted Nick, glancing over to ensure Jameson was sheltering as best he could. Linda ducked but prepared her aim at the jet ski to the left. Nick brought the Rattler around to be resting on the transom and aimed for the jet skier on the right. He double-tapped the trigger and two 300 Blackout expanding rounds hit the right-hand jet ski rider, one in the centre of his chest and the other in his neck just above the collarbone level. There was no visible damage caused by the chest shot other than an entry hole in the guard's body armour but the guard's neck exploded to the rear as the expanding bullet exited, taking a large chunk of neck tissue and bones with it. The chest shot had also caused considerable internal damage and the guard's body fell from the jet ski into the river; he would be dead in a matter of seconds. The unmanned jet ski had lost acceleration once the guard had let go of the accelerator lever and glided across the water, running aground at the side of the river.

At the same time, Linda had taken a couple of shots at the left-hand jet skier but he was still outside accuracy range and her shots hit the front fairing of the jet ski. This allowed the guard time to fire off a few more rounds as he swerved to one side to avoid further hits.

Wilmott's boat suddenly veered to the right towards the centre of the river and causing Linda and Nick to lose their balance. Nick looked towards Wilmott to see what he was trying to do only to see him slump backwards into his chair.

"Man down!" shouted Nick making Linda look around, first to the Prime Minister and then across to Wilmott.

"David!" she shouted. "No!"

"Lin, get over there and steer the boat," said Nick thinking on his feet. "I'll see if I can hold off this lot behind us. Check on Dave when you can."

Linda made her way over to the wheel keeping low in case of any more shots. She reached the wheel and steered the boat, levelling it out now central in the river. They had been fortunate that Wilmott had staggered against the wheel, knocking it to the right. If it had been to the left, they would have run aground at the river's edge.

They were now passing Chiswick Eyot, a small isle in the river, and were entering a narrower part of the Thames so Linda kept the boat in the centre as she steered it around the bend in the river. She glanced around quickly to look at Wilmott. He was slumped on the chair with blood running down one side of his face from around his temple – unconscious or worse. Linda had to leave him as he was for the moment as the boat was travelling too fast and the river too narrow at this point to stop concentrating on steering – her priority was for the people in the boat that were definitely living at this time.

On one of the two remaining chasing jet skis, Jenkins waved on the other pair forwards.

"Take them out! Now!" he shouted menacingly.

The rider of the other jet ski managed to find a little more speed from his vehicle, spurred on by the deadly look on the face of Jenkins, and they moved off gaining on the boat ahead. He turned to be side on to the boat so his passenger could fire off a couple of shots. One of the shots hit and went through the transom, narrowly missing Nick's side and ending up embedded in the deck. Nick returned a couple of shots from the SIG but he didn't have time to aim as more shots were heading his way. His shots weren't far off though as they fizzed past the jet ski rider's head making him duck involuntary and turn sharply, heading back where he came from. He performed another 180 degrees turn as Jenkins's jet ski caught up with him so that they were both alongside each other again.

"What the fuck are you doing!?" screamed Jenkins at the rider.

"We're outgunned," shouted the rider in reply. "They've got rifles against our pistols."

"I don't care if they've got fucking cannons, get back there and kill them," he said pointing his pistol at the rider.

The jet ski rider decided it was safer to pursue the boat rather than stay beside Jenkins so he increased speed again, lessening the gap. Nick took advantage of the jet ski approaching head on and took aim on what was becoming an increasingly larger target. He steadied his MCX on the transom again, knowing he was safe to show himself for a few seconds, and took aim at the largest target at this range; the rider's torso. He fired off two rounds and hit the rider in the chest with both shots. The 300 Blackout rounds were too powerful for the rider's body armour passing through it as if it wasn't there, one bullet expanding, entering and bursting the rider's heart, the other doing the same to his lung. He released his hold on the handlebars and slumped off the jet ski into the water, dead before he landed.

The passenger, now exposed, fired off a few shots in Nick's direction, causing Nick to duck down before he could shoot again. He slid forward on the jet ski, grabbed the handle bars and powered the vehicle in chase of the boat again. This guy was an accomplished rider and a crack shot which meant that, once the jet ski had become steady, he was able to steer and throttle with one hand and shoot with the other. This he did every few seconds, keeping Nick pinned down as he closed the gap on the speeding boat.

The boat had now reached Barnes Bridge and Linda steered it through the centre arch. She had glanced back just before reaching the bridge and saw that Nick was being kept pinned down as the jet skier was approaching. Looking ahead again, she saw a large object floating in the water between 50 and 100 metres away and recognised it as a fallen tree branch. What she could see of it was about 3 metres long and at least 50 centimetres in diameter.

"Hang on tight," she shouted as she steered straight for the driftwood.

Jameson had already secured himself down low on the deck and Wilmott was wedged into the driver's seat so they were okay. Nick heard Linda's shout and had no idea why but trusted she had a good reason to call out so he grabbed some hand-holds and hung on tightly.

Linda quickly glanced between the route ahead and the advancing jet ski behind. She kept low as she was now the only visible target for the jet skier to aim for but he seemed to be conserving his rounds and only firing sparingly to keep Nick from shooting, concentrating more on catching the boat. He was now only about 20 metres behind and still gaining.

Linda kept looking from front to back, she needed to judge this accurately if her plan was going to work. If it didn't, the jet ski would be upon them and they would be open targets.

The large branch was floating lengthways on to Linda's approaching boat so she steered for its centre. One more glance behind showed that the jet ski was now only about 10 metres away and the next glance forward found the large branch at an equal distance ahead.

Linda whipped the wheel fully clockwise causing the boat to lean over sharply as it steered as quickly right as it could. Had the passengers not heeded her warning shout they may have been tossed out from the boat such was the sudden and dramatic angle it made in the water as it conducted such a sharp turn. The boat sped past the branch so close that a high-pitched noise could be heard above the engines as the hull scraped one end of it. As soon as the boat was clear of the floating branch, Linda performed an anti-clockwise turn of the wheel to settle the boat and return it to an even course.

The jet skier had no time to react to Linda's sudden course change and the boat had been covering his view of the river ahead so he was met with the sight of a huge piece of driftwood only a few metres ahead in his path. He tried to steer away from it but it was too late for any manoeuvres to work and the jet ski hit the branch side on at speed. The front of the jet ski hit the middle section of the branch causing the vehicle to flip upwards and out of the water, with the momentum forcing it to perform a full backward circle in mid-air. This all happened very quickly and the rider was still clutching the handle bars and in a seated position as the jet ski tried to continue its mid-air somersault. He ended up performing another half circle so that his body was upside down when gravity took over and brought the jet ski and him back down to the river. The rider's head struck the water and the continuing momentum of the jet ski caused it to snap back with a loud crack as his neck became violently broken. The sound of his neck breaking was the last thing the rider ever heard as he was dead before the jet ski had crashed into the river with a large splash, leaving his lifeless body floating in the Thames.

Once the boat was relatively steady, Nick took advantage of the distraction and brought his MCX back up onto the transom to assist with his aiming. The last remaining jet ski with a driver and Jenkins as the passenger, was now about 100 metres back and Nick could see they had recovered from the shock of the crash and Jenkins was preparing to fire on the boat. Nick held the MCX as steady as he could and took aim at the approaching jet ski rider.

The rider was making no attempt of weaving about to try to put off Nick's aim, keeping his craft steady so that Jenkins may be able to get off some accurate shots. This was his downfall as, from Nick's point of view, his target was only getting increasingly larger in his sights. Nick held his breath and checked his aim once more as he fired two shots in quick succession. One shot missed, whizzing harmlessly past the jet ski driver, but the other shot hit him fully in his right shoulder, expanding and exiting to the rear, taking a sizeable amount of bone fragments, body tissue and blood with it. The rider could no longer steer or accelerate with his right hand due to a chunk of his right shoulder now being missing and he slumped slightly as he let go of the handle bars to be able to clutch at his wound. This caused the jet ski to veer sharply to the right and the vehicle to run aground onto the rowing boat launch slope beside Chiswick Bridge. The increased friction between the jet ski and the concrete slope caused the vehicle to stop abruptly and its occupants to be hurled into the air, landing heavily onto a couple of parked cars further up the bank.

Jenkins's impact, though heavy, was cushioned by landing on the car's bonnet which crumpled and broke his fall. He climbed off the bonnet and gingerly stumbled back to the edge of the river. Amazingly he still had hold of his pistol which he raised and used to shoot through the arch of Chiswick Bridge at the fast-retreating boat. The distance was already too great for the shots to land with any accuracy and they hit the water harmlessly, causing small splashes some distance from Linda's boat.

"Shit, shit, shit!" screamed Jenkins at the top of his voice as he stormed back up the concrete slope towards the cars.

A small crowd of people had assembled around the impacted cars having been in the rowing clubhouse at the time of the incident and a few onlookers had stopped on the bridge to search for the cause of the crash noise. They were all fast retreating since the shots were fired but a couple had stayed to try to assist the injured guard who had landed against the side of a car.

"Get away from him!" screamed Jenkins, pointing his pistol towards the couple as he advanced upon them.

The couple backed slowly away, a look of terror on their faces as they stared at the barrel of the pistol. As they moved away, Jenkins could now see the guard who was on the ground in a seated position with his clothing around his shoulder now sodden with blood. He wasn't going anywhere without medical assistance.

Jenkins glanced across to the bridge. The people who had been there attracted to the noise of the crash had either moved away or ducked for cover so Jenkins was satisfied they weren't seeing what was going on any longer. He turned towards the scared couple and, without further thought, shot them both in the head, killing them instantly. He then turned back towards the guard who now, through the grimacing, had a knowing look on his face. Jenkins shot him in the head too and his lifeless body remained sitting with his head slumped to one side.

Jenkins checked his own pockets for his mobile phone but they were empty; it must have fallen out during the commotion. He went over to the lifeless guard, checked his pockets and pulled out a mobile dripping with the guard's blood. He wiped the phone on a dry area of the guard's clothing and then tapped in a number that was answered on the first ring.

"I need a clean-up team and transport to the rowing club beside Chiswick Bridge now!" he shouted, still sounding hysterical. "And I want the local police kept away from the area at least until I'm clear. And I want a boat that's headed up river from Chiswick Bridge intercepted. And I need it all NOW!"

He glanced back under the bridge arches along the river and could no longer see Linda's boat.

"Shit, shit, SHIT!" he screamed again.

Further up the river, Linda hadn't slowed down even though she could no longer see anyone chasing them. It may be only a matter of time before somebody else may start up the pursuit again. Nick had seen the jet ski crash into the concrete launch slope so took advantage of the quiet time. He worked his way forward in the boat, first checking the Prime Minister was okay and then moving on to Wilmott's unmoving body, checking him for vital signs.

During glances backwards, Linda saw what Nick was

doing.

"Jeez, Nick. Is he …?" she asked in a worried tone.

"It's okay, Lin. He's unconscious but breathing fine. The head wound looks worse than it is. It's a deep graze and may need a stitch or two. Lots of blood but no serious damage. Half an inch to the side and it would've been very different."

Linda smiled and looked relieved. "I thought he was dead."

Nick opened a storage compartment beside the chair and found a first aid kit.

"I'll patch him up for the moment and let him sleep it off until we dock. He's likely to have one hell of a headache when he wakes up."

Linda laughed and turned to fully concentrate on steering while Nick found some liquid skin and sprayed it along Wilmott's head wound creating a temporary seal.

Whilst this was going on, they had travelled under the railway and road bridges of Kew and were now speeding past a long island in the river known as Brentford Ait. About a mile ahead Linda could see another island named Isleworth Ait situated at a bend in the river and, in the distance, high to one side, a helicopter following the path of the Thames, flying towards them.

"That can't be for us, can it?" she shouted to Nick gesturing towards the distant aircraft.

Nick followed her gesture and saw the helicopter was getting lower as it was approaching.

"Too early to be sure but I wouldn't put it past Jenkins to have called it in. Who knows how many people he's got on side?"

He watched closely as the copter slowed its forward travel and began descending.

"It looks like it could be getting into position to intercept us around Richmond Bridge."

The helicopter was doing what Nick had suggested. It was hovering low above the river over Corporation Island beside Richmond Bridge. As it stabilised into a controlled steady hover, the side door opened to reveal two more Parliamentary guards strapped in seated positions. Each of them had long-barrelled SIG MXC assault rifles with high powered sights. They both readied themselves, covering the river at the exit from under Richmond Railway Bridge, waiting for Linda's boat. They had both been trained for precision sniper fire from helicopters so their target area in their sights appeared very steady.

The lead sniper took his aim away from the railway bridge and refocussed on the boat across the Royal Mid-Surrey golf course, tracking its progress along the river. He spoke to the other sniper over their headset comms.

"Orders are to take out the occupants of the target boat. We'll get a clear shot when it comes around the bend in the river by Isleworth Ait and then straightens up for the approach to Richmond. I'll be our 'eyes' until it exits our side of the railway bridge, you keep targeting the bridge arches and take out the driver as soon as it clears the bridge. Then we can both concentrate on the passengers. Orders are to shoot to kill where possible."

"Yes sir," said the second sniper as he swept the arches in his sights in preparation.

The lead sniper changed channel on his comms and spoke again.

"Sir, we are in position and ready. The area has been secured as best as possible for such short notice; local police have cordoned off Richmond Bridge and are in the process of moving people in land from the river side. Can I confirm permission to shoot?"

"Yes, yes, yes," came the unsteady voice of Jenkins over the comms unit.

On his orders, Jenkins had had his mobile patched through the helicopter crew to brief them of his intentions. He had just been picked up from the Chiswick rowing club and was speeding towards Richmond.

"Permission is granted to fire at will. But keep me in the comms loop. I want to hear what's going on."

"Yes, Sir," replied the sniper, switching his comms back to the helicopter crew but now leaving Jenkins connected too. "Permission to shoot granted," he confirmed in a professional tone. "Pilot, keep us hovering here, Sniper Two keep your aim at the railway bridge and I'll update on their progress. Clear?"

"Yes, sir," came the reply from the other occupants.

"They're alongside Kew Gardens, approaching the next bend by Isleworth Ait. ETA about 90 seconds at current speed."

Back on the boat Linda and Nick were still concentrating on the helicopter and, even from a distance, could make out the side door opening and a couple of people sitting, facing out.

"Pretty sure you were right, Lin," said Nick as he kept the helicopter in view. "It looks like they're preparing a welcoming party for us and I doubt it will be friendly."

The Prime Minister, having been watching proceedings from his area of low cover, had come forward in the boat to see what was going on now that the shooting seemed to have stopped.

"What's happening?" he asked.

"More of Jenkins's sympathisers up ahead in a copter with a welcoming party for us by the looks of it, Sir," Nick said. "Please return to your cover in case they start shooting again but be prepared to leave the boat in a hurry if we give the shout. We may need to get away quickly if they have what I suspect will be superior fire power."

"But how can we get away from a helicopter?" asked Jameson as he was returning to his place of relative safety.

"Leave that to us please, Sir," said Nick. Then he turned back to Linda. "Plan B I think, Lin."

"Yeah, Plan B it is," agreed Linda. "We need to get Dave conscious and ready to go too."

"Yeah, working on it," said Nick as he moved over to Wilmott and started to try to gently awaken him.

"They're approaching the end of Kew Gardens now," said the lead sniper, "about to enter the river beside the golf course."

He quickly panned his sights along the river ahead of the boat and then back to it.

"Once they get in line with the end of the golf course, they'll be out of sight for approximately 30 seconds or so as they round the river by Isleworth Ait. We won't see them until they're past the Ait and then they'll be under and out the bridges within 30 seconds from then. All prepped and ready?"

"Sir," came the reply.

They were ready to release a deadly fusillade at the boat and its occupants.

"They're definitely waiting for us," said Nick straining his eyes to try to see more clearly. "From here it looks like they're ready with rifles, waiting for us to come out from under Twickenham Bridge. As we near the end of the golf course I won't be able to see them for the trees but I don't think they're moving so we should be okay."

Linda pulled back the throttle a little.

"Unless they make a move while we can't see them. I'll slow down a bit," she decided, "and give us a little bit more time if they're not moving."

Nick turned back to the slumped body of Wilmott and gently shook him by the shoulders.

"Come on, Dave," he encouraged. "We really need you awake now."

His efforts were met with a few murmurs but nothing else.

"Dave… David…. WILMOTT!" he ended up shouting. "We need you conscious and with us NOW!"

A few more murmurs greeted him but Wilmott remained unconscious. Nick glanced forwards again and saw they were only about 300 metres from the near end of Isleworth

Ait. His sight moved on to the helicopter still hovering near Richmond Bridge and what looked like gunmen waiting to shoot them all. At that moment the tree cover increased meaning he would no longer be able to see the helicopter and therefore wouldn't know if they decided to move in on them whilst they were unsighted.

He decided there was no choice but be cruel to be kind; getting Wilmott conscious may be the difference between life and death. He slapped Wilmott hard on one cheek then the other then repeated the strikes gently and slowly.

"Dave!" he shouted, "we need you with us now! DAVE!"

The lead sniper was still relating progress to his crew and to Jenkins via his comms.

"They're approximately 100 yards from the Ait. They may have slowed slightly but still coming towards us at pace. They're about to go behind tree cover. At latest speed I estimate they'll be out of sight for 30 to 40 seconds until they've rounded the bend in the river and got past the Ait. Okay, they're out of sight.... Now. Sniper 2, confirm readiness for engagement."

"Ready sir," came the reply.

"Received," acknowledged the lead sniper. "They were central so, unless they move, they should be coming through the middle arch."

"Take them out," shouted the voice of Jenkins appearing on the headsets of the helicopter crew. "Shoot to kill. You understand me?"

"We have your orders and are prepared and ready, Sir," acknowledged the lead sniper. "We are good to go."

He turned his sight to the near end of Isleworth Ait which would be the next part of the river where he could see the boat when it clears the tree coverage.

"Forty," he started counting down. "They'll be at the start of the Ait now," he estimated.

"Thirty," he continued. "Now alongside the Ait"

"Twenty…"

"Ten… They should be approaching the end of the Ait now."

"Six…"

"Five…"

"Four…"

"Three…"

"Two…"

"One…"

"Now!"

There was a moment of silence as the boat was yet to come into vision.

"Hold position," said the lead sniper. "Hold position…"

"What's going on?" shouted Jenkins through the comms set. "Tell me now!"

"They've yet to appear sir," said the lead sniper still sounding calm and in control. "They must have slowed further. They should be in sight any moment, Sir."

Jenkins considered the situation for a moment and didn't like what he was thinking. "They've turned around," he shouted. "They're going back. Track them now!"

The lead sniper reacted quickly to the orders given by Jenkins.

"Pilot, move out and follow the river. Let's find these bastards. Sniper One keep your aim active. We take them as soon as we see them. Moving in track mode now Sir," he related to Jenkins.

The helicopter remained low but tilted nose down slightly and accelerated forwards following the course of the river. It skimmed over Richmond Railway Bridge and Twickenham Bridge and continued at the same height heading towards Isleworth Ait, all three occupants scanning the river for any sign of the boat.

"What's happening?" demanded Jenkins. "Tell me now!"

"No sight so far, Sir. Just reaching the Ait so nearing where we lost visuals."

They flew over Isleworth Ait above the trees so they could see the river on either side of it and there was no sign of the boat.

"No sign of the boat around the Ait, Sir," the lead sniper continued his narrative. "You may well be correct. They must've turned around."

The helicopter arrived at the end of the Ait and banked right to follow the bend in the river. It straightened out and they could now see a long, straight stretch of the Thames as it flowed first beside the Royal Mid-Surrey Golf Course and then beside Kew Gardens. It was straight enough for them to be able to see approximately 2 kilometres before the next bend in the river. The pilot brought the copter to an abrupt hover as, for the entire 2-kilometre stretch, there were no vessels on the river.

"We have no sight of the target," reported the lead sniper over the comms.

"What the hell do you mean you have no sight of it?" demanded Jenkins.

"We have flown over the river at the Ait and can now see down as far as the Brentford Ait beside Kew Bridge and the river is empty of craft, Sir."

"The boat has disappeared!"

CHAPTER 27

Southampton

In the concealed sub-basement levels of the Self-Store-It warehouse, Southampton, Keith Turner was again studying the latest satellite pictures of Diabolus island off the Canaries. For once he had been home to freshen up and change clothes and was now wearing a fresh tee shirt with 'Gone phishing' written across the front.

Keith's assistant, Tony Chapman, ambled into the room carrying a couple of large cups of steaming coffee. Keith looked at his watch and then, with a curious expression, back at Chapman.

"It's not the usual time for coffee, Tony."

"I know," said Chapman smiling, "but there was a new van outside giving out promotional coffees so I got us one each. Black with no sugar for you, right?"

"Perfect, thanks," said Keith taking a cup and gulping down a mouthful.

"Wow, that is hot." He grimaced a little. "And it's a bit bitter. There's a sachet of sugar around here somewhere."

He rummaged around his desk and then his top drawer until he found the sachet he was looking for. Holding the sachet tightly, he bit the corner open and poured the contents into his cup, gently swirling it to mix. He took a sip and smiled.

"That's a bit better. Still a bit bitter. Not as good as the one from the usual van but pretty good for free. Thanks."

"That's okay," said Chapman sipping his. "Mine doesn't seem bitter but maybe it's the milk that obscures it. Still, as you say, not bad for free."

He looked at Keith's pictures and asked, "Found anything?"

"Yes mate," said Keith, tapping on his keyboard to show a split screen of pictures, "I think I have."

"What've we got?" asked Chapman pulling up a chair.

Keith took another gulp of his coffee.

"I'd ordered a few sets of HD satellite images so I could zoom in closer and I got lucky on these last three I looked at."

He used his mouse pointer to indicate the bottom of the island on the left-hand picture on the big screen.

"This is a picture of the island taken about two hours ago. If you note its position from the latitude and longitude lines that I've marked on it, then compare it to the middle picture you'll see it's definitely moved in the forty minutes between the two pictures."

"Moved!? Are you sure?"

"Yes mate," answered Keith, "and, if we look closer at the third picture, there's another point of interest."

Keith stood up from his chair in order to walk over close to the large screen. As he did so his view of the room started to spin slightly and he stumbled as he lost balance.

"You alright, Keith?" asked Chapman.

Keith steadied himself against the wall, shaking his head to try to stop the spinning.

"Yeah, I'm okay thanks mate. Think I've been sitting for too long then stood up too quickly."

He moved unsteadily to the screen and pointed to a couple of lines of crested water just off the south side of the island.

"In this picture taken another forty minutes later, we were lucky enough to capture these marks in the sea just south of the island."

"And what are they?" asked Chapman, watching Keith closely.

"After a bit of studying," said Keith pointing to the marks on the picture, "I came to the conclusion that the marks are being made by water jet propulsion units."

"Jet propulsion?" asked Chapman.

Keith looked up from the screen and over to where Chapman was sitting. He had to concentrate hard to keep Chapman in focus.

"Yes, jet propulsion. Like the type used by jet skis. Couldn't believe it myself at first but pretty sure that's what the marks are. It's not an island, mate. It's a floating vessel, a giant disguised boat."

"You have got to be kidding," said Chapman. Then he added, "You sure you're okay?"

Keith took a step back towards Chapman and stumbled again. The room spun more violently and his vision went in and out of focus. He placed his hands on each of his temples as his head started to pulsate in bursts of pain and his stomach churned as a wave of nausea swept over him. A frame of darkness started to close in, shutting off his vision as the room appeared to turn on its side as he fell to the floor.

"The coffee," he mumbled in realisation. "There's something in the coffee. Must be."

He gasped as the pain at his temples became unbearably strong. He tried to move his limbs but they now felt so heavy that he had no choice to leave them in the position they were. He tried to speak but could no longer move his lips properly. All that came out was a low mumble.

Through the ever-enclosing darkness of his peripheral vision he could see Chapman pressing his hands to his temples and stumbling unsteadily towards him. He tried to call out "The coffee" as a warning again but now no sound came from his mouth as his lips and vocal cords could no longer move. The last thing he saw was Chapman falling to his knees beside him.

Then everything went black.

CHAPTER 28

Isleworth

Making up part of the slow but steadily moving traffic along Park Road beside Syon Park, a dark blue Porche Cayenne Turbo was heading north, passing the boundary of West Middlesex University Hospital. The car was capable of a top speed of 178 miles per hour and an acceleration of 0 to 60 miles per hour in around 4 seconds but, today, it was being driven at a steady pace, tracking the surrounding vehicles and trying to remain as inconspicuous as possible. The privacy glass that was usually fitted to the rear had been specially upgraded on this vehicle to include the front windows too and the windscreen was directionally highly tinted so it was difficult to see into but allowed perfect outward vision.

Nick Saten was driving the Cayenne with the British Prime Minister, Chayton Jameson, sitting in the passenger seat. In the rear seats, Linda Andrews was tending to David Wilmott's head wound using a medi-kit that was kept in the car. Whilst keeping sight of the traffic ahead, Nick was continually checking his rear view and wing mirrors as well as peering upwards out the windscreen for any signs that the helicopter crew had spotted them.

So far Plan B seemed to be working perfectly. As they were approaching the Isleworth Ait, as soon as they had reached the point where the line of sight to the helicopter had become obstructed by the terrain, Linda had steered the boat sharply across the river to a point in line with the end of the Ait. At this point on the riverside, there was a small mooring area for about half a dozen boats with a small car park beyond it.

Before the trip to the Houses of Parliament, they had driven in two cars, the R8 and the Cayenne, to the car park where they had parked the Cayenne, leaving Wilmott and continuing in the R8 towards Westminster. Wilmott had a mooring for the boat here and had jumped on board and cast off towards Westminster by river having first reserved the mooring space in case they needed to return there.

It was this reserved space at the end of the mooring line that Linda had quickly steered the boat into, deftly controlling the throttle and wheel so that they moored quickly without bumping the moorings and caused only a small swell in the water that was quickly dissipating. Nick had then quickly jumped out and secured the boat so it looked like it had been there a while and then he ushered out Jameson and helped a still-groggy Wilmott out with Linda following to the rear.

They had quickly travelled the few metres to the car parking area where they had got into the Cayenne and had slowly pulled away, joining the modest traffic. This had all taken less than a minute to achieve so, by the time the helicopter had realised they were not exiting the bend in the river past the Isleworth Ait and had flown to investigate, they had effectively disappeared from view.

Nick continued glancing in his mirrors, it couldn't be much longer before the helicopter crew realised what had happened and started searching for them. They had reached a tee junction and were in a short queue of cars waiting to turn left into Twickenham Road when Nick noticed movement high up in his rear-view mirror.

"They're here," he said calmly, keeping sight on the copter in the mirror. "Approaching from behind. Coming slow, checking the vehicles. They must've sussed what we've done. I was hoping it'd take a bit longer before they were searching in the right area for us."

"We should get out. Run for cover," said Jameson looking and sounding nervous.

"No, stay put and keep calm, Sir," said Nick, putting a hand up to indicate quiet. "They don't know what car we're in. They're only guessing at the moment. We're pretty much blacked out in here. They won't be able to see in unless they hover right in front of us and peer through the windscreen which they're unlikely to do unless we look suspicious to them. Many cars have tinted windows nowadays and this blue is popular so we should blend in pretty well."

Whilst keeping the helicopter in sight, Nick angled his vision lower in the mirror so he could see Linda and Wilmott in the rear seats.

"How's he doing?" he asked sounding genuinely concerned.

"I'm doing fine," answered a hoarse-sounding Wilmott. "Thanks for asking."

"Sorry, Dave," said Nick smiling into the mirror, making eye contact with Wilmott. "Didn't know you were still alive."

"Oh, that is nice," said Wilmott pretending to be hurt. "You're now off my Christmas card list."

"Sorry, mate. I wasn't sure you were properly back with us. You were still pretty groggy when we pulled from the boat."

"I'm in good hands back here. Linda has performed her best nursey actions. 'Kin headache and I must look good in a bandage but otherwise okay."

"That's good, mate," said Nick smiling. Then, looking at his mirrors again he added, "Okay, not so good. They've come in low and are using their floodlight to shine into the cars at the back of our queue. I think that light may penetrate the tint on the windows."

"What are we going to do?" asked Jameson. "Move around the queue and make a run for it."

"Not a good idea, Sir. Unless we have to. One, it will give away our position and two, we're in a fast car but the helicopter is capable of outrunning us and so could easily keep us in sight. I'd much prefer we blend in but will take off if we have to and sort out the consequences if necessary."

One car ahead had found room to turn left into the main road, leaving two more ahead of them waiting. Nick kept his eyes on the copter in the mirror.

"They're three cars behind, down low and lighting up the cars like it's daylight inside them."

Nick looked from the cars ahead in line and back to the mirror.

"Two cars behind now. Hang on to something in case I have to speed off; these cars have quite a kick to them."

Another car in front turned left, allowing the waiting queue to move up closer to the junction; only one car in front of the Cayenne now. Nick glanced behind again and saw the copter was looking into the car two behind them now having flown over the one third in line.

Linda was also looking out the rear window at the helicopter.

"They're one car behind now, Nick. This is getting a bit close."

"I know, I know," said Nick edgily, now keeping one eye on the mirror and the other on the traffic ahead.

In his head he was assessing the road sides so he had an idea of how he could use the verges to jump the queue if necessary. Looking back via the mirror he could see the copter was close enough to be able to see its searchlight lighting up the car behind as it was passing over head.

The car in front pulled out into the main road and Nick moved the Cayenne up to the junction waiting for a gap. In the mirror he saw the search light sweeping across the bonnet of the car behind and heading towards the Cayenne.

He started to move his hand on the steering wheel in preparation of having to turn it sharply. Continuous traffic passed across the Cayenne. There was no gap, not even for a fast car to pull out into. If they tried, they would draw too much attention and either give themselves away or, at least, invite further scrutiny.

The searchlight inched nearer to the back of the Cayenne and the cross-traffic on the main road kept coming without a break. Nick nervously glanced from front to back. If he pulled out into traffic and caused another to brake or sound its horn then that would really draw attention to them.

"C'mon, c'mon," he said out loud.

"Nick, the light's touching the boot," said Linda.

"I see it," he replied, still glancing from windscreen to mirror.

"C'mon. Come on!" he shouted.

"It's reached the rear window, Nick. We need to go now!"

"I know. I know," he said. "Working on it!"

The edge of the search light beam was now starting to brighten the inside of the Cayenne as it started to shine onto the edge of the rear seats. Linda and Wilmott leaned forwards keeping themselves out of the beam for a few seconds more.

"Nick....! They're about to see us."

"I see 'em," he replied, riding the brakes, allowing the Cayenne to inch forward closer to the junction boundary lines.

"Surprisingly busy here. Didn't think we'd have trouble at this junction. We may have to make a run for it."

He peered at the cars passing in front, willing them to disappear. Then looked back at the copter which was now filling the rear-view mirror.

"Come on!" he shouted through gritted teeth, his tightened grip on the steering wheel now causing his knuckles to turn white.

"Come on!"

Then there was a gap.

Nick pressed down on the accelerator and the Cayenne moved into the gap in the traffic, quickly matching the speed of the other cars and leaving the searchlight now shining on an empty piece of road. The helicopter also joined the route of the main road as there were no more cars to check at the junction but it was now many cars behind the Cayenne again and checking them was a slower process now as they were moving at speed.

"Jeez!" exclaimed Linda. "That was a bit close."

"Tell me about it," said Nick breathing a sigh of relief.

The traffic on this main road was relatively fast moving so, at the moment, the copter was getting farther back as it had many more vehicles to check. Nick easily kept pace with the other cars and they were now making good progress. In a minute or so they would reach the right turn at a roundabout that would take them onto a dual carriageway where they could increase speed and head towards the M3 motorway and back to base at Southampton.

"Where are they!?" shouted Jenkins through the headset of the helicopter pilot. "How the hell could you lose them? You had them in sight. It's a river for Christ's sake, not a 'kin maze!"

The pilot was suffering a number of emotions at this time. He was angered at losing them on the river, frustrated at not being able to find them again and nervous as to what Jenkins may do to him when he returns to base.

"They had a contingency plan, Sir. They moored at a point in the bend in the river where we were unsighted. It took time to realise what they'd done as they chose a mooring with similar boats. They must've been prepared for this as, in the short time it took us to realise they weren't exiting the bend in the river and then fly there, they had already moored their boat and transferred to a vehicle."

"And where's the fucking vehicle now?" screamed Jenkins.

The pilot swallowed hard.

"We didn't see the car, Sir. So, we're in the process of

examining all vehicles as we fan out from the mooring."

"Don't be so fucking stupid!" shouted Jenkins, his voice booming in the pilot's headset. "They could be in any vehicle on any 'kin road. They're long gone. You lost them and I will not forget this."

The pilot gulped again and tried to keep his voice calm.

"Sir, we had no idea they —"

"Shut up!" interrupted Jenkins with a hysterical scream. "Get your arse back here now and pick me up. I need to get to the airport. Radio ahead and get the Lear jet prepared. No, I'll do that. You just fly me to Diabolus Island in under four hours and you may just redeem yourself."

"Yes Sir," said the pilot. "On our way now."

Jenkins cut off the helicopter and then phoned a number from memory. It answered on the first ring.

"Get to the Lear jet now," said Jenkins hurriedly. "I'll meet you there as soon as I'm picked up. We need to get to Diabolus fast and ramp up production."

The person on the other end of the line acknowledged the instruction and hung up the call. Jenkins now dialled the number of Westminster security. That call was also answered on the first ring.

After identifying himself Jenkins said, "The Prime Minister has been abducted. Nicholas Saten, Linda Andrews and David Wilmott have gone rogue and have disappeared along with the PM. They must be found as a priority. Launch Emergency Protocol Alpha Omega One. The Prime Minister must be found and made safe. For his abductors, Saten, Andrews and Wilmott, you have authority to shoot to kill on sight. I repeat, you are authorised to shoot to kill."

CHAPTER 29

The remainder of the journey back to Southampton was uneventful. After evading the helicopter search in outer London, Nick had driven the Cayenne steadily all the way, ensuring that no speed cameras were triggered nor any possible speed traps were alerted. They hadn't stopped on route and the two marked police cars that they had passed had ignored them, having no reason to be suspicious. Wilmott was making a good recovery from his head wound, the spray plaster being strong enough without the need for stitches and, by the time they had reached the outskirts of Southampton, he was feeling well enough to be complaining about the fuss being made.

After around ninety minutes travelling, they drove into a space in the car park of the Self-Store-It warehouse, Southampton. Nick exited the car first and, confident the coast was clear, waved the others out. They walked into the entrance door doing their best to shield the Prime Minister from view.

"Hmm, that's unusual," said Wilmott as they entered the reception area. "There's no one on the desk."

He looked around the room and found nothing out of order.

"Maybe they're just on a break."

He went over to the desk and swiped his pass through a hidden reader towards the back of the top drawer then placed his thumb on a fingerprint reader that lit up beside it. On the underside of the desk, a small panel slid out revealing a Glock 26 pistol. Wilmott took the Glock and drew back the slide, arming it. "Just in case," he added as he led the way to the lifts.

The quartet entered the lift and Wilmott performed the swipe and fingerprint routine again to reveal the hidden floors and tapped the icon for the office and lab level. As the lift reached its destination the doors opened to reveal the second reception desk which was also unmanned. Wilmott held the Glock facing downwards and quickly glanced left and right out of the lift. Seeing no one he stepped out and motioned the others to follow.

"There's another Glock in a similar location in this desk, Nick."

Nick moved over to the desk and obtained the Glock using his swipe card and moved beside Wilmott so they could cover one another. Nick and Wilmott motioned for Linda and Jameson to stay behind them and they started to move down the corridor towards the labs in a cover and move formation.

They reached Keith's lab room without seeing anything out of order. However, inside a chair was on its side and a couple of coffee cups were on their side on the floor with spilt coffee puddling around them. Keeping silent and communicating only in signs, Nick and Wilmott searched the lab finding no one in there. Nick held up his hand to indicate Linda to stay in Keith's lab with the PM as he and Wilmott moved on to search the other rooms on that level. As they reached the farthest lab, Wilmott took up covering position at the doorway and Nick entered, gun at the ready. He stood there surveying the room for a few seconds and motioned for Wilmott to remain where he was and continue covering.

Nick knew there was something wrong in this room. Whether it was like a sixth sense, intuition or just down to experience he didn't know but he did know something was wrong. He intensified his visual scrutiny. Everything seemed to look okay. No, in fact that wasn't the case. At the far end of the room, beyond the final benches, there was a faint variation to the shadow on the floor, as if someone or something was blocking one path of light. It was unmoving but didn't look right compared to the other rows of benches.

He motioned to Wilmott to stay where he was and to continue to cover him. He crept forward towards the end bench, Glock outstretched, watching the unmoving faint shadow and the area of the bench above it, ready to react to any movement. He moved slowly across the floor, making no noise, ensuring as much as possible that he kept the bulk of a bench between him and the space at the end of the room. His pulse quickened and a few beads of sweat ran down his temples – this was the point at which an unknown assailant or assailants could move from the cover of the far benches and take him out. However, there was no going back now – he'd crossed the line of safety so may as well continue. After all, he thought to himself, he had Wilmott as cover at the door.

He arrived at the near side of the bench and still there had been no movement from the shadowed area. His heightened senses told him that there was definitely someone there.

Did they know he was on to them? Were they waiting for him to show himself? It was now or never.

Glock extended, finger on the trigger pressing slightly so a shot could be quickly taken, Nick leaped around the bench, aiming where he estimated the torso of a hiding person would be –

And he stopped, shoulders dropping slightly in a show of grief.

On the floor, behind the bench were the two

receptionists and two lab assistants all dead on the floor, bullet wounds to each temple and pools of blood around their heads where they lay. The gun man or men could still be around so the professional in him still ensured he checked the surrounding area was clear before waving Wilmott over.

Wilmott walked over to be beside Nick.

"What is it, mate?"

Then he saw the lifeless bodies lying on the floor.

"Shit!" he exclaimed quietly as he looked around the room. "How the hell did they find us, Nick?"

"Haven't a clue, Dave," said Nick still surveying the area. "And where's Keith and Tony? I expected them to be here at this time."

"I dunno, mate," added Wilmott. "This isn't good. Not good at all."

They searched the rest of the level, finding no further bodies or signs of upheaval and made their way back to Linda and Jameson in Keith's lab. Wilmott quickly logged into the network using Keith's terminal making a few mouse clicks.

"That's this level locked down, secure, in case the hostiles are on another level. No sign that they're still here though."

"Did you find anyone?" asked Linda.

"The techies and reception staff are dead," Nick replied. "All shot through the head."

"Jeez!" Linda said. "What about Keith and Tony? Them as well?"

"No, not them, Lin. No sign of either of them."

"Look at this," cried Wilmott, waving everyone over to the screen on Keith's desk. "I've quickly run the CCTV playback and found something."

Once everyone was looking at the monitor, Wilmott tapped the play key to start the video running.

"I've looked through the multiple screens and nothing seems to be happening apart from in this lab."

On the screen a view of the room from one corner was displayed. Keith was sitting at his desk as Chapman came into view with a small tray with two coffee cups. Keith took one of the cups and both men drank. Soon afterwards Keith then rose from his chair clutching at his head, staggered and collapsed to the floor. Chapman then made similar motions a few seconds after. The screen then went blank.

"That's it," said Wilmott. "There's no further recording after what we've just seen. Someone's gone in and cut the recording and erased everything from the reception cameras and all data from Keith's lab camera from the point they fall over."

"I didn't think that could be done," said Linda with a puzzled look.

"In theory it shouldn't be possible, especially with the system we have" added Wilmott. "Whoever doctored the recordings knew what they were doing."

"Jenkins must be behind this," Linda speculated.

"Well, he has enough people at his disposal," Wilmott added. "Who knows how many he and this Caymes bloke have on side and, if he declared it a national security matter, he could even involve those not on their side."

"So, what do we do now?" Linda asked to all present.

"I think we carry on as planned," said Nick. "We make our way to this Diabolus Island and do our best to stop Caymes from going any further."

"Agreed," said Wilmott.

"And," continued Nick, "we don't know if Keith and Tony are still alive or have any idea where they are at the moment. The fact that they're not here suggests they may have been taken. So, the best way to save them, if we can, is to stop Caymes."

"Agreed again," said Wilmott.

"Seconded," said Linda.

Nick turned to the Prime Minister. "Sir, we have no way of telling, in the short term at least, who is and isn't on side with us. So, the best way to protect you at the moment, is for you to stay with us."

"Agreed," said Wilmott and Jameson at the same time.

"Here, here," added Linda smiling. "It's beginning to sound like a Parliamentary debate."

"Yes, but without the argument," added Jameson smiling too. "But, how do we get to this island if we cannot involve other national bodies?"

"Good point," said Wilmott adding, "but I still have a few old contacts I can use, calling in a few favours. Leave it with me, I'll get on to it now."

With that, he strolled over to a corner of the lab already tapping out a number on his smart phone.

"Meanwhile," said Nick, "Linda, you go to the armoury and start kitting us out ready for the journey. I'll stay here with the PM and go through the CCTV recording again to see if there are any backups that have been missed."

Linda headed off towards the armoury, and Nick sat at Keith's desk running through the CCTV backup systems in the hope that something would give an extra clue as to what went on.

As Linda, Nick, Wilmott and Jameson were preparing to move out from Southampton, at an airfield outside London, Jenkins and his chief security officer and pilot, Tucker, were disturbed by the bleeping of Tucker's phone. He tapped his earpiece to answer the call, listened for a few moments and then requested the caller to hold.

"Sir," he said with a relieved tone, "we have a report that the PM, Saten and Andrews have been spotted entering a Self-Store-It warehouse in Southampton."

"Southampton?" questioned Jenkins. "Is this report likely to be accurate?"

"Caller is reliable, Sir. And the description of persons appears to be accurate."

"Okay," said Jenkins quickly adding, "mobilise units down there. Remember, the PM must be saved if at all possible. The others I don't care about."

"Yes sir," said Tucker tapping his earpiece back online from being on hold. "Yes, authority granted to mobilise to the site. Rescue the main subject as a priority. Residual subjects do not need to be taken alive. Authority for the kill shot is green. Go, go, go!"

Fifteen minutes after setting out from Keith's lab, Linda returned from the armoury having selected a range of weapons and gadgets she thought would help if they ran into trouble. Wilmott was still in the corner of the room chatting on his phone and Nick was still studying the playback from the CCTV. She looked around the room once again.

"Where's the PM?" she asked in a worried tone.

Nick looked up from the monitor and gazed around the room.

"Oh, he's still not back. He … er… went to the … er…"

His stammering was interrupted by the sound of a cistern flushing coming from the toilets two doors down.

"Ah, that's where he is. Fair enough. In fact, seems like a good idea. Maybe we should all follow suit. You never know when we're get the next chance."

"You may be right, Lin," Nick murmured. "Might as well as I'm getting nothing exciting from re-watching these videos."

He turned off the video playback leaving the live CCTV feed on the display.

"Okay we're sorted," Wilmott said as he ended his call and returned from the corner of the room. "We can get to Southampton Airport and fly out to the Canaries and pick up a boat from there. Once we've loaded up the car and then driven to the airport, a private jet will be waiting for us."

"I'm impressed," Linda muttered, smiling. "Just how many people do you know?"

"Well, you know what they say. It's not what you know or who you know. It's what you know about who you know that makes the difference."

"I won't ask how you know what you know about who you know," added Linda smiling.

"We've got company!" shouted Nick sounding alarmed.

"Company?" asked Linda and Wilmott together.

"Yep, live CCTV feed shows a vehicle arriving at the front entrance and uniformed, armed guards alighting from them. Can't see any insignias on their outfits again. Don't think they're here for a friendly chat."

"How did they know we were back here?" asked Linda.

"They're either returning on the off chance that we may have turned up or there are bugs planted here that we haven't swept for yet."

"Whether they know we're here or not, they're coming in," stated Wilmott. "Time we were off."

"Another vehicle arriving," added Nick. They've got the car park covered. We're not getting out of here quietly."

"We may have a chance," said Wilmott as he watched the events on the monitor. "In order to keep these levels secret during the initial build, there's a link from the multi-storey car park next door to a small loading/unloading car park on the upper hidden level of this building. It allowed us to bring in all the equipment unseen from the storage side. That's why there's a multi-storey car park beside each Self-Store-It warehouse. It's not known by as many people as it's only used for the 'special' deliveries and emergencies; our visitors may not know to look out for it. It may give us the edge to get back to the car with less hostiles to contend with."

"But we can't load the weapons I selected," complained Linda. "We can't carry them all in one journey."

"I suggest," continued Wilmott, "that we each take a Glock loaded with the armour-piercing ammo, some spare clips and a TASER. Where possible we can use the TASER as it'll be silent and won't attract the attention of others."

"Okay, let's go before they reach these levels," suggested Nick, turning to Jameson and adding, "Sir, you stay between

Linda and me." The PM said nothing and just nodded so Nick finished by saying, "Lead the way, Dave."

Wilmott took one last look at the CCTV feed on the monitor.

"It looks like they're not coming straight down to these hidden levels. They're searching the storage levels and no-one has so far accessed the secret levels in the lifts. That may buy us a little more time."

Nick added, "But somebody must know about this area. We have a number of bodies in the lab to vouch for that."

"True," agreed Wilmott, "but no-one's coming this way as yet. Let's use the advantage while we have it." Wilmott led them to the armoury, keeping slow and quiet in case any hostiles had reached the hidden levels. They didn't encounter anyone on-route and so, as suggested, Wilmott, Linda and Nick grabbed a Glock and a TASER each, along with spare clips for the Glocks and spare battery packs for the TASERS.

Being a non-public facing branch of MI6, they had access to the latest technology weapons and the ammunition for the Glocks and the TASERS were no exceptions. The 9mm rounds for the Glocks were made with a hardened core and a special mixture of propellent which allowed them to defeat body armour and helmets at a range of 75 metres. The TASERS were still in the experimental stage and, so far, had not been issued to any law enforcement agencies worldwide. Where conventional TASERS carried their stunning bolt of energy through thin wires fired at the target, these ones fired a line of ionising particles creating a charge path in the air that the energy bolt could travel to its target. They were as effective as conventional TASERS at a range of 50 metres and, due to there being no wires, had the advantage of being multi-shot. The ionising function meant the battery packs were slightly larger but the rest of the TASER looked much like its predecessor.

Equipped with their weapons, they followed Wilmott through a hidden doorway within the armoury that led to the small loading/unloading car park. At the far side of the area was a set of double doors marked 'Generator – 3 Phase. Beware 400V. Authorised personnel only'. They looked old and unused but opened on well-oiled hinges without a sound. There was no generator beyond the doors, just a corridor.

"This leads to an identical set of doors in the car park next door," said Wilmott quietly. "I suspect we'll have some company beyond them so be prepared when we reach them."

He didn't wait for any acknowledgements, just carried on down the corridor as faint LED lighting systems automatically detected them and lit up a few metres ahead of where they were.

It didn't take long for them to reach the other end of the corridor. There they gathered by the double doors.

"I hope these are as well-oiled as the others," said Nick as he gripped the handle.

He turned it gently, ready to react quickly if it made any noise. It was, however, well maintained like its counterpart at the other end of the corridor and made no noise as he opened it slightly so that he could look through the small gap. He pushed the door to close the gap and turned back to the others.

"I can see four," he said in a hushed voice. "Two standing by the exit and two searching through the parked cars – not that there's many of them. They've started with the ones farthest from here. They presumably still don't know what car we are driving. We've only got the three TASERS so I suggest we move in and you two take one each of the ones at the exit and I'll go for the two searching."

"Before we go," cut in Wilmott quietly, "in the space facing the exit is another Cayenne. A black one this time. It's ours so we can head for that rather than get back to the storage car park. I've got the key with me but it's keyless entry anyway so, when we get there, any of us can start and drive it."

"You're full of surprises, Dave," said Nick adding, "So, same take down plan but meet by the black Cayenne."

He turned to Jameson finishing with, "Sir, you keep right behind us, stay down below the cars and get in the rear seat when you can. Okay all, let's go."

Nick inched the door open again and peered through. The two guards were still stationery at the exit and the other two had moved on searching other cars but were still on the far side of the car park to the door. Nick opened the door wide enough for him to slip through and, picking his moment when all the guards were looking the other way, he silently darted across to the nearest car and crouched down beside it out of sight. He held up the palm of his hand towards the doorway signalling everyone to stay there and stole a glance through the car window. When the guards were facing away again, he waved his hand and Linda ran out at a crouch to join him. He did this manoeuvre two more times so that now all four of them were crouched beside the car. He pointed a finger to himself and then two towards the two guards who were searching then moved the two fingers to Linda and Wilmott and then to the other guards at the exit. He finished by making the okay sign with his hand and, after receiving the same in response from Linda and Wilmott, he moved off at a crouch keeping within the cover of the parked cars. Linda and Wilmott stayed crouching and moved off slowly from car to car, making their way nearer to the two guards at the exit, signalling for Jameson to follow low when safe.

The exit was open to the outside and the guards searching were not doing it quietly which made it easier for Nick, Linda, Wilmott and Jameson to move around without being heard. However, the nearer they all got to the guards the quieter they needed to be. As they all neared their targets Jameson stood on a small stone creating a slight grinding sound, just loud enough to be heard over the ambient noise.

Instinctively Nick froze on hearing the sound then

ducked down lower for cover. He was now only two car widths away from the searching guards but could no longer glance up to see them for fear they had turned to see what had made the noise. Linda had dragged Jameson down behind a car nearer to the exit and she could still see the two searching guards so signalled, palm up, to Nick for him to remain still.

Nick remained crouched behind a car listening for the guards' footsteps. He had his TASER ready but, not knowing exactly where his targets were, he had no idea whether he would be able to hit both of them before one could fire back. He kept low, hugging the side of the car, listening to the footsteps getting closer. Linda continued signalling for him to remain where he was but he could see that she was beginning to feel concerned. He was concerned too. Even if he could hit the two guards near to him, were the others in a position to take out the two near the exit.

The two searching guards had heard the grinding noise and had changed course to investigate, walking slowly towards the car where Nick was sheltering, assault rifles at the ready. Nick kept crouched down, willing for the them turn away. He looked across to Linda and could see that she seemed a bit calmer now; he could tell she had a plan.

Linda made a series of hand signals at Nick, first indicating she was using the car she was behind as a template for his one. She then pointed at angles to two areas beyond the car, giving Nick a clue as to where the two guards were in relation to him. She then gave a gesture with both hands indicating distance, then pointed to her feet and held up all fingers from one hand and one from the other indicating a distance of around 6 feet. She then gestured to herself and Wilmott and then over to the exit, giving the thumbs up indicating they were ready to go. She then made an 'okay' symbol with her hand and Nick returned the same.

The searching guards were now nearing the car Nick was sheltering behind, their footsteps sounding like they were now beside him. It was now or never. He held his TASER ready for firing and, with his other hand, he held up three fingers towards Linda and Wilmott and visibly counted down.

Two…

One…

Zero.

Nick jumped up, surprising the nearby guards. It was that moment of surprise that gave him the advantage. In that split second it took for them to regain composure, Nick had assessed where the two of them were. He brought up his TASER, lined up with one guard's neck and head area and he pulled the trigger. In a matter of milliseconds there was a slight crackle as a charge of around 30 thousand volts transferred along a path of ionised air, virtually invisible, hitting the guard and causing him to fall to the ground completely immobilised.

The advantage of the new TASERS immediately became evident at this point as, with previous models, Nick would have had to keep the TASER pointed at the target and the thin conducting wires would still have been connected to the weapon. With the new cordless version, Nick was able to immediately change his aim to the second guard and fire again with similar results. This had taken place in the space of around a second so neither of the searching guards had had the time to react to Nick's appearance before they were TASERED.

However, the two guards at the exit had seen what was going on and had started to react, bringing their weapons up towards Nick's direction. He was in the open with no cover nearby. If they got their shots on target, he would be going down.

Following the countdown reaching zero, Linda and Wilmott had remained hidden for the time it took Nick to fire his first shot. That gave enough time for the exit guards to have their attention diverted to Nick's direction. At that moment, Linda and Wilmott also jumped up and, having already decided who was aiming for which guard, they fired off their TASERS, hitting the targets, causing them both to fall to the ground, shocked and incapable of any voluntary movement.

Linda and Wilmott raced over to the Cayenne, picking up the fallen guards' weapons on the way, dragging the Prime Minister with them; there was no time at the moment for pleasantries. Nick joined them moments later and they all jumped into the vehicle, Nick driving with Wilmott in the passenger seat and Linda and Jameson in the back. Nick hit the start button and the engine roared into life. He selected 'sport mode' on the auto selector and floored the accelerator. The Cayenne sped off, straight out the exit, its traction control allowing maximum acceleration with minimum wheel spin, pinning the passengers against the back of their seats. It sped out onto the road still accelerating as Nick steered it left having spotted a number of guards standing beside a Range Rover Sport a hundred metres or so to the right.

"They've spotted us," shouted Linda. "They're getting into the car."

"I see 'em," Nick replied as he eyed them in the rear-view mirror. "When they get close, shoot out their tyres, Lin. I'll slow down a little to let them catch up a bit."

"Don't worry about that," cut in Wilmott as he tapped out a message on his smart phone. "I'll handle them when they get closer. Leave them to me."

No one commented on Wilmott's offer, trusting in his confidence.

"You concentrate on getting us to Southampton Airport, Nick. I've messaged the ground crew and the plane will be ready for us on arrival."

"Okay boss," said Nick as he kept one eye on the road and the other on the mirror. "At this speed they'll be catching us pretty quick."

"That's fine," said Wilmott as he moved so he could see behind via the wing mirror.

Traffic was almost non-existent at this time on the roads

out of Southampton so the Range Rover driver had no problems in catching up with the Porsche at the speed it was going. Two of the passengers wound down their windows and drew their assault rifles, aiming at the Cayenne. They both fired simultaneously on full auto, causing the few other cars to either veer off or brake sharply to avoid the confrontation. Three of the rounds hit the rear window of the Cayenne, creating indents in the glass rather than smashing through.

"Bullet proof glass?" Nick smiled, glancing at Wilmott. "What next? Smoke screen or oil from the rear?"

"Better than that," chuckled Wilmott. He placed a finger on a hidden print reader on the touch screen on the dashboard bringing up a keypad and a four-digit pin input screen. He tapped in four numbers, then placed another finger on the print reader and a new set of icons appeared. One icon was entitled "Spikes" and showed a small picture of a three-pronged spike. He hovered his finger over the icon and looked again at the wing mirror. The Range Rover was gaining, the driver going flat out to catch up with the Cayenne and Wilmott could see the two shooters preparing to fire again.

"Duck!" shouted Linda as she peered out of the rear window. "They're about to fire again."

Wilmott tapped on the icon on the touch screen and a compartment in the rear bumper opened. From the opening a large quantity of razor-sharp, three-pronged, triangular spikes fell out and scattered across the road behind the Porsche. The Range Rover driver spotted the spikes falling and jammed his foot on the brake pedal but the car was too close and going too fast to stop before reaching them. It drove across the scattered spikes, many of them cutting deep into the tyres causing all four to blow out simultaneously. The driver fought with the steering wheel but couldn't stop the Range Rover from veering out of control across the road and smashing hard into a parked car. All the airbags in the vehicle deployed preventing major injuries to the occupants but, none of them were wearing seatbelts, so they were still considerably jostled around inside the cabin. The front of the vehicle was damaged the most, causing the radiator to be crushed and scalding steam to erupt from the exposed pipes. The crumple zones of the vehicle were overcome due to the speed of the impact, distorting the chassis and side pillars. The vehicle would not be going anywhere soon. Though cushioned, the guards were still stunned by the force of the impact so, by the time they recovered and gingerly climbed out of the window cavities, the Cayenne was nowhere in sight.

The passengers of the Cayenne saw this taking place, Nick and Wilmott in the mirrors, Linda and Jameson through the rear window.

"Impressive," said Nick slowing down a little now they didn't have anyone chasing them. "What else have you got on that screen?"

"I'll have to brief you on that one of these days," replied Wilmott. "For now, though, let's get to the airport and head off."

The road they were now on was long and straight and Nick could see that some of the few other cars on the road had stopped and someone was standing and making a phone call.

"Emergency services are probably on their way," he added. "Someone's phoning back there."

"Let's keep to the speed limits now then," said Wilmott cautiously. "We don't want to attract any more attention to ourselves as we don't know who's on our side or not."

Nick slowed down to within the limits and the rest of the journey to Southampton Airport was quiet and uneventful. They arrived there ten minutes later and, with Wilmott showing his credentials and his advanced preparation messaging allowing them to be expected, they were guided straight through to park up beside a Learjet 75. As they boarded the aircraft Wilmott headed for the cockpit while the others surveyed the plush interior of the latest plane that Bombardier produce.

Capable of sitting up to nine passengers in extreme comfort, with Honeywell engines that generate 3,850 lbf of thrust, the Learjet 75 can travel at a top speed of Mach 0.81 at a maximum altitude of 51,000 feet and has a maximum range of 2,080 nautical miles. The cabin has a private, quiet executive suite where conversations can take place with minimal noise disturbance. It was in this room that the four passengers were meeting, Wilmott having got there following a final briefing with the pilot.

"Strap yourselves in," he said whilst doing so himself. "The pilot says we'll be taking off in a few moments."

By the time they had sat down and clicked on their seat belts, the plane was taxiing towards the end of the runway. As soon as they had turned in line for take-off, the pilot announced that clearance had been granted, seatbelts should be fastened and they should prepare for immediate take off. He then powered the aircraft along the runway forcing the four passengers back into their seats, eased back on the yoke and the Learjet 75 soared into the air, banking towards the Isle of Wight and then levelling out in the direction of the Channel Islands.

It wasn't long before the pilot announced they had reached cruising altitude and that they could remove their seatbelts and sit back and enjoy the next four hours and thirty minutes of the flight. Now, the three agents visibly relaxed a little, thinking they were relatively safe whilst in the air. However, the Prime Minister still looked tense.

"Nervous passenger, Sir?" asked Linda, smiling politely.

"A little," replied Jameson trying to return the smile. "It's just the events of the past few hours catching up."

"Just relax now if you can," she continued. "I suspect we'll have a bit of a de-briefing in a few minutes." That triggered nods from Nick and Wilmott. "For the moment, I spy some bottles over there. Would you like a drink, Sir?" she added as she headed for the drinks cabinet. "That goes for you too," she said looking towards Nick and Wilmott.

"Erm, a G and T please if poss," said Jameson.

"Scotch on the rocks for me," said Wilmott.

"If it's there, Irish whiskey for me please," said Nick. "And have one for yourself too, waitress," he added smiling.

"Oh, very funny," she said playfully giving him the middle finger sign.

"That's right," he said smiling and returning the middle finger salute. "Just the one." He then changed his hand to produce a vee sign adding, "Not two."

That broke the tension in the room and, once drinks were poured for all, they swivelled the seats around and pulled out a table so they were now two to a side facing each other.

"So, now we're in the air, "said Wilmott, "it's time we had a de-brief about what's gone on and, more importantly for the time being, what we're going to do when we get to the island."

Linda spoke up first. "Well, I don't think we really know all that's going on." That received nods of agreement. "We do know they're making picobots as weapons but we don't know what they intend to do with them. We know they're manufacturing them on Diabolus Island and we know the person on the inside is your Private Secretary," she looked towards Jameson, "but we have no idea about his boss, this Caymes bloke."

"Jonathon Caymes," added Nick, continuing, "I've tried to look him up and there seems to be no records of his existence on our databases or on the internet in general."

"I've done a secure database search for him too," said Wilmott, "and, other than the data that Keith had discovered and entered, there's nothing. "And that's another thing," Wilmott continued, "we assume from the video that Keith and Tony have been captured. Their bodies weren't at the storage facility, so I'm assuming they were taken. If these people want their coding or these bots re-programmed then they couldn't've picked two better computer geeks to assist. So, I'm hoping we'll find Caymes,

Keith and Tony on this island and find a way to stop production of these bots."

"And I take it," Nick added, "this orthotope thing that started this whole thing going, is to power these picobots and we don't know if they've been successful in developing this superconductivity any further."

"Spot on," said Wilmott. "Hopefully they've either not got further with that or they're developing that on the island too as we don't have any other known locations for them; what we know from the encrypted USB is all we know."

"That sums up the past," Jameson spoke up for the first time since they sat down. "Now we need to know how we're going to go forward. How are we going to get to this island and stop these people?"

Nick spoke again. "We have no layout of the island nor the buildings on it so, I can only suggest we go in the front entrance and knock on the door – well, maybe blow the door down if necessary. Well, seriously, I think we're going to have to think on our feet as we go. We don't know the extent of the guards on the island nor how many people are working there. We can only assume they will be heavily armed so, will have to go in stealthily until we're ready to pounce.

"I suggest we travel as close as we dare by motor yacht then either swim in or make our final few hundred metres by inflatable. Whichever we feel is best at the time; we need to finalise our plans when we see exactly what we are up against."

"Yes, agreed," said Wilmott. "Not the greatest of plans, if you can call it a plan at all, but it's the best we can do. We need to get in there as quickly as possible not knowing how soon they intend to use these things in anger.

"We're landing in Lanzarote and transferring to La Villa Lujosa, a private villa in the south on the hills of Playa Blanca. You can stay there, Sir," he continued looking at Jameson, "as we can't risk you coming along to the island." He then addressed the others. "I've not seen it but I'm told it's a location of ours so is kitted with what we need to go in aggressively. I've got the SATNAV coordinates for it so we can get there easily. There's a track leading down the hillside to a private beach where there'll be a boat there to take us to the island when we're ready."

"Sounds good to me," said Nick adding, "Well, don't know about you lot, but I'm gonna put my head down for a few hours and see if I can get some sleep while I've got the chance."

"Agreed said Linda," as she spied agreeing nods from Wilmott and Jameson. "Maybe we can formulate more of a plan in our sleep."

They all swivelled their chairs around to be facing the front of the aircraft and then tilted them so they were near horizontal. From a cabinet at one side of the room Wilmott produced a blanket for each of them and they all laid back and covered themselves. Now it had been mentioned, they all realised they'd had no sleep for a while and, within minutes, they had drifted off.

CHAPTER 30

Nick came to as his subconscious registered the jet engines reducing in power and the aircraft commencing its descent. He glanced around the cabin and noticed that Linda and Wilmott were also stirring. Jameson was already awake and was tapping on his smart phone. Seeing Nick's quizzical look, he gestured towards his phone.

"Couldn't keep asleep. Thought I'd go through my old emails to keep me occupied. Didn't want to wake anybody."

Nick smiled and was about to reply when the pilot's voice came over the PA system announcing they would be landing in ten minutes and that seat belts should be fastened.

"Nothing from Jenkins I presume?" he asked.

"Erm, no, nothing" Jameson replied. "All boring stuff I'm afraid."

They all belted up and looked out the windows as the aircraft banked around Playa Blanca then straightened out to be flying in line with Lanzarote's southerly coast line. Descending, the plane passed the many motor yachts moored at Puerto Calero Marina then on past the white hotels of Puerto del Carmen and then the long sandy beach of Los Pocillos before landing at Arrecife Airport, the

Aeropuerto de Lanzarote. It quickly slowed and then taxied a short way off the runway where it came to a stop.

Nick was up and opening the main door before the others had removed their seatbelts.

"I bet you're one of those holiday passengers that remove their seatbelt before the seatbelt sign has been switched off and get on all the other passengers' nerves," said Linda playfully, receiving another one-fingered sign in reply and a smile.

As he lowered the door for it to form into the steps, Nick could see beside the aircraft was another Cayenne.

"Just how many of these cars have you got?" he asked looking back at Wilmott.

"They're damn fine cars," said Wilmott smiling. "So why not have one in every port."

"I thought that supposed to be a girl in every port," said Linda, smiling.

"I tried that and found Porsches were cheaper," responded Wilmott, also smiling.

They boarded the Cayenne, this time with Wilmott driving, Linda in the passenger seat and Nick and Jameson in the back.

"We've been pre-cleared at immigration," mentioned Wilmott casually. "We have special diplomatic clearances. Well, the PM had it anyway, so I thought I'd bump up ours to be the same. That way they didn't have to find out just yet that you're on the island, Sir."

"Fast cars in every port and the jump on customs and immigration," smiled Nick. "You have some big friends in high places, Dave."

"No point having connections and not taking advantage," replied Wilmott laughing.

With that he started the Cayenne, programmed the SATNAV and drove off and out of the airport, on to the LZ-2, heading in the direction of Playa Blanca. The journey lasted around 30 minutes and the roads were very quiet once they were a couple of kilometres away from the airport so they were all relaxed as the SATNAV announced the turning to the villa was approaching.

As the Cayenne turned onto the private driveway, they could see a sturdy metal gate about 100 metres ahead. As the car approached, the gates opened automatically, triggered by a sensor in the Porsche, and once through, they automatically closed sealing them from the outside world. They drove for another 100 or so metres and arrived at a large, modern-looking villa, duplex in style with large glass concertina doors on the ground floor and balconies leading from the bedrooms on the first floor. There was space for about five or six cars at the front and Wilmott chose the one nearest to the front door.

They all exited the car, stretching as they stood on the gravel drive, the contrast from the cool air-conditioned interior of the Cayenne to the thirty-degree heat in the sun causing their clothes to cling to their skin.

"We'll soon get the air-conditioning on inside," said Wilmott leading the way to the front door, "then we can get to our rooms and freshen up. I could certainly do with a shower."

"You certainly could," said Nick laughing.

They were all smiling as Wilmott took out his ID card and swiped it across a small receiver beside the door. A couple of clicks could be heard as the locks disengaged and he pushed the door open ushering them all inside. Last in, he closed the door behind him and tapped a couple of buttons on the wall-mounted control unit, switching the air-conditioning system on. They all walked through the main entrance hall, into the lounge area and –

Six people in combat outfits faced them, pointing assault rifles in their direction.

"Stay where you are!" shouted the one with 'Alpha' written on his helmet. "Arms in the air and quiet."

Nick spun around, prepared to lead the others back through the front door at a sprint, to find it opening again and another half-dozen armed people entering to cut them off. He turned back to face the others and raised his arms, gesturing for the others to do the same.

"How did they know we'd be here?" asked Linda quietly.

"We received a message," said a familiar voice, "giving us notice of where and when you would be. So, we then thought we'd arrange a welcoming party for you."

The speech came from the person entering the front door. As he entered in to the hallway the effect of the sunlight behind him, causing a silhouette, faded and the familiar form of Kit Jenkins came into view.

"Shit!" said Wilmott under his breath.

"I heard that," said Jenkins. "Surprised to find us here ahead of you? It helps to be on the inside."

"Who told you about this place?" demanded Wilmott. "This is… was top secret."

"It was our mysterious Mr. Caymes if you must know," volunteered Jenkins. "He passed me all the details."

"But how did he know?" mumbled Wilmott under his breath.

Jameson took a step forward and directed his voice towards the combat team.

"I think we've heard enough from Mr. Jenkins now," he said with a calm authority. "I'd like to take over at this point."

"And I'd like you to shut the fuck up and do as you're told like the rest of your pals," said Jenkins confidently. "You're not in charge here, Jameson."

The Prime Minister stood his ground against the words from Jenkins and was about to start speaking again.

"Mr. Prime Minister," cut in Linda, raising her hand slightly to delay him speaking. "I don't think we're in the ideal position to issue instructions at the moment."

"Quite correct Ms. Andrews," added Jenkins with a smug grin as he looked around at the combat team. "I'm the one issuing the orders here."

"No, you don't understand, Mr. Jenkins," continued Jameson, still calm. "Perhaps I said it wrong before." It was

Jameson's turn for the smug grin. "When I said I would like to take over, I meant I am taking over at this point."

The combat team continued to train their assault rifles on Linda, Nick and Wilmott but the ones that were pointing towards Jameson turned and now pointed at Jenkins.

"What the fucks going on?" shouted Jenkins, the smug grin being replaced by a puzzled, nervous expression.

"Shut up, Jenkins!" shouted Jameson as he walked over to be beside the man with 'Alpha' on his helmet.

A mixture of confusion and a hint of realisation was appearing on the face of Wilmott.

"You don't seem surprised that we were ambushed, Sir," he said in a curious tone. "How did you know? I had received no intel on this happening."

"I knew we would be ambushed," Jameson laughed. "I knew because I arranged for it to happen, you idiot." He laughed again, louder than before. "I've been in control here the whole time." He gestured to the second six-man combat team. "Tie them up and sit them in the lounge out of reach of each other."

The combat team immediately sprang into action, producing thick tie wraps which they placed around the wrists of Linda, Nick and Wilmott, then sat them on the floor as instructed. Jenkins was still looking confused but didn't say anything as Alpha's assault rifle was aimed at his head. Alpha kept his assault rifle moving from Jenkins to the DAHRT team as he waited for further instructions from Jameson.

"Move them down to the boat a soon as possible so we can get on our way to the island, said Jameson. "We have no time to waste."

"You want them kept alive?" asked Alpha seeming surprised.

"Yes, for the moment. They may be good motivational tools to get other people working to full capacity."

"If you're sure," said Alpha.

"Sure?" shouted Jameson. "Are you questioning my

orders?"

"No, Sir," said Alpha sheepishly. "Just making sure I understood correctly."

"Well, now you do," said Jameson menacingly. "Now get them to the fucking boat and no more pissing around!"

"Yes sir," said Alpha, gesturing to his men to carry out the orders. "Right away, Mr. Caymes."

A further hush came over the almost silent room as Linda, Nick, Wilmott and also Jenkins realised the truth – Chayton Jameson, the Prime Minister of the United Kingdom, elected by the populace, was the mysterious Jonathon Caymes.

CHAPTER 31

The silence was broken by Jenkins. "You are Jonathon Caymes," he said sounding amused.

"Yes, that's right," laughed Caymes. "Under your noses all the time and no-one realised."

"You are Caymes," Jenkins repeated. "I shared office space with you. I sneaked through old wings of Westminster to take calls from you. Actioned some vicious orders from you whilst, much of the time, sitting opposite you in your office. And you never told me you were Caymes."

"I couldn't reveal my identity," said Caymes, walking over to Jenkins then turning so he faced his captive audience.

"I took a risk inventing the name," he continued, theatrically. "Using the letters in 'Chayton Jameson' to create 'Jonathon Caymes' was risky but fun. If anyone had worked it out, we would've soon had them eliminated."

"Glad I'm no good at anagrams then," said Linda aggressively.

"Would you have got this one," said Nick. "ing-fuck-case-nut."

"Oh, that one's easy," smiled Linda. "It's fu¬¬ –"

"Shut up!" shouted Caymes. "You think you're funny

but I'm the one who should be laughing. Once you have served your purpose on the island, you people are dead."

"Y, you're not including me in that statement, are you?" said Jenkins nervously.

"No, of course not," replied Caymes, smiling. Jenkins relaxed a little and responded with a slight smile. "No, you've served your purpose already." Caymes nodded at Alpha. "Has his DNA been programmed?"

"Yes Mr. Caymes," Alpha replied.

"Okay, go ahead," instructed Caymes.

"W, what's happening?" stuttered Jenkins as Alpha took out a small metal box from inside his combat vest.

"N, no. What are you doing? I can still help you."

"You've made too many mistakes recently," explained Caymes. "Anyway, you're still helping. You are about to be involved in a very important experiment."

"N, no, please," Jenkins begged.

Alpha looked over to Caymes who gave a slight nod. Alpha pressed a release catch on the underside of the box and a lid on the top sprung open. Immediately a grey cloud emerged from the box and started to spread out around the room, heading towards each person there. The slightly dispersed cloud reached Alpha and headed for his face. Parts of the cloud reached other members of the combat team and then Linda, Nick, Wilmott and Caymes.

Other than a slight irritation from where the cloud remained around the eyes, nose, mouth and ears, it didn't seem to be bothering those people. When the cloud reach Jenkins, the initial moment of irritation changed to pain as more and more of it entered his eyes, nose, mouth and ears. At the same time, the parts of the cloud that had spread to the other occupants in the room, floated away from them and headed towards Jenkins. In a matter of seconds, the cloud seemed to have moved around all the people in the room and had singled out Jenkins. Now the whole cloud had surrounded him as more and more of it entered his orifices. The pain was excruciating and Jenkins screamed and jerked his body violently as he tried to free himself from the ordeal.

Linda, Nick and Wilmott stared in horror as they watched Jenkins writhing and grimaced as his screams echoed around the room. The combat troops looked on uneasily knowing they dare not say or do anything for fear they may get the same treatment; some of them had seen similar things happen before.

With one final gut-wrenching shriek, Jenkins went quiet and slumped to the ground, dead. Seconds later, the cloud exited from his eyes, nose, mouth and ears, leaving a small trickle of blood from each location and quickly drifted back to the metal container. Once the cloud had settled back into the box, Alpha pressed the catch and the lid closed, sealing it in.

"My god!" breathed Linda. "That's inhuman."

"Yes, Miss Andrews," goaded Caymes, "I suppose, technically, you are correct. There was no human input to that."

"You're sick," she continued, unable to help herself from commenting.

"Sick!" yelled Caymes. "You call me sick. Oh no, I disagree. It takes a leader to make these tough decisions."

"And what," she added, "allows a leader to afflict torture upon another person?"

Caymes was becoming visibly angry the more Linda continued but his arrogance forced him to defend his position.

"All my troops know the consequences of failure," he shouted as he became red in the face."

Linda could see she was antagonising Caymes and, so far, getting away with it. Could she make him angry enough to drop his guard and allow them a chance to form an escape? It was risky. Not enough and he would just enjoy the chance to gloat, too much and he could just as easily kill her. For the moment, she decided to continue.

"Troops?" she chuckled. "Troops? What have you

formed, your own army? Oh please! I can see all the clichés now. You've become the stereotypical cinematic villain!"

Caymes was now scarlet in the face and spittle was leaving his mouth as he shouted.

"Shut up!" he screamed. "A good general needs his troops and has to make difficult decisions between life and death during times of war."

"War?" she shouted. "What war? We're not at war."

"Not at war!" Caymes responded. "We've been at war for years! How many years now have we stood back and let other countries beat us at manufacturing, take our brightest talents, lure our businesses away to Europe."

"That's not war," Linda shouted. "That's politics and competition. They're the sort of things you're supposed to be sorting out as a politician."

"Politics is too slow, Miss Andrews. We could take years to get results if we go down the political route. Using my methods, we can get things sorted quickly."

"You are truly mad," Linda said exhaustively. "And what did Jenkins's death have to do with your war?"

"He did not die in vain. Miss Andrews. He had led my troops on the ground for much of the conflict but, recently, he was making too many mistakes and had to be sacrificed for the cause."

"But, in that way?" she pleaded. "Was that really necessary?"

"It is necessary for a general to keep discipline within his ranks. Anyway, Jenkins was the key in a very important experiment. What you saw there in action, were the latest version of my picobots. Remotely programmable, able to communicate with one another, both virtually instantaneous and now powered by a near-superconductive battery source that allows them to operate almost indefinitely. They are my new indestructible troops."

"I take it back," Linda growled at him. "You're not just mad, you're insane!"

"Shut up!" he screeched, moving over to Linda and

slapping her hard across the face.

Nick went to move towards Caymes in Linda's defence but was hit in the back of the neck with the butt of a rifle and fell back to the floor dazed.

"I've said too much," said Caymes, turning to Alpha. "In fact, I've had enough. Kill them all."

Alpha brought his assault rifle up, pointing in the direction of Linda, Nick and Wilmott. His finger moved over the trigger…

CHAPTER 32

MI6 Headquarters, Vauxhall

Andrew Fleming sat at his large desk in his large office. On one side of the room, a number of LCD displays were showing news broadcasts from strategic points around the world. He currently wasn't watching the transmissions and had muted all feeds, choosing to read the document in his hand whilst facing the Thames through the one-way glass that made up two walls of the room.

His was an unusual route to be head of MI6 in that he hadn't risen up through the ranks but had been brought in specially to run the agency. His army intelligence record was substantial as was his experience of field operations but what he lacked in his knowledge in espionage was made up by having knowledgeable people around him. He seemed to be doing okay in the job as he had received no negative feedback so far.

The document he was reading was a briefing note regarding the incident at the Houses of Parliament. Though the contents of the note regarding the apparent disappearance of the Prime Minister had placed the country on high alert, Fleming was calmly scanning the contents.

Never one to panic, he tended to keep a cool head, known for analysing situations clearly and not going into knee-jerk reactions.

A knock at the office door stopped him from reading through the briefing note again.

"Enter," he said, raising his voice loud enough to be heard through the solid wooden door.

The voice recognition system running in the background, triggered by his wording, established the voice-print was identical to that stored on the security network, and released the door deadlocks allowing it to be opened. As the door swung silently on its well-lubricated hinges, Fleming's personal secretary, Sir John Wetherby, entered with a multi-page document in his hand.

"It's here, sir," he said enthusiastically. "The full report on the Palace of Westminster incident."

"Dispense with the formalities, John, please," Fleming asked through a slight smile.

"Okay Mr. Fleming," said Wetherby uncomfortably.

"Oh John. It's not "Mr. Fleming" or even "Andrew", it's "Andy" unless we're in public."

Fleming spun round in his chair to face Wetherby and took the report he was being offered.

"I take it you've read it, John?" he asked, receiving a nod. "In that case, please give me a precis of its contents."

"Okay, er, Andy. It appears the PM was lured out from the conference and then abducted by boat. Sir Kit Jenkins gave chase along with the security services but they left the Thames around Isleworth and must have had a car waiting."

"They lost them whilst on the river?" asked Fleming, sounding frustrated. "Our top Parliament security lost a boat on the river?"

"The abductors were prepared, Sir… Andy. And from CCTV picked up within the House, it appears the abductors were two ex-special forces operatives, Linda Andrews and Nick Saten."

"And we have no idea where they are now?"

"No… Andy. We picked up a message from the Air Force saying that they were taking Sir Kit to Lanzarote so we suspect he knows they have gone there. We also logged a private jet take off from Southampton Airport shortly after the jet with Sir Kit took off from RAF Stoney Cross. That jet was also headed for Lanzarote but showed no passenger list on the system. We therefore suspect the PM was on that plane. Why they were heading for Lanzarote, we don't know and, as yet, we haven't heard from Sir Kit."

"He must have had intel they were headed to the Canaries. Get my car ready to take me to RAF Stoney Cross and contact them to arrange for a jet to take me to Lanzarote."

"You're going to Lanzarote on a hunch, Sir… Andy?" asked Wetherby.

"Yes, John, I am. If Kit has gone there, he must be pretty sure that's the correct place to head for. And, with the PM involved, I feel I should be out there too."

"With due respect, sir, if the PM is there, you'll need me with you to keep the press and media off your back."

"No, John. I'll need you here to deal with questions from the police and ministers."

At that moment, the red telephone on Fleming's desk rang. With the PM out of circulation, it could only be the Deputy Prime Minister, Michael Cooper. Fleming picked up the phone, gesturing for Wetherby to remain.

"Yes, Mr. Deputy Prime Minister," he said then, after a pause, added, "Michael. How can I help."

Another pause as he listened. "Ah, so you have seen the report. I have just gone through it now with Sir John."

Another pause. "Yes, I believe he would not have flown out there if he wasn't sure that is where the PM has been taken."

A further pause. "Yes, I intend to fly out there and take charge as soon as we have finished our call."

A further pause. "Er, no. I feel John would be best placed here dealing with the media."

Another pause. "Er, yes I suppose he could deal with them at the scene. And, yes, he is experienced at dealing with people at all levels."

Another pause. "Yes Sir… Michael. As you say, we'll be on our way as soon as we end our call."

Another pause. "Yes, Michael. I… we will keep you informed of our progress."

The line went dead as the Deputy PM hung up the call. Fleming calmly placed the phone back on to his desk and looked over to Wetherby.

"Okay, John, get the car and the jet sorted. We are going to Lanzarote."

"Yes, Andy," said Wetherby turning to leave Fleming's office, heading towards his own in order to make arrangements from there. As he closed the office door behind him, he couldn't help but allow a little smile to form on his face.

CHAPTER 32

"Wait!" shouted Caymes.

Alpha kept his assault rifle pointing towards the trio but removed his finger from the trigger and held fire. Caymes brought out a vibrating smart phone from his pocket and swiped the answer icon.

"Yes," he said listening intently then, after a few more seconds he said, "Okay" and then ended the call. "Don't kill them now," he ordered, "I said we may need them as a convincer when we get to the island and now, I'm told they may prove useful even after that. Keep them tied and guarded and get them to the boat, now. I want to be on the island within the hour."

"Yes sir," said Alpha as he gave a nod to some of the other troops.

In response to the nod, three of them withdrew a different pistol from within their combat armour, each choosing a different target from the choice of Linda, Nick and Wilmott. Without further pause, all three fired and small darts hit the neck of each target. All three winced at the sting of the dart then, within a few seconds, their vision started to spin fast and quickly reduced to darkness as their legs gave way beneath them and they slumped to the ground unconscious.

Nick was the first to awake. He felt nauseous and one side of his neck was sore. He remembered the dart hitting him and then everything going dark. He opened his eyes fully and his sight started to come back into focus. He was on a bed in a large room. He could see two other beds with Linda and Wilmott laying on each of them. He swung round and sat up on the side of the bed and the room appeared to spin causing his nausea to increase. He sat there for a few moments until the nausea and the spinning calmed down then got up and walked over to Linda. She was laying very still so he felt her neck for a pulse. He was satisfied she was just unconscious so went over, checked Wilmott and found him to be in the same situation.

Content with them being okay, Nick took more notice of the room. They were in what looked like a large suite from a five-star hotel, three large beds, spaced out with bedside cabinets for each occupied one side of the room whilst a drinks cabinet and a small table and chairs were on another. The carpet was a thick, luxurious pile and the ornaments placed around the room all looked to be very expensive. A large TV screen was on another wall and a number of plump cushions had been spread out across a sofa that had been placed for maximum comfortable viewing of the TV. Unlike regular hotel suites, the room had no windows, making Nick suspicious that it was underground, and the main door was locked with no visible means of opening it from the inside.

Wilmott let out a few murmurs signifying he was stirring so Nick went over to help him up.

"Slowly does it, Dave," Nick advised as he supported Wilmott to a sitting position.

"Shit," said Wilmott holding his head in his hands. "What the hell did they put in those darts?"

"I dunno, mate," said Nick shaking his head, "but I think I'll stick to pints in the future!"

Wilmott smiled then winced as it made his head hurt more. Then, feeling a little better, he glanced around the room.

"Lin?" he asked, concerned.

"She's okay," Nick assured, indicating with his head where Linda was laying on the third bed. "The mark on her neck indicates she was also hit by a dart. If it had the same tranquiliser as in ours, chances are she'll be out for a bit longer, having less body mass."

Happy with the answer, Wilmott took more time to look around the room.

"Where are we?" he asked.

"Well, I've been in some worse cells in the past," joked Nick, "but it appears that we are in one now, all be it, with many creature comforts."

"Please, Mr. Saten," sounded Caymes's voice from hidden speakers whilst, at the same time, he appeared as live video on the TV screen, "don't think of it as a cell. Think of it as a home from home."

"So, you're listening in on our conversations," Nick spoke into the room, not knowing where the cameras and microphones were. "Not something I'm used to be subjected to at home, Caymes."

"Okay, I stand corrected, Mr. Saten, though some people may have their houses bugged but, in other ways, you can treat it as you would your home."

"I'm not confined to one room at home," protested Nick.

"Oh, is that what's bothering you?" laughed Caymes as a loud click could be heard as dead bolts were released at the door. "There, that's better, isn't it? You're now free to wander around the island."

Nick walked over to the door, opened it and discovered three armed guards standing outside, each one showing their names on their body armour, 'Beta', 'Gamma' and 'Delta'. Nick shut the door and walked back to be beside Wilmott as Caymes continued.

"Oh, your escorts are stationed outside and will accompany you purely for your safety and security," he laughed again. "We don't want you to come to any harm… prematurely," he continued laughing.

The sound of Caymes's and Nick's voices along with the door opening and closing had caused Linda to wake up.

"Ah, I see Ms. Andrews is now with us," continued Caymes, obviously still monitoring the room in real time. "Perhaps you could bring her up to speed on my hospitality and then join me in the meeting room in, say, twenty minutes. Your guards will show you the way. Just ask them when you are ready. I look forward to seeing you, we have much to discuss."

With that, the screen became blank and the speakers became silent. Nick moved over to help Linda get through her nausea phase of awakening and continued speaking to Wilmott.

"Well, I think that answers your previous question, at least partially. We appear to be on Diabolus Island and appear to be of value alive, at least for the moment. Perhaps the reason for that will become clearer in twenty minutes."

They each took turns to freshen up in the bathroom and then Nick and Wilmott spent some time updating Linda on the few minutes' conversation with Caymes she had missed.

"And I suggest," concluded Nick, "that we are mindful of what we say out loud as the room appears to be constantly monitored." He looked from Linda to Wilmott then continued, "Oh well, shall we go and see what Caymes has to say for himself?"

With no objections, Nick led them to the door and opened it. Outside, Beta, Gamma and Delta were still standing by the door, blocking any chance of them getting out of the room unseen. Nick addressed the one with 'Beta' written on his body armour.

"We come in peace," he smiled. "Take us to your leader."

Beta's stern face, just like the other two guards, didn't

change in response to Nick's comments. All he said was, "Follow me," as he turned and started walking away. In trained formation tactics, the two other guards stepped back allowing Linda, Nick and Wilmott to exit the room and walk behind Beta whilst they followed on behind, cutting off any chance of the trio lagging behind or changing course.

They strolled for a couple of minutes, passing some undesignated doors. Quick glances through the windows in the doors revealed what looked like lab areas with a number of technicians in white coats, some staring down microscopes and others sat at computer terminals. They soon arrived at a door with a name plate reading 'Meeting Room A' on it. They were shown inside and asked to sit down at a large table that had six chairs along each of its long sides and two at each end. It looked like a typical meeting room that could be found in any corporate building – a large monitor on one wall, ports at each table position to plug in laptops or tablets and a conference telephone module in the centre of the table. There was no-one else in the room so they chose their seating positions. They sat spaced out at one end of the table, Wilmott taking one of the two end seats and Nick and Linda sitting, one each side, at the first two side seats from Wilmott's end. Nick leant across the table and pressed the line out button on the telephone module. There was no dialling tone and the LCD display was blank. Nick shrugged his shoulders.

"It was worth a try," he smiled.

At that moment, the door opened and a grinning Caymes strolled in. As he came through the doorway, the guards could be seen standing outside.

"Please don't get up," he laughed as he walked around the table and sat in one of the two chairs at the end opposite Wilmott.

"Thank you for coming," he added.

"Like we had much choice," grumbled Linda.

"You always have a choice, Ms. Andrews," cackled Caymes. "I personally think you made your choice wisely.

The choice not to come would have been met with some forceful tactics and I would hate to see you damaged."

"Damaged?"

"Well, beaten up then if you prefer."

Wilmott tried to progress the conversation. "So, what are we meeting here for?" he asked.

"All will become clear, Mr. Wilmott," answered Caymes. "You are here, and still alive, to provide motivation."

"You haven't exactly got us here motivated to motivate others," continued Wilmott.

"I'm hoping that keeping you alive is the required motivation. Otherwise, there is no need to keep you," Caymes said menacingly.

"So…?" prompted Wilmott. "I can tell you're itching to tell us why we are here and what you are doing. Just like every cinematic villain you've got to explain the plot to us before we are left to die in some contrived way that we can then escape from and save the day."

"Your goading will not work with me, Mr. Wilmott. And, I can assure you that, once your value has been exhausted, you will just be shot. Nothing complicated."

"Oh well, that was worth a try too," said Wilmott, speaking to the room. "So, spill the beans, you nut job!"

Caymes laughed off the insult and addressed his seated audience.

"For too many years we have been at the mercy of bureaucrats and unelected politicians from within Europe. In fact, beyond Europe in some cases. Decisions are made for us that aren't necessarily in our best interest and we have to abide by laws that do not function well for our isolated island, the UK. This lack of quality leadership has had a fallback in our country and caused it to attempt to split into individual, independent countries, taking even more power away from central government. And, for all this, we pay vast sums that prop up the expense accounts of these unelected MPs. Well, the time has come to stop this out of control, incompetent governing body and I am going to be the one to do it."

"What!" exclaimed Wilmott. "Isn't that what referendums are for? To allow the people to decide. Isn't that what Brexit is supposed to do?"

Caymes laughed again. "Referendums are useless, Mr. Wilmott. The people don't understand what is best for themselves. And Brexit doesn't go far enough. European Parliament is still there and still having 'back door' influence in our daily operations. It needs to be eliminated."

It was Wilmott's turn to laugh this time.

"Listen to yourself, Caymes. Your speech signifies you are not trying to represent the people, just dictate to them. And, I suppose you've decided that you are the best person to take over rule once the European Parliament has been, as you say, eliminated."

"I have considered it carefully, Mr. Wilmott, and recognise I am best placed as I do understand what is best for the people."

Wilmott was still smiling. "I have no doubt that's what they all say. Anyway, whatever you think, you'll never convince the rulers of other countries to stand down and let you take over."

Caymes began to cackle again. "Of course, they wouldn't. I know that. That is why I wouldn't even try to convince them. There is no need. There is a conference to discuss future governance to be attended by all major nation's heads of state at the Houses of Parliament next week. During the main speeches, when all have pledged to be present, they will be eliminated leaving me to take over in their place."

"Their countries won't accept you, no chance."

"They will have no choice, Mr. Wilmott. My picobots have been placed within the main conference chamber. At the time of the main speeches, they will be released, eliminating any opposition. Once the world has seen the destructive capabilities of my picobots. They will have no choice but to accept my rule. As we speak, canisters of my bots are being distributed around the world and, once their capabilities have been demonstrated, the threat of them being released amongst the general population will ensure everyone is kept in check."

"You're mad," said Wilmott as Linda and Nick sat at the table shocked at what they were hearing. "Surely you'll be at this conference too. Won't wearing a protective bubble suit make the others a little suspicious?"

"I have thought of that, Mr. Wilmott. I'm not stupid you know." Wilmott raised his eyebrows in disbelief. "We have developed the capability for the picobots to analyse the DNA of the subject they have entered and to ignore any matches that are pre-programmed into their memory banks.

"They communicate with each other in real time so can guide themselves away from any friendly DNA sources they encounter. The thing we are lacking at the moment is the ability to remotely program them in real time. If we need to change or add DNA profiles into their avoidance system, we need the ability for it to be transmitted from distance. This is being worked on as we speak and the reason for you being here as the motivation I mentioned.

"In fact, it's time we found out how the programming is progressing." Caymes pulled out a smart phone from his pocket and tapped an icon on the screen.

Within a second a voice could be heard in the earpiece of the phone, "Yes sir."

"Get in here, now, with a full report of programming progress." ordered Caymes aggressively.

"Yes sir," replied the voice in the earpiece.

Though it couldn't be heard that well, there was something familiar about the voice. Nick glanced at Linda and then Wilmott and could see they mirrored the puzzled look on his face. He gave a slight shrug signifying he couldn't place the voice. It was too faint to hear clearly. Linda and Wilmott shrugged indicating they were struggling to place it too.

Their puzzlement was short lived as, around thirty

seconds later, there was a loud knock on the meeting room door.

"Enter," ordered Caymes.

The door opened as a voice said, "Yes sir," and all heads turned to see the incoming person. The voice was now easily recognisable, being spoken directly rather than faintly from a phone's earpiece.

Entering the room, leaving the door open, was Tony Chapman.

CHAPTER 34

"Tony?" questioned Linda. "No…"

"Oh, yes, Ms. Andrews," Caymes appeared to take great delight in saying. "You mean you had no idea?"

"You bastard!" growled Wilmott, going red in the face as realisation hit him like a sucker punch. "You were responsible for the security breach at the Southampton storage centre? Responsible for all those technicians's deaths?"

"No, you really can't blame Tony for that," came a voice from the other side of the door. "I must admit that was down to me."

"No….!" exclaimed Wilmott in disbelief, having recognised the voice straight away.

"Yes," continued Andrew Fleming as he walked through the doorway closing the door behind him, "I take responsibility for the casualties."

"Casualties!" shouted Wilmott, red-faced and veins bulging in his neck. "Casualties! They were innocent people, some of them had families."

"There is always collateral damage at times of war."

"War?" spat Wilmott. "Not you as well. We are not at war."

"It's just a matter of interpretation, Dave," said Fleming nonchalantly. "We had to get Mr. Turner out of the Southampton base and we couldn't allow any witnesses to seeing it was Mr. Chapman that instigated the extraction."

"Keith as well," exclaimed Linda.

Fleming smiled at Linda and moved closer to her. "I would like to be able to say Mr. Turner is on-side as we require his assistance, but I'm afraid he is not. In fact, that is the reason you are here and alive. We have him working on our remote real-time programming code and we need to be sure he is working as fast as he can. Once he sees his friends are here and their lives are dependent on him cooperating, I suspect his output will increase."

"He won't assist just to save us. He knows we know the risks involved in this game."

"I think you underestimate him, Ms. Andrews. He has already started working with us with only the threat of your arrival. You forget, I know him. I sat in on his interview and wrote his file."

Linda decided to be quiet now. She had no further come backs, not until she had more knowledge of the situation, perhaps by seeing and speaking to Keith. Whatever was actually going on, at least it sounded like he was still alive.

"I don't really begin to understand his views on all this," said Wilmott pointing at Caymes, "but you, Andrew, you are betraying your country and its people."

"I became disillusioned with the country long ago, David," replied Fleming, "and when Jonathon pitched his ideas to me, I could see the benefits of, excuse the cliché, a new world order. And the general population of the world have memories like goldfish; they will quickly forget the tactical moves and soon accept the new ways once they realise, they will be better for it."

"And you really believe this?" asked Wilmott incredulously. "In fact, don't answer that. I think I've heard enough from you."

Nick decided to add to the conversation. If they could

get Caymes angry enough maybe it would create some sort of advantage. Slim chance but all he could think of at the moment.

"I think I can speak for us all when I say we would rather die than be any sort of catalyst for your world domination by any other name."

"I have already said that I want to save the world, not dominate it," roared Caymes.

"And you intend to save it by taking control?" enquired Nick.

"I intend to keep everything in order," added Caymes. "That's all."

"If that's not domination, we need to re-write the dictionary. You treat your country no, all countries, with contempt. From birth, I was taught to respect my country. I grew to serve it and would never betray it. I was born to die for the freedom of my country and its people."

"Oh, nice speech. Very moving," sneered Caymes. "Of course, we are all born to die, Mr. Saten. It's just that some of us will die sooner than others."

"After you," said Nick with mock politeness. Linda and Nick smiled whilst Caymes said nothing, eventually moving the conversation on to detract from his flushed face.

"Enough!" shouted Caymes. "Guards, in here now!"

The door opened immediately and the guards from outside quickly entered. Caymes turned towards Chapman.

"Take them to the lab. Demonstrate to Mr. Turner that he can keep them safe by co-operating then lock them back up again."

"Yes sir," said Chapman as he directed the guards.

Chapman led the way from the room with Linda, Wilmott and Nick behind him and the guards very close behind them. They walked along a small maze of corridors until they came to a door locked by a digital key card system. Above the door was a large sign reading 'Main Lab. No admittance unless authorised.' Chapman opened the door, entered and motioned for them to follow.

"Are you sure you're authorised to enter, Chapman?" asked Nick. "It doesn't say 'except lowlife scum' on the sign."

"Shut the fuck up," shouted Chapman, giving a small nod to the guards.

One guard raised his rifle and brought the butt down on the back of Nick's neck. It wasn't hard enough to knock him unconscious but it dazed him. He continued walking, slightly unsteadily, determined not to show how much it had hurt.

"Any more shite from your mouth," threatened Chapman as he swiped a card across the reader, "and I won't ask him to hold back."

The door clicked open and Linda moved over, holding up Nick, allowing him to enter the lab.

"Are you okay?" she whispered.

"Yeah," Nick replied softly adding a little wink. "I think I'm wearing the guards down now."

The lab was large, approximately 50 metres square, and consisted of a number of work stations, each with a monitor, mouse, keyboard, scanner and printer. The work stations were unoccupied except for one. Seated at one of the central desks was a figure staring at the monitor and typing speedily. Printed on the back of his tee shirt was written 'and lost by a short head' and, as he rose from his chair upon seeing Linda, Nick and Wilmott heading towards him, the slogan 'I joined the space race' could be seen on the front.

"Guys!" he shouted as a big grin appeared on his face.

"Keith," Linda shouted. "Are you okay?"

"Of course, he is okay, Ms. Andrews," Said Chapman confidently, "and he is helping us with our experiments," he added.

"You can fuck off, Chapman!" shouted Keith.

"Not sure if he's that keen to help," added Nick.

"Then we'll give him a reason to be keen won't we," continued Chapman as he gave Nick's guard a slight nod.

Using the butt of his assault rifle, the guard hit Nick on the back of the neck again. This time it was hard enough for Nick's sight to fade and for him to fall to the ground. The guard then turned his rifle around and pointed it at Nick's chest, preparing to fire.

CHAPTER 35

Houses of Parliament, Westminster

The Deputy Prime Minister, Michael Cooper, was sitting at his desk trying to remain calm under pressure. Since the abduction of the Prime Minister, he had had the press office badgering him for information to release to the media, the security services informing him hourly on the little progress they were making, heads of other countries offering their advice and assistance and The House wanting half hourly updates. On top of all that, the Peace and Security Summit was scheduled to be taking place in the House in a few days. Heads of all major nations would be attending – in fact, many of them had already arrived in the UK in preparation – and, before the abduction, the Prime Minister had told him that nothing must stop it going ahead; it was too important to the world for it to be stopped or even postponed.

He couldn't remember the last time he had slept and this was the first time since word had got out that he had actually had any time alone. He looked at the pile of memos on his desk and the emails piling up in his inbox at the rate of a couple every minute. He closed his eyes but immediately opened them again as he felt himself drifting off to sleep. His private secretary had been keeping him topped up with strong, hot coffee and he realised a fresh one had been recently supplied as the one on his desk was no longer steaming. He took a gulp from it and felt the heat warming his stomach making him realise that he must eat something in the near future.

His thoughts of food were interrupted by the ringing of his smart phone. He was always surprised when it rang as so few people knew the number. He took it out from his inside pocket and was further surprised when he saw 'PM' as the name of the caller. He swiped the 'answer' icon.

"Cooper," he said tentatively.

"Mike," said the voice at the other end of the line.

Cooper's surprised look increased further.

"Chayton… Is that you?"

"Yes, Mike. It's me."

"Are you okay? Where are you? Do you need help? Are you safe?"

"I'm okay, Mike," said Jameson. "Fleming sprung me. I'm in a safe place, currently under his protection."

"Thank goodness, Chayton. I was getting very concerned to say the least as we hadn't heard anything about you since the disappearance on the river. I can inform The House and the media you are safe."

"No!" said Jameson abruptly. "Don't say anything for the moment. I realise that puts the pressure firmly on your shoulders but, until I get back to the UK, I think it would be safer for all if my status remains unknown."

"Okay, Chayton, I'll try to keep the press and The House at bay but, you know how rumours manage to surface without any effort."

"Do as best you can, Mike," added Jameson. "I appreciate your efforts."

"Thanks, Chayton. Where are you? Will you be back soon?"

"I'm somewhere around the Canaries so should be back

to the UK in about four hours or so."

"Okay, I think I can hold off the media and other questioners until then."

"I do appreciate this, Mike," said Jameson sounding sincere. "There is one other thing."

"Yes?" asked Cooper.

"The Peace and Security Summit," said Jameson. "It is still going ahead, isn't it?"

"It hasn't been cancelled," said Cooper cautiously, "but, being only a couple of days away, many of the national leaders have already arrived in the UK ready for it. And many of them are using the example of your abduction as a reason that it must go ahead whether you are there or not. In your absence, we had decided not to change the venue from the Houses of Parliament and we have upped the security and threat levels within the House as a precaution. Do you want it cancelled?"

"No!" Jameson said abruptly once more then slowed himself down. "It's too important to stop or even postpone. If there are any heads of state that feel uneasy about attending, please stall them from making any decisions until I get back. I should be flying back to a UK air force base later today so should be back in my office for this evening or tomorrow morning. We can announce my return tomorrow morning then I can take the flak from the media allowing you some space to get things organised."

"And get a bit of sleep perhaps," added Cooper

"I'll ring off now, Mike," said Jameson, "Fleming is approaching and wanting something." There was a brief pause then Jameson continued. "Ah, yes. Andrew has reminded me. In light of the security issues, he has insisted on some additional security measures to be in place during the summit. As well as additional operatives from 'Six' being stationed in the House, he has made available a number of smart alert receivers. They can be used to raise a local alarm around the summit table rather than the general alarm of the House. They have been delivered for your attention. They are designed to clip onto the Bluetooth translation table speakers and sound an alert through them if the need arises. Can you ensure that they are clipped into place, one on each table?"

"I'll get that in motion as soon as we're finished."

"Thank you, Mike," said Jameson. "Much appreciated. See you later today."

"That's okay, Chayton. It's great to hear you're alive and wel –"

The phoneline went dead.

"Oh well," thought Cooper, "he's a busy man and been through a lot. Now, how do I go about continuing the organisation of this event and its security without mentioning the man has been found safe?"

Caymes put down the phone he had been using to call Cooper and turned to Fleming.

"We need to get me back to the UK quickly, Andrew. We need to return triumphant that you successfully rescued me without me being harmed."

"I can organise that now, Jonathon. Give me twenty minutes and we can be on our way."

"Good," said Caymes looking happy. "We need for all the heads of states to see I am unharmed. It's crucial they all attend the Peace and Security Summit; we can't afford for any of them to be missing."

CHAPTER 36

Diabolus Island

"No!" shouted Keith.

Chapman gave another slight movement of his head, this time a shake, and the guard withdrew his weapon and returned to his watching position.

"You see, Mr. Saten, your safety along with that of Ms. Andrews and Mr. Wilmott will ensure Keith remains very keen at all times."

"There's no need for this," pleaded Keith to Chapman. "I'm already helping you aren't I."

"Yes," replied Chapman smugly. "And long may it last if you want your friends to be safe."

"You bastard, Tony!" snarled Linda as she bent down to assist Nick.

"Words, Ms. Andrews. They have no effect on me. Anyway, I'll leave you all to re-acquaint. No doubt you have much to catch up. Have no fear of escape. The door will be locked and two of the guards will be stationed outside."

With that he turned on his heels and headed out of the door followed by the guards. As the door clicked shut, two of the guards remained outside the lab as Chapman and the third guard walked off.

Keith rushed to where Linda was checking Nick.

"Are you okay Nick?" he asked.

Nick sat up and replied rubbing the nape of is neck.

"Yeah, mate. I'll be okay in a minute but my neck's beginning to tell me to keep my mouth shut in front of guards with guns."

Chapman walked into Caymes's office as he'd been instructed to do once finished with Keith Turner's motivation. As he was approaching, he could hear Caymes was in frantic conversation with Fleming but they stopped abruptly as he entered.

Caymes turned so he was facing directly at Chapman.

"Ah, Tony," he said loudly, "have you some good news for me?"

Chapman felt the hairs on the back of his neck stand. It was at times like this that Caymes was unpredictable. Sometimes when Caymes received bad news, the bringer would be held responsible and would be punished – one known occasion being where the person had been subjected to the bots. Other times, Caymes would just laugh it off. There was no way of telling the response until it came.

Chapman swallowed hard. "No, Mr. Caymes. Not yet." Chapman could see no evidence of a smile forming on Caymes's face so he decided to continue speaking quickly. "Er, but I'm sure we will get a breakthrough soon."

"I hope so, Tony," said Caymes smiling. "I really hope so."

Being afraid of bad developments forming during times of silence, Chapman decided to continue with an update.

"Er, but I am overseeing Mr. Turner's work on the remote programming issues."

"You are telling me that we still cannot program the bots with the DNA profiles?" he asked aggressively.

Chapman swallowed again and felt a bead of sweat trickling down his temple.

"Er, no, Mr. Caymes," he said tentatively. "That's not quite correct. Er, we can't program them remotely as yet but the swarm communication still works correctly. So, we got around the issue by manufacturing some bots pre-programmed with the DNA profiles you require. They were then introduced to the swarm and, within seconds, the new programming was peer-transferred to them all."

"Excellent," said Caymes. "And we can quickly change their programming again if we need to?"

"Er, yes and no," said Chapman seeing Caymes's stare intensifying. "Let me explain. Yes, they can be easily re-programmed. However, the only way to do this at the moment, is as I explained before – pre-programmed bots need to be introduced to the swarm for the new program to propagate."

"So, just to confirm," Caymes asked menacingly, "the ones sent to the summit have all been pre-programmed with our DNA profiles?"

"Er, yes sir," replied Chapman. I oversaw their programming myself. I certainly don't want to be around those things if they don't recognise my DNA."

"Excellent," Caymes said again. "Andrew and I have to get back to the UK now. We need to reassure the visiting heads of state that it is safe to attend the summit. You stay on here and make sure Turner cracks the remote programming. Tell him you'll start killing his friends if he doesn't demonstrate progress. Then join us at the House tomorrow so that we all show a united stance ready for the summit to begin the day after."

"Yes sir," said Chapman, relaxing a little as Caymes and Fleming left the room to begin their journey back to the UK.

With Caymes away, it was now time to demonstrate his capabilities. He'd been in the shadow of Keith Turner for too long and it was now time to show Turner who was now in charge. He would make him produce this coding, threatening his friends if necessary, then, once Turner had produced the goods, he would kill them all.

Back in the lab area, Nick was still massaging his aching neck whilst Keith was explaining the situation.

"They've managed to produce microscopic nano bots. In fact, they are so small we may have to create a new title for them. Pico bots may be a more fitting description. They're so small that, when they fly, there are so many of them they look more like a cloud of smoke. In fact, as they fly, perhaps they should be called pico drones."

"Yeah, whatever they're called, we've seen them in action," said Linda in disgust.

"Oh, you have," said Keith. "Well, somehow, they've successfully perfected the combination of 3D biological printing and fusing that with robotic parts to create them. Microscopically, they look a bit like flies but behave a bit more like bees or ants – successfully coordinating themselves for maximum effect. They can communicate with each other in real time and can be enabled remotely, tapping into Wi-Fi, blue tooth or the mobile networks using their own comms system when nothing else is available. They can be programmed to follow complex instructions and are relentless at carrying them out."

"But, how do they inflict damage to people?" asked Linda.

Keith continued. "They are small enough to enter the body through any orifice and, once in there, they can attack and over power any organ, inflicting so much pain that the 'infected' person usually dies in agony before their organs shut down."

"Jeez!" Linda said revolted. "How do they know who to attack? When we saw them in action, they targeted one person in a room without harming us."

"Miniaturisation hasn't stopped them being sophisticated. They are able to analyse DNA within a fraction of a second of entering a bloodstream. How they do it so quickly, I have no idea. And they are programmed to attack a certain DNA, or multiple DNA profiles, when they encounter them. As soon as one, or more, of them identify the target, they can summon the others that are in the vicinity. And, any that enter a body and discover the DNA profile is not a target, they leave that body without inflicting any damage. When you were witnessing the attack, chances are some entered each of you but didn't identify you as a target and left you without attacking."

"These things are a nightmare," said Linda shuddering as she remembered their attack on Jenkins.

"So, where's their weakness?" asked Nick.

"They generally don't have much in the way of weaknesses. However, they currently have something lacking. They are unable to be re-programmed remotely at the moment. They can be programmed during manufacture but remote programming is not getting through. Remotely, they can be sent individual instructions, 'attack', 'go', 'stop', those sorts of things but can't be re-programmed. They just seem to ignore a remote firmware update. That's why they brought me in. They think I can work out what's going wrong with remote programming."

"And…?" Nick enquired.

"And… so far, I have no idea."

"So, can't we just let them fly around for a while until they run out of steam?" suggested Linda.

"Not so long ago that would have been a viable solution," said Keith. "The reason they wanted the orthotope was to create the power lines for these things. They now have virtually superconductive circuitry so can keep going for a long time. Before getting the orthotope info they could only be powered up for just a minute or so tops. Plus, they discovered that a few need to be programmed at the manufacturing stage then introduced to an existing swarm of the things and the new programming gets spread amongst them within seconds. Remote programming still doesn't work but re-programming by propagation is successful but only if they have access to the swarms they want to be updated."

"Jeez!" said Linda again. "As I said, these things are a nightmare."

"So, how do we stop them?" asked Nick in a hopeful tone.

"You don't stop them!" said Chapman menacingly as he opened the lab door and walked into room followed by the two guards.

"Just thought I'd ask," said Nick flippantly whist making a mental note to be careful what he says out loud in the vicinity of what must be hidden microphones.

"They are unstoppable," continued Chapman, ignoring Nick's remark, "and, with them, we can control the world and bring about peace."

"Yeah, yeah," said Nick, trying to goad Chapman. "We've been through that debate already with your boss. We had to agree to disagree."

Their talking was interrupted by the sound of a helicopter taking off nearby. Chapman's bravado was increasing in the same fashion as Caymes's now he was in charge on the island.

"And there goes the boss on his way to bring about these changes," he said with conviction, his enthusiasm growing.

"And, how does he plan to instigate these amazing so-called changes?" asked Nick moving closer to Chapman to emphasize his aggressiveness.

The two guards moved closer behind Chapman in order to bring their weapons to bear if necessary but Chapman was getting too confident now and, with a slight shake of his head he signalled the guards to stand easy.

This is what Nick was hoping would happen and he moved a little closer as he continued his verbal attack.

"He doesn't have a chance of overpowering all the major nations. Some, if not all, will rebel."

Chapman's confidence was getting the better of him now and he took a step towards Nick, pointing his finger at him aggressively.

"I don't think so, Mr. Saten. At the Peace and Security Summit being held at the Houses of Parliament tomorrow, all the world major leaders will be present along with most of their deputies and their defence ministers. We have all the leader's blood banks held locally as a security measure and, from them, we have obtained their DNA profiles. The bots will be released within the meeting area programmed with these profiles and, when released, will kill all the leaders leaving Prime Minister Jameson to control the various remaining minsters with the threat of their death too."

Chapman confidently took another step closer to Nick so that his threatening finger was now only inches away from Nick's face.

"They won't know that our bots will ignore them as we don't have their DNA on record." Chapman laughed in Nick's face and the guards joined in laughing too.

"You see, Mr. Saten, there is no way you can stop this."

"I can have a damn good try," said Nick, moving into action fast.

As he had hoped, Chapman and the guards had relaxed thinking that the prisoners had succumbed to their fate.

This gave Nick an advantage.

In one smooth movement, Nick bent down, leant into Chapman's body, picking him up off the floor and flinging him at the guards. It all happened so quickly that Chapman nor the guards had time to react. The three of them tumbled to the ground in a heap. Nick quickly bent down and grabbed one of the guards' rifles that had been dropped, picking it up and firing a quick double tap into the chests of both guards, ensuring neither of them would be getting up.

Linda had had her suspicions that Nick was planning something when he kept moving closer to Chapman so she was the first to react when he made his move. She ran to the dead guards, picked up the second rifle and pointed it at Chapman who was still sprawled on the ground.

"Don't even breathe!" she threatened him.

Chapman produced a nervous smile.

"N... No need to shoot, Ms. Andrews. I... I'll assist you in whatever you want."

"I know you will you arsehole," responded Linda still aiming the rifle at his torso, "otherwise I might feel the need to start with your kneecaps. Now get up slowly and keep your hands on your head, fingers clasped."

Chapman slowly got to his feet and adopted the stance as instructed. Nick checked the two guards, picking up a spare magazine of ammunition and a security swipe card from each. The assault rifles were both fitted with large suppressors and Nick's shots had only made a muffled thumping sound so had not alerted any other guards to what had happened. Both guards had radios on their belts but hadn't had enough time to use them. Nick switched them off and tossed them on to the floor.

"Everyone okay?" he asked, looking around the room at each person in turn, receiving nods from them all.

"Okay, we need to get out of here and off this island."

"I don't think you'll be able to do that," said Chapman, seeming a little more confident. "The island is teeming with guards. You'll never get past them all."

Nick walked over to Chapman and hit him in the stomach with the butt of the rifle, hard enough to wind him.

"Firstly, you'd better hope we get off the island because if we don't, nor do you. Secondly, I don't think there are that many guards on the island. I've only seen the same ones since we've been here. I don't think Caymes was intending to have many visitors so didn't post a large security network."

"And thirdly, said Keith as he was busily shutting down his laptop, "they probably didn't feel they needed a large security presence as they could move the island to any place they wanted, effectively making it disappear."

"Move it?" questioned Nick. "What do you mean, move it?"

"We're not really on an island as such," added Keith. "We're actually on a giant boat or raft with what looks like an island plonked on top of it."

"You're kidding," said Linda.

"Nope, no kidding going on. It's what I had discovered back at base before Chapman gave me a drugged coffee. I had satellite photos taken a few days apart and discovered that the island was at a slightly different location in one set compared to the next. It was moving in the water with no loss of land mass. I concluded it was a vessel of some kind but, before I could alert anyone, I was drugged and dragged here."

"In that case," decided Nick, "before we get out of here, you can take us to the control room for this vessel, Mr. Chapman."

Nick dragged Chapman in front of him and held him steady with the suppressor of his rifle pressed against the back of his neck.

"Lin, there's some tie-wraps in the guards' inside pockets. Get some out and secure this bastard's hands."

"With pleasure," said Linda as she carried out the instructions.

Nick went through Chapman's pockets and found a smart phone. He threw it over to Wilmott.

"Dave, until we find our own phones, can you use this one to arrange some fast transport back to London?"

"Consider it done," said Wilmott already tapping the screen as he headed to a corner of the room to make a quiet call.

"While that's being done," said Nick turning back to the now quiet Chapman, "it's time you told us where the bots have been placed in Parliament and how they're going to be released."

A nervous look appeared on Chapman's face.

"I don't know," he mumbled.

"Don't give me that shit, Chapman," said Nick menacingly, pointing the rifle at Chapman's left kneecap. "Last chance, where are they?"

Chapman started to breathe heavily and fear showed

prominently in his eyes.

"I… I really don't know," he said quickly moving his view from Nick's eyes to the suppressor at his knee. "Mr. Caymes only told those that needed to know. He always kept control like that. I think he told Andrew Fleming. In fact, I think they both decided where to place them but I don't know where. And I don't know how or when he intends to trigger them." He glanced between Nick and the rifle faster and faster. "Y… you've got to believe me. I don't know any of that."

Linda spoke to Nick but didn't take her eyes from Chapman.

"I think the little shit may be telling the truth. Look at him, he's a snivelling wimp. Maybe you should go for one kneecap to make sure."

Nick moved the rifle around to side of Chapman's knee.

"No!" screamed Chapman. "Please, no!"

Nick moved the rifle away from Chapman's knee.

"I think you might be right, Lin," he said calmly. "Maybe we won't waste any ammo on him at this stage." He turned to Chapman and added, "Your knee is safe for the moment, mate but, if I even think you might be lying to any of us, I really won't feel guilty about doing it. Do you understand?" Chapman nodded but kept silent. "Right," continued Nick, "first thing you can do to save your knee is to take us to the island's control room."

"Okay, no problem," mumbled Chapman. "This way."

"We wait until the phone call is finished and Keith has all he wants to bring with him. The we move, quickly and quietly."

"Do you think the fact that no-one has found what we've done as yet," said Linda, "means they're in wait for us somewhere?"

"I suspect," replied Nick, "that the lack of guard backup and us not being found so far, is another indication that, one, they're not very professional and two, there's not many of them. Is that right Chapman? How many guards are there? Answer!"

"There's only about half a dozen left on the island," mumbled Chapman. "One for each lab and a couple spare for breaks. The rest have already been dispersed as most of the work here has been done."

"Okay," added Nick, "you'd better hope I don't find you've been bending the truth at all. Have you?!"

"No," Chapman mumbled again. "That's it as far as I know."

"Okay," said Nick again, then turned to the rest of the room. "Guys?" he asked. "How we doing? We really should be on our way now. Getting a bit nervous here, staying in one place."

He was acknowledged by Wilmott finishing his call and Keith shutting down his laptop and grabbing it and a few USB drives, both of them then heading over to where Nick, Linda and Chapman were standing.

"Okay," Nick said yet again, prodding Chapman gently with his rifle. "Let's go…. Slowly."

They headed out of the lab with Chapman leading, Nick behind him, then Wilmott and Keith together and Linda at the rear.

Checking the corridor was clear, Nick spoke quietly to Wilmott.

"Okay, Dave, how are we getting out of here?"

Wilmott replied quietly just so the group could hear him.

"There's a chopper coming over from Tenerife to fly us back to the airport where a jet will take us back to London."

"I do wish I had your connections," said Nick and, prodding Chapman again, continued," after the control room we want the helipad. Okay?!"

"Yeah, okay. I heard," snarled Chapman.

Chapman led the group down some long corridors passing some large laboratory-type rooms, all of them deserted. He gave brief descriptions of each lab as they passed as if he was giving a guided tour.

Keith increased his pace a little so that he caught up level with Nick.

"I've only been to the control room once, Nick, but I'd swear this isn't the quickest route," he whispered.

"I was beginning to wonder," whispered Nick in reply. Then he raised his voice. "What are you playing at, Chapman? You leading us round in circles?"

"N… No!" Chapman stammered. "I'm leading you the route with the least chance of running into the guards."

"And, why should you do a thing like that?" asked Nick suspiciously.

"Well, I don't want to get caught in the middle of a shoot-out, do I?"

"I don't trust him to do something like that," Keith continued his whispering to Nick.

"Don't worry, mate," replied Nick, "nor do I." He prodded Chapman with his rifle. "Come on Chapman. I'm not a complete fool. Stop fucking about!"

"Trust me," Chapman muttered, "we're nearly there now. We're just approaching it now. It's just around this next corner and we'll be there."

As Chapman moved to walk the group around the corner, Keith jerked to a halt.

"Stop!" he shouted.

The group stopped except for Chapman. He had reached the corner and suddenly started into a run, leaving the group.

Nick brought his rifle to bear and glanced around the corner and immediately jerked his head back as shots rang out, some of them digging holes into the wall where his head had been moments before.

"Keep back!" he shouted holding his rifle at arm's length, firing a few shots blindly around the corner."

"He's been describing his journey all the way," declared Keith. "He must be miked up and has broadcast our journey to the guards. He's been leading us into a trap."

The group went silent for a moment realising they'd been had and the gunshots had stopped now that Nick's head was no longer visible to the shooters. The silence was broken by the sound of footsteps approaching the group from behind along the corridor.

"We've got company coming from the rear, folks," said Linda drawing her rifle, covering the corridor behind them. "They sound a few corners away at the moment but they're heading this way. We're surrounded!"

The area of the corridor where they had come to a halt consisted of bare walls; there were no windows or doors that they could escape through. Ahead of them, around the corner, were Chapman and his guards and, behind them, around that corner, were the approaching footsteps of more guards.

They had nowhere to go.

They were caught in a trap.

CHAPTER 37

Somewhere over the Atlantic Ocean, heading for the UK.

The Airbus A319 is a medium-range, twin-engine jet aircraft capable of a maximum range of 4287 miles and a maximum speed of 541 miles per hour, carrying a maximum of 156 passengers. This particular A319, on route from Tenerife to London had been modified internally to luxurious standards. Capable of carrying a maximum of 18 passengers, all seated in deluxe leather chairs, it incorporated an executive rest room, a fully-stocked bar and even a master bedroom.

On this occasion there were only two passengers with one member of staff in attendance. The two passengers were Jonathan Caymes and Andrew Fleming. Both were enjoying a cocktail made by the attendant whom they had then dismissed so they could talk in private.

"It seems a waste destroying the island with all the production facilities on it, Jon," said Fleming staring into his glass, watching the small bubbles forming around his olive.

"No, no" replied Caymes. "When I mentioned destruction to you, I meant to the people on the island, not the island itself. Not a good idea to destroy our main production facility before the new, larger one has been made. Oh no, I shall not be destroying the island, Peter."

Caymes pressed a button on a plate embedded in the wall beside his chair.

"Do we have mobile phone coverage in here yet?" he asked impatiently.

"Yes, sir," came the voice of the pilot, sounding relieved he could answer positively. "Now we're airborne the mobile signal repeater in the cabin is functional as is the mobile to satellite converter. It should be seamless now, sir. Just make a call as you would normally."

Caymes released the button and picked up his smart phone from the table in front of him and tapped a speed dial button.

"Ten minutes countdown," he smiled. "That should give them enough time to reach panic level."

"Are you sure it's wise to give them time to think about it, Jon? Doesn't that give them time to cause some damage before the event takes place?"

"All computer systems are locked down at the start of the countdown, Peter. The network is only responsive to my phone signalling. There'll be no trouble."

"As long as you're happy," said Fleming sipping on his drink.

"Oh yes, very happy," said Caymes laughing. "And now for Chapman, the last of our loose ends."

He tapped another speed dial button.

"No countdown for him."

Fleming formed a puzzled expression.

"Oh, you don't know, do you?" said Caymes looking very pleased with himself. "With all the technicians on the island, when supposedly taking blood samples for DNA processing, we injected a number of bots into their bloodstreams. As we had Chapman's on file already as part of the crown servant database, we had to invent another reason for him to be injected but we got them into him too.

The bots remain dormant until triggered by a call from me. I dealt with the technicians as we left and now it's his time."

"What about Saten and his team?" asked Fleming.

"They can't get away," Caymes replied triumphantly. "Chapman would have been guarding them up until now. If he's with them, they'll be panicking that the bots will be heading for them next. "Anyway, when the countdown gets to zero, they'll be dealt with very efficiently. There's no escape for them."

Caymes smiled and leant across the table, presenting his glass to Fleming. Fleming clinked his glass again Caymes's.

"Cheers!" they both said together.

They sat back in their comfy leather chairs, Caymes smiling and sipping his cocktail, Fleming also sipping his but looking very pensive.

CHAPTER 38

Diabolus Island

The footsteps were getting louder as the guards got nearer to the trapped group.

"We've nowhere to go," said Keith nervously. "What do we do? There's at least a couple of guards ahead with Chapman and it sounds like at least another couple behind us."

"Okay," said Nick, thinking fast and keeping his voice low, "Chapman and his goons should be keeping back for a while following my covering shots. The two coming from behind should be a bit wary after hearing the shots and won't know exactly what to expect." He laid down on the floor and beckoned to Linda. "Lin, remember Afghanistan, I'm shot and dying, you're trying to keep me alive. The rest of you gather around, look concerned and don't raise your weapons when they turn up."

Linda remembered the ploy but looked concerned. "You can't be sure this will work, Nick. We were lucky last time."

"It'll be fine," assured Nick. "They're amateurs. Besides, what choice do we have."

Nick positioned himself on the floor, on his back, head pointing towards the corner from where the two guards were approaching. He kept hold of his rifle; arm bent so the weapon was also pointing towards the approaching guards. Linda knelt over Nick and started chest compressions, too light to be effective but hard enough to look good. Keith and Wilmott stood over them, looking anxious.

"Come on!" she shouted as she pressed down onto Nick's chest. "Don't give up on me. Come on!"

After a few seconds, from around the rear corner a guard glanced around, took in the situation and jerked back quickly. A further couple of seconds later the two guards advanced from around the corner with their weapons raised. "Don't move!" one of them shouted.

Keith and Wilmott glanced up at the guards and then looked back down at Linda and Nick. Linda didn't look up and just carried on with the chest compressions. Nick lay on the ground, unmoving. The guards advanced slowly, one pointing his rifle at Keith and Wilmott, the other covering Linda and Nick.

Linda continued her heart massage with one eye on Nick and the other on the approaching guards, begging in her head that the guards didn't get trigger happy.

"Come on! Don't give up on me," she yelled again.

The guards came closer to Nick and Linda, distracted by what was going on. They were now within a step of where Nick would want them to be so Linda yelled again, louder this time.

"Come on, Nick!"

They took a step closer.

"Don't give up on me…"

Another step.

"…Now!"

On the command of 'now' Nick, whose supposedly lifeless eyes had been watching Linda's giving him a clue to the positions of the two guards, quickly raised his rifle and fired one shot into the chest of one guard and, before the other could react, changed his aim and fired another shot into his chest. Both guards fell to the ground, both shot through the heart. They would be dead in seconds.

Linda and Wilmott reacted quickly and grabbed the assault rifles from the stricken guards whilst Nick jumped up, covering them.

"As I said, amateurs."

Seeing the guards were no longer a threat, Nick turned his attention back to the corner ahead of them, knowing the guards with Chapman would react to the commotion here. Linda, frisking the guards for any spare magazines, found something clipped to one's belt that surprised her.

"Nick," she shouted, unclipping it and throwing it to him.

Nick caught it and, in a hushed tone, said to Keith and Wilmott, "Stun grenade. Now we may have the advantage. Shield your ears."

Nick recognised the flash bang device as being one that has a two-second fuse. He advanced to the corner around which he knew Chapman and his guards were lurking. He jerked his head around the corner and back again, observing that they were still there and that there were two more guards with Chapman. He fired a shot blindly in their direction to keep them back and then pulled the pin on the grenade. He held the device for a count of one and then threw it hard around the corner, immediately covering his ears and squinting his eyes.

Following a couple of thumps where the grenade hit the floor and bounced, it detonated with a sound louder than 170 decibels and a blinding flash of around 7 megacandela. Around the corner from the detonation, the light was still bright through squinting eyes and the sound was still loud through shielded ears. However, in the vicinity of the detonation, the sound and flash were of the strength to temporarily disorient the two guards and Chapman.

A second after the detonation, Nick raced around the corner and fired two shots into the chest of each guard, grabbed Chapman and called for the others to join him. As he neared where Nick was standing, Keith looked at the two guards.

"Hey," he said to anyone listening, "they've got stun grenades too. How come they didn't use them on us the same way we used one on them?"

Nick answered. "They probably knew the guards were coming up behind us. Probably in contact, wired up like Chapman was. They perhaps didn't want to get the other guards caught in the blast from one of those things and thought they could leave us to them. Whatever the reason, I'm bleedin' glad they didn't."

"Yeah, second that," said Keith.

Just beyond the fallen guards was a set of double doors with glass windows taking up the top third of each. Nick peered through and saw a room containing a few desks with computers on them and what looked like a bank of servers covering one wall. It appeared to be empty so Nick ushered everybody in, dragging Chapman in with him.

"This has got to be the control room," he said confidently.

"This is definitely the main control area," agreed Keith. "I've only been here a couple of times but this is where they control the picobot production and steer this overgrown boat."

"Okay, Chapman," Nick shouted, "I wanna know how to stop production and stop this island."

Chapman was still stunned by the grenade hearing only a ringing and still blinded; only seeing shapes and shadows.

"It's no use talking to him at the moment," said Wilmott. "He'll be stunned for at least another twenty minutes."

"Okay," said Nick moving over to one of the desks, "let's see if we can fathom out how to stop these things."

He looked over the array of controls on a touch screen and tapped a button to see if he could get anything displayed that he may recognise. As he tapped, all the monitors on the room displayed a red background with white figures that started counting down from '10.00' in one-second intervals.

"What did you do, Nick?" asked Linda looking at all the red displays.

"I don't think I did that," said Nick. "I only tapped the

'Enter' key to see if I could get any life out of the system."

"Well, you certainly got that," Linda added, "and I must say, I don't like the look of this."

"Nor me, Lin. Looks suspiciously like someone's done our job for us. I have the feeling we've got, er, nine minutes and thirty-four seconds to get off this island."

He looked across at Wilmott.

"Er, Dave, any news on getting us out of here?"

"The helicopter should be here any minute, if not already. If some sort of destruct sequence has been initiated, which it certainly looks like, we need to get clear of the place as quickly as possible."

"Right," said Nick, turning to Keith. "You know the quickest way to the helipad, mate?"

"Yes, Nick, this way," said Keith leading them towards another door the other side of the control room from where they entered.

"I suppose we'd better bring him with us," said Linda, looking disgustedly at Chapman.

"Yes, I suppose so," said Nick, grabbing Chapman by the arm again, preparing to guide him to the door.

At that moment Chapman jerked violently and began to scream.

"What the…!?"

Out of Chapman's screaming mouth came a small grey cloud that split into six smaller clouds and entered into his nostrils, eyes and ears.

"Bots!" shouted Keith as Chapman's screaming increased and his body writhed in agony. "They've booby-trapped him as well as the island."

"Oh, Jeez!" exclaimed Linda. "let's get out of here."

"If they were programmed for us, we would know by now," said Keith as he watched Chapman collapsing to the floor, now silent. "We probably haven't noticed but a few of them would have spread out to us already. If they had any of our DNA programmed, we wouldn't be standing here now."

"Well, let's get out of here in case there are any other bots around that are programmed specially for us."

"Okay, Nick," agreed Keith. "Let's go."

Keith led them through the door and they filed out of the control room, leaving the lifeless body of Chapman on the floor and the banks of monitors showing '5.49' and counting.

As Keith led the way along a maze of long and similar corridors, he spoke out in panted breaths.

"The other tech guys are all here against their wills. They'll be locked in the labs. We've got to try to save them if we can."

"Okay," Nick agreed. "Where are they?"

"They're just down here," Keith said breathlessly.

He reached a door similar in appearance to the others but this one had a key pad that was glowing red.

"They're in here," he said looking through the window. His voice then changed, becoming lower in volume and sadder. "Oh…… The bastards!"

Linda approached and peered through the window.

"Jeez!" she said in a saddened tone. In the lab, still at their desks, were the scientists that had been forced to work fearing for the lives of their families. They were all lifeless with each one of them showing small trickles of blood from their eyes, noses, mouths and ears.

"They set the bots on them all," she said hitting her balled fist against the door. "We've got to get them, Nick. We must make them pay for what they've done."

"Agreed," said Nick, "but we've got to get out of here first if we're going to do anything. And we must have around 3 minutes left now before the countdown reaches zero."

"Three minutes and 3 seconds," said Keith as everyone looked around at him for an explanation. "It's appearing on my laptop now as well as all the monitors in the place. Don't worry though, it's my laptop so I know it's not been tampered with. There's no hardware destructive mechanism in it to my knowledge. It's just tapped into the countdown."

"Okay," said Nick, "keep us informed every thirty seconds

or so."

Keith nodded his agreement and led them on through the corridor maze. As he rounded the next corner, he stopped abruptly then immediately jumped back causing the others to bundle into him. Linda was about to ask what the problem was when the answer became apparent. A couple of shots rang out from around the corner hitting the wall in front of the group.

"Guards!" gasped Keith. "Two of them. Armed… obviously."

"For fuck's sake!" exclaimed Nick. "Surely they're aware of this bleedin' countdown. Why is it, when there's an ominous, impending event you still get a couple of 'do-gooders' intent on blowing your head off rather than running for it?"

He edged towards the corner, stopping before showing himself to the guards.

"Do you two realise this place is probably about to blow up in about three minutes?!" he shouted.

He was answered by another couple of shots hitting the edge of the corner near his head. He took a step back from the edge.

"I s'pose they don't know or don't care."

"Two minutes, 30 seconds!" shouted Keith.

"Thanks mate," shouted Nick in reply.

"You did ask," Keith explained.

"Yeah, I know, mate."

"Chopper's here," shouted Wilmott.

"When the countdown reaches 30 seconds, tell them to get out of here whether we're with them or not. I get the feeling there won't be much of this place left after we get to zero. Which reminds me, we need to get out of here."

Nick bent down low and quickly glanced around the corner then darted back before the guards had time to adjust their aim. The guards were standing about ten metres along the corridor, one on each side, flat against the walls, aiming their assault rifles in Nick's direction. His old teamwork with

Linda came into force now. As soon as she had seen him bend down and glance around the corner, she readied her weapon and came to stand behind him. Without looking back, knowing she would be there behind him, he put his left hand in the air, opening and closing his fist twice indicating ten metres. He then pointed to himself then pointed left indicating he would go for the guard on that side of the corridor. He then closed his fist and opened his fingers one at a time approximately one finger per second. As he opened his fifth finger, he dived across the floor into the opening of the corner, rifle at the ready. As he dived, he adjusted his aim and fired two shots at the guard on the right, hitting him in the chest. As the other guard started to react to Nick's appearance, bringing his rifle around in Nick's direction, he was hit by two shots from Linda as she had followed Nick's dive a split second later. Both guards fell to the floor, dead or dying. Linda and Nick got up from the floor and shouted for the others to join them.

"Two minutes," shouted Keith.

"Thanks, mate," shouted Nick in reply. "Are we anywhere near the outside?"

"Yeah, Nick, it's around the next corner, along the corridor and through a couple of double-doors."

"Great, mate," thanked Nick as he ran off around the next corner.

He ran along the corridor and approached the set of double-doors Keith had described and peered out as he waited for the others to bunch up behind him. About a hundred metres ahead the helicopter could be seen on the helipad with its rotors still spinning in wait for them.

"One minute, 30," shouted Keith as they all grouped together by the doors.

As Nick started to open the doors, one of the windows shattered as a high-powered bullet smashed through it, followed by the loud bang of the gunshot a split second later.

"Oh great! A 'kin sniper now!" yelled Nick as he dived back

away from the window and into the group, forcing them down and away from the doors.

"Lin?" he gestured towards the door as he headed for the far side with the shot-out window. Linda joined him on the other side of the door so she could glance out the intact window.

"Any idea where the shot came from?" she asked.

"No idea, Lin" he said glancing around at where the bullet had hit the wall behind him. "Must be over to the right somewhere, behind the chopper."

He glanced around the side of the broken window to see if he could get an idea of the sniper's location. He felt the bullet fly past within millimetres of the side of his face and heard it hit the wall behind him at the same time as the bang from the shot reached them.

"Fuck that!" he exclaimed darting his head back away from the open window. "That was way too close!"

"Still no idea where he is," asked and stated Linda in one sentence.

"Still out there on the right but didn't have a chance to spot him," replied Nick. "We're stuck here if we can't get at him. And we've got…?" he asked, looking at Keith.

"60 seconds," Keith acknowledged.

"Shit! A minute before the island potentially blows," added Nick.

"What do we do now?" asked Linda. "Make a run for it? He can't get us all."

"Prefer if he didn't get any of us, Lin," said Nick, "but we haven't got the time to flush him out. I'm open to suggestions," he said to the group.

"Hang on," shouted Wilmott from the rear of the group. "I've been in contact with the pilot. He's got an idea. He asks for us to keep the sniper occupied."

"Okay, I'll just stick my head out the window," said Nick, "blowing my brains out should keep him occupied."

"Try my jumper on the end of your rifle," suggested Keith as he took it off and handed it to Nick.

"Okay, thanks. Dave, tell the pilot we're doing it now."
Wilmott spoke down his phone and Nick lifted the jumper up into the area of the broken window. The jumper deformed as it was hit by a bullet followed a few moments later by the sound of the gun shot from the sniper. Nick brought the rifle back down to reposition the jumper when the sound of another shot was heard from outside.

"The pilot says we can get outside now. It appears he got him. We have a sniper for a pilot."

"That's handy," said Nick as he held the jumper up to the window again. On receiving no shots this time, he opened the door and ushered everyone out, handing the jumper back to Keith.

"Thirty seconds," shouted Keith as he poked his finger through the new hole in his jumper.

"Let's get out of here," shouted Nick. "Run for it. Dave, tell the pilot to take off as soon as we're on board. We haven't got much time!"

"On it now," shouted Wilmott, his voice sounded erratic as he was sprinting along.

The helicopter's side door was open, awaiting their arrival and the pilot had done as requested and was spinning the rotors readying for take-off. However, they were still at least a twenty second sprint to the chopper and twenty-five seconds was now showing on Keith's tablet.

"Count us down from ten if you can," shouted Nick.

"Will do, boss," replied Keith breathlessly.

They all sprinted at top speed towards the chopper aiming for the open side door, Nick leading with Keith trying to keep up at the rear. They were still nearly 100 metres from the chopper when Keith's voice interrupted their concentration.

"Ten, nine!"

"Oh, jeez!" shouted Linda. "We're not gonna make it."

"Eight, seven!"

"Just concentrate on the door," shouted Nick, "not the numbers." Though inwardly he agreed with Linda; they didn't have enough time left.

"Six, five!"

The rotor blades could be seen increasing their spin speed.

"Keep going!" shouted Wilmott.

"Four, three!"

"Maybe there's a delay between zero and the explosion," Keith added hopefully.

"Two, one!"

There was still too far a gap. They weren't going to make it before the countdown ended.

"Zero!"

They were still too far to jump into the side door so they all dived to the ground, bracing themselves for the anticipated explosions.

Nothing happened.

"What the...?" questioned Keith. "Nothing?"

Nick lifted his head and looked around, wondering what was going on. Due to the noise from the rotors spinning, he was unable to hear the multiple clicks that occurred all over the island. However, he was able to see what happened as a result of the clicks. At equal grid points around the island, canisters that were embedded in the ground clicked open and a grey cloud emerged from each one.

The nearest canisters to the helicopter were around the perimeter of the helipad and Nick could see the grey mist formed by the picobots as they emerged.

"Get on the aircraft quickly!" he shouted. "Bots incoming!"

He jumped up and started running for the chopper again with the others following close behind.

Nick arrived at the side door, dived in and immediately turned to help steady the others as they followed him in. He could see the grey clouds combining and heading towards Keith at the rear of the running. Keith wasn't operationally fit like the others, being a desk-bound techie usually, so was finding it difficult to keep up with them, and he wouldn't let go of his laptop so found it difficult to get into a natural rhythm.

"Keep running," Nick shouted to them all but was trying to encourage Keith. "Don't look back, just concentrate on the door."

Wilmott was next to arrive at the chopper. As he dived in, Nick shoved him so he rolled sideways, leaving space for the next person. The next person was Linda and Nick did the same for her. As Nick peered out, he could see Keith was only a few metres away but a large grey cloud was only a matter of centimetres behind him.

An isolated few of the leading bots reached Keith and positioned themselves to enter his body in the standard ways: heading for his ear canals, eyes, nostrils and mouth. Unable to feel this occurring, Keith took another stride towards the helicopter; he could see Nick waving him on and ready to grab him as soon as he was within reach. More bots reached Keith as the ones that were already on him were making their way nearer to their entry ways.

Nick could see the cloud gathering behind Keith.

"Keep going, mate," he shouted. "No slowing down."

More bots had now reached Keith and many of these were at his entry points. They prepared to move in, communicating with themselves and the other approaching ones. Keith took another stride nearer the chopper and –

He moved into the downdraft of the rotor blades that were now getting near to take off speed. The bots that had reached Keith were blown from him and the grey cloud that had been behind him was dispersed away from the helicopter.

Keith reached the doorway and dived for the gap

"Nothing's happened," said Keith relieved. "It was all a joke."

"I don't think Caymes knows what a joke is," Nick said ominously. "You didn't see behind you. Look out there."

Keith looked out the open door and could see many grey clouds of bots rising from the ground.

"Oh my god!" he exclaimed. "They intended to kill all the people on the island not sink it. Jesus, Nick, we were seconds from death."

"Yeah, mate," said Nick as he slid the chopper's side door shut. "Make's you glad Dave didn't order an escape plane. It would've only blown away the bots that were behind it." He turned to face the cockpit. "Okay," he shouted, "we're all onboard. Get us off this 'kin island fast."

The pilot quickly got the rotors up to take off speed and lifted the aircraft off the island and started to fly in the direction of Tenerife. As the chopper passed over the island, they could see that grey clouds of bots were emerging all over.

"Jeez!" exclaimed Linda. "There must be millions of them. Anyone on the island wouldn't've stood a chance." Then she thought for a few moments. "Oh god, what about when they fly over to the Canaries? They'll get the millions of people on the islands. And can they move further out from there?"

Keith had been watching the bot clouds as they were flying over them.

"Unless they've been programmed to head for the Canaries they won't go, Linda. The way they're loitering around the island, it looks like they were programmed to seek out anyone there. Without further instructions, they'll just fly around the island searching for people until their batteries finally run out. The Canaries should be okay."

Linda looked relieved.

"You're sure about that, Keith?" Keith looked around down at the swarms of grey bot clouds and nodded the affirmative. "Thank god for that," she added.

The helicopter took them to Reina Sofia Airport in Tenerife where they transferred to a waiting Gulfstream G450 jet, arranged by Wilmott, to take them back to the UK. Once the aircraft had taken off, they gathered together to relax for the first time in days. Wilmott made them all drinks from the bar and they sat and silently pondered the current situation for a while.

"So, what do we do now?" Linda put out the question to all.

"We've got to stop Caymes from releasing these bots."

Nick spoke out. "I've got a plan," he said enthusiastically.

"Oh, yes?" questioned Linda.

"Well, not fully thought out yet," explained Nick, "but we now have around four hours to mould it into some sort of workable process."

"So, you mean you want us to sort out a plan? Is that what you're saying?" Linda teased.

"No, not at all," said Nick feigning tearfulness. "It involves us all and I think it may work."

"Okay, let's hear it then," said Linda, Keith and Wilmott all together.

Nick sat back in his comfortable chair and motioned for the others to sit back and relax too. He took a sip of his drink and started outlining his plan to Linda and Wilmott as the aircraft took them across the Atlantic towards the UK.

CHAPTER 39

Houses of Parliament, Westminster. The day of the summit.

Originally called the Victoria Gallery, the Royal Gallery is the largest room in the Palace of Westminster and, as such, is used for important occasions including state receptions, dinners and ceremonies. It is highly decorated with portraits lining the walls, gilded stone statues guarding the doorways and stained-glass windows depicting the arms of the kings of England and Scotland.

With its history and splendour, the vast room was chosen as the location for bringing together the heads and deputies of most of the major countries of the world to attend the first Peace and Security Summit.

It was regarded by the media to be a diplomatic triumph by Prime Minister Jameson as there had never before been a single gathering of so many heads of state. The Prime Minister had labelled it in the Press as a huge opportunity for the world to be governed by one collective voice and it had increased his ratings in the opinion polls by six points.

The summit was due to officially start in two hours but, before the formal commencement of proceedings, Jameson had allowed this extra time for mingling and informal chatter. It was actually in place for Caymes to ensure no heads of state would be late for the official start time – he wanted to ensure they were all in the room at the same time. There seemed to be an enthusiasm for this summit, due somewhat by the world's media latching onto the importance of a positive outcome, and already most of the delegates had arrived at the Gallery, not wanting to be reported as being the last to attend. Prime Minister Jameson had declared that security for such a unique event would be handled directly by the UK Security Service and that Andrew Fleming would be taking personal charge at the event.

Whilst smiling politely at the attendees that came into eye contact, the two of them were meeting at an end of the room that was farthest from the buffet and therefore quieter.

"You've got all exits covered?" asked Caymes, keeping his voice low.

"Yes, all security here are ours," whispered Fleming, staring ahead and keeping up the fake smile at anyone that made eye contact. "Their DNA is on file so they will be ignored the same as us when the time comes. It was a good idea to change the programming to ignore the DNA set rather than target. That allows for any late changes or additions; they'll still be sought out rather than missed. They have instructions to keep all exits locked down once the release is triggered so no one will escape."

"Good, good," said Caymes in an excited manner. "In a few hours' time we will have all the major nations reporting to us. We will have control of the world's oil, precious metals and stones. Hell, we'll even be governing the heroin, meth and cocaine industries."

Fleming moved around so he was standing in front of Caymes.

"May I suggest, Prime Minister, that you refrain from talking about it. Walls and ears…"

He moved back so they were once again side by side now Caymes had stopped talking.

"And, I don't know why you allowed them in," he said still smiling towards the crowd, "but that news crew are heading this way. Be prepared for a barrage of questions and a camera in your face."

"Leave them to me, Peter," said Caymes, still smiling, now for the camera rather than the crowd. "I can deal with them."

He looked towards Fleming so that the camera crew could no longer see his lips moving.

"I asked Deputy PM, Cooper, in his role as Marketing Minister, to allow one independent news crew in to cover the event. It also means we will have live coverage of the release until the crew are consumed and then we can use the TV link to broadcast our message to the world."

"It's still a risk," worried Fleming. "We don't know them. We don't know them at all."

"Let me worry about that," assured Caymes. "Just as you're about to let me worry about what to say to them now."

The news crew consisted of two people. The reporter was a woman with shoulder length blonde hair, tanned skin that looked like it may be from a bottle and features that betrayed the fact she was a little overweight; cheeks and chin swollen and puffiness below the eyes. Her eyes were hidden behind tinted spectacles and an attempt to disguise the fullness of her figure was unsuccessful due to her evening gown being a size too large making it loose around her body rather than hug her figure in the way it was designed. She had an earpiece fitted with a built-in microphone that wrapped around the side of her face to her mouth and she also carried a cordless microphone for use during interviewing.

The cameraman had a similar earpiece and wrap-around microphone and his face was partially obscured by the LCD display section of the Steadicam system he was strapped into which he kept very close to his eyes as if he had forgotten to bring his spectacles with him. His hair and features were very similar to those of his colleague and his tan also had the look of being fake. They were currently following Michael Cooper, the Deputy Prime Minister as he was heading for Jameson and Fleming.

Cooper reached the Prime Minister and stood close by next to him.

"Prime Minister, may I introduce er, Angelica Clements and er, Archie Lord. Independent news crew, here to film the event as requested."

"Hello," said Jameson gruffly.

"Hi," said Angelica in a forward way, betraying a strong Irish accent, "my friends call me Angel or Ange."

Archie kept quiet and continued filming the introductions.

"Well, Ms. Clements," Jameson emphasised the 'Ms.' keeping his gruff sounding voice, "you are required to keep close to me and film as much of the events as you can manage. You have a live feed to the major channels, don't you?"

"Yes Mr. Prime Minister, we are live now and will be interviewing leading up to the summit and then filming the whole thing live."

"Good, good," Jameson replied. "Okay, get on with your work then."

"We are Mr. Prime Minister," smiled Angelica. "We are."

The news crew backed off but continued filming Jameson, Fleming and Cooper.

Jameson turned to Cooper.

"Where the hell did you get those two, Mike?" he said gesturing at Angelica and Archie.

Cooper turned towards Jameson.

"With respect, Prime Minister, you asked me to find an unbiased news team and those two are freelance; not connected to any channel. And, yes, as Angelica said, they have a live link into many of the world's major news channels."

Jameson kept his eyes scanning the gallery as he spoke to

Cooper.

"Excellent Michael, excellent. They should be ideal for my requirements."

His scan of the gallery halted when he reached the doorway leading to the entrance.

"What the fu…," he said, stopping himself going any further, knowing the camera was broadcasting his every move.

"Is everything okay, Prime Minister?" asked Cooper.

"Er, yes Michael, fine. Please leave us now, I need to talk to Andrew. And ask the news team to film elsewhere for the moment."

The Deputy Prime Minister nodded his acknowledgement that he would act as instructed and retreated, taking the news crew with him.

Fleming had been looking towards Cooper and the news crew and had not had the wandering eye like Caymes so was surprised when he let out the expletive and had dismissed his deputy and the news team.

"What's the matter, Chayton?" he asked quizzically.

"What's the fucking matter," Caymes retorted. "How the fuck did he get in here?" he said motioning towards the main doorway. "In fact, how the hell is he still alive?"

Fleming followed Caymes's gaze over to the main doorway and scanned the people standing there. Framed in the centre of the doorway, looking over towards Fleming and Caymes, wearing an immaculate dinner suit, crisp white shirt and bow tie was Nick Satan.

Fleming's service training took over and he showed no sign of surprise.

"I see Saten is here," he said quietly. "Like you, I am at a loss as to how he got off the island unscathed and how he got in here."

"So, what do we do now?" asked Caymes with a slight quiver to his voice.

"We continue as planned," said Fleming calmly. "He can't stop us even if he is here. He doesn't know when we will release the swarms and has no idea where we will launch them from. For whatever reason he didn't die on the island but he will die today. The swarms will have an extra body to deal with."

Nick kept eye contact with Caymes and Fleming for a few moments then smiled smugly and started a slow walk across the gallery towards them. He maintained his pace all the way to where they were standing and he stood to their front, close to them.

"Surprised to see me again?" he asked, looking from one to the other.

Fleming replied whilst Caymes stood quietly seething.

"Mr. Saten, we don't know how you got away from the island but there's nothing you can do here. Try to stop us before the event and we'll have you taken away as a madman. Try to warn anyone in here and they will laugh you out of the place and try to alert the guards and you will find them very uncooperative. If you remain here, you will die with the rest of them out there."

He gestured towards the delegates in the room as he spoke.

"You have no chance of your plan working," Nick cut in confidently. "We know what's going on and we're here to stop it."

"You say 'we', Mr. Saten," Fleming smirked, "but I don't see any evidence of anyone but you. If you are going to bluff, you have to have an air about you of owning a winning hand. We have a royal flush. Goodbye Mr. Saten, we have people to see."

"You should never get over confident, Mr. Fleming," Nick threatened. "It can be your downfall."

Nick turned sharply on his heels and walked slowly off, blending into the crowd, not looking back.

"How much do you think he knows?" asked Caymes.

"He's bluffing," answered Fleming. "If he knew as much as he would like us to believe then he would have come in here and closed us down."

"Sounds logical but are you sure?"

"I'm sure, Jon," Fleming said reassuringly. "I know the rules that he and his teams work to. I helped write some of them."
He stopped talking and pondered for a few moments.
"But, perhaps we should bring everything forward by a couple of hours. There's no need to take any chances."
"Okay," agreed Jameson, scanning the faces before him, catching the eye of Michael Cooper and summoning him over.
"Yes, Mr. Prime Minister," said the Deputy PM as he arrived.
"Michael," continued Jameson," we have decided to bring forward the summit by a couple of hours. Can you put the word out that we will be starting in," he looked at his watch, "twenty minutes. That should allow time for any stragglers to get in here once the announcement is made."
"Oh, okay, Mr. Prime Minister," stuttered Cooper, "I'm on it right away."
With that he headed away to carry out his instructions."

A few minutes later, in a corner of the room, trying to make himself look inconspicuous, Nick stood supposedly looking at a painting whilst sipping on champagne. Hidden by his shirt collar was a covert throat microphone and inserted in his ear was a miniature cordless receiver. These were wirelessly linked to a small transceiver concealed under his arm.
Nick was speaking into his covert comms system now.
"I think they've called my bluff. When I told them they wouldn't succeed, they didn't flinch and, when I told them we were here to stop them, that had no effect on them either. Watching their body language, they never gave a clue as to where the bots are being stored nor how they intend to trigger the release. We're in trouble here if we're not careful. We'll keep mingling this end and see if we can get a clue of where these damn bots are stored. In the meantime, we could really do with this program being cracked."
Nick's transmission was being relayed to a further, more

powerful, transceiver situated in an area in the grounds of the Palace of Westminster which, in turn, was transmitting onto the main mobile cell network.

Sitting in a remote location, in front of his laptop, typing furiously was Keith Turner, also wearing a covert transmission system.

"As we speak, I'm working on it as fast as I can, Nick. Still getting the same prog crash when I try to transmit a reprogram command as I did on the island. Still bugging me, this end."

"If you don't suss it soon, mate, it'll do more than 'bug' us at this end."

"I know, Nick. I know. Going through the code again now. I'm sure it's there in front of me, so to speak. Somehow, I'm missing the obvious. I'm sure of it."

"Well, I don't want to add to the pressure, mate," said Nick, "but, perhaps I did get them a bit worried after all. They've just announced they're bringing the summit start forward by a couple of hours which means it begins in about 15 minutes. We've no longer got a two-hour cushion to get this sorted."

"Shit! Shit! Shit!" exclaimed Keith. "Working on it."

"Okay," said Nick sounding calmer. "We'll stake out the room this end. If we can find out where these things are stored and physically stop them launching, we won't need to reprogram them. Keep in touch."

"Will do, mate," said Keith still tapping away on his keyboard, fingers a blur."

CHAPTER 40

Nick wandered around the room slowly, looking for anything that seemed out of place but, at the same time, not wishing to cause a scene that would give Caymes the excuse to have him removed. Nick thought that, as it stood at the moment, Caymes probably felt pretty invincible and would therefore let him remain here to see the events unfold. He'd thought of creating a bomb or fire scare but, if the guards were on Caymes's side then they would calm the situation, label him as a troublemaker and have him kicked out. No, he had little choice but to stop the bots somehow so, in order to do that, he first had to find where they were being housed.

Nick scanned the room and the many people that were in it. It's possible that Caymes could've planted someone in the room to carry the things but he doubted it. He wouldn't want to rely on someone else, he would want the container or containers to be within sight so he knew things were okay. Caymes or Fleming, or both, could be carrying the containers themselves but he doubted that too. If they were called away or taken away due to an emergency or a security alert, that would mean the bots would go with them. No, it's far more likely that they were spaced out in a few locations throughout the room to allow an even release and

340

to allow for a built-in redundancy if any of them were to fail. He took in the pictures on the walls, none of them looked like they'd been disturbed for a long time so, not obviously there. The tables and chairs looked pretty standard, a writing pad, pen and pencil for each delegate plus, per table, a tray of still and sparkling water with glasses and a small loudspeaker designed for translation from the orator's language to that of the local delegate's to be relayed rather than each delegate having to wear headphones.

Nothing else.

He kept looking. What was he missing? He checked his watch, about ten minutes until the start now. Things needed to move fast.

Keith stopped typing and quickly scanned through the new code he had written. All looked good so he hit the button to start the compiler working.

"This has got to be it," he said to himself.

In his latest read through the coding, he had spotted that the remote programming function wasn't turning the bots off first before sending the new program This meant, he thought, that, when the new program was remotely received by the first of the bots, they were in the minority as most of the bots still had the old program in memory. Therefore, as they all kept in contact with one another at all times, the newly programmed bots were regarded by the others to have the incorrect software and would transmit the older code, overriding the new coding. Keith figured that, if he sent a code to momentarily turn them off then on again, then immediately sent the new code, the bots would accept it before they had a chance to compare it to their existing memory and would therefore keep it. That had to be what was causing the supposed non-programming remotely.

The compiler had completed so Keith hit the transmit button, sending the new program and instructions across the internet to the remote bots. Concentrating the picobot program to search for recipients in the Westminster area,

Keith had been alarmed to find that the software had registered that there were many millions of the things lurking somewhere in that region. Unfortunately, the program could only narrow the location down to the area showing the room where they already knew they were, showing the swarm as a blue mass superimposed over a map display.

He watched his laptop screen as the program showed the new code had been received by the bots, turning them from blue to green. Then the mass on the map turned black showing they had been turned off then quickly turned back to green again, showing they had been switched back on. Then the left-hand side of the mass started to turn red showing the new code was being programmed.

Keith watched the monitor as the red area grew larger heading to the right.

"Yes, yes!" he shouted to himself as he watched.

Then the progression of the red mass slowed down until it stopped before a third of the swarm had changed colour.

"No!" he shouted this time.

The mass then started to turn back to green from right to left until, within a few seconds, the mass was completely green again.

"No, no!" he wailed.

Keith hit the comms button that connected him to Nick and Nick responded almost immediately.

"What have you got for me, Keith?" he said hopefully.

Keith sounded defeated.

"It still didn't work mate. I really thought I had it that time."

Nick was gutted. Did this mean they were too late to save the delegates ... and themselves. But he wasn't going to show his disappointment. The bots hadn't been launched yet so there was still a chance. He remained sounding up beat.

"What, no change at all?" he asked.

"Exactly mate. No matter what I've tried when re-programming, the existing firmware over writes the update

before it can get a hold. I really don't know what else to try."
Nick glanced at his watch. It showed five minutes to go
before the start of the summit.

"Look, mate," he said with as much enthusiasm as he could
muster, "I don't pretend to know anything about these bots
including their programming. However, I imagine them to
be just mobile computers which are just the same as desk
computers except they're, er, mobile. Does that make sense
so far?"

"Well, yes, Nick," said Keith wondering where Nick was
taking this conversation.

"Well," Nick continued, "Whenever I try to run a firmware
update on my pc and it fails, it reverts back to the version
prior to the update attempt."

"Exactly, mate," said Keith. "That's what I'm saying. That's
exactly what I'm trying and exactly the result I'm getting. I
just can't get them to keep the new code."

"So," continued Nick, "when I get a situation where my pc
won't accept an update of some kind, rather than update the
code, I delete it from memory and install new coding that
includes the new update already written in." That seems to
work when –"

Nick was cut off mid-sentence by an animated Keith.

"Oh my god, mate!" he exclaimed. "How could I have
ignored that method. I've been so intent of going for an
update rather than a re-install, I've ignored a full reset;
haven't tried it at all. Oh my god!"

"Is it worth a try?" Nick asked.

"It's worth more than a try," Keith replied already typing at
speed on his laptop. "I think you've sussed it, mate. Leave
it with me for a few minutes and I'll see what I can do."

"Okay," agreed Nick, "but we only have a few minutes
before the start. If this doesn't work, you get far away, mate.
Don't let Fleming and his goons catch up with you."

"It might not come to that," muttered Keith whilst still
typing, his fingers a blur. "Caymes may not set them off
straight away. They could get some speeches out first."

"Can't rely on that, mate. I've riled them up to bring the summit forward so I can't see them hanging about with the launch. Unless we can find them and stop them this end or you can send them our reprogramming code, everyone in this hall except for Caymes, Fleming and their loyal guards may as well kiss their asses goodbye."

"How long have we got?"

"Well, it can't be long now. I can see Caymes and Fleming are heading for the top table. It won't take long for others to follow. A few minutes at most, I'd say."

"Okay, working on it," said Keith, his voice almost drowned out by the sounds of his computer's keys tapping.

Nick continued to wander around the gallery, keeping one eye on Caymes and Fleming and the other looking for where the swarms could be stored. He also kept the comms connected so he could listen for any update from Keith. All he could hear at the moment was the fast tapping on Keith's keyboard.

CHAPTER 41

The news crew were doing their rounds too. Michael Cooper was heading for the top table to join the Prime Minister but he was blocked off by Angelica Clements and Archie Lord.

"Deputy Prime Minister," asked Angelica, "may we have a few moments of your time?"

Cooper stopped and considered the request for a few moments, glancing across to the top table and seeing that Jameson and Fleming had yet to reach it.

"Certainly, Ms. Clements. How can I help you?"

"Thank you, sir," Angelica said as Archie moved to get Cooper in frame over Angelica's shoulder.

"Could you tell us how you feel about hosting the first Peace and Security Summit?"

Cooper smiled to himself. This was the sort of question he could give stock answers to.

"Well, Ms. Clements," he spoke confidently, "it is of course a privilege and an honour for the UK to be hosting the inaugural summit. We hope that it will lead to less fighting and disagreements in the world and that there will be many more in the future if they are needed."

Angelica smiled.

"Thank you. And would it have gone ahead without the Prime Minister if his abduction was still on-going?"

Cooper glanced towards the top table and saw that Jameson and Fleming had taken their place. He made a subconscious look at his watch to convey time was pressing but continued to smile; he had a stock answer for this question too.

"We consider the summit to be far more important than any one attendee so, yes, of course it would have gone ahead. Though it would have been under a grey cloud if the Prime Minister had not been rescued; one of the reasons for the summit is to stop things like his abduction from happening."

Angelica also looked across to the top table and saw that it was now only awaiting the arrival of Cooper to be fully occupied. However, she continued with her questions.

"With the Prime Minister's return so close to the start of the summit, he has hardly had time to recover from his ordeal. Can you give our audience the assurance that he is in the correct state of mind to be hosting such an important event?"

"Yes, I can confirm he is okay, Ms. Clements," Cooper continued, still smiling. "He was checked out by physicians when he returned and they all gave him the go-ahead to take part in the summit, saying that the abduction appeared to have had no adverse effects on him mentally or physically. In fact, I can give you an example of his positive frame of mind. Moments after he was rescued, before commencing the journey back to the UK, he phoned me and was more concerned that the summit tables had been laid correctly than anything else."

Angelica looked curious.

"Oh really, Mr. Deputy Prime Minister. Are you able to elaborate on that?"

Cooper habitually glanced at his watch again but continued smiling for the camera.

"I really must be taking my seat now, Ms. Clements,

thank you."

He started to make a move away from the news crew but Angelica stood her ground causing him to pause.

"If you could answer that one final question, Mr. Deputy Prime Minister, I think it would be good to give the viewers that example of how unscathed, both mentally and physically, the Prime Minister was, er, in fact is."

Having been led into giving another answer, Cooper was determined to ensure this would be his final speech. He continued with his best smile for the viewers.

"Okay, Ms. Clements, I'll tell you this as my final comments. The Prime Minister was very level headed at the time of being rescued, he insisted that the summit should still go ahead though, as I said, it would have gone ahead whether he had been found or not. He also was of the frame of mind to ensure that the smart alert devices that Mr. Fleming had procured had been set out on each of the summit tables. In fact, to demonstrate how much he cares about the summit, I have to say he was more than just curious the table was laid out correctly, he was insistent; questioning me directly to ensure I had either personally performed or overseen the addition of the smart alert devices. That's the sort of man he is, Ms. –"

Angelica cut Cooper off from saying anything more. She held up a hand in front of his face, glanced around at Archie and saw that he was nodding.

"Can I stop you right there for a moment, Mr. Cooper?" she asked in a tone that betrayed it wasn't actually a question.

Her hand went to her ear and when she spoke again, her Irish accent had disappeared.

"Nick! She said urgently, still applying pressure to the device in her ear that enabled the comms including her hidden throat mic, to operate, "they're in the small devices clipped to the table speakers; one per table."

"Copy that, Linda," replied the voice of Nick Saten. "I'm on to it right now."

Nick scanned the room. There were too many tables to count and each of them had a speaker and each speaker had a device clipped to it. They'd never be able to move them all, nor move everyone out the room, before Caymes would see what's happening and launch the swarms. He tapped his comms link to Keith.

"Mate, we think we know where they're being stored – on every table in here. We're well and truly up shit creek if we try to remove them all. No way we can do it without being seen. How about you?"

Keith had finished typing moments before Nick had made contact.

"Was about to contact you, mate. Ready to send."

"Go for it," Nick said. "Now!"

Keith tapped the 'send' key and watched his screen again. The visual display of the picobots went from blue to green as the latest update was received then became black to show that the reset command had been received. The display then started to become red, left to right on the screen, as the reprogramming started.

"They're reprogramming, Nick," Keith said triumphantly. "It's working."

"Great, Keith," Nick replied. "Let me know when it's complete?"

"Okay, mate…. Fuck! Fuck! Fuck!"

As he had said 'okay' the growing red area had stopped and the green was spreading back across the screen showing that the bots were programming themselves back to their original code again.

"Shit, Nick!" he exclaimed. "It didn't work. It didn't fucking work! I'm so sorry, mate."

"Okay, Keith," said Nick solemnly. "Not your fault. What happened this time? It seemed to take longer for you to say it failed."

"Yeah, mate, there seemed to be more of them taking the new code before the collective decision to reject it took over. The reset seemed to work at first and then they seemed to 'remember' they shouldn't be accepting new code."

Linda, in her disguise as Angelica Clements had been listening in, still holding the deputy PM at bay, spoke up.

"It's almost as if there's a safety feature built into the things to stop them being re-coded."

Wilmott, in his disguise as Archie Lord, added, "Is there a security bit set to allow or reject re-programming, Keith?"

"Yeah, there is, mate," said Keith, "but the reset command should overcome that and allow the re-coding to go ahead."

He paused in thought for a moment.

"Unless …"

He started typing furiously again.

"Unless what?" enquired Nick.

"Unless the security bit hasn't been coded to allow external programming to disable it."

"What does that mean, mate?" Nick asked

"It means that I may have to find where the security bit coding has been stored and re-program it. It may be that the bots need to be reset and, due to the security coding, either having a bug or being deliberately programmed that way, they might have to request a re-program to accept it. Working on it."

"Have to ask you to work fast, mate. I think we have minutes at the most before this thing starts," Nick added, then spoke to Linda and Wilmott. "In the meantime, Lin, we need to start going around the tables and removing these things. Can't see we'll have time to remove them all but we have to try."

"Okay, Nick," said Linda with an upbeat tone. "Maybe we can shift enough of them to stop them reaching everybody in here."

"Maybe," added Nick hopefully. "Dave, you hold the deputy PM whilst Linda and I start collecting these things."

"Sure thing, Nick," said Wilmott taking a small sidearm from a hidden area within the Steadicam. Pointing it

Cooper's way whilst keeping it from view of others, he ushered the deputy towards a corner of the room, making it look like he was still filming him.

Linda started to make her way across the room towards Nick, pausing at each table to supposedly reposition the drinks tray and speaker but actually unclipping and pocketing the security devices. Nick started towards Linda, doing the same, hoping to meet in the middle.

Keith was scanning screens full of code looking for the security sub-routine. It can't be that well-hidden, surely. He glanced at the clock. It had been one minute since Nick told him they only had minutes. He looked back at the screen and continued scrolling the code up the screen.

It must be here somewhere.

CHAPTER 42

Jonathon Caymes and Andrew Fleming stood in their places at the top table, choosing not to sit until everybody was in their places.

"I think everyone is here now," whispered Caymes to Fleming. "We can start the proceedings."

Fleming kept surveying the crowd in front of him whilst whispering in reply.

"We should hold off until the rescheduled time. Ensure all delegates are here. Plus, we want the news team in place to ensure filming goes ahead. Where are they now?"

Caymes scanned the heads of his audience until he found the crew.

"The cameraman is over in the far corner filming Cooper but the woman is wandering across the room away from them. What is she doing?"

He continued watching for a few moments until he saw she was heading to meet Saten whilst momentarily stopping at each table.

"Oh my god, Andrew!" he exclaimed. "They're collecting the swarm containers. They're unclipping the containers and pocketing them."

Fleming turned his attention to where Caymes was gesturing.

"Why is she helping Saten?" he wondered. "And, how the hell did they discover where the bots are being stored?"

"I've no idea," said Caymes in an alarmed tone, "but I'm launching now." He reached inside his jacket pocket, withdrew his smart phone and unlocked it."

Nick had been keeping watch over the top table knowing it wouldn't be long before they were spotted. He'd hoped it would have taken longer than it had.

He met Linda in the middle of the room.

"We've been spotted," he said to Linda and to Keith and Wilmott via his comms. "I've been reading Caymes's lips. He says he's launching now. We're out of time. Keith, you got anything?"

Keith's voice came over the comms network sounding stressed.

"Think I've just found it, Nick. Re-programming now. I need a few more seconds to finish and compile."

"We really don't have any more time," said Wilmott over the comms. "I can see Caymes is tapping codes into his smart phone now."

"I'll see what I can do," said Nick as he started running. "Keith, get it sent."

He ran through the crowd of delegates heading for the top table. Once he got to a clear view, he could see Caymes was still tapping his smart phone.

"Caymes!" he screamed at the top of his voice causing the crowd to look his way. It also made Caymes glance up from his phone to where the shout had originated. As he'd shouted, Nick withdrew a ceramic knife from a hidden inside pocket of his evening jacket.

The knife, being made with no metal parts, had passed through the security scanners without raising any alarms. However, being ceramic, it could still be sharpened to have a blade like a razor. This knife had been designed for throwing and Nick gripped it in the military half-turn throwing style then sent it on its way towards Caymes.

Nick was a specialist knife thrower and the ceramic blade hit its target and embedded itself to the hilt into Caymes's neck. Caymes fell to the floor in shock, dropping his phone to the floor beside him.

Fleming watched the action quickly play out in front of him; from the shout of 'Caymes' to the knife's impact had taken around a second. In that time, Fleming had taken his sidearm from his shoulder holster, aimed at Nick and fired twice. His aim was true, Nick was hit and fell around the crowd's feet.

Many of the delegates screamed in alarm and started heading for the exits finding that, in response to one of the first commands from Caymes's phone, the guards had closed and locked the doors; everyone in the room was now trapped in there.

Linda had withdrawn her ceramic knife and now threw it at Fleming, hitting him in the shoulder. He fell next to Caymes. Linda pushed through the crowd to where Nick had fallen and bent down to check on him. His eyes were open but he looked pale and had a sheen of sweat covering his face.

"Leave me," he said grimacing in pain. "Get the phone."

Linda forced her way through to the top table to find Caymes and Fleming collapsed on the floor. It was obvious that Fleming was bleeding out badly, her knife had probably nicked his brachial artery, and he was already looking weak. Caymes's knife wound hadn't severed any major arteries but had sliced into his windpipe causing his lungs to slowly fill with blood. However, due to this being gradual, when Linda arrived, he was still conscious and would probably survive with medical intervention and was still able to laugh weakly as he tapped the final code into his smart phone.

"No….!" screamed Linda but it was too late as the command had been sent and all the clip-on containers, including those in her and Nick's pockets, sprang open, releasing the picobots into the room.

The bots flew into the air and, quickly coordinating, landed upon each of the people in the room, entering their bodies through their eyes, ears, nose and mouth and immediately checking their DNA against the database in their memory.

The bots that had entered Caymes, Fleming and the loyal guards in the room, sent out a message to the millions of others that these people could be ignored. For all the other people in the room, the bots started to attack from inside.

Linda, Nick, Wilmott, Cooper and all the delegates began to scream in agony as their internal organs were overwhelmed and every nerve in their body felt like they were on fire.

The pain was too great for any of them to do anything but to scream uncontrollably.

CHAPTER 43

The compiling ended and Keith hit the send button immediately. Over his comms system he could hear the screams from the room coming through the throat mikes of the team.

"Come on!" he shouted. "Come on!"

His screen showed the usual mass of the bots within the gallery turn from blue to green showing the bots had received the new code.

The screams could still be heard over the comms system.

The green mass then changed to black for a couple of seconds as the reset was carried out.

The screams continued and Keith could do nothing more than watch his screen and shout, "Come on!" again.

The mass then started to turn red from left to right showing that the new code was being programmed.

Keith held his breath. This was the point when all other programming attempts failed.

The red continued to stretch on to the right-hand side of the mass.

Keith stared hard at the screen. Though the red was still spreading across, the original coding could take over again at any moment and delete the update.

The screams continued from the gallery making Keith cringe.

Pixel by pixel the mass continued to fill with red. There was now more red than green pixels on the screen.

"Come on you bastards!" Keith yelled at his monitor.

The screams over the comms system seemed to get louder. All Keith could hear were the people in that room and all he could see was the programming screen in front of him.

The pixels stretched to the far right of the mass. There were now only four lines of green left.

Keith was transfixed by the graphics.

Three lines…

Two lines…

One line…

All red.

"Yes!" he shouted. "Yes, yes, yes!"

The mass on the screen turned from red back to blue to show the new code had been accepted.

The screams coming through the comms system stopped.

In the gallery room the bots had stopped attacking the people and their agony had relented almost immediately. Caymes, in his weakened state, looked confused. Why had it stopped? Fleming was also still conscious and also had a confused look on his face.

Then the new programming took over.

The bots checked the DNA of the bodies they were in against the new database in memory. Now their instructions had changed. Those bodies with DNA the bots were originally programmed to ignore were now the targets and vice-versa.

The few bots that were in the bodies of Caymes, Fleming, and the loyal guards now called for the others in the room to join them. The bots inside the delegates all left their bodies by the various orifices and formed a dark grey cloud as they swarmed towards their new targets.

Laying on the floor, Caymes could look up and he watched as a huge quantity of the swarm flew towards him and Fleming. He stared in horror as they reached him and then started to scream in realisation as millions of them entered him through his wide-open eyes, open mouth, ears and nostrils. The remainder of the bots spilt up and entered Fleming and the guards.

There were many more bots per person now that only a handful of targets were in the room and so the attack and accompanying pain was more severe than for the delegates.

The screams from Caymes, Fleming and the guards filled the room.

Linda had felt the bots leave her body and seen them join the cloud that headed for Caymes and Fleming. She could now only watch in horror as the two men convulsed in agony as the bots attacked from within.

The attack was by so many and so devastating that, within seconds, the screaming stopped and seconds after that, Caymes, Fleming and the guards were dead.

Keith shouted over the comms system, "What's happening there? What's going on?"

Linda responded quickly.

"You did it, Keith. The re-programming worked. You saved the delegates. You did it."

"Thank god," said Keith, now finally breathing steadily. "Are you okay, Lin?"

"Yes, I'm fine," she replied.

"And Nick and Dave?" Keith enquired.

"Dave's okay," Linda said then paused for a moment. "Nick was shot, Keith. Fleming got him. I don't know how he is. On my way to him now. Standby."

Linda headed back towards where she had left Nick. There were now a crowd of delegates circled around that area. She started to push her way through the people, shouldering them out of the way.

"Let me through," she said in a raised voice, "stand back, give him some space."

She pushed her way through the final layer of people and reached the stricken body of Nick laying still, on the floor. She knelt down beside him and felt his neck for a pulse and immediately took her hand away as her fingers were now covered in blood.

"No, no, no!" she cried as she saw the blood was trickling from the side of Nick's mouth and pooling around his neck where his collar circled. His eyes were now shut and she couldn't tell if he was breathing or not.

She unbuttoned his evening jacket and pulled it aside from his torso revealing a large bloodstain on the left side of his chest.

"No…!" she shouted again and then looked up to the crowd of people. "Someone, get an ambulance crew here now!" she screamed.

"What's happening?" Keith cried down the comms system.

"Nick's down," she cried, "in a bad way. Gunshot wound to the chest. It looks bad, Keith."

She looked around the crowd of faces staring down at her.

"Has someone called for the ambulance crew?" She received a nod and a shout from somewhere confirmed they were coming.

Wilmott came pushing through the crowd with Deputy PM Cooper close behind. "Lin?" he enquired staring down at Nick's body.

Linda had felt for a pulse again as Wilmott arrived. At the sound of his voice, she turned to face him and, with her eyes glassy, she shook her head slowly.

CHAPTER 44

The Royal Gallery, Westminster. 1 hour later

The first ambulance crew arrived on the scene quickly; there was always a crew within the Palace of Westminster on standby, in case of emergencies. They were able to start triage on the room's occupants and before the arrival of the external ambulance crews who took over and tended to the most badly injured.

Only two of the delegates were badly injured from the bots' attacks; they were elderly and had suffered heart seizures brought on by the intense pain. They were still alive and expected to recover. The rest of the foreign attendees were treated for shock and for minor bleeds from the various orifices where the bots had entered them and they were expected to make a full recovery. This meant that the DAHRT Team's interaction had saved all the delegates and stopped a global catastrophe from occurring.

Linda was laying on a wheeled stretcher having removed the prosthetics and latex that had made her into Angelica, waiting to be taken to an ambulance. She, like all the others that had borne the brunt of the attacks, would be taken to hospital for a body scan to ensure there was no internal injuries that needed treatment.

Wilmott, also having removed his disguise after explaining to Michael Cooper, walked with the Deputy PM over to her side.

"Okay, Lin?" he asked.

Linda turned her head to face the source of the question and grimaced slightly as a migraine-like headache suddenly mustered itself. She still managed a weak smile and looking at Wilmott replied, "Dave?" then looked from Wilmott to Cooper and said, "friend or foe?"

Wilmott smiled back and said, "Friend."

"Are you sure?" she continued questioning.

"To be fair," continued Wilmott, "I wasn't sure at first but the few bots that attacked us before the re-program took over, continued to attack him in the same way they attacked me and then they left both of us when re-coded so that gave me a confidence level that he was okay. I've had a bit of a chat with him whilst we've been waiting for the paramedics to do their thing, he knows about us and what's going on now"

She nodded gently. "You both look okay," she said wearily.

"Yes, Lin, we got off lightly. I'd taken the DPM at gunpoint to what turned out to be the farthest point from the launch areas so we had less bots to attack us. We're regarded as the 'walking wounded' and will still have to have a scan but less urgently than the rest of you."

"And Nick?" she asked tentatively. "They took me away from him and won't tell me anything. It didn't look good. Did he make it?"

Wilmott looked around the room rather than at Linda and her heart sank and her eyes became glossy again.

After a few seconds, he finally found what he was looking for and made a beckoning gesture with his hand.

"You may as well ask him yourself," he said smiling as another stretcher was wheeled up beside Linda's.

Linda turned her head and came face-to-face with a very

pale but smiling Nick Saten. "Hi," he said weakly, "thought they'd got me, did you?"

"Oh, Nick!" she cried, her glassy eyes now producing a few tears, "I really thought you were dead."

"It was a close thing apparently," he whispered, "but, thanks to the wonders of graphene covert body armour, one shot was stopped but cracked a couple of ribs. It was the other one that caught me as I spun around. Went in at the side of the armour and got me under the arm, straight through. Missed anything vital but caused quite a bleed hence, when you saw me, I probably looked like a gonna!"

"Yeah, at a quick glance, it looked pretty bad."

"Well," Wilmott joined the conversation, "between the both of you, you delayed Caymes long enough for Keith to get the new code loaded. Good idea of yours, Nick, to get the targets reversed in the new code. It did our fighting for us in the end."

Part of Nick's plan had been for him to goad Caymes into revealing where the bots were being stored and then, if they couldn't be disposed of, to get Keith to reverse the coding so that who were the 'safe' people in the room – Caymes, Fleming and the guards – then became the targets and vice-versa.

"Yeah," said Nick wincing, "I had every faith that Keith would find how to transmit the update code."

"He cut it a bit fine though, didn't he?"

"I had every faith…"

The paramedic stopped Nick from having to say anything further about his 'faith'.

"Okay, Nick, we've got to get you to hospital. You need stitches. That superglue won't hold forever."

"Is there room for two?" Nick asked gesturing towards Linda.

"Oh no, Nick," she said, "I'll wait my turn. There's probably more injured people in front of me."

"No, it's okay," smiled the paramedic, looking at Linda, "the badly injured are sorted now, we can take you as well."

"In that case, two it is then," said Nick.

"What about you, Dave?" Linda asked Wilmott.

"I'll catch you up later," Wilmott replied. "As I said, the Deputy PM here and I weren't caught up in the main attack, so we can make our own way for a check-up."

"Well, make sure you do," Linda ordered jokily. "Both of you that is."

"We will," smiled Cooper. "There's just a few things I want to discuss with Mr. Wilmott before we go."

Linda and Nick smiled and were wheeled off to join the remainder of the delegates on their way for treatment. Cooper and Wilmott surveyed the room and tried to take in the devastation that was in front of them. The police forensics teams had arrived some time ago and had erected small tents around the bodies of Caymes, Fleming and the dead guards and were busy gathering evidence. Keith had effectively switched off the picobots by sending a reset code causing them to fall to the ground dormant and a couple of the forensics team were sweeping them into evidence bags.

Cooper looked around the room as he spoke to Wilmott.

"Lots of noise and movement going on in here David. Perhaps we could retreat to my office to continue our conversation before we head off to the hospital."

"Lead the way Mr. Cooper," said Wilmott ushering towards the main door. "Please lead the way."

EPILOGUE

1 week later. Vauxhall Pleasure Gardens, across the railway lines from SIS HQ, Vauxhall Cross

The midday sun was shining brightly in a cloudless sky, allowing very little shade for anyone to shelter. There was a soft breeze blowing along and off the Thames cooling the skin of those people who had chosen to meet outside rather than in their air-conditioned but fresh-airless offices.

Lunchtime in London tended to consist of an hour sometime between 11.30 a.m. and 2.30 p.m. so, on a pleasant day like this, at midday, there were many people sitting either on benches or on the grass, eating anything from a few biscuits to shop-bought sandwich meal deals to full picnics.

On a section of the gardens far from the main entrance, near to the boundary with Vauxhall City Farm, four people were sitting on a picnic blanket with an open basket in the middle of them with mostly empty food trays and beer bottles spread out around it.

"I don't know where you get those tee shirts from," said Nick Saten. "In fact, let me re-phrase that, mate. I don't want to know where you get those tee shirts from."

363

"Why, what's written on this one?" asked Linda Andrews.

Keith Turner, the wearer of the tee shirt in question, turned at an angle so that all could see the logo 'My intelligence is artificial' written across the front.

"You have to have the right connections," he said smiling then added, "How's your arm Nick?"

Nick's arm was in a sling to reduce any movement of the stitches under his arm. He lifted the sling slightly and seemed to be inspecting his wounds.

"It's coming on nicely thanks, mate. Still reminds me who's in control of the pain from time to time but it's early days yet. The docs tell me I should get around 80% of movement back within about 3 weeks."

"That's good news," said David Wilmott, "and you don't even seem to be suffering too much."

"Well, I'm on a good combination of painkillers at the moment. Nothing hurts and another benefit is, if I have a drink, they make me pissed quicker."

"That could be handy I suppose," said Keith seriously. "Less time in the bog."

"What?" puzzled Nick.

"You know," continued Keith, "in the bog, whoosh, piss finished, done."

Nick stared at Keith for a few moments taking in what he said.

"Not 'piss quicker', 'pissed quicker' you burke! You know, drunk … in quick time."

"Oh, I thought you meant," a wave of the arms to indicate a fast flow of liquid. "Oh, never mind …"

"I'm beginning to think your intelligence is artificial," laughed Nick. They all joined in laughing, knowing all was said in jest.

Wilmott got the conversation back to business.

"Now we're all fed and watered, let's get business out the way. Nick, you were going to inform me of the permanent members you want on your DAHRT Team."

"Well," said Nick looking around the small group, "Linda already knew she was in the team." This brought a little smile from her. "I've already asked Keith if he would join as our IT expert and he has agreed if I'm not mistaken." This got a 'yeah' of approval from Keith. "However, I'd also like to ask you, Dave, to be the fourth permanent member. You certainly proved your worth out there."

"Ahh," said Wilmott, "you've caught me out asking that."

"Oh?" questioned Nick. "I thought you'd be pleased I asked."

"Oh, don't get me wrong," continued Wilmott. "I'd like to be in the team and, with your approval, I'd join in whenever I could. However, and this is just for your ears until the official announcements. The soon to be new UK Prime Minister, Mr. Michael Cooper, will be appointing me as the new chief of Six."

Everybody smiled and a chorus of 'That's great', 'Well done' and 'Right on' went around the picnic blanket.

Nick spoke up over the congratulations.

"We'll I'd be happy to have you on the team whenever possible, Chief. And, does that mean it's you we come to for a pay rise?"

"Nick, 'k… off," was the only reply he received.

They all spent the next hour relaxing in the sun with the continuing light breeze keeping them cool. They'd said enough for the moment and all kept silent listening to the leaves rustling in the trees and the faint murmurs of other people speaking in the gardens. In their relaxed state, even the sounds of trains on the nearby tracks, going in and out of Waterloo Station, were soothing.

The silence was finally broken by Wilmott.

"Well, you lot, I've got to get back to the office now, I have a meeting with Mr. Cooper."

He stood up and packed the empty trays and bottles back into the picnic basket ready to take it with him.

"I'll take this back to the office save any of you coming back. I'll be in touch with you all tomorrow."

"Okay, Dave. Take it easy," said Nick as Wilmott took his first steps towards Vauxhall Cross.

"I will, don't worry. And what will you three being doing for the rest of the afternoon?"

"Well, I suggest we go and find a quiet pub," said Nick smiling. "Don't know about you lot but, for some reason, I fancy a game of darts!"

ABOUT THE AUTHOR

Lee Faulkner was born in the 1960s and has had a varied working life, starting in electronics and IT with the latter part of his career being involved with the police service. He is married and lives in Hampshire where he is currently working on the next installment of Nick Saten's adventures with DAHRT.
This is his first novel.

Printed in Great Britain
by Amazon

33125060R00208